M000165828

BLOOD FROM THE SKY

BLOOD FROM THE SKY

a novel by Piotr Rawicz

Translated from the French by Peter Wiles

With an Introduction by Lawrence Langer

First Paperback Edition

YALE UNIVERSITY PRESS/NEW HAVEN & LONDON

First published 1961 by Editions Gallimard
First American edition published 1964
This paperback edition published in the United States by
Yale University Press 2003

© 1961 by Editions Gallimard
English translation © 1964 by Harcourt, Brace & World, Inc., and
Martin Secker & Warburg Limited
Introduction © 2003 by Lawrence Langer

Originally published in France under the title Le Sang du Ciel

All rights reserved. This book may not be reproduced, in whole or in part, including
illustrations, in any form (beyond that copying permitted by Sections 107 and 108
of the U.S. Copyright Law and except by reviewers for the public press), without
written permission from the publishers.

Printed in the United States of America.

ISBN 0-300-07830-7 (pbk. : alk. paper)

Library of Congress Control Number: 2002115063

A catalogue record for this book is available from the British Library.

The paper in this book meets the guidelines for permanence and durability
of the Committee on Production Guidelines for Book Longevity
of the Council on Library Resources.

10 9 8 7 6 5 4 3 2 1

INTRODUCTION

Lawrence Langer

Nearly thirty years ago I wrote in the preface to *The Holocaust and the Literary Imagination*: "Among the works of unusual distinction which I have omitted with regret are Piotr Rawicz's *Blood from the Sky* and Charlotte Delbo's *None of Us Will Return*." Since then I have written extensively on Delbo's memoirs but seem never to have found an occasion to discharge my overdue obligation to Rawicz. I welcome the chance to do so now. With the exception of Anthony Rudolf's brief *Engraved in Flesh: Piotr Rawicz and His Novel "Blood from the Sky"* (1996), to which all readers must be grateful for information about Rawicz and his masterpiece that is available nowhere else, virtually no detailed critical commentary has appeared in English or any other language. For a distinguished book whose French original (*Le Sang du Ciel*) was published in 1961 and its English translation three years later, this is an unusual fate; its emergence from the limbo of neglect will restore a rich and original creation to the already considerable body of Holocaust literature and, one hopes, inspire the critical community to examine its merits.

Piotr (Pinchas) Solomonowic Rawicz was born in 1919

in Lvov, then part of Polish Galicia, later absorbed into Soviet Ukraine as a result of the Ribbentrop-Molotov pact of 1939. For nearly two years Rawicz lived under Russian occupation, but his plans to enter the university were dashed by the German invasion of June 1941. He and his companion (later his wife) Anka managed to escape the liquidation of the ghetto in Lvov, spending the next year in flight from the Germans while concealing their Jewish identity. They were thus refugees from life and refugees from death, enacting a common if ironic drama of the Holocaust era: trying to survive by denying the self. The plight provided Rawicz with a central theme of *Blood from the Sky*, whose protagonist, Boris D., manages to save himself by persuading his captors that he is not who he is.

No memoir equivalent to Primo Levi's *If This Is a Man (Survival in Auschwitz)* has yet turned up among Rawicz's papers to confirm the details of his *Wanderjahr* fleeing from the SS units that were systematically shooting or deporting the Jews of Ukraine. His novel mixes invention with truth so that one must be wary about using its fiction to verify his fact. But sometime between the end of 1942 and early 1943, Rawicz was arrested and sent to Auschwitz, not as a Jew but as a Ukrainian. Presumably he was considered a political prisoner and hence would not have been threatened by the gas chamber. Rudolf reports that from his wife (who had avoided arrest and survived the war with false papers) Rawicz was even able to receive letters and packages—a privilege not afforded Jewish prisoners. Rawicz occasionally spoke to friends about his Auschwitz interlude and the immunity from the ultimate horrors of the place that his precarious deception granted him, but any version of the episode is conspicuously absentfrom his novel. Perhaps he felt that Auschwitz exceeded the limits of artistic representation. More likely, he saw that any of the Auschwitz experience would have disturbed the design of *Blood from the Sky*, whose tensions develop from the nomadic quest for refuge, not the more localized ordeal of imprisonment. Had he chosen to write about it, however, the results would probably have resembled the mixture of irony, cynicism, and dark humor that inform the Auschwitz tales of Tadeusz Borowski.

Rawicz remained in Auschwitz until 1944, when he was transported to Leitmeritz, a camp in the vicinity of Theresienstadt. He was freed from captivity at the end of the war, presumably by the Russians. He returned to Lvov, traveled around Poland, and then received a scholarship to study in Paris, where he settled in 1947. Like Elie Wiesel, almost ten years his junior, he worked as a correspondent for foreign newspapers, in the meantime absorbing the language in which he would write his novel. It is an odd if significant coincidence that several survivor-authors, including Wiesel, Aharon Appelfeld, and Jerzy Kosinski, chose not to use their mother tongues in their fiction.

Although Rawicz decided not to draw on his deathcamp experience in his novel, his encounter with atrocity affected—one might even say "afflicted"—his view of post-Holocaust culture. A master of many languages, including uncommon ones like Sanskrit and Hindi, Rawicz was sensitive to how words could shape and reshape our understanding (and misunderstanding) of the human scene. The verbal manipulations of Nazi discourse helped to deceive a generation of Jewish victims, as well as a world that did so little to aid them. In *Blood from the Sky* verbal dissimulation becomes a principle of being, both an instrument of death and a guide to staying alive. Perhaps writing in French rather than his native Polish would free Rawicz from the temptation to lapse into familiar patterns of speech. Indeed, so skeptical had he grown of the candor of human dialogue in the era of Nazi inhumanity that he used the following exchange as the epigraph to the first chapter of his novel: "How can you tell Man?" "By the fact that he can bark." Readers are thus warned from the outset to be wary of any definition of the individual as a creature who talks.

One of the many complex strengths of *Blood from the Sky* is that its vision of life is often contradicted by its achievement as art—a paradox that incidentally serves equally well to describe the poetry of Paul Celan. The mistrust of words that thematically infuses the text with pervasive suspicion opposes the creative intelligence that seeks an ordering form in the midst of the chaos of extermination. Or as Boris, one of several narrators of the novel's action, asks in a tone of self-mockery: "Composition on the subject of decomposition?" What serious Holocaust author has not faced a similar dilemma? Boris's repeated close escapes into further flight are interspersed with accounts of German cruelty that keep the reader's attention grounded in the reality of extermination. Were the subject less gruesome, one might speak of Rawicz's strategy of playfully maneuvering our expectations between hope and despair in a spirit of mischievous glee. Just as we are cheered by one more successful effort by Boris to avoid disaster, we are forced to confront the grim danger that surrounds him as he decamps. That very word, with its sinister echoes, reveals the taint that the Holocaust has inflicted on the purity of a once-innocent vocabulary.

Still, speech and voice play substantial roles in controlling the impact of *Blood from the Sky*. Rawicz invents an anonymous narrator to tell its story, which is based on "papers" left by Boris D., a Jewish resident of Lvov, who is posing as a non-Jew. Boris in turn includes in his "notes" episodes concerning the destruction of the Jewish community of the region, all of which he could not have witnessed himself but has written down from the testimony of actual observers. We are thus faced not with a single chronicle, or indeed a single chronology, but with a constant shifting of time and place to reflect the disorder that always lies at the heart of the event we call the Holocaust. Moreover, we encounter not a report but a reconstruction of that event, drawing on multiple sources ranging from the author to his principal narrator to his protagonist Boris to the keeper of the Jewish cemetery to the head of the Jewish Council in the ghetto to the administrator of the Jewish hospital (misguidedly considered the only safe haven in town) to the chief of the German SS detachment that arrives unexpectedly one day in the hospital to deport or execute its staff and patients. The novel thus fuses as part of its very structure the intricate issues of what happened, how to impart what happened, and who should be relied on to divulge it. Its sense of artistic urgency is driven less by moral fervor than by the compulsion to witness, to leave a legacy for future generations that turns history and memory into art.

The friezes of horror scattered through the text sabotage any impulse to search for a heroic center in the narrative. Boris is lucky to outlive the disaster, but on its deepest level the purpose of his witnessing is not to celebrate his own life but to commemorate the death of others. The anonymous narrator informs us that he has tried to remove the "pseudo-lyrical bits" from Boris's account, but the prudent reader will note that he has not always prevailed. After all, Rawicz is the master-controller of the novel's style

style, and there are moments when he seems determined to visualize atrocity with a poetic imagery that will engrave itself indelibly on the reader's imagination. For example, as the SS are removing the patients from the ghetto hospital to trucks waiting to bear them to their doom, they find it too cumbersome to carry out on special stretchers the postoperative cases from the surgical section. "Muller," the officer in charge instructs his Sergeant, "help me tidy up this ward." The narrative continues: "Striglitz paused beside the first bed, discreetly drew his automatic, and leveled it at the patient's forehead. 'There, that's taken care of. No more suffering for you, little brother,' he declared with unfeigned tenderness. He proceeded on his way, followed by the Sergeant. A hefty gardener and his frail, slender assistant, full of trust in his master. Both seemed to be engaged in a soundless rite. The clicks were barely audible. The patients lay there waiting, long, white plaster dolls. Their eyes—fat June bugs, dark and shiny—flew up toward the ceiling, then fell back, sinking lower and lower, their wings broken off" (123). "Pseudo-lyricism" is in fact an exact designation for the precise recital of atrocity that Rawicz dramatizes in a tone of ironic understatement and feigned compassion. As we peer through the dusk of the creative gesture at the ghastly subject that inspired it, we cannot avoid a feeling of friction between the horror of such historical moments and their metamorphosis into fiction. T. W. Adorno was not the only one to express concern about this dilemma. If art in general opens us up to life, Rawicz knew that in some instances it also opens us up to death. The need to write surmounted this hurdle, but it did not suffuse the artist's heart with satisfaction or joy.

Indeed, a mood of loathing fills many of the pages of *Blood from the Sky*, and not only for those guilty of the crimes it records. In a notebook that Boris turns over to the novel's anonymous narrator, we find some peculiar definitions of literature: "anti-dignity exalted to a system, to a single code of behavior. The art, occasionally remunerative, of rummaging in vomit" (134). It is as if the disgust inherent in the theme of mass murder, through some kind of osmotic infusion, corrupts aesthetic vision and defiles the innocence of its disposition. "Dissecting the world into tiny bits," Boris continues, "covering paper with tiny scribbles that aspire to be unique: that is the posture in which the brotherhood of man and insect—hideous, if the truth be told—manifests itself in the purest form, with the utmost obscenity" (134–135). Such language provides insight into the Holocaust-afflicted imagination, pursuing its artistic endeavor while steadily aware of the diminished human stature that Nazi brutality has introduced into the world.

Rawicz's fellow artist and countryman Czeslaw Milosz, writing in 1942, used similar imagery to reflect on that reduced human status: "Death makes no more of an impression than the drowning of an ant makes on its comrades, parading beside it on the tabletop. A certain insectivity of life and death, as I'd like to call it, is created. I suspect that we are beginning to look at man partly as a living piece of meat with tufts of hair on his head and his sexual organs, partly as an amusing toy that speaks, moves—but all one has to do is raise one's hand and squeeze the trigger and an ordinary object is lying in the same place, as inert as wood and stone."[1] In our age of increasing atrocity, Milosz's vivid description of the idea that Nazi Germany has formally bestowed on modern consciousness—a "certain insectivity of life and death"— seems less alien than we would wish it to be. The distress that Milosz shared with Rawicz was the difficulty—often, it seemed, the impossibility—of finding a center of ethical authority, whether in a religious institution or in an innate sense of humane values, with which to oppose effectively the amoral ruthless power of Germany and its cohorts. The foe both Milosz and Rawicz faced as writers finds succinct expression in the diary entry of a young SS officer who witnessed the massacre of the Jews of Zhitomir: "Liquidations, executions, purges. All these words, synonymous with destruction, seem completely banal and devoid of meaning once one has gotten used to them. It is a vocabulary which has become general usage, and we use such words just as we talk of swatting disagreeable insects or destroying a dangerous animal. These words however are applied to men. But men who happen to be our mortal enemies."[2] As words corrupt deeds, so deeds corrupt words, and one goal of the artist's vocation is to try to reverse the stain before it grows indelible.

How to rescue existence from the "insectivity of life and death" that spread like a contagious disease during the years of German rule in Europe was no easy challenge for Rawicz as he surfaced still alive from the carnage. The spectacle of loss that threads through his novel lay across the landscape like a mantle of decay. To sustain a heart that loves in a world where violence and murder prevailed was, Rawicz found, not a simple task; he approached it with simultaneous resolve and a lingering doubt. Interspersed through *Blood from the Sky* (much as in Charlotte Delbo's Auschwitz trilogy) are brief poems and verse fragments, traces of lyric pain that condense the author's vision of a world gone awry into the utterances of a wounded mind. One short stanza reads:

And it howls like an injured dog,
The past,
And I lick its blood.
(Butnat-butnat-butnat

ural

ly!) (p. 77)

Converting the unnatural in history into the natural expression of an artistic temperament could not subdue a past drowned in bloodshed without a strong ironic sense of how familiar words decompose in the very process. The alliance with Celan is once more evident in these lines.

Blood from the Sky can easily be classified as a prolonged cry of lyric pain from a region that the reader can trespass only through the enticing structure of a narrative form that Boris calls his "circuitous tale." Like the anonymous editor of Boris's papers, we as readers are forced "to impose a certain shape—and what a shape!—on this jumble," and like him, too, we must quickly "abandon any ideas of fishing for authentic 'values'" (206). Indeed, under Rawicz's guidance, our "hook" descends into areas of experience where only the subtlest master of invention could lead it. Over the years we have been reminded repeatedly that the "real" story of the Holocaust will never be told because its secrets are locked in the knowledge of those who did not return. But Rawicz cunningly finds a way of penetrating that silenced realm. He gives us a verbatim account of one of Boris's dreams, set in a large synagogue, which seems "a cross between the Temple of Solomon and the hospital in our town," thus traversing, in a single image, ancient Jewish tradition and modern Jewish doom. In the dream Boris encounters hallways and doors, much like Kafka's Joseph K in *The Trial* wandering the corridors of bureaucracy, pursued by the same "gnawing disquiet" that is the hallmark of Kafka's fiction. But in the post-Holocaust era, as evinced by Boris's nocturnal vision, the claustrophobic threat assumes a menace not to be found in Kafka's world, despite claims to the contrary by many critics: "I learned (though from whom?) that I was under sentence of death, a penalty that I associated with asphyxiation." Boris tries to flee, but guards prevent him: "The atmosphere of no exit, the feeling of being stifled and walled up, was intensifying" (208). He speaks of this as his "crucial dream," and we share it as a fierce epiphany, an imaginative insight into that ultimate instant when being and nonbeing united during suffocation in the gas chamber. Without naming it, Rawicz evokes the terror of extermination, thus paying quiet tribute to the appalling locale that he decided to omit from his novel.

But what of transcendence, of Jewish belief, of the reconciliation destined to come with the arrival of the Messiah, a conviction that lies at the heart of Jewish faith? Sholom Aleichem's Tevye the Milkman carried on dialogues of dissatisfaction with his Deity whenever his misfortunes proved too burdensome to bear. But Tevye's misery was all too human, part of the common lot; his discontent could be tinged with a melancholy humor. It had strict limits, approving reproach but shunning scorn or disavowal. Just as extermination exceeds the verbal scope of a term like "misfortune," however, so Rawicz's Boris must contend with a God whose role in the doom of European Jewry—whether through presence or absence—warranted a far more severe vocabulary. Boris gains access to the diary of a young boy who works in the hospital, a diary whose entries reflect a cruelty that is the daily diet of his existence. "I spend quite a lot of time staring into garbage cans," he writes, introducing a withering image of universal nihilism worthy of a Samuel Beckett: "May it not be that the Universe itself (along with that bitch, Eternity) is the refuse from something which manifestly doesn't exist? And God perches on it like a giant cockroach lulled to sleep by the sun. What can God's dreams be like?" (101). The reader is tempted to reply "They can't be worse than Boris's!" Rawicz here allows Milosz's "insectivity of life and death" to invade divine realms without necessarily endorsing it, although it gains the status of possibility by its inclusion in the verbal scenario of his novel. The role of the Creator in the destruction of European Jewry remains one of the troubling subterranean themes of *Blood from the Sky*, matching the ambivalent attitudes of the novel's creator himself.

Anka Rawicz, who was separated from her husband but still on close terms with him, died of cancer in the spring of 1982. A few weeks later, on May 21, Rawicz went to her apartment and committed suicide using a pearl-handled revolver that he had bought for the purpose. It seems useless to speculate why. Perhaps, as a result of Rawicz's corpse-strewn memory, Boris's conclusion at the end of the novel that "the future is an abscess to be lopped off" had finally caught up with Rawicz. But this is only conjecture. Living with *such* death in the way that Rawicz must have drains the energy in ways unknown to those of us who were spared the ordeal. How the Holocaust experience had invaded his mind during the postwar years may be detected in his admission that "for every writer the language in which he writes is a kind of concentration camp. But when you write in a language not completely your own then it is a kind of prison within the camp, a second degree prison."[3] Maybe he slowly succumbed to the shock of recognition, and the futility attached to it, that one can be alive after Auschwitz without having survived Auschwitz. Of destruction Rawicz had had much to say in his novel. In the last gesture of his life, he chose to leave the mystery of self-destruction as the final but unexplained legacy of his tempestuous career.

But while retreating into his zone of silence, Rawicz could not carry with him his art. He spent the war years in what Milosz and others have called anus mundi, the cloaca of the world, and like Milosz he sought to understand "what it means to bear such an experience inside oneself." For many this remains the ultimate question of our time, and *Blood from the Sky* provides a partial response. In the novel Rawicz forged a paradoxical tension between life and art, bizarrely affirming annihilation for our consciousness by giving it a form. No less than his Polish compatriot he instinctively resisted the principle that Milosz could not avoid restating after the havoc of the Holocaust lay strewn across the plains of history: "Horror is the law of the world of living creatures and civilization is concerned with masking that truth. Literature and art refine and beautify, and if they were to depict reality naked, just as everyone suspects it is (although we defend ourselves against that knowledge), no one would be able to stand it."[4] Rawicz extended the frontier of artistic expression, as so much Holocaust literature does, by giving the unbearable a bearable frame. He knew with Milosz that "life does not like death," but would have added that death, and especially mass murder, was utterly indifferent to that aversion. And he certainly would have been even more skeptical than Milosz of the idea that "what takes place in *anus mundi* is transitory, and that harmony is enduring."[5] Fortunately, this uncertainty kept neither Milosz nor

Rawicz from practicing their craft.

Notes

1. Czeslaw Milosz, "Letter to Jerzy Andrzejewski," in *To Begin Where I Am: Selected Essays*, ed. Bogdana Carpenter and Madeline G. Levine (New York: Farrar, Straus and Giroux, 2001), 192–193.
2. Cited in Richard Rhodes, *Masters of Death: The SS-Einsatzgruppen and the Invention of the Holocaust* (New York: Knopf, 2002), 146.
3. Cited in Anthony Rudolf, *Engraved in Flesh* (London: Menard, 1996), 75.
4. "Anus Mundi" in Milosz, *To Begin Where I Am*, 371.
5. Ibid., 372.

PART I

The Tool and
The Art of Comparison

"How can you tell Man?"
"By the fact that he can bark."

CHAPTER 1

I'm scared of your cops, of your summonses, of your justice, of just plain you. So I'm not telling you straight out what kind of tool the title refers to. You'll get no strong language out of me. Later on, you will see for yourselves. When a man's papers aren't in order, when ambiguity—strained and creaking ambiguity—is the one remaining bridge which occasionally allows him to steal, in the evenings, into the encampment of the human, it is better for him not to expose himself to the censor's thunderbolts. You won't be cheated, though. As time goes by, you will see what tool I mean . . .

I can disclose without fear, however, what the words "art of comparison" mean. There is nothing scabrous about them. Not in the opinion of the authorities, anyway. The point is that I want to open this tale—which aspires to be antiphilosophical, aphilosophical—with a comparison. I shall use it. I shall abuse it. It's an old-fashioned and maybe idiotic way of going about things, but I'm not going to deny myself. Standing, utterly destitute and without a stitch of clothing, on the threshold of maturity—that foul-smelling soup kitchen wherein we are called upon to change from jeering to jeered-at spectator—I cry in a toneless voice: "No more self-denial!"

I should like to compare life to a waiter, to the waiter slowly bestirring himself outside the café where I am opening my story, as one would open a shop. It stands resting its back against this or that table. It is neither altogether bald nor altogether hairy. A few bashful tufts on its hideous head. Its jacket, which is meant to be white, is not very clean but will pass muster. It serves drinks at a rhythm which is not that of those who are drinking, and its drinks are neither particularly hot nor particularly cold; a bit sharp, a bit sickly; turbid, but in no way perturbing. It is lined and weary, with a jaundiced look; it expects tips, but is left cold by them . . . It casts about for dignity and serves it up, well knowing that dignity does not exist. It is pale and will die before long. Do please continue to draw upon my comparison yourselves. It isn't exhausted yet, but it no longer amuses me.

As I say, I have opened this story as one would open a shop. An oblong. The counters are there, and the shelves. Wet paint. A vacuum . . . like an accordion. One can pull it out and push it in. I want to play with it for a moment. Just time enough for the merchandise and the customers to make their appearance. One of them—but is it in fact a customer or an item of merchandise?—is beginning to take shape on the horizon.

My shop is open, then, and outlined on the horizon is the newcomer I couldn't make up my mind about just now. Is he an item of merchandise? Is he a customer? In relation, I mean, to my shop, to my narrative, to the tables outside the café. Or are we dealing with a poster snatched by the wind from its wall retreat, washed out by rain and by the numberless glances of the strolling crowds? A poster taking off in tatters and flapping its wings . . . You are going to be able to judge for yourselves.

He vacillates among the chairs.

The terrace is crowded. The weather is cruel, as an afternoon in the Boulevard Montparnasse can be, in mid-August, at five o'clock. The damned of the earth surround us. They are poor and very important in their own eyes. There is a little old man who for forty years has been claiming that destiny has made a mistake. It is he who ought to have been organizing fake bull fights in Saint-Paul-de-Vence and speculating on the Bourse and taking young, ever younger, wives, whereas the Other . . . it was for the Other to have spent all these long years propping up the same bar in the Boulevard Montparnasse . . . Then there is the fellow with the beard who is jealous of Soutine. He should have been Soutine, but not be dead. You want to know about his paintings? The light forsook them decades ago. For good and all. Let someone—with a cruel streak—mention Picasso, and he will asseverate: "THAT gang, if you know what I mean, THAT gang are simply coining money. And why? Because they have no shame. They've lost all sense of it. If you are willing to pay that price, it's easy. They shrink from NOTHING . . ." For his part, he shrinks from everything; and everything shrinks from him. As in a dream. He remains demurely in his transparent, chloroform-filled test tube, which has acquired a meaty smell with his advancing emaciation. To pay for his cup of coffee he hunts desperately for the small yellow coin in a pocket whose interior I would rather not imagine. His fingers swoop on the fifty francs like birds. And he revels, and he exults . . .

There is only one among them whose company does not

appall, with whom I associate without fear: David has a little golden goatee, and his fingers are like ten benedictions. He draws the vanished world. His light pencil strokes humble my memories. He is clean. He is depersonalized. Like a goldsmith: "I'm stupid, I know that well enough. But what about THEM—the clever, the pushing? What have they achieved that is so wonderful . . . ? My shirts are white . . ."

The whiteness of his shirts . . . Good grief! By drawing—with a judicious sprinkling of minute pencil strokes—every cajolement of his flesh and of his mind, he is living out his memories and the memory of his memories. On their side, they—the others—are no longer living out their lives, nor their dreams. They are TALKING them OVER, in search of a release that is denied them, and their words are like so many splashes. But is a man who loves modesty, restraint, and calm capable of closing his heart to the arrogant, the squalid, and the loud?

A third, a fourth . . . They grow agitated, they fidget, they sweat—those, at least, whose puny bodies retain the paltry gift of being able to sweat. They sip cups of coffee and murder the idioms of the confines of old Europe.

The unhungry among them appear as proud, perpendicular islets.

Here comes my customer, the merchandise I'm on the point of selling you. Reeling, walking, flying. Can I compare him to a fly whose wing has been ripped off? Or to a slow movement tending only to immobility? His appearance suggests the tired feeling one gets before starting work. Legs that drag along like a pair of rawboned horses. Having spotted me, he makes for me like a magnetic mine for a ship. Blindly, stumblingly, but with assurance.

Fashioned from a dark metal, very thin and very straight, he must once have been not bad-looking at all. But since, between him and myself, the "now" has been pitilessly exposed at the start and does not exist, while the "once" still flourishes, he ISN'T bad-looking. Only, he does not fit in with his surroundings. Paris has not assimilated him, even though it swallows up the diversity of all things. Paris has not mastered him, and is starving him by way of revenge . . . His skin is dried up, and the color of tobacco ash. His hair is thick and flaxen; the whiteness of his teeth is a dead whiteness. His long legs have retained a surprising autonomy in relation to his body, just as his body has in relation to Paris. The moment his oblong, his morbidly oblong eyes close, there is a cutting off, a distinct severance. And without fail the question arises: Will they ever open again? I shall say no more about his eyes.

Now that coffee has been ordered, we wake up to the fact that 1961 has been merely an illusion, and a pale and macabre one. The present is present like a lump of dead meat dried up by the malevolent sun. It isn't even putrefying now. It no longer gives off a stench, this dead lump. It is a worm-eaten substance that saps us, yet remains dehydrated. It shortens our lives, and yet remains dead and dumb itself. An illusion . . . Paris is one as well, with all its bustle. So is the building across the street. But the butcher's shop which forms part of it is less of one. And the red meat, with the black flies on it, isn't one at all.

"The tale of the tool approaches
Like a plane
In the blue sky[1]

[1] Our customer's narrative begins in quotation marks. I hope these quotation marks will get lost as we go along.

* * *

An average-sized town in the Ukraine.

July 12, 194–.

A boat. A floating island made of crystal. Such, then, is this past solidified for all time, like men turned to stone at the sight of the Gorgons. We shall die, and so, with the blood from our brains, will our memories; they will be soaked up by the sand that the high seas lap against. But the boat, full of frightened faces, of faces lit up by hope, of dead faces, and also of bodies of every age and every degree of beauty, the boat will go silently on and cleave breathless eternity, rusty eternity.

And never again will the island, with its lights, descend to these depths which go by the name of Earth.

CHAPTER 2

On July 12, 194–, we were ordered to pack our belongings—
forty pounds per head—leave the doors of our flats and
houses open, and assemble in the main square, which on one
side was bounded by the river. Thousands of fag ends glim-
mering expectantly on a bronze ash tray, and above them a
hand clutching the pylon-shaped extinguisher.

It is with subdued suffering that one sees a town where one
has lived, and where one's family and friends have died, turn
into past history before one's eyes. So I, and I alone, was going
to come through the impending slaughter alive. To be sure,
a human being who has not attained to Wisdom is incapable
of envisaging his own death. As their every hope proved ill
founded, I was giving edge to my spleen. I had loved them in
the old days, when they were alive, but it was not a com-
plaisant love. Was it too vast? For years, for centuries, they
had striven to tarnish the image of my love. They had not
succeeded. And the burdensome love that I felt for them
foreshadowed the unparalleled, the glorious era of unrestraint
that was soon to open out before it. They were all going to die,
and I was experiencing a foretaste of the love for these dead
that was to swallow me up forever, just as the twilit landscape
swallows up the distant shadow of a child. I knew that the

moment that lay ahead was to provide me, not only with a lifetime's bitterness, but with an eternal alibi. And I am too weak, I always was—*my customer continued*—to live without an alibi.

Well, all these smart people around me were holding papers in their hands. No men and women any longer: just hands, hands like so many screams, a forest of hands. No hands any longer: just papers, documents. The most wonderful documents with which an Empire could provide human beings. Each of these safe-conducts proved conclusively that the Millennial Reich could not win the war, or even survive another day, should any harm come to a single hair of the holder's head.

The chemist's wife, a good-looking piece at whom I used to make eyes in the old days, was manufacturing heavy guns to keep the war going. It was important, it was vital to the power that had assembled us here, that she should not be disturbed, even in the most dire emergency. A blonde thirteen-year-old girl was a collector of scrap iron. Hands off—insisted her pass—she enjoys the lofty patronage of the Supreme Commander of the Guard. And old Senator Gordon, Gordon who—so it was said in our town—had never slept with a woman, not once in his life; who, spurned by beauty, courted ugliness and poverty alone, so that he might succor them and perpetuate them; who—as all the poor in our town knew —lived on plain bread, and one might almost have thought on roots and herbs, so that he might distribute the whole of his pension to beggars, honest and otherwise . . . His noble mission was acknowledged, encouraged even, by the invader, who had put him in charge of mutual-aid activities in our province. What was he thinking of, this old senator whose high-sounding title and bilious disposition were encased in a tall, stooping, hacklike carcass, and who had been elected, in error, thirty years before, coming near the bottom of a national and messianic poll? Did corpses engage in "mutual aid"? Was it possible to putrefy in a seemly and an unseemly manner? Was putrefaction a process or an individual who would generously distribute alms to my brethren? And if it were an individual how was I to portray him, in what colors was I to depict him, in the account that I should have to compose one day? Composition on the subject of decomposition? Does this vulgar pun stand up for itself unaided, or am I going to have to stand up for it sword in hand . . . ?

However, I woke to the fact that I was projecting my own obsessions into the senator's gaunt head.

There were some quite acceptable-looking girls, whose breasts and hips were beginning to fill out. Unripe apples that were soon to be picked. I was overcome by a feeling of jealousy at the thought of their end, of the flame that was to usurp my place and lick these breasts and hips to death. A jealousy fiercer than that which I felt for their lives . . . Oh, out of all these girls to fashion just one, to peel off the veils and coverings item by item, to drink the acid juice, to drain it to the dregs . . . The thought of this was assuredly more exhilarating than "The Ravishing of Astarte"—a poem that I had been writing, or rather *not* writing, for years . . . So this was the revelation: these girls of my early years were to become, forthwith, as ancient as Astarte and as divine. For was not the Great Void about to engulf them as concealed from mortal view as the home of the goddess . . . ?

I stood distributing smiles. I was not brandishing any papers. My two empty hands were a betrayal, a betrayal of the others' hopes . . .

Shulamith's uncle was there, the hunchback with four thousand years of history inscribed on his bony face. He spoke neither the language of the gentry nor that of the local peasants. His hair was gray and black. Two colors which invoked the end, just as my own blond mane, even if it did not save me, marked a foothold on the steep climb to survival. There was no corner of the globe where this humpbacked rabbi could have concealed what he was. He shot me a glance that carried more weight than any form of words. He was not asking for the advice, offered at death's door, which I voiced out of sheer cruelty: "You must get hold of some counterfeit papers and make out you're one of them . . ." Oh, I knew that he could not follow my advice. I knew that later, after the boat had sailed, I would remember my cheap joke and my expression of arrogant superiority, afforded me by my fair hair and by my excellent, my impeccable pronunciation of the enemy's tongue.

A train whistle blew. Or was it a distant factory siren? "Stack your luggage at the side of the square. Hand over all gold, jewelry, and money. Men on the left—in fives . . ." Suspense, renewed suspense. The helmeted and unreal soldiers stood around the gently vibrating square like the angels of the Lord. No sooner had the moorings been cast off than, slowly and deliberately, the vessel got under way.

CHAPTER 3

The mossy stone doing service as my headrest had been merely a blind. The stillness of my body as it lay hidden behind the rock constituted a broad royal road to survival. Once the thin cough of the machine guns had died away, the hours caressed the sky like dark birds . . . From the depths of my pit, where I lay as flat as a flounder, reduced to two dimensions, I watched the sky breathing calmly in and out: On, to murder the sky, to see blood from the sky . . . The images dispersed, and with them the words that had never been uttered. With a movement so furtive that it seemed to originate elsewhere, I directed my eyes toward the plain. I was seeing it from a very long way off, as though through the wrong end of a telescope. A pair of children's shoes, a doll that had come through unscathed, a silk brassière . . . There lay the fountainhead. In the interlude between the slamming of the gates just now and the opening of a museum at some future date, this brassière lifted and rustled like a butterfly in no man's land. An old family snapshot, all this: the huge flesh-and-blood dolls, the sky and the plain. The spell wore off, and survival came gushing forth, like a splash.

* * *

After swimming the river under cover of dark, I felt immortal. A nocturnal trot through the streets of the walled-up town. With their doors standing wide open, the tenements and their solidified vestiges of life were indulging in the luxury of gaping very theatrically. Wearying of such hackneyed theatricalism, I made my way underground, where, in spite of all that had happened, a few living persons still crossed my path. The network of subterranean hide-outs, so picturesque and so dank, remained in operation—at a reduced rate, it is true, like a broken spring. I testified before witnesses who in their turn, as I very well knew, would shortly disappear and enrich my future testimony. The trading bug dies hard. I managed to sell the few items of gold that were all that remained of my former wealth. I was asked to relate "in detail" what had occurred over on the plain. What mattered to them was the morning, the happening. For my own part, I was still inhaling the twilight mists . . . The large stone and the river felt at hand, as did the night. The machine guns earlier that day, and these people showering me with questions, were now merely the bricks of a monument that I was never to erect.

Naomi was there in her underground hiding place, fast asleep, safe and sound. To me, waking somebody I care for has always seemed harder than killing. Yet it was essential to disturb her sleep and submit to the liturgy of renewal. A final grooming—carried out with such resources as were to hand. We were about to plunge into a world that was not our own. As though into a grave . . . False papers? Here again, the trading bug offered its services, in the shape of a foolproof document attesting our importance to the war effort. There were those who were willing, for a monstrous sum, to fit us up as workers of utterly incontestable economic value. All this rubber-stamped by the Guard and the Army, and duly endorsed by the State Police . . . But such assets belonged to the past. One asset alone continued to keep its value. Its market price was colossal, but we had been rich in the old days. As a man bestows a precious jewel—with a courtly bow—I had presented my mistress with a slender phial of cyanide.

CHAPTER 4

Leo L.—for the sake of convenience let us call him L.L.—
was the greatest orator I have ever come across. He was
THE orator. Among my elders, the memory of the great
haranguers of the October crowds was still alive. As a boy of
ten, I still used to meet wealthy tradesmen, small landowners,
priests and rabbis who would relate how, as they had stood
listening to Lev Davidovich, they had felt carried away by
some obscure force, snatched up by some wild animal that
trampled on their interests and lacerated their deep-rooted
convictions and habits. One old man—a builder of the Trans-
Siberian Railway, a clearer of virgin forests, who'd had a
barony conferred on him by the Czar immediately after a
wave of pogroms had swept through the towns of the
Ukraine—would assert that by the end of one of Trotsky's
speeches he was ready to enlist in the partisan army which
had just burned down his town house and slaughtered his race
horses.

Another story: the detachments of the Red cavalry were
entering Odessa to deliver it from the White terror. Was it
the presiding spirit of those parts? Was it the solemn character of the day, or did what occurred result simply from the

consumption of a considerable amount of vodka on an empty stomach?

The old traditions were stronger than the new doctrine. A handful of Odessa's liberators strayed into the narrow streets of the Jewish quarter, where they were given an ovation that left them gaping.

"Nikolai Ivanich," said one of the liberators, turning to his sergeant, who was wearing a grave expression and whose horse seemed to be drunk, "Nikolai Ivanich, what are we going to do with these sons and daughters of Jerusalem? Do we give it to them?"

"But of course we do, boys. It's the thing . . ."

A minor pogrom ensued, and the day after there was the devil to pay. Lev Davidovich was reviewing the victorious units. I can imagine, more or less, what he must have said to his troops. I find it harder to imagine HOW he could have said it.

"I am proud of you, my beloved comrades. And so are working people all over the world. By liberating Odessa, you have accelerated the liberation of the whole of humanity. At the same time, your political training has in some cases not yet attained the desirable level. That is quite understandable. Czarist exploitation and the Civil War have allowed little opportunity for theoretical studies. A handful of our glorious comrades, doubtless carried away by the high spirits resulting from victory, have committed an act that might give rise to unfortunate misunderstandings. There must be no confusion between the Red Army on the one hand and Petlyura's and Makhno's bands on the other. Consequently, it is unavoidable that the comrades who embarked on a minor pogrom yesterday should be hanged outside the city hall today. You must understand my position. I can neither pardon them nor even reprieve them . . . They have every excuse, these poor misguided comrades, and my gratitude and fellow feeling toward them are wholly undiminished, but any unfitting leniency could well be misconstrued. I do not know who the offenders are, my staff has not succeeded in bringing their names to light, but I am sure that they themselves will realize the political necessity that forces me to act. Let them therefore own up. I am waiting . . ."

What do you say to that? Nikolai Ivanich and his five comrades did not hesitate even for a moment . . . Trotsky shook hands with each of them, after which they were hanged amid scenes of jollification. Birds straight out of folk tales—crows, in all likelihood—flew round and round the hanged men's heads, cawing all the time, in black and brownish circles. And these circles grew smaller and smaller, less and less real. Until circles and heads, heads and circles, had entered the realm of shorthand signs, the abrupt realm of dots.

As a child, I would take these tales with a pinch of salt. The miracles to which I was inclined to attach credence had nothing to do with the orator's art. I was cool in my attitude to the messianic doctrine that had hypnotized my elders, prior to stripping them of their estates and their thoroughbreds. I never heard Trotsky. The fact that he did not believe in God made him, in my eyes, the strangest of beings.

But the first time I heard Leo L. speak in public, I realized that my uncles' stories might be true. My eyes were suddenly opened to an entirely new direction which it was possible for a man's inner powers to take.

I had known Leo L. from my earliest childhood. When he dined at our house in those days he was capable of putting away two whole chickens and five full bottles of wine. He was a friend of my father's and used to take me on his knee. The bluish smoke from his cigars would surround his mane with a dense halo. For a long time I was unable to make out the nature of the strength with which, as I could feel, his entire being was brimming over. He was known to lead a scandalous love life. His name was a famous one in the capital. He had a crazy and unbearable wife whom he had married in order to pay the debts accumulated in the course of a fairly stormy youth. I also learned later that there was mistrust among his colleagues of the rather theatrical nature of his talent. His wild and splendid tirades, his noble outbursts—while incontestable works of art—had cost the lives of more than one of the clients whom he had defended before staid and hostile juries . . . There were slanders concerning his love of money. His scale of fees, his competitors claimed, was certainly on a par with the quality of his work, but not with its effectiveness . . . For a long time this elderly chitchat left me supremely indifferent. And then—our friendship began.

One night there was a meeting of the lodge of which my father was president—a gathering initially quite indistinguishable from any other, and organized to help raise funds for a theater that was to present the works of our classical playwrights. I was there. I was anxious to parade the fledgling self-importance of my seventeen years, and perhaps also to polish off a few budding actresses who—I hoped—could not fail to be impressed by my high-sounding name, if not by my studied melancholy and my passivity in amorous games.

Smoking long cigarettes, and discreetly glancing at my watch, I had endured the ten or so speeches interlarded with quotations from the classics on which these people were proposing to nourish us, when the eleventh and final speaker was announced: Leo L. took his place on the improvised rostrum and set about proving that it was absolutely essential for our town to have its own theater. And at once all the old tales about Lev Davidovich came flooding back into my mind.

Gone was the barrier that I was arduously erecting between
my prefabricated spleen and the audience. So we needed a
theater, did we . . . ? On Leo L.'s high and bulging forehead, the bumps of genius were ablaze. I was now simply one
of the dazzled and enthralled crowd. I was ready to give
up my passions, my solitude, my abandoned ways in order
to hear the plays of Anski and Peretz in the theater that WE
were going to build. I was even prepared to give up my horse.
And my horse had eyes beyond compare. They shone with
kindness and sadness, like the eyes of a philosophical cow being led to the slaughter at twilight. And nothing mattered
any longer, except this heavenly theater which my father's old friend was voluptuously describing. Was it the
metallic ring of his voice, or his choice of images, was it the
lively and forceful harmony between thought and expression . . . ? I could not have analyzed it, but I was overcome . . .

When the meeting was over, I went up to L.L. He was
not impervious to flattery. My words afforded him obvious
pleasure. It was I who now set forth the momentousness of
our task, while the Old Gentleman, behind a thoroughly mischievous smile, displayed regal indifference: "Do you really
think any useful purpose would be served by having a theater
in this backwater? We already have a number of poorhouses,
several orphanages, an institution that provides dowries for
marriageable girls from seedy backgrounds . . . A theater
founded by philanthropists and run to suit their tastes? Don't
make me laugh! After Danchenko and Meyerhold, after
Wakhtangov and Stanislavski? . . . It's true, you didn't
know Petersburg as it was in 1900. But even so! At your age,
it is perfectly reasonable for a boy who isn't entirely brainless
to conceive a passion for drama, by which I mean for actual

plays. He OUGHT to conceive a passion for actresses. But as for the theater . . .

"Incidentally, Boris, how about paying a visit to the White Bear? I don't feel like going home. There comes a time when there is only one light in which a man can consider the contents of his own mind: that of a circus. And the circus, at the moment, appeals to me even less than your 'theater' . . ."

We spent the night in a gypsy night club and christened our newborn friendship with a bottle of Martell's, which did not seem at all out of its element in our northern clime.

Subsequently I was to bring to our friendship quite a few things that I regarded as the best I had to offer, and that were simply the mirroring of other men's ideas; all this being by no means devoid of pretentiousness: I rambled on to Leo L. about Artzybashev and the modernists and the surrealists. I expatiated on pan-sexual theories and launched into descriptions of "organic landscapes." It was all a crib, in fact; an avowed crib, it is true. The Medieval Revival played a part in it, and so did my cabalistic spells. On the one hand there were my wanderings in neglected graveyards and through stretches of waste ground, my peregrinations *ad limina* and the weeks that I spent at the court of some saintly miracle worker; on the other there were the days of debauchery, which to me was the sole possible expression of the sacred. He set me talking. He tried to get me to write. The admiration that I poured out to Leo L. was unfeigned. The fact that he realized it opened the door to his friendship. As for my youthful raptures, I myself was more ironical toward them than he who was trying to show me their intrinsic value. If one of us indulged in lampoonery and poked easy fun at the emotions, it certainly wasn't the old lawyer. In his huge library one drank exaggeratedly, unreally scented China tea.

When our region, which all through history had been
nothing but a magnet attracting pogroms, began to undergo
the final pogrom, Leo L. was appointed head of our community. In his absurdly sumptuous office, with its plush curtains
and soft, dark red carpeting, the king of the walled-up town
was treated to the special attentions of the experts who had
been sent to our part of the world. He was required to hand
over gold, furs, and chinaware, together with real tea and coffee, which were in cruelly short supply in that period of enforced isolation; men and women, too. The weight of his
responsibilities was not devoid of grandeur. "Our demands
are trifling this time," a little sergeant of the Guard would an-
nounce with a smile. "Eight hundred men over the age of
sixty. They are to be at the railway station by tomorrow evening. You have unlimited powers, and our complete trust
in the bargain. I'm sure you realize that if the goods are not
delivered we shall have the factory after us, and so will you.
And if that happens we shall help ourselves to those eight
hundred, and to a few hundred more besides."

So the old lawyer would comply. He would confer with his
colleagues, distribute orders and sign them, attend to the necessary paper work. It was through the efforts of our own
constabulary that word became flesh, and flesh—smoke.

The rhythmic advance of the disposal work, and his pathetic and silent dependability, invested the Old Gentleman
with real majesty. Whenever I talked to him at that time, I
would see the crucial sequences of our long history unfold before my eyes. As soon as I set foot in his study, where he dis-
charged his duties surrounded by a comic opera guard—sham
cops who were really undertakers, armed with puny truncheons—he would send the others out. At once we were back
to our old chatter. In its present context, it took on a pitiful
quality, like the private parts of a pretty woman, shaved for

an operation, in the glare of the surgery lights . . . We both sensed it, and may even have conceived the same image.

One evening, when he saw me walk in, Leo L. rose ponderously from his chair.

"I've only one last wish before I die," he said, "as I will do soon enough now. Only one last wish: to be back on my country estate, strolling around the big pond and catching the scent of the aquatic plants."

It was not this sudden love of nature that struck me, but the succinctness and directness with which it was expressed. True, the high walls kept the open country hidden from us; but to make up for this, despite the urbanization that had been wished upon us, we ourselves were becoming an integral part of nature, in an ever more palpable manner. Death and starvation confronted us whichever way we turned. In the middle of the road, we would stumble over bodies with old newspapers draped over them. The elementary processes —putrefaction, combustion, transformation of living saps into dead liquids—monopolized our senses. Brotherly cohabitation with rats, fleas, and bugs opened our eyes to the universality of pullulation—the common, inglorious lot of all living matter. The physical proximity of the flames and decomposition which were already devouring our race made us share more directly in the universal afflatus. Moreover, in that period of siege, we who were not yet hungry made love like men possessed. Each new day was a penetration of the hidden recesses of time—of time which was preparing to engulf us. Each penetration was . . . a New Day, like yet another nail driven into the flesh of our stubborn continuance. Never before had the sky, the pale sky of our northern clime, been so carnal. It was an accursed sky, that sky which was killing us a thousand times over, and killing us also with the shafts of cold sensuality that it was directing at us. Whole worlds went into the shaping of this sensuality, and dozens of girls. There was an autumnal song which proclaimed:

> When spring's dainty violets come shooting up,
> They'll be shooting up over our heads . . .

"You'll soon be sniffing the violets from the root end," friendly soldiers would assure us, taking a glass of wine with us before making off with a Persian rug or a piece of antique silverware.

I was about to tell my old friend of these observations concerning our intensified participation in the work of the Creator-Destroyer, when—quite uncharacteristically—he broke in on me.

"Forgive me, my dear fellow, but I find it hard to listen to variations tonight. The main theme is quite enough for me, and by that I mean: what is happening, what we are doing and what we are not doing. The concept of 'responsibility' . . . What an ugly word it is, and how lucky I am not to believe in such a notion. I have practiced as defending counsel for too long to be taken in by it . . . Should we be capable of fighting, of fighting with our bare hands? I've been guilty of some silly mistakes, perhaps even of crimes. Granted. Indeed, there is no 'perhaps' about it. I could level the most damning indictment of my career against the things I do, and what I have turned into. There is nothing that I can put forward in my defense, nothing apart from this conviction that I have acquired rather late in life: that human beings have no worse enemy than the State of Being. So I am freeing them, those who are particularly dear to me, I am freeing them from this eponymous enemy."

He paused . . . I tried to slip in a remark, but already he was pursuing his reflections: "What distinguishes a human being, a specimen of *homo sapiens*? The fact that, try as

he may, he cannot spit in his own face . . . And yet, and
yet: perhaps it isn't so very impossible? One would have to
make a study of mechanics, of hydraulics; one would need a
torrential enough flow of spittle and a complicated system of
pipes. Let's see, now . . ."

These scientific terms made me reflect on the striking intellectual qualities with which my friend was endowed . . .
This humanist, who was quite at home with at least a dozen
languages, was capable, if the need arose, of making triumphant excursions into the realms of the so-called "exact"
sciences. On one occasion, appearing for the defense in a per-
plexing case of murder by poisoning, Leo L.—having slept
with the lady accused—had spent months studying chemistry
so that, on the day of the hearing, he would be able to con-
found the most highly regarded experts in that field.

"You may remember," L.L. continued, "that, a year before
the war started, Harvard University offered me a professor-
ship. I could be over there today, picturing what is happening here and making things hot for the head of the faculty. I
didn't go, because I had no wish to be a professor. Not yet. A
question of vanity. Possibly also on account of my wife, whom
I loathe and whom I have grown used to ill-treating—only
mentally, of course . . . In America I should have had to put
her in an asylum, and that displeased me. What! Be false to
a madness that had become one of the shared possessions of
marital life? How despicable! And, believe me, I'm glad that
things have turned out the way they have. That I am here,
with you, with all of you, with all of us. I wouldn't want to
be without us. Absence, in itself, would have been a crime, an
unforgivable crime. Besides, just think what a pleasure it is
for me, in the evening of my days, to be giving a performance,
a true performance—what am I saying?—to be participating
in the theatrical event of a lifetime. For, setting aside a few

technical details, I am cast in the role of—no, I AM, I have become—the Head of the Sacred Community . . . let's say of Frankfurt, at the time of the Black Death. The Medieval Revival. And you have to admit that those who have us in their keeping have supplied the appropriate trappings . . ."

He reached for a volume of Heine: *The Rabbi of Bacharach* . . .

When we looked up from the book, he held me back: "Wait a moment, there's still a bottle left in this cupboard . . ."

All this was in March—a cold, bleak month, indistinguishable from eternity.

And now, after my morning in the square down by the river, I met L.L. again. Most of his flock had stayed behind in the square. He did not ask me for any details. The grapevine was still operating, possibly thanks to the efforts of a few wretched members of the constabulary who had escaped the shooting and were incapable of living without the "lawful authority" which, despite all that had happened, was still embodied by my old friend. The three of us were sitting in a comfortably furnished cellar. In the dark-toned copper candelabra, the candles were burning down. We might have been in a temple. It was all so bitter and so monstrously lovely. Time was hurrying past. I knew that L.L. was bound to be the last of the people with whom I should sit talking like this in the world that I was preparing to turn my back on. There was nothing whatever original about our leave-taking. He kissed me on the mouth. He kissed Naomi, not without caressing, in so doing, her firm and ample bosom. He was making no effort to ward off solemnity. Even as I myself made the effort, even as I restrained my breathing, which grew suddenly heavy and rapid, I could not help admiring his *savoir-faire*. The old lawyer was not afraid of pathos.

"You are leaving, my children, and goodness knows you are right to do so. All of us who remain here are going to perish in the weeks ahead. I'm not saying that isn't a pity. Anyway, as tamer of my own downfall—and of yours, too—I may still have a chance to mold that fall, to break it in as I would a goat. And it will come and eat out of my hands.

"Of you who are leaving, a few may survive. I am by no means certain. But should you happen to do so, remember everything, remember carefully. Your life will be no life. You are going to become strangers to yourselves and to everyone else. The only thing that matters, that WILL matter, is the integrity of the witnesses. Be witnesses, and God keep you . . ."

Patiently, with steady hands, Naomi started to unpick, from my gray suit and her gray costume, the yellow stars of the Poet-King.

CHAPTER 5

The one who is listening chimes in: The tables outside the café have started to empty. My roaming eyes are brought up sharp by one of the remaining groups. There they sit, four or five of them, a minor forest of weight-supporting elbows. Yellowy hands. Rimose fingers, with knobs running after one another, chasing one another, exploding. Poor men's hands. Proud but featherless cocks, tubercular and dreary. Without stirring from their seats, they are revolving around . . . Around whom or what?—It's the Knitter. He came to Paris, just as they did, some forty years ago. But, unlike them, he is not angular. All bulging curves and half-smiles, his body achieves realization and affirmation through kindly little folds, through obliging acts of guile. The Knitter has forfeited his soul, in his own eyes, but he has been successful. His small factory is a going concern. For him, hunger is only a memory. His twelve-year-old son will go to the École Normale. He is being groomed for an eminent position. What the Knitter says about painting is little further from the mark than the observations of those about him. They know it, and this knowledge is like a shameful disease. Their pride is aggressive. The Knitter's is discreet; it smiles. Is he going to buy a picture, half a picture, five per cent of a picture? They haven't yet got that far. The question has never even been formulated. They are biding their time. At the moment they are concocting a theory about art sacred and profane . . .

"Abstractionism?" declares the Knitter. "Old Moses, the fellow who carved the gravestones in our little town, was practicing it years ago. And believe you me, he practiced it better than most of your false prophets, even though he had never heard of the word . . ."

His audience is discomforted. In their heart of hearts they are in agreement with the manufacturer. Their sensibilities are as like as twins. But what agony for them to feel that they are on the same side . . . The talk moves on, breaks off, starts up again. They condescend to argue. Their ulterior motives and dissembled feelings are quite apparent to the Knitter, but he wants none of this truth. He is reveling in his role as patron. Only one of the painters seems not to be participating in the sitting race. Georges produces his sketchbook and scrawls something that the others are not supposed to notice. And then—plop!—he jackknifes right into the middle of the conversation. He rips a page from his sketchbook and hands it to the Knitter: "I've turned out a little portrait for you, old boy. Yes—just like that. With me, it's a matter of instinct . . . I'll be sitting here idly, and the moment the others start to chat I'll find myself sketching. Anything. Anybody."

The Knitter's smile becomes set, like a yellow lamp. It isn't a gay smile.

"Waiter, charge everything to me," he says. "As though you need telling!"

The Knitter's fingers go on poking about in his wallet. With a conspicuously discreet gesture, he slips a small piece of paper toward Georges. It is a five-hundred-franc note. I

glance at Georges's eyes. Is there any embarrassment in them?
Merely a glint of relief and unalloyed happiness.

The solemn face-bearers get up, one by one, and make
their way across the street—only to gather again in a grubby
restaurant and continue the conversations begun half a century ago. The waiter propped against a table sagely savors the
stillness of the moment. His presence bothers us. A barely
perceptible breeze caresses the tall trees along the boulevard. My customer stares uneasily about him.

"Waiters scare me," he says. "Everything scares me, except death, and I'm none too sure of that any more . . . How
do I feel about life here? About life pure and simple? One
tries to go through the same motions as other people, and one
gets worse and worse at it. And one's sense of weariness
grows . . ."

Now that the departure of the little old men is over, we
have become a somewhat indecent island, a pair of voluntary beasts of burden, saddled with the story that is only just
beginning.

"Let's go somewhere else," suggested my customer.

If there is any virtue in Paris, it is her indifference. Time
is dead. The houses in the Rue de Rennes: piano keys on
which no one has played in all eternity. Our footsteps make
an aggravating sound in the dusk. On the Île Saint-Louis,
below the Hôtel de Lauzun, a gas lamp is lapping at the darkness, whose bitter-tasting sap is flowing nowhere. Now we
are sitting on an upturned rowboat. The river is still. A
weary river, fatigued and out of breath. A few late rats, like
bulky army tanks, are making their way home to their boat-
houses. Envying my customer's mood of final and unshakable
renunciation, I am—for my own part—far from remaining

deaf to the soundless voice of the city. I picture myself filling the Hôtel de Lauzun with images that I have been fondling for a long time past; using it as a place to house my collection of various textures of skin, various sounds of panting. And I think: Let it be fulfilled anticipation that metes out death. Fulfillment of anticipation? My customer seems not to believe in it.

"And how did your friend Leo L. meet his end?" I ask.

He doesn't answer at first. The wheels have to be set in motion again.

Well, I didn't see it with my own eyes, he said, for next day Naomi and I left town, never to return. But later, much later, in another chapter, his final months and his death were described so clearly to me that it was as though I were there myself.

After the morning on the riverside, the last morning that I lived through in our town, the trucks arrived. A special detachment of our own constabulary—under special supervision—was entrusted with the task of stripping the corpses of absolutely everything, including hair and gold teeth. By now, the walled-up town numbered only a few thousand inhabitants. Maggots burrowing in a hunk of cheese that was turning into hard wood, turning into steel. Like a huge head without a body, the Communal Council continued to hold its sessions, surrounded by the surviving members of the constabulary. The latter still had their truncheons, but there were few people left for them to hit. The tombstonelike walls were battered down and replaced by barbed wire. The winds caressed our final nakedness, the few old houses to which the once sizable township had been reduced. This final nakedness could scarcely be destined to last. The fifteenth-century temple, standing right beside the Council Office, was turned into a warehouse for the clothing and personal effects taken off the bodies of the dead. Fifty men were in there night and day, with heavy chains on their feet, engaged upon the task of sorting. The clank of these chains could be heard even inside the Council Office, where my dear Leo L. held sway in the midst of the "twelve" . . . He was said to take drugs. No one ever caught him doing so. He managed to get his hands on a single cyanide capsule and made his wife take it. Was this an instance of supreme sacrifice or, on the contrary, an act of hatred? Who will ever be able to decide for sure? Cyanide had at that time become as costly as pride.

The belongings of the dead had been transported elsewhere and the fifty chain-wearers liquidated (now that the familiar clanking had ceased, it was only right that the expansive silence, the new silence, should arrive with some unknown shell on its back) by the time the Captain of the Guard, Werhahn, drove up in a black limousine and demanded to see the President. No one knows what happened in Leo L.'s office . . . What is certain is that, an hour later, the officer came bouncing out of the room, followed by Leo L., who was shouting: "I am President of the Corpses, Captain, but you mustn't get the idea that it was you who chose the position for me. I chose it for myself, years ago, for there was nothing else for me to do. Nothing else. Thanks all the same."

The twelve Councilors were hanged on the first-floor balcony. They were like an anecdote. They swung as the wind willed, like twelve black overcoats on invisible hangers. A few moments later, Werhahn ordered the parade of the constabulary. They were shot slowly, row by row, and as they saw their comrades fall some of them began to piddle with fear. The urine mingled with the blood, to form puddles of indeterminate color . . . Leo L. stood gazing at the scene and kept on with his "Thanks all the same, Captain . . ."

Since there was now no constabulary to order about, Werhahn asked Leo L. to fetch a leather suitcase from his car. He had appeared to hesitate for a moment or two. When Leo L. returned, the Captain opened the suitcase with the aid of a small key and produced—guess what . . . ? He produced a gorgeous plain red shirt, extremely wide and extremely long, a shirt-big-enough-to-wrap-a-bus-in.

"It's a present for you," he said to L.L. "Do please put it on at once . . ."

There was also a papier-mâché crown, and as soon as Leo had donned this garb they made him dance. He began with a waltz, then came a tango in the course of which Leo clasped an imaginary partner to him in a manner that could not have been more suggestive. He was already gasping for breath when the Captain called for a spot of folk dancing. From that moment onward, things started to deteriorate. During the Cossack dance, Leo got his legs entangled in his shirt. He tripped and fell. Before his wondering eyes, a gigantic henhouse took shape. Its bars were of fluorescent metal. A blinding light was being shed, but where on earth was the source of it . . . ? Perching on the bars were purple-colored hens and earnest, winged archangels. This entire gathering intoned a chorale, launched into a strident symphony, keen as a blade, which was escaping—O wonder!—from Leo L.'s gullet. It took him some little time to realize that all these images and all this music were stemming from his own being, from his own entrails. But wasn't the reverse true? Wasn't he the very center of this henhouse, which was imprisoning him by means of bars fixed to his retinae?

"If the henhouse is inside me, then I am vast, vaster than the planet," Leo L. said to himself. And, in essence, that is what he had always struck me as being. "But if I am inside this fiendish contrivance, who can have put me here—and when?"

By this time, the Captain was not alone in giving orders. His adjutant and a number of N.C.O.s were joining in. One of them called for the Russian kamarinskaya, whereas the rest were keener to see a polonaise, and two or three cognoscenti were intent on being treated to a thoroughly Jewish dance: a mayoufess or a rikoudekle. The lawyer's pale face grew as red as his shirt, and the veins in his forehead as azure-blue as the Mediterranean on a sunny day. In the joyful hubbub, no one could even be sure who had fired the first revolver shot, as restrained and rational as a "Shush!" directed by an overtaxed schoolmaster at a class of rowdy boys.[1]

[1] Later, much later, said my customer, when war gave way to a period of factitious calm in the world, I gave a certain amount of thought to the significance of the moment that I have just described to you. In firing his revolver, the enemy supposed that he was performing a relatively commonplace task, annihilating just another cell among all the millions of cells in the organism that he was preparing to kill. But unwittingly he had aimed true, he had aimed at the very heart of the peril. When, some years later, in one of the enemy's ancient cities, an attempt was made to pass judgment on the misadventures of the period, many of the races formerly under the heel of the vanquished gave voice to their experiences. Before going to the gallows, the accused had to sit in the dock and endure the indictments of these injured races. True enough, there was talk too of the furnace chamber through which we others, we members of the murdered race, were passed. But our race was missing from that stately hall. No gramophone record had been found which emitted anything like the sound of its voice. The verdict was earless, and the gallows—sightless. The enemy's leaders, today so much closer to their victims than to their judges, secured this posthumous victory thanks to the unknown N.C.O. who had killed the old man in the huge scarlet shirt. For he alone would have been capable of speaking for us.

CHAPTER 6

in which we go back six months

If the Seine didn't have embankments—*said my customer*
—Paris would be a city more after my own heart . . .

While I was still quite young, I was struck by an analogy,
without ever mustering the strength to get it out of my system, to turn it into a story or a poem, to pin it down. The
comparison-making bug had taken hold of me. Having considered the concept "humanity" for the first time, I caught a
glimpse, as it were, of a glass model of the human brain. This
model was made up of two thousand million strictly identical cells. Confined in each is a little worm. Greenish, pale
pink, or some such color. The worm stirs, it tightens and
loosens its fragile coils. It is doing the same as each of its
two thousand million (minus one) counterparts. The
devil only knows for what reason he would like to break down
the transparent wall that separates him from his neighbor.
Were he to succeed, he would make love to it, or devour it
perhaps, or be devoured by it, or all three at once . . . But
never in all eternity will he succeed in shattering the glass,
the splinters from which would draw his greenish blood.
Endlessly he will reperform his absurd gymnastics and remain in solitude (you can say that again!), though parallel,

though identical, to his two thousand million neighbors (minus one) . . . all as "solitary" as he.

And yet, and yet, unless my religion has been pulling our legs, at the end of time the Great Hand (the one which, at the beginning of my story, was holding the pylon-shaped extinguisher), the Great Hand will pick up the glass brain and, in the sport which the Indians call *lila,* hurl it to the floor . . . I haven't the breath (by which I naturally mean the divine afflatus) to describe what happens to the tenants once their huge transparent sphere has been broken. One small detail: the cosmic Pekinese, the Pekinese in divine attendance, will pee on them, thus enriching the scene physiologically, so to speak, as well as from the standpoint of the visual arts . . .

Could it be that the Messiah is afraid of the hermetically closed cell, of the solitude which alone would allow him to share in the destinies of human beings . . . ?

But let us turn our eyes from such apocalyptic glimpses! The little episode that I am about to relate to you took place some five or six months before my departure with Naomi and more than a year before the death of my old friend Leo L. Do forgive me if I lapse into altogether too epic a tone. It is the subject matter that compels me to do so.

The race which for thousands of years has been boasting that one day a true Messiah will emerge taintless from its midst has in the meantime produced a whole pleiad of Messiahs false, semigenuine, and suspect. You are as familiar as I am with the cases of Sabbatai Zebi and Jacob Frank, to say nothing of a certain Karl Marx and at least a dozen People's Commissars and Deputy Commissars.

Let us go further: which of us, if only for a moment, has not imagined himself to be the Messiah in person . . . ? In the seventeenth century, when the Cossack hetman Bogdan

Khmelnitski had caused several hundred thousands of our people to be cut down, drowned, and impaled, the handsome Sabbatai appeared in Smyrna, promising the strewn corpses justice and resurrection; millionaires in such peaceful countries as Holland sold their homes for a song in order to join Him whose coming had been foretold. These enterprising, level-headed shipowners, these kings of commerce, climbed onto the roofs of their ancestral homes and awaited the wind, the divine tempest, which—in the twinkling of an eye—was to convey them to the feet of their Messiah. Apparently the God-given wind did not come. Once Sabbatai had performed his act of perfidy, once the Messiah had donned a green turban and the Sultan had appointed him court chamberlain (according to some) or governor of an Aegean island (according to others), the majority of the shipowners and merchants went back to their business. True, they rebuilt the fortunes squandered at the Messiah's behest and, to some extent, in his honor. But the incident left a scar, one more scar to be perpetuated in the lives of their children.

It was to one of us, to one of the great members of our race, that the honor fell of creating the Golem—that fearsome clay monster whose deadly powers were reputed to compensate for lack of divine spirit. It is only fair to recall that, in principle, this brute force was intended for use solely in the service of our race and to the detriment of its slayers. But that was only "in principle." For in practice, as you are well aware, events didn't transpire without a number of highly regrettable complications. From being a tractable instrument in the service of the Holy, the Golem turned into a raging beast slaughtering the very people whom it was supposed to be protecting. And why? If you really want to know: on account of a ferocious longing for the soul which it had been denied at the outset. And, come to think of it, wasn't this longing, this

noble grief prompted by emptiness, as good as a real soul, a
soul undeniably present? In the last analysis, the Golem
turned killer as a result of a kind of sentimentality, of an un-
voiced need for kindness. So that, in this respect, the Golem
was merely the reverse, the "other side," the *sitra akhra* of
the Messiah. It was simply addressing reproaches—not altogether unjustified—to its venerable creator, the Chief
Rabbi of Prague, for conjuring it out of the air without en-
dowing it with that fundamental discernment between the
black and the not so black, between the cruel and that which
is less so, between good and evil in fact, of which even the
lowliest living creatures could not—in all fairness—be devoid. I frankly admit that, confronted by this dialogue between the Holy Man terrified by the consequences of his act
of creation and his blood-smeared Golem, it is to the Golem
that my pity goes out first.

Thus, for centuries, false Messiahs and more or less gory
Golems have been issuing from our womb; but have you ever
pictured what their interbreeding might one day give rise to?
It is in periods of extreme distress that the emergence of
both becomes most frequent. So now listen:

At the beginning of the period in which the story of "the
tool and the art of comparison" is set, there was in our province a man named Garin. Was he a merchant or a ship-
owner? I can reveal only a few flimsy details concerning his
life till then. He was equally avid in business and travel. He
devoted his days to gold, and to the people and objects relating to gold. He was as skilled in handling his gold as an able
musician in handling his harp and a poet his dream. He was
as skilled in handling it as a dream, an imperious dream,
handling its poets. In addition there were checks (some of
them even stamped "Insufficient funds"), bills of exchange,
bonds, dividend payments, foreign stocks, lists of market

prices, telegrams—a whole glittering-gold subcontinent in which an entire lifetime could admire its reflection. All of this sprinkled with a rather shady sensuality. One of those men who are incapable of regarding a pear in any other light than as a slightly perfected apple. Fat account books with their stout green bindings—antediluvian fauna, lunar fauna attended by a positive army of little black clerks, all so agile and so withered—indulged on their vast shelves in a sleep that was haunted by cruel landscapes and infinite horizons.

Once the invader arrived, once the first corpses—still looking a little unreal—lay strewn across the streets around the castle that overlooks the old regional capital, once the funerals started, carried out in keeping with our ancient rites, with hired mourners following the coffins, the struggle began between old Garin as he had always been till then, his bygone commonplaceness, and his secret wound. Like Jacob, he grappled for a whole night long with what struck him as his past mediocrity—a mediocrity that he imagined to be utterly misleading, and to have been forced upon him by other people and by an epoch of inordinate calm. Early next morning, one more savior was born to us. Garin the rich, Garin the manipulator, Garin mobilized his millions and used them to gain access to the Governor General. This was a spectacular achievement, even in a time that was disaccustoming us to the unspectacular. The Governor General could easily have taken Garin's millions without receiving a member of the accursed race in the castle of the country's former kings. He could have fleeced Garin and killed him, without having to account to anyone . . . Yes, but Garin was armed not only with his own millions, but with the promise of easy THOUSANDS of millions. To achieve his ends, he went around bribing lackeys and lackeys' lackeys. The result surpassed

even his wildest hopes: in the great hall, beneath por-
traits of ancestors who were not his, the false king breathed
a false religion into the false Messiah: "It is work—yes, that's
it: work—that can save you and your race," he said. "Neither
you nor your fathers nor your forefathers have ever known
the meaning of work—yes, that's it: of work, of the task well
done. When you have learned it, my men will have no further
reason for killing you . . ." The Governor's clean-shaven
face was like a clearing, in the sunshine, in the heart of an
unknown forest. "You must cease to be parasites; otherwise,
within a short space of time, you will cease to BE!" added the
Governor, and he dismissed Garin, who, that very day, dis-
patched a cofferful of age-old jewels to the castle . . . together with a memorandum concerning the industrial call-up
of the appropriate sections of the population.

And Garin, who imagined that he had thereby bought his
personal security for several months to come, left no stone
unturned in an attempt to make his coreligionists share in
the conviction that the Governor had inspired in him. Armed
with impressive passes and with the blind strength of his
will, he journeyed back and forth between the little towns of
our province, as in days gone by he had journeyed between
the capitals of the old world and the new. He traversed the
low-lying plain where peasants, with hate in their hearts,
were sharpening their knives. Preceded by his legend, a pitiless salesman traveling in false hopes, he went from one
backwater to another, calling together the elders and the
influential and the rich, who became his agents and in their
turn preached Work as the one, infallible method of surviving.

"Garin Workshops" sprang up everywhere, like mushrooms in the humid forests of Polesie. In these were produced
a whole range of more or less nonsensical items—baskets

and brushes and gloves and rag dolls—which became more
precious than emeralds or pearls or gold. It took influence,
power, and money to get one's sons, still more one's daughters, into this community of redemptive work. The coddled
daughters, the loveliest daughters of the Chosen People,
were packed off by their parents to the Garin phalansteries,
where, in driblets—like an elixir—and in exchange for
large sums of money, the documents of survival were handed
out. Garin employment cards bearing the Garin stampmark
were to fill the gas chambers with clean air and to cause re-
volvers to vanish from hands. "It's good to work for the
army," people said. "It's even better to clean out latrines and
empty spittoons in one of the Guards' barracks. But the only
thing that really puts you in the clear is a job at Garin's . . ."
They parted with fortunes, they brought their own machinery and wool and wood and cotton, in order to participate
in the Divine Service of Survival that was being celebrated in
Garin's various establishments.

Am I to boast of my perspicacity? *said my customer.* It
wasn't wisdom, but rather . . . lack of experience. Since my
eyes were not bemused by too many glimpses of the past, I
did not find it at all impossible to conceive of a situation from
which there was no way out, of a sealed-off room in which
there was neither a window nor even the smallest hole. Besides—*and in my customer's somewhat Mongolian eyes I
thought I caught a ghost of a smile*—besides, isn't a window,
the very concept "window," diametrically opposed to the
concept "house"? In which case, despair being a house . . .

Be that as it may, in the face of everything and everyone,
I did not believe in the magic efficacy of Garin's Message.
This sacrilegious skepticism was not designed to increase my
circle of friends.

All the same, even though I myself hung back, I made Na-

omi enter one of the workshops. No doubt there was an un-
derlying malice in my decision. The Princess of Israel with
the oh-so-white hands had to spend long days toiling at a
bench with a needle. Had she defied me, "public opinion"
would have cried shame. In the eyes of everybody, I was doing
the best I could to ensure her safety—even to the point of
neglecting my own. At the same time, I was still free to do
as I liked with my days, and with my nights too. My secret
contriving and basically innocent Machiavellism (since
there was no cure for the situation, not even Garin's places
could do any serious harm) were not without drawbacks. At
the end of a twelve-hour spell at the sewing table, Naomi
burst into tears. "It's all right for you!" she shouted at me.
"You cling to your freedom, you go on doing nothing, you go
on writing your shady poems—don't deny it! They're all
aimed at me, I don't have to read them to know that. And
you pack me off to that factory, which is worse than all the
gas chambers put together. I won't stand for it!"

"It's for your own good. As long as I live, I mean you to
have as good a chance as any. Besides, all your friends work
there: the Chief Rabbi's daughter, and Lawyer V.'s, and
young Baroness G. If your parents were here, they would
have sent you."

I had selected the names that constituted the best possible
alibi for the social constraint to which I was subjecting Naomi and with which now, in her sixteenth year, she was
having to comply for the very first time. But the list was ill-
chosen to quell the dark flame that was hissing louder and
louder, sputtering hatred as it did so. The names of Naomi's
young companions did indeed conjure up other things for
me: silken skins, hidden folds, the bittersweet of armpits,
blouses skillfully unfastened, a collection of moments each of
which was in the old days worth all eternity.

It was easy for me to imagine, when it was too late, what Naomi might have thought: There he goes—lining me up with the rest, cataloguing me, comparing me . . .

My concern for security was seen as a kind of act of betrayal directed against our joint destiny, which she refused to visualize as being other than completely different from everyone else's. It was in the course of a November evening three weeks before—dark, and empty, and extremely calm—that I had made a woman of this little girl who was now kicking against what, to her, seemed my first betrayal.

I cupped her breast in my hand.

"You MUST stay at Garin's," I said. "Anyhow, it won't be for very long."

As indeed it wasn't: a few weeks later, the news arrived like a sparrow hawk. The "big sweep" was due to begin. Leo L.'s associates were feverishly compiling interminable lists: of the old and the young, of the productive and the nonproductive, of those who worked with their hands and those who worked with their brains. What personal or social qualification was to provide immunity, this time, from what was demurely termed "conveyance eastward"? This was a question on which people held not one view but a thousand—and all were contradictory. One day, it would be families living on the dole who were allegedly sure to embark on the long journey. The starving multitude who, only two days earlier, had been begging for the vouchers that entitled them to a frugal meal would now besiege the Council Office, making a show of factitious wealth and demanding that their names be struck from the list of those in need of aid—aid for which they had previously gone down on their knees. Another day, a well-informed speaker would recall the hatred that the invader had always shown for the well-off. Men high in the commercial world would disguise themselves in caps and overalls, hoping to look like factory workers. Next, the threat was said to be directed against children under six: they were to be sent to holiday camps from which there would be no return. That very day, a long queue of importunate parents would invade the Registry Office, to get their offspring's birth certificates doctored. Afterwards there was not a single child under the age of six left in our town. In case of need, even a babe in arms was able to prove that he had been born before the war. Only a week later, supplies of henna were completely exhausted at the news that it was the old who were to be taken—to special rest homes. The puppet show was uneasily poised. Every night I would call at Leo L.'s for news. He would confess his ignorance. "The big sweep is coming," he would say, "but I wouldn't like to say who is going to suffer. Perhaps all of us? Or perhaps not yet?" And once again he would turn to the subject of the theater, which was, as it were, the symbol of our friendship: "When all is said and done, how grateful we should be, how grateful *I* should be, to our destroying angels . . . I am not very partial to the word 'cosmic,' but there are times when it is difficult to avoid using it. Therefore, I say, we should be grateful to them— more: we should be respectful of them—for this whole, 'cosmic' *mise en scène*."

He would enlarge on this with an ever-so-slightly ponderous volubility: "The entire universe, with its Milky Way and all its internal and external astronomies and with all that we 'know' and 'feel,' for good measure . . . the whole thing is a giant walled-up town—what am I saying?—the whole thing is a miniature ghetto, with God as head Kapo, as Chief Elder of our own race and of those that surround us. A label is stuck on you: what these insects call your name and trade. And even your face: Professor This, Rabbi That,

Doctor the Other. And this is the first mask. It isn't the most grotesque. Your own body—that is the second. Then comes your soul. And everything that lies, or doesn't lie, beyond it. Up to, and including, time and space, existence and nonexistence, and Nothingness. What a collection of cloaks! And may not Nothingness itself be, by extension, merely a cloak for Nothingness . . . ?"

L.L.'s eyes were growing deadly pale behind his heavy tortoise-shell spectacles. His eyes no longer existed; they had become diluted, merging with spectacles which themselves barely existed.

"They have thrust the whole thing under our noses," he resumed. "This Performance of Nothingness, this puppet show which—say what you like—is less misleading than everything else: they have thrust it under our noses and they have even notched our eyelids, just to make absolutely certain that we don't miss seeing it. The pattern that they have devised serves the truth; it is the truth. No display of gratitude, no act of sacrifice, can be too great. Not even the sacrificing of a little comfort. My bathroom is out of action. They've cut off the gas. No doubt they've found a better use for it than warming our bones.

"I'll tell you a little secret: what draws me to them and divides me from all of you—even from you, Boris—is that you still regard the act of killing, of killing oneself or killing others, as something important and dramatic."

And he steered me toward a volume of the *Zohar*.

One sunny afternoon, I left the enclosure to pay a call on a friend of mine, a young psychiatrist. Not being one of us, he lived in the town's free zone. He was very fond of me, this boy. Every time we met, I had to begin the uphill struggle against his crazed generosity all over again: he was intent on our exchanging skins and destinies. He would heatedly rebut the charge of generosity: he made it sound as though this exchange could only be beneficial to his pride, if not to his life. He made it sound as though my destiny, our destiny, was superior to his, superior to God's.

Were the arguments that I used against him sincere . . . ? As I walked along I girded myself, without displeasure, for yet another dispute, knowing that it could not conceivably pass off without our consuming several bottles of wine. At that time, the high wall did not completely encircle the quarter that had been set apart for us. Staring into the sun, I had forgotten, if only for a moment, the star that I wore on the back of my jacket. Viewed in conjunction with the very cool and gray and fathomless sky, the world and everything that it might contain, including myself, seemed insubstantial, without either volume or consistency. Striding out along the streets that were covered with our thick, yellowy, vernal mud, I had forgotten both of us: not only myself but my bizarre social position. I had even forgotten the fear which, whatever I may say now, held us, without respite, in its viselike grip. Nothing existed apart from this spring, at once present and distant—like love, or like dewdrops.

Suddenly, even before I had glanced about me, I felt an alien consciousness weigh on my insides like a dead fetus. A truck was crossing my path. Slowly our glances met: mine and those of the soldiers sitting in the back. With their vacant blue eyes, they were gazing intently at the yellow star, as though at a field to be harvested.

When I got back to the ghetto, I woke up to what everyone else already knew: Captain H.'s special brigade had arrived and was to begin the big sweep next day.

The night with Naomi might well be the last. I still had a drop of port left. Naomi was humming a strange old song:

> My boat is hewn from water,
> It has to cross a wooden lake.
> Where am I to find the strength to row?
> For I am burning to join you.
>
> With oars made of water,
> How am I to row on the wooden lake?
> My strength deserts me, and my soul cries:
> "How can I ever reach you . . . ?"
>
> Your lake, beloved, is made of water
> And your wood is truly wooden.
> I shall have to die and be born again
> If I am to be with you.

While our naked bodies clung to each other like two mouths, each of us was listening to the heartbeats of the new-born day. United, we were appraising our all too distinct sense of apartness.

CHAPTER 7

I got up early, feeling much too wide-awake and full of mistrust for this abrupt transition from night to day. The dense intermediary fog, the no man's land which always used to serve me, which still serves me, as a BRIDGE between the dark light of dreams and the world of solid objects—this was cruelly absent. The bed was empty. For months now, the crowded and exhilarating routine of the Garin Corporation had been making its mark on the Princess's habits. Naomi was already at work.

A glance out of the window was sufficient to inform me that the star turn—scheduled to appear any moment now —had not yet begun. The show was still only warming up. When I went out into the street, I walked slap into the midst of a bustling activity unusual at this early hour. People were endeavoring, not to avert the inevitable, but to put their final affairs in order, to dispose of such commitments as continued to link them to their old lives. Picture a ship going down. Her captain, knowing that she is sinking, stands tidying his bookshelves. The comparison, though not exhaustive, is honest enough. Like plasma cells under a microscope, groups were forming and re-forming. Gold rubles and sweets were on sale, cyanide and cigarettes. A poison-vendor, formerly a chemist—a bald, emaciated figure wearing a meek, forlorn expression—was quietly puffing his wares: "What a pleasing selection I offer! This little pill coaxes you off like a lullaby. And this one acts like lightning. Its performance is scientifically attested. It takes but three seconds. And here we have a very special mixture. I call it a *mille-feuille*. It's as sweet-tasting as the honey cakes that my grandmother used to bake for the Purim festival. You who love your children, let them sample these delicacies . . ."

I bumped into Dr. Hillel—a scholar unrivaled in any matter relating to post-Biblical history. His collection of monographs on the Talmud's sources was among the finest in the world.

"You two must get together. I love and respect all cranks," my cousin, young Baron L., had said long ago, introducing me to old Hillel. And we did indeed get together, in the course of the long winter evenings. After familiarizing me with his handsome collection of dirty photographs, the doctor initiated me in the convolutions of the Sanhedrin text, which sheds a very different light on the doings of the Nazarene and his apostles from the Church's official history. The old doctor's lewdness was equaled only by his passion for history. The setting in which he entertained me was as heavy as overripe fruit. The dark curtains, the oaken shelves, the books, the hard-of-hearing footman: these created a homogeneous realm of weightiness in sharp contrast to my host's unbounded agility.

Now he held me back with a gesture: "Do stay awhile. I'm all alone. My daughter ran away, hoping to make a dash across the front line. I've just had news. She was captured. My footman was arrested in the course of the last roundup by YOUR constabulary. For my own part, I'm taking steps to die tonight. Call it an old man's weakness, if you like. I feel

like saying a few words to someone before I go. It may as well
be you. You at least know something of the researches I was
engaged upon. I was trying to reconstruct the Great Name so
that I might foretell the future. I started keeping a journal,
writing anticipatory memoirs. I've got as far as July in the
year seven thousand. A queer tack for a historian. Everything
has gone into it: my youth, my wife, the love I bore my
daughter, and money too, lots of money . . . Oh, by the way,
I know you slept with her. You weren't the only one. But that
is neither here nor there . . . In the days when I hankered to be a historian, I wanted to become one—how sub-
limely naïve!—so that I might indulge in memory, so that I
might conjure up the past. I used to think: The bygone ages
are here somewhere, locked in a chest, up in some attic.
They're covered with rust. The mice are hopping about on
them. All one has to do is find the chest and open it. That
was the bottom rung of the ladder . . . Later, my researches
—and it was this that earned me a reputation as a lunatic—
were directed toward foretelling the future . . . I was a
rung higher; but still so low, so very low, on the ladder. Folly
still, and not divine folly . . . Believe me! At every moment,
what we regard as 'life' is turning into 'the past.' Can it be
that life is a solid, and the past a liquid? Ought the 'march
of time' to be regarded as the transformation of solid into
liquid? But where, in that case, is the Squeezer, the Squeezer,
the Squeezer?! This senseless query came crowding in upon
my nights. Now I know. Something quite different was involved. Old blockhead that I am, it was only thanks to our
soldier-friends that I found out; and by then it was too late.
All the same, I shall always be grateful to your friend Captain H. Both past and future must be destroyed so that
they may be integrated in the solely existing present. In this,

one seems momentarily to spot the glint of an infinitely sharp blade. That is what is happening now. And THAT is eternity, immortality. There is no other!"

The fleeting shape of an old beggar detached itself from the group surrounding us. I felt a wave of sickness come over me. This starved-looking figure was the poet Isaac D. He and Dr. Hillel had been much at loggerheads in the old days, though for precisely what reason I did not know. Isaac D.'s voice seemed to reach us from a long way off. He was speaking from the far side of the Ocean of Hunger, which we had not crossed. Not yet.

"Don't listen to that old lunatic, Boris. His brain is addled, while as for his heart . . . he has never had one. He doesn't understand the first thing about eternity. He's a dabbler. He remains one even today, when we are to die. Eternity . . . Now me, I used to hunger for eternity, as though for bread. Has it even so much as occurred to you that all that divides 'immorality' from 'immortality' is a paltry 't'? What does it imply? 'Theology' according to some people, 'theater' according to others . . .

"And did you also know that the best rhyme for 'cherish' is 'perish'? You hadn't thought of that, had you? Do slip me a few rubles or a few potatoes, though . . . You're a nice boy —oh yes you are!—I know you. It's only fair that this day of sadness should be a bit more cheerful for me than for the others. Just look at me . . . My fleas are far better off than I am. Even when there is no more flesh or blood for them, they can still stave off hunger by devouring my skin. But what about me? I'm not asking for something for nothing. I shall recite a little poem for you, a very cheerful little poem that I composed while queueing outside the Council Office for a bowl of free soup—when they were still providing free soup.

That was exactly a week ago. Those were the good old days."

Screwing up his face, he began to recite his poem;

> Mankind will pass away
> And will not even form
> A geological layer.
> What manner of place will our sufferings
> Fertilize?
>
> Eyes rend the landscape
> Which will pay them back in their own coin
> A few steps, and then a few more, in the murk
>
> Toward final immobility
> Toward finality immobile
> Final finality
> O skimped panting creature . . .

He let out a bellow of laughter and suddenly, putting an end to his clowning, he shot a conspiratorial glance at me. Then, in a thoroughly sober voice, he said: "Life has lived up to our dreams. Even our cruelest dreams. Hasn't it, Boris? The cosmos is a nurse who, having inflamed our passions, has now begun to minister to them. But she is a nurse-cum-whore. Where are my rubles? And my potatoes?"

My pockets were empty. I managed to slip away. For a few seconds I could still make out Dr. Hillel's gray and tousled mop of hair, then the crowd separated us.

Senator Gordon was taking the air.

"Boris," he said to me, "it's the end of the world. Yesterday I went out into the free zone, to call at the Welfare Office. I had to report on the running of the orphanage. Of the three hundred children in my care when I started, two hundred and twenty-two were taken away in the course of the earlier sweeps. The remainder are alive and flourishing. And they are my pride. My greatest pride. They don't go hungry. I've begged from the Council, from the hospital board, even from the constabulary. I've begged, as I've been begging all my life long. That just about sums it up. And yesterday—would you believe it?—the superintendent of the Welfare Office looked at me, all innocence, and said: 'Now look here, Gordon, what have you been up to with these children? An incredible death rate! You must be selling their rations on the black market and keeping a mistress on the proceeds . . .' The swine! It was he himself who gave orders for the children to be deported . . . What stopped me from killing him wasn't that I was afraid. It was the thought of the children who are still with us . . .

"Listen, Boris, when the sweep starts couldn't you get L.L. to arrange a swap? We keep the young, they take the old. How can they deport children, little children . . . ? I myself would gladly go. In the first batch. Though as for finding someone to take my place here . . ."

He gestured helplessly.

CHAPTER 8

The only garden left in our walled-up town was the old cemetery, whose earliest graves dated back to the thirteenth century. It was densely overgrown. Picking one's way to its remoter corners meant battling through whole armies of ferns and weeds. One advanced like a diver among the plants on the sea bed. In the old days, around the tombstones of the great and the holy, one used to find thousands of little cards bearing intimate prayers scribbled by God-fearing supplicants. They implored the dead to intercede on their behalf in the High Court of the Beyond. Stirred by a curiosity which was yet devoid of blasphemy, I used to enjoy ferreting out the mighty secrets of the humble by surreptitiously reading these pious petitions. I remember on one occasion chancing upon the prayer of a widow calling for the death of her only child—a girl whose cosseted upbringing had entailed endless sacrifice, but who was guilty of harboring love for a renegade.

Today I did not find a single one of these faded little cards in the old cemetery. Were our people praying elsewhere? Had faith in the decisive influence of the Great Dead been extinguished? Or in their infinite kindness? All the same, a few cheap candles were still burning on the carved tomb of Tori Zahav, author of one of the key commentaries. Likewise on that of the Golden Rose, who—four hundred years earlier—had succeeded, by means of a miracle and a sacrifice, in deflecting a Tatar chieftain's wrath from our overgrown village.

My state of mind in these hours: that of a reporter making the fullest use of his eyes and ears with the aim of wiring a special dispatch to his paper. But what *was* my paper . . . ? I fought my way through the resistant vegetation till I came to the mortuary. A group of beggars stood intoning psalms over close to a hundred bodies. Old Yaakov, who knew me well thanks to the frequent bottles of vodka that I used to slip to his mendicant crew of saintly songsters, whispered in my ear: "Fifty-eight suicides last night alone. And let me tell you this: who are they? Not ordinary folk. Not the men and women who are dying of hunger. Bigwigs, every one of them: the ones who even today could afford to keep the cold out and eat better than the rest of us ate before the coming of this Angel of Death."

Scandalized, but obviously proud of the social position of his corpses, he led me around in a thoroughly proprietary manner: "There's Professor Caro and his good lady. They used gas. Don't suppose they felt anything. And that's Urias the banker—the fellow who, three years ago, shelled out three million toward the restoration of the Main Synagogue . . . And this one? Don't you recognize him? It's Tarnovski the poet. Hanged himself. Just look at that bruise. He had no money for poison."

I remembered the fine translations from Homer and Dante, and the bridge that Tarnovski had sought to throw across the Bosporus, linking Mount Olympus and Mount Zion. He had told me of this bridge of the future, and of how it was to be ornamented, of the gargoyles and grotesques that he had thought of adding.

I nearly jumped: Shulamith's body was there, lying on a narrow oaken trestle. Her black tresses set off her delicate, exceedingly white frame. I recognized the fold of skin below her left breast.

Were those eyes—mirroring the yellow candle flames, and so still and glazed and staring—trying to send me a message? For a split second I relived our first night together and saw again the bloodstains on the sheet at our first awakening, an awakening more distracted and more decisive than the early hours. Neither of us was yet twenty. The act that we had performed, the bond that we had established and discovered, this strange new quantity that had come into being between us—these seemed so much more important than ourselves. Had I been in love with Shulamith, or with her virginity, or with the nameless force that had impelled me to take her? In every fiber of my being I re-experienced the tough resistance of the secret parts that I had rent with a determination which—as I had felt even then—belonged not to my own self but to an outer, encroaching universe.

And afterwards, the weeks in the mountain country, among the lambs and the sheep which used to wake us with their bleating. The silvery torrents, the trees, the hidden tracks high in the Carpathians, where—two centuries earlier—the *Baal Shem Tob,* or Master of the Good Name, had met the mountain-bandit leader Dovbush and revealed the mysteries of Divine Will to him.

You who were so silent, Shulamith, must accompany me on the journey for which I am preparing. In the course of it, silence will be the one token of fidelity to the selves we were.

I reached out, meaning to stroke Shulamith's tresses. Old Yaakov stopped me.

"Mr. Boris, you are not allowed to touch the bodies. You belong to the Kingdom of Priests, and such contact would defile you. Is it for me to teach you the Law?

"In the days when things were normal, you weren't even allowed to set foot in here or so much as look at the bodies. But I have taken this sin upon myself. You believe in God and you give charitably. Go now, and should we survive this day do not forget me. With things as they are, it isn't easy for a man to keep body and soul together when all he can do is recite psalms. I've got work to do. They must all be cleansed, so that they may be granted the Burial of the Just, in accordance with the holy rites of our people."

I left Yaakov to his work, which he performed like a black and agile spider; but my walk in the garden was not over. After gazing at the death of human beings, I was confronted, on my way out, by the death of stones.

Along the main pathway, under the supervision of a sentry in *Feldgrau,* ten or a dozen rickety marionettes were jerking sledge hammers about—not to mention their bones. Another group was hauling wheelbarrows. The party was demolishing some old tombstones. The blind, deafening hammer blows were scattering the sacred characters from inscriptions half a millennium old, and composed in praise of some holy man or philosopher. An *aleph* would go flying off to the left, while a *he* carved on another piece of stone dropped to the right. A *gimel* would bite the dust and a *nun* follow in its wake . . . Several examples of *shin,* a letter symbolizing the miraculous intervention of God, had just been smashed and trampled on by the hammers and feet of these moribund workmen.

Once the dissolute army of letters had broken free of its

ordained contexts, was it going to invade the world of the living, the world of so-called secular objects, hunting down all
that was harmonious? Was it going to deal blind and deadly
blows like a whole band of Golems run riot?

What a tremendous flood of energy these dying, makeshift
workmen were setting loose! Were the fragments about to
turn into white-hot shell splinters? Once their journeyings
through so many towns and nations was at an end, were the
sacred letters—lonely now—going to reorganize themselves
into a new community, creating a simple, cruel order, the
very opposite of the one that had just been destroyed before
our eyes? Was the secret life of these murdered tombstones
going to continue in these chips and granules, scattered
here, there, and everywhere, lurking in unsuspected holes
and corners?

The working party stank—even in the open air. Under the
eye of their grubby sentry, they dared not beg aloud. Death
—that of their fellow men, of the stones, their own—had become unimportant to them; but hunger hadn't. Though the
sound had been barely audible, like the sigh of the wind, I
caught the word *lekhem,* which means bread. I didn't have
any. I plunged my hand into my pocket and, with a quick
jab of the wrist, tossed a small piece of chocolate in the direction of the group. Three or four of the workers flung themselves down. It wasn't their hands that moved, but their long
skinny necks, as they gobbled a mixture of dust and tiny
scraps of chocolate.

Fear said: "You mustn't become like them!"

A voice said: "You must espouse their condition, their
stench, before you die. You mustn't miss this unique opportunity. The divine door is open. You must plumb the
depths."

The tombstones were giving way before the thudding

blows of the sledge hammers. Like a child who has constantly thumbed through the same picture book, I knew the bas-reliefs by heart, and their simple, ageless language:

A candlestick: a God-fearing woman, mother, and spouse.

Two palms set in an attitude of benediction handed down from the time of the First Temple: beneath this stone there lies a priest.

A felled tree: this man died before fulfilling his earthly destiny.

Fish: all living creatures perished in the Flood except those who dwelt in the waters. The flood of God's wrath exterminates evildoers. He who lies beneath this stone was just, and he will survive as the fish did.

The Lions of Judah and the stags and the winged dragons and the books carved on the tombstones of the Doctors of the Law were going down under the hammer.

I must escape, I thought, I must rescue the old cemetery . . . Shall I ever be able to take it upon my shoulders, like a black cloak? Muffled up in the old cemetery, as though in the sky, I must start on my journey toward distant lands, and may we not be recognized! May nobody recognize us!

CHAPTER 9

"Well, young Boris, next time we meet, it will be on the shelves of Smiechowski's shop . . ." As he cracked this now extremely stale joke, my friend Abracha lit up the dark cellar with his smile. I smiled back. Smiechowski owned a soap factory, and on his products there had lately appeared three enigmatical letters: "R.J.F." In the opinion of the race which had considerable experience in solving such riddles, they stood for *Rein Jüdisches Fett.*[1] Abracha was working as an electrician at the time—though actually he was a jack-of-all-trades and a good friend to the whole town.

His skilled touch was greatly appreciated by those who were commissioning underground hide-outs equipped with every ingenious device.

Where was he from? Nobody knew for certain. Accounts were rife concerning his origins and peregrinations, but they were more often contradictory than complementary. He had traveled a lot and lived for a time in France and Persia.

"After I'd got to France and spent the last of my money," he told me one day, "I had to find a job. Well, I found one all right. It was in a toy factory. For eight hours a day—some-

[1] Pure Jewish Fat.

times twelve, when there was a rush on—I was at my bench stuffing teddy bears' bellies. Day in, day out, for eight months. It was worse than being a machine. At least a machine goes out of action at times. But not me. At the end of eight months, the foreman comes up to me and says to me in their lingo—I'd picked up a bit of it by that time—anyway, he says to me: 'I've got good news for you. You're a good worker. The ones we had before used to throw up the job as soon as they'd put a bit by. But you're reliable. You've stuck it. We're grateful. So, from tomorrow on, you're promoted. You won't be stuffing bellies any more. You'll be stuffing ears!'

"No need to tell you: I beat it the very next day. In Marseilles I joined the crew of a boat that was sailing for Iran . . ."

"And was Iran pleasant?"

"Pleasant? My eye!" Abracha's face assumed an expression of intense distaste. "They say Persia is the land of the thousand and one marvels. If you ask me, it's the land of a thousand and one farts. They didn't even have any vodka. A bottle of whisky cost—let's see now—something like a week's wages. And in comparison with the locals, I was making a fortune. And not even wine. I was happy when I was able to clear out. That would have been in—let me think —that would have been in 193–."

To have been a Red Army soldier in Budënny's cavalry, Abracha must have been over forty, but the alertness of his movements, the mocking expression in his eyes, and his inexhaustible cheerfulness were those of a man of twenty-five . . . if that. He was the buddy of everyone, and everyone was his buddy. The events of the past year had in no way affected his spirit, exercised no influence over his inner metabolism. He remained exactly as he had always been. He was doing well for himself, but was incapable of holding on to money. With a perpetual cigarette butt in his mouth, thin, wiry, passionately addicted to zakuski and coarse jokes, he put one in mind of a liaison officer—not only between different streets, but between the various social strata of our melting community. The news that he passed on might assume a comic guise, but it was always accurate. He enjoyed free access to the occupying army's barracks. Our Council would have been only too glad to employ him for certain delicate tasks. Abracha had charm and courage, and these did not spring from any failure to recognize danger. His contacts in the part of the town that was closed to us constituted a considerable asset, but Abracha was in no hurry to bring them under official control.

"If you're ever up against it, let me know," he said. "I'll get you over the wall and through the lines. That goes for your girls too. In reasonable quantities, of course."

"You know I don't want to leave. After all, this town more or less belongs to me. As far as I'm concerned, those who are dying are the only possible companions . . . My family, my landscape, my cemetery. It's absurd, but I have the feeling it would be a cheap way out not to pay for all that I have received from my God. But what about you, Abracha? There's nothing to keep you here. The front is only two hundred miles away."

At this, he began to open up.

"I've done enough traveling to last me to the end of my days. I've lived with the Kazaks and with the Tatars. I had a wife in Tashkent. I spent two years in the Moscow jail . . . I suppose you don't know the Great Steppe of Hunger? Not far from there—well perhaps 'not far' isn't quite accurate— live the Tungus and their shamans. Incredible customers. They can turn the sunlight on and off, as and when they choose. They use moonbeams to make silvery milk for their youngsters. Then there's the Uzbeks. They move with their flocks, from one grazing ground to another. Whenever they have a guest, they dish up a couscous. At the end of the day, you all sit telling jokes and everybody gets under the same lambskin rug: grandma and grandpa, and father and mother, and little girls. I didn't miss my chances . . . Farther on, along the road to Tashkent, there are rose plantations right in the heart of the desert. The biggest plantations and the biggest roses in the world. The scent lulls you and makes you tired as death. And the Uzbek girls flit about among the bushes, smiling and silent, snipping off flowers with their scissors. Very silent, they are. Just a quiet click now and then. Attar and babies—that's all they make down there . . . The water from artesian wells smells of roses. Even the dung smells of roses . . .

"I could go there. It's true. I could go on living, but my old lady won't hear of it."

He blurted this out with apparent reluctance. A silence formed between us, which he was the first to break.

"You don't know my old lady. Nobody in this town does, though she has been living here for years. Ever since her accident. You don't know what you've all been missing . . . Though it's been my own fault. If you can call it a fault. Come with me now. You'll find it's worth it . . ."

The outside of the house had a mangy look. There were only two windows on each floor. The stairs were dark and narrow.

"It's on the third floor," said Abracha. "She never goes out. I take her her food. She doesn't go short of anything. Wait a moment . . ."

He knocked four times. There was no sound of movement. He began to shout: "It's me—Abracha. You asleep?"

"Have you got someone with you?" asked a low, distinct voice.

"I've brought a friend to see you, Lena. You'll have to entertain him."

He gave the door a shove, and it creaked painfully open. We were in a room filled to bursting with crates and trunks which appeared to be substitutes for chairs and tables and chests of drawers. An extremely wide bed took up half the floor. I was unable to make out the features of the woman who lay beneath innumerable raspberry-colored blankets, with two big fat cats beside her motionless head.

"There isn't anything you need?" said Abracha. "Well then, I'll leave the two of you. Have a good time. I've got to hop back to the hospital. Their X-ray machine needs mending. See you later."

Suddenly I was overcome by a feeling of having been here before, of reliving a scene from the past. Sitting myself down on the bed, I began to stroke one of the purring cats and strove to attune myself to this somewhat bizarre setting. What was I to say to this bedridden woman? The silence was beginning to weigh on me. Why the devil had Abracha been so keen to bring me to this attic? I made an effort.

"So you're his aunt, madame? He has never mentioned you. I thought he was all alone in our town. Is there anything I can do for you?"

She didn't answer right away. Suddenly the rays of the setting sun lit up her emaciated face, which I had failed to discern till then. The head, which put one in mind of an icon, was weighed down by an enormous mass of red hair. The skin was of the purest whiteness. The nose, slightly tilted, clashed with the tragic look of the large, deep-set, motionless eyes.

Finally she spoke: "You're Boris, the young Baron, aren't

you? Abracha has been telling me about you. It seems you
are being difficult, you don't want to leave. Is that so? Well,
you must. It is written in Genesis: 'Therefore shall a man
leave his father and his mother, and shall cleave unto his
wife . . .' I'm not telling you to cleave unto ONE woman, but
unto all those whom you are going to have in the life that
lies ahead of you . . . Besides, what is a woman? Have you
ever asked yourself that? She is concavity, emptiness. And
for you . . . emptiness does not even come to meet fullness.
There is no process of meeting, of identification. For you
. . . emptiness IS fullness. It is always like that in the beginning. Is it for this that you must survive . . . ? The one true
emptiness is the life that you are going to lead after we are
dead. It isn't you who are in any way exceptional. Your
destiny is somewhat so."

I attempted to smile.

"Don't make me out an exceptional being, madame. Everybody thinks he is, so I know that I am not. If I really
were, I would know. And if I had that knowledge, I would
know it was false. Let us come down to earth."

She broke in, with a note of displeasure: "I am not flattering you. It isn't you who are exceptional but your destiny.
Perhaps you are not yet ready to share ours. Or worse: you
are not worthy of it. Or rather, I am expressing myself badly:
the great, the exceptional destiny belongs to the people, to
all of us. Yours is dusty and commonplace. You see—I am not
flattering you. On this earth, the smallest child is related to
somebody. But not you. You have never been able to accept
that other people are the blood that flows in our veins. You
have lived without that fluid. For you, other people were
merely a plaything, a toy; and by other people I mean all of
us. Even those you have claimed to love. So you trifle with the
blood in your veins. The day you find yourself without your

toy—and that day is coming—I shan't envy you. The abyss
will be your only friend, the fall into it your only lawful mistress. And the Town will become a thorn in your flesh. Inside, within the walls of this thorn, which will go on growing
and growing, the Town will be reborn, with its little
wooden houses, its little gutted houses."

Suddenly, wordlessly, she grasped my left hand. I surren-
dered to her . . . And then: "Now, Boris," she said, "get up
and look out of the window . . . "

Should I have resented it? I have never been capable of detecting real malice in human beings. I have never found any.
Mad or not, Lena radiated goodness. Obeying her command,
I went over to the window. The house nestled at the foot of
Eagle Mountain. Gilded by the sun's last rays, the old straggling town was still there, faithful to its usual image. Mute
belfries. Cornices like dead birds. The broad, willow-
lined river. The Mountain of Prince Daniel, who, before
founding the town, had ordered the blinding of his beloved
brother Michael, to avoid the possibility of dynastic complications . . . The forests, the old shanties. The houses,
chapped like faces. The unseeing windows.

I knew it by heart, this view unfolding like an Egyptian
bas-relief. There was no perspective to impose scales on this
landscape; all its components beckoned the eye TOGETHER
from an equal distance. I knew by heart, I felt in every fiber,
the coolness of the river water, the shade of the oak forests,
the history of the castle, and even—or so it seemed to me—
the histories of the men and women living in the old slum
dwellings: their hours of merriment and their times of hardship, their loves and their hates, their dreams and their awak-
enings. Too extreme, the involvement of my senses and my
soul. Too generous, this gift pouring into me through the
grimy windowpanes of this unswept attic room. I was being

overwhelmed by a prodigal, untamed simultaneity that was the source of wild and painful wealth. The scene, flat as a fresco, as a crude backcloth, was hurling its splendors and horrors at me in a single mighty sweep. Its present was there, and its past. It was through here that the Varangian troops passed, and the caravans from Arabia and the Byzantine Empire. Here the merchants from Scandinavia pitched their camps and exchanged their goods with the doubly nomadic Jews. It was from this town that Dov Baer, Holy Bear of Meseritz, went out into the woods every Sabbath evening to talk to God, eye to eye, brow to brow.

Simultaneity of crowding images: a mighty extendable staircase that suddenly, as one is about to climb it, rears in front of one in a gigantic, inaccessible vertical. A waterfall, abruptly stilled and challenging.

The low, panting town, the russet-haired town was racing, like a basset hound, against its own disappearance. And now the town was turning into a rapid, and the rapid into a snake. An anemic snake crawling among blazing bushes. All that remained of the snake was a few withered scales reflecting the sunlight. And now only one scale, one solitary scale turning into a piercing memory.

My legs buckled. I sank back onto Lena's bed, my head spinning. Silence. The seconds were buzzing around us like dark insects.

A very gentle voice said: "Forgive me, Boris. It's all over. I knew that in your case I'd have to resort to the view. There are others to whom I could do this with just an inkstain or candle flame. I am an old woman. Years ago, lots of people used to come and see me. Grand Dukes, even. That was in Orlovsk, near the old capital. It was I who told Grishka Rasputin the very day on which he would die. It is hard to break such news to others. And yet, it is enough to have felt just

once, but felt truly, that time is ONE, never afterwards forgetting what you have felt . . . Then you see what people
call 'the future' in the same light as you suddenly see the
curve of a road that you have walked along hundreds of
times before. For nothing passes away; everything endures.
Abraham, Isaac, and Jacob are here in this room. And so is
the bleating of their sheep. What is the use of trying to fight
it? You are going to leave here and acquire a new self. You
won't be 'Baron' Boris any more . . . This town, which you
love so much and which gave you such a fright just now, will
be burned to the ground, but it will still be here . . . At
least, it will always be somewhere. Don't worry. One day you
will find the road that leads back to it. If only I had more
strength I'd tell you a story, the saddest story of all, a story
about you: about a man who doesn't like fighting, but who
fights. He fights against his own zodiacal sign. And, maybe
to have its revenge on the man, that sign abhors him and galls
him . . ."

She gave a cough: "You haven't got a decent cigarette on
you, have you? I'm fed to the teeth with *makhorkha*; that's all
Abracha ever thinks of bringing me."

The smoke that she was exhaling filled the room with
the shapes of castles, bridges, and towers, which hung motionless in the air for longer than my tired eyes could focus
them. Leave here? Why should I? I wasn't especially keen to
live. The thought of being confronted with my new self,
which—if I was to believe Lena—was patiently awaiting me
somewhere beyond my present life, filled me with disquiet.
What about my everyday self? I found that quite hard
enough to get along with. I am anything but an adventurer.
Is that why adventure came in search of me? The way ahead
had seemed clearly marked out for me, so brief yet so broad,

ending in the mass paupers' grave in which I would share the fate of my fellows.

There was something else too, a far from negligible detail barring the way to this outside world which was so repugnant to me. A perfect excuse. More than an excuse.

It was as though Lena were reading my thoughts.

"I know," she said, "you are thinking of the tale. It's real and serious. Great suffering is ahead of you. Vaster than your body and your soul. But when the time comes, it will not hold you back . . . How shall I describe your suffering? It is of the nature of the black fire, of the shades, of the bottomless pit. Not that of light. For the shades suffer, and light too is subject to pain. And suffering itself suffers likewise. As do stars, rays, and lines.

"A man once told me about these things: 'It hurts the triangle,' he said, 'that it should be condemned to inflict suffering with its corners, condemned to go on gashing and hurting the universe for evermore.'

"All this is complicated, too complicated for my old head. But I am only a messenger. And the day will come, I know it will, when you will remember my saying this . . .

"I've no wish to hurt you, but there it is: you haven't earned the right to stay."

Coming out of Lena's, I found a small, dirty, crumpled piece of paper lying in the road. It was a birth certificate made out in the name of Yuri Goletz, christened on August 4, 192–, in St. Basil's Church, Svanovo. Father's occupation: farm hand. I'd heard it said that people sometimes paid in dollars for papers of this kind. Mechanically, I folded the paper and put it in my pocket.

CHAPTER 10

Haven't you ever been interrogated by electric current? *asked my customer*. I don't know whether they use it in this country. In the most advanced nations of my acquaintance, it's a commonplace practice. The manuals (for internal distribution only) of certain institutions, which have carried research into the human animal further than the medical profession, likewise indicate HOW the current should be used in order to rule out any effective resistance on the part of the interrogated. It's simple. They put a steel ring around your penis. I don't know exactly what the routine is in the case of women, but they are sure to be endowed with some equally sensitive region . . . You don't feel a thing apart from the cold, which is in no way unbearable. The room is well furnished and newly painted, preferably pale gray. The portrait of some leader, on the wall, is extremely apposite—I would even say indispensable. His mustache absolves all sins, even before they are committed.

Whoever is interrogating you sits down at his desk and runs his fingers over a button. Obviously, however much you are affecting indifference, you can't help looking at him. For his part, he doesn't look at you: only at the button. The moment he moves his finger toward it, you screw up all your strength: I must resist, I will resist! You clothe yourself, in anticipation, in your thickest armor. You bid agony come, and set it at nought. He can pluck the living heart from me, and I won't cry out, I won't confess to anything. I'll pull through. You have summoned all your resources: huge they are, haughty as a mountain. All the same, you take a peep at the switch. And then: click! The figure at the desk has pressed his button. The shock?! Where is the shock . . . ?! It hasn't come. You have expended yourself in anticipation, your resistance has been whirring away to no avail. You were as strong as a lion, as steadfast as a martyr of the Church, and all for nothing. And just as you are saying to yourself: "What a pity, I'd have been splendid!" the shock arrives, savage and excruciating, too much for your resolutions, too much for you. "You" no longer exist. Then, but only then, you start to scream, and after that . . . it's cards on the table.

All this is down in writing, in the official handbooks. It's old-hat. But generally the procedure is practiced on individuals. The day I went to the old cemetery, he who was the enemy of our everyday and the friend of our eternal peace employed the same method on a collective scale. He pressed the button. Our town was watching him. But the current hadn't been turned on. Not yet. The pogrom didn't materialize. Evening found me back in my cold cellar, tired and unappeased. On her return from the Garin Workshops, Naomi warmed me up, hair tangling with hair, skin against skin, lip to lip.

CHAPTER 11

The Golden Mountain

Nor did anything occur in the next six days. Captain H.'s lusty boys were camped around the wall. They would shoot compassionate glances over the top, at the buildings, at our constabulary, and at the girls. Was this the vibrant complicity that arises between artist and raw material before the act of creation begins?

They would sing jolly army songs and sluice themselves down at the pumps.

The Council strove to achieve a calm beyond the realms of possibility. The Captain, it said, would go off in search of other pastures. The Captain had given his word of honor. A contribution would have to be paid; the sum had yet to be determined . . .

On Thursday evening the Council's messengers made their rounds: all women whose surname was Goldberg—Golden Mountain—were to report at the main gate.

I knew six who had gone into hiding, not without drawing upon themselves the spiteful remonstrances of their neighbors: "They'll be the death of us. And fancy bearing such a pretentious and plutocratic name in times like these! Fancy parading one's gold under THEIR hungry noses! It's people like them who have brought our sufferings upon us . . ."

Twenty-seven Goldberg women made their way to the guardhouse by the main gate. Name and pallor excepted, not a feature in common. They were made to stand in a long line, like the fragile keys of a spinet, the youngest four years and two months, the oldest eighty-nine. Five tradesmen's wives, comparatively well fed. One tense, red-haired militant Communist, one dressmaker, one earnest, resolute streetwalker. Being entitled to share the fate of respectable women counted for more in her eyes than the nature of that fate, which was concealed from her, as it was from her companions.

Leo L.—I think he must have fortified himself with a few drinks—was determined to make a short speech:

"O Goldberg women . . . The bond that united you to one another may have seemed slender, entirely fortuitous. The majority of you, I will wager, have never given an ounce of consideration to those hidden vibrations, to that imperceptible aura, which a NAME gives off when we utter it, or even when we do not. Vibrations of a kind that release the hidden springs of destiny. Which of you can ever have devoted even a moment's thought to the relationship between the NAME and the man or woman who bears it? And yet . . . I shall make no mention of the so-called 'scientific' truths. In the light of the great times in which we are living, they are truly stripped of their power—what am I saying?—they are eroded, invalidated.

"You have lived out your little lives in close proximity to one another without detecting the link that exists deep down between you, without ever concerning yourselves with the hidden paths of destiny that today—who knows?—may be singling you out for the great task of redeeming our sacred, ageless community. Unless it is elevating you to a higher path, to the path of seemingly pointless sacrifice. But there is no such thing as pointless sacrifice.

"All the same, it is my hope and wish that my final supposition shall prove to have been quite unfounded!

"O Goldberg men!" he flung at a terrified group of males. "Close your hearts to sadness! If not your wives themselves, at least the sacred memory of them will be restored to you before long . . ."

He had intended to go on, but the Captain's adjutant appeared at the gate and whispered a few words into the ear of the old President, who then concluded: "Ladies, all that I am in a position to add is that I profoundly envy you your fate, without—alas—being able to share it. My name and sex have never seemed such a heavy burden . . ."

An unknown soldier was scanning the faces attentively. He seemed to hesitate. Then: "Forward march!"

The Indian file of Goldberg women disappeared through the gap in the wall. They were never seen again.[1]

[1] There is a danger of this chapter's remaining incomprehensible to readers, as it is to the author. All I could get out of my customer was a strange unconfirmed rumor, according to which one of the Captain's associates had caught gonorrhea from a Miss Goldberg. In view of the laws of the occupying power, which punished all contacts between the races—the pure and the impure—the soldier in question could not officially proclaim the motive for his revenge. On the other hand, he enjoyed complete latitude in exerting it. Other reports claimed that it was all a mistake. Soldier Handtke had made love to a girl called Goldstein—Golden Rock—but, being somewhat hard of hearing, he had muddled the two names, which were, after all, so similar . . .

CHAPTER 12

It was on a Saturday morning, more than a week later, that the sweep began. I shan't inflict a full account on you. If you haven't memories of your own to call on, rummage in your imagination, rummage among certain of your dreams—in which I am fully prepared to trust. As for Naomi, myself, and a few other persons whom I have mentioned in my account of the preceding days . . . well, we all came through it alive—even old Yaakov and his team of psalmsters. All except Dr. Hillel, who hanged himself in his library on the very day of our last meeting.

Can it be that courage and cowardice constitute an inseparable duet, a *dvandva,* a tandem like emptiness and fullness? To tell you the truth, and I'm not boasting, I made no attempt whatever to escape the big sweep. At the time, dying struck me as easy and pleasurable. And death's response was that of the eternal woman. Since I did not flee, she turned her back on me. I spent hours in hiding places that were reputedly unreliable. I would go out in the middle of indiscriminate roundups, without a document to my name, running an unpaid messenger service between parties who had been separated by the sudden beginning of a sweep hitherto so frequently postponed. My fair hair and my well-cut suit and my easy gait did not especially invite the attentions of Captain H.'s boys. For all that, there were certainly moments of cowardice and intense fear. These generally assailed me in the evening, when—their working day over—the troops left our quarter and made their way back to barracks, a song on their lips.

Suppose the old woman was right, suppose one day I was free of this merry-go-round—how would I live? Who would I be? A man who has undergone plastic surgery must experience the same fear prior to seeing the new shape of his nose reflected in a mirror for the very first time. Can a burrowing mole survive in mountain air?

Between the passing of youth and the coming of "social maturity" there stretches a no man's land, habitat of the ill-adjusted and the luckless . . . My fears were borne out one day, much, much later—but how could one tell? Already, in the moments that I am describing, I had forebodings of that dark and pestilential region. Living among enemies is nothing in comparison to a life spent in an environment of indifference.

From the street came screams and the chatter of guns. I leafed through some of my old notes. I was startled by the ugliness of my own verses. Let the soldiers come! All my will power was strained in the direction of these soldiers, who would be bound to bring me the final, conclusive message. Was that why, was it on account of this straining will power, that they did not come? For the conclusive message did not exist. In vain did I hunt for it among these old jottings of mine:

> Time is a conveyance
> Bound for the black hole.
> Time is a commentary

(It will have commented on nothing).
Time is a lancet
Peeling away, peeling away:
From skin, its luster;
From our bones, their skin;
Nondecay
From the decay of our bones;
Luster from nonluster

                 etc.

Or again:

     I have it on a leash,
     The past,
     Trailing it after me like
     (But naturally!)
     Like a dog.

     Like the dog on a leash
     I trail it after me,
     The past.

     And it howls like an injured dog,
     The past,
     And I lick its blood.
     (Butnat-butnat-butnat

                 ural
                   ly!)

The screaming and gun-chatter came through the window. They were getting closer. I began to write, deliberately, in a controlled, painstaking hand:

"If Boris's poems were to be brought together in a single volume, they would bite one another till they drew blood, they would kick up a shindy, they would devour one another. But set your mind at rest! Boris's poems will never be brought together in a single volume. The volume will never exist. The poems will never exist. Poetry does not exist. Nor does Boris."

Was that why the soldiers did not come?

A grub, a favored grub, ensconced in a juicy, overripe pear and threatened with transfer to a hard green apple, must go through similar moments. But enough of these all too personal recollections. Basically, these chapters ought to have only three heroes: a bridge, a mill, and a hospital. The living merchandise—*was* it living, though?—was stored in the mill. The bridge led to the railway sidings. And the hospital? Its turn will come. As for the fourth hero, Mr. Garin, the false Messiah whom I mentioned earlier, he arrived in town at the height of the catastrophe. To those who had to go, for whom there was no way out, he brought the gift of a few days' hope. He paid for his mission from Above with his life and with his death. I was to see his corpse. Death brought an openness to his face, which in his lifetime had always seemed shut tight. Far be it from me to speak ill of Mr. Garin. The present that he made my town was the only present it wished to receive.

Mr. Garin saw his structure crumble when, with the beginning of the sweep, Captain H.'s troops invaded the Workshops. It didn't even have anything to do with the Workshops or those who, by dint of faith, had transformed them into an illusory safety zone; it was simply that a quarrel had briefly arisen between the Captain and the town's Mayor.

The Mayor—a well-meaning Rhinelander deposited in our native plain by the victor's service transport—had affirmed before our community councilors, struck with wordless admiration: "Those who are working for the Mayor have nothing to fear. They are going to come through this war alive! This I guarantee. That's official!" And indeed, it was not his guards, but the Captain's soldiers, who, within a week of this solemn declaration, burst into the Workshops to take away two thousand young men and girls.

"To hell with the Mayor!" the Captain kept shouting, in response to the timid protestations of the personnel manager. Even after his mission was accomplished, he continued for several days to harbor a thoroughly military-minded contempt for the Mayor's administrative softness. "Oh, the people they send us as civil administrators!" he would confide to his associates. "They don't understand the first thing about this backward country. Not the first thing!" A reconciliation was effected only on the occasion of the banquet in the officers' mess, given by the Mayor for the Captain and his team, the night before they left town.

A vibrant emptiness had thus invaded the huge Garin Workshops. A few dozen survivors—a framework with nothing to support, a cadre without an army—were singing hymns for the dead when I stole into the premises to spend the night there. What I found, I shall tell you later. My own day had been no less eventful than that of the Garin Corporation. A lady in her fifties—a one-time *poule de luxe* who, in exchange for resoundingly hard cash, had offered us her hospitality—had got me out of bed at six in the morning.

"Mr. Boris, you must leave at once. And your lady too. I'm terribly sorry, but patrols are out searching every house for members of your race. New notices have been posted: anyone caught hiding them is to be shot instantly. See for yourself."

I have to admit that it was nerves and embarrassment that were making me yawn. Not the remnants of sleep. For the first time in my life, I was being turned out. I stood shaving with hands that did not entirely belong to me. Naomi was trying to negotiate: "I'm so sleepy, Madame Olga, won't you let us stay just one more hour . . . ? Perhaps the patrols will move to another district. It's so warm here in your house, so nice . . ."

I sneaked a glance out of the window. There was a country look about this small, select quarter on the edge of town. Such peace and quiet! A squirrel was darting about among the leaves of an elm tree.

"Mr. Boris, Miss Naomi . . . Had I known the troubles you were going to bring down on my roof, I would never have taken you in, not even for a thousand gold rubles . . . Anyway . . . If the young lady wishes to stay, well, she has good papers and her face isn't known hereabouts. I shall say she is a cousin of mine, from Rostov. They're brunettes, the girls in Rostov. Nobody can prove anything. Rostov is on the other side of the front. You see, while you two were sleeping, I was racking my brains. But as for you, Mr. Boris, you're a man—and you can say that again . . ." A fleeting smile lit up her time-worn face. "It's different for a man. If you'll pardon the expression, they'll have your pants down in a jiffy and we'll all be caught like rats in a trap."

Thus the question of the tool was taking on the color of reality.

I drained all the resources of my eloquence in an attempt to persuade Naomi to accept this offer which, in view of the circumstances, was lacking in neither sense nor generosity. The old dear was right: notwithstanding my fair hair and apparent calm, it was indeed I who was principally liable to bring about the extermination of this peaceful little household. The sign of the Covenant, inscribed in my body long ago, as it had been inscribed in the bodies of my forefathers and THEIR forefathers, could be made out all too plainly by those taking part in the hunt that was going on in our town. It was within the capacity of the dimmest oaf from Bavaria to interpret this hieroglyph, which meant certain death for me, for Naomi, and for our good hostess.

The only effect of my words had been to increase the speed with which Naomi got dressed.

"You are not leaving here alone," she said to me. And then: "Thank you, Madame Olga, thank you all the same . . ."

The old girl was wavering. She had expected opposition from us. Perhaps even entreaties. The prospect of death was receding with our departure, but so was that of untold easy pickings. True, when we left her house we would be taking death with us, but we would be taking life as well. Madame Olga would be left with nothing but her once glittering, now tarnished, memories and the slow rhythm of her days as a woman of independent means.

A touch of coquetry for my benefit. A smile: "You needn't leave in quite such a hurry. The samovar is on the boil."

Plucked from this cozy interior, whose alien fustiness had been a haven, and pitched into the bright, shelterless street, we recognized our own trembling as the enemy, the main enemy. Why couldn't Madame Olga's house take on the properties of cloth? If only we could tailor ourselves a flowing cloak from it and become invisible! If only we could be turned to dust, cease to exist—anything rather than have to bridge this alarming gap which was luring us on and lying in wait for us at every step.

The gray-green soldiers were advancing along the other

side of the street. They were looking up at the sky. Were they scanning it for the game that existed in such profusion only a quarter of a mile away, within the walled-up town?

In this peaceful quarter, thoroughly Christian and thoroughly Slav, it was their mission to track down such of us as might have fled the encirclement of walls and men. A combing operation which, all in all, held out little promise of being fruitful. Were they envying their colleagues, immersed in their labors at that very moment?

Suddenly an idle glance came to rest on us like an obscene caress. And that was that. Another two seconds and the question would come, polite and impersonal: "Your papers please?" Naomi clutched at my arm, and already I was tugging her zestfully toward the patrol.

"What *is* the exact time, Corporal? My watch is up to its tricks again."

A fraction of a second went by. The blue eyes unhurriedly probed our two exteriors. And then came the answer: "Twenty to eight, sir. No, twenty-*three* minutes to eight. I'm bound to be fast."

Slowly and deliberately I produced my Tula-silver cigarette case, a present to my grandfather from his brother, the miracle man of Miropoly. Intrinsically, the object was reasonably attractive, but of no great value: nothing to shout about. It was on account of its original owner, who'd had the reputation of sanctifying everything he touched, that the Zaddik's devotees offered me enormous sums for this piece of antique silver.

The "Lion of Miropoly" was a rabbi renowned among his peers and in his generation, and extraordinarily vehement in his dealings with God. It was with admiration that his followers passed on his sayings—a source of incessant scandal in the eyes of his adversaries. One night, on the eve of a great feast, the Rabbi ordered his disciples to entreat the Lord not to deliver our people before all the other peoples of the world had been delivered. "What would I myself be, what would any of us be," he reasoned to his bemused followers, "if we were not flooded with love for our people? This love is the precious gift that comes to us from above. Now, would you be capable of loving the man whose belly is full, if those about him are starving?"

And to make his meaning plain to all, he related this little parable: "A poor woman going out to do her shopping leaves her children in the care of a neighbor as poor as she and endowed with as large a brood. The children start playing together and are soon making too much noise, so the neighbor offers them some sweets. Naturally, there are not many sweets in the house. Perhaps not enough to go round. To whom should the poor woman offer them first?" the holy man asked his disciples with a knowing smile. "You will hardly think it should be to her own children . . . ?"

The private conversations which it was the Lord's practice to accord the Lion of Miropoly on the eve of great feasts were, for the most part, characterized by tremendous violence.

In his role as defender of his people, the Rabbi would sometimes deliver impassioned pleas that verged on blasphemy.

One of these conversations is preserved in the record published after his death by one of his disciples:

In reply to the Rabbi's remonstrations, in which he upbraided the Lord for the sufferings endured by his people, the Lord God had started enumerating the iniquities of which recent generations had been guilty: the hardheartedness of the rich, the inordinate pride of the men of learning and the contempt in which they held the simple-minded; the innumerable transgressions of the Written and the Oral Law.

Whereupon the Rabbi broke in upon the Lord: "All this is true. I am all too aware of the sins of my brethren, and of my own sins too. But who is to blame? Of whom is it written that He created good and evil and that He sowed the seed of evil in the heart of man? Who, then, is the author, the sole author, of this impious farce enacted on this impious stage? Besides: it's all very well for You to preach goodness and nobleness and pity, sitting up there on Your marble throne, surrounded by winged lions and angels and flames. The lamentations of the world, and the smoke from our sacrifices, come to You from far, far away, from far, far below. And You are wrathful at the transgressions committed by Your creatures, delivered to their weaknesses and their despair and their hardships? What would You say if in order to feed Your family, You had to roam day in day out the fairgrounds and market places, where the peasant buying Your shoddy merchandise may at any moment turn into a savage cutthroat? If You had to wear Yourself out in petty scheming, despicable but unavoidable, and to contend with a petty tyrant who threatens to evict You and Yours from Your miserable hovel unless You pay the rent, which is long overdue, while You don't know where the next penny will be coming from? If You were the permanent target of every kind of mockery and cruelty and yet, in the teeth of it, had to survive? To survive, not because You love life (You are much too tired for that) but from a sense of duty, so that someone survived by whom Your Law would be more or less rigorously observed? If You had to endure the hunger of Your children, without being able to feed them, if You had to stand helplessly by and watch their dying and their death?"

Now it was the Lord's turn to break in upon the Rabbi: "And do you really suppose, you numskull, that I am unaware of all that? That I am not personally familiar with it, that I do not experience it? It is in My own flesh and My own blood that I share the sufferings of every one of your brethren. I am with the peddler trudging the pitiless plain in search of a living and realizing at the approach of darkness that his shabby bundle weighs as much as it did at daybreak, and that his purse is empty. I am with the father who sees his child dying, and I am with the dying child. I am that father and that child. I am that death. I am with the helpless old man, mocked at by his killers before they murder him, and it is I Myself who am that innkeeper evicted by the landowner for being behind with the rent. I am with the blasphemer who turns against Me because he can stand no more, and I am the blasphemer and his blasphemy. I tramp all the dusty roads of your sins and adversities. I am with the thief, with the trickster who repents and the trickster who does not repent . . ."

To which the Rabbi replied: "True. And yet: You are with all of them, with all of us, in the manner of a king who disguises himself as a beggar or a highwayman in order to become acquainted with the lives and death of his people. You are like a rich man spending a night in a flophouse, secure in the knowledge that once the masquerade is over, once he has gained all he wants from the experiment, he will fling off his rags and return to his mansion, there to delouse himself in a hot bath and relax in the bosom of his household. Even in the harshest of ordeals, You still have Your resources, the resources of Your divinity. It's all very well You sharing in our every hardship. You know that Your splendor awaits You, and—like so many palaces—Your endless series of universes, not to mention the everlastingness of Your bliss and the bliss of Your everlastingness."

But God retorted: "And what about you? What about all of you? On the hither side of your worst hardships, have I not extended the same resources to you, have I not opened the gates to the same palaces? Is not the least among you that same rich man disguised as a tramp?"

This interview, it appeared, left my great-uncle prostrate for several years. He fell ill; his haughty manner changed to an unbounded gentleness and humility. Several times he begged the Lord to pick another spokesman, another guardian of the age, from among his peers. But this prayer was never granted.

Was the old miracle man going to save us now?

It wasn't my brain but my whole body that was laboring and battling against these crucial moments. It would be a mistake to offer a cigarette to this soldier of death. I mustn't give the impression that I was seeking to win his lousy good will. I didn't need it. I was a person of note. A young man of good family.

The blue eyes had been following the movement of my hand with a certain disappointment. Were my hands shaking? Was the color going from my face?

"Could you give me a light, Corporal?"

"Why certainly, sir. Here you are . . ."

Could it be that the small flame sheltering within his thick, screening fingers was more ephemeral than our two lives? A hidden link was forming between OUR flame and his. It mustn't be the soldier who blew either of them out . . .

"There, that's it. Thank you, Corporal . . ."

His heavy footsteps rang out in the morning blur, a long way off already and drawing farther and farther away. I inhaled greedily. Was this really my last cigarette . . . ? Naomi did not smoke. How could I make her share a little of the ecstasy I was experiencing? I looked around. No one in sight. I kissed Naomi on her full, red, moist lips.

Where were we to go . . . ? All exits, from whatever part of town, were closely guarded. No point in trying. All civilians had to show their papers. The men had to drop their pants. And this had been going on for days, ever since the mobile brigade arrived. As for seeking shelter with friends in the Christian quarter, the troops were even now pasting up notices: local inhabitants hiding escapees from behind the wall would be shot instantly; local inhabitants handing them over would receive twenty rubles in Occupation currency, plus a two-pound bag of sugar. Sugar was scarce.

In a peaceful square we saw a small boy tugging feverishly at a soldier's sleeve: "Over there, behind that garden gate. I saw three of them making a run for it, with my own eyes. Oh, quick, sir, hurry up!"

"Well, Naomi, where are we to go?"

"Well, Boris, where are we to go?"

Sentries were making their way through the municipal park, asking the courting couples for their papers. The churches were shut. The whole world was shut.

We turned back.

Behind the castle ruins, the very place where the soldiers were at their thickest, there was a dried-up well. In preparation for an emergency and in utmost secrecy, some of the Council members had arranged the repair of a subterranean passage that linked the basement of the assembly room to this disused well. The work had been carried out at the beginning of the war. Those who had been in on this now valueless secret were no longer of this world. I repeat: the secret turned out to be valueless, for nobody knew at the outset that

the other town, THEIR town, was going to be hostile, actively
hostile. There were dreams of combined sorties, of guerrilla
units. These hopes died well and truly with those who had
cherished them. A couple out strolling in our Sunday best,
we leaned over the edge of the well. No one about. From the
haze over the river, a slightly watery sunlight. I vaulted over
first; a few seconds later, I caught hold of Naomi and we
dropped together to the bottom of the well, which was
strewn with rubble and with other, unspeakable things. I
was feverishly trying to dislodge the cluster of bricks concealing the passageway. Sounds carried to us from above. It
needed only a child to lean over the edge. Had not I myself,
as a boy, got a morbid thrill out of peering down deep wells?
Out of listening to the low rumble of empty space? We had
no means of telling what was happening up on earth. In
any case, what good would the knowledge have done us? With
my bare hands, blackened and bleeding now, I labored to
free these few bricks, whose immovability would spell
death for us. Our lives depended on the spot where a tiny
plant might have chosen to sink its roots between a pair of
clammy bricks . . . Suddenly the wall yielded. The passageway reached to a fair height, but was pitch-black. There
were faint squeaking sounds, suspicious rustlings. I went first,
holding on to Naomi's hand for all I was worth. Was it the
dampness? Was it the draft? I just couldn't get my lighter to
work. Something soft and heavy plopped onto my foot. Rats.
The ground underfoot was getting slimier all the time. We
were beginning to bog down. Every time one succeeded in
extricating a foot from the sticky substance was a victory,
every step forward, a risk—one's foot feeling its way blindly,
unable to remain poised in the air.

   "Let's take a breather," said Naomi. "Just a short one."

A shrill scream, instantly stifled.

"It's a rat! A rat jumped on my shoulder! Suppose someone heard me scream? Boris, forgive me."

No choice but to keep on the move in this confounded passage. The rats were confusing us with the walls, with the rubble, with the permanent fixtures of their landscape, which for them must exist not as something seen but as something felt. They were jumping on us, living clusters, animated by the feeling that this was their home ground. It was at this moment that I began telling Naomi a story, a tale taken from a zoology textbook (though I now have my doubts about its having been a textbook).

"Haven't you ever heard of that enchanting animal known to naturalists as the King Rat, or Royal Rat?

"It sometimes happens that one hears squeakings and pipings and yelpings coming from a rafter in some old loft—different and louder than those usually made by rats. It gets on your nerves and you pick up an ax and split the rotten beam. Whereupon it releases a monster, created out of sickness and starvation in the cramped and filthy nest: a score or so skeleton-thin rats have become so conjoined, their legs and their long tails have grown so fused and knotted, that it is no longer possible for them to disunite; the blood system of this collective organism is now one, the same blood flowing through the entanglement of tails and legs. None of them will ever again be capable of leading an independent existence. They will have to live communally, enjoying the incomparable bliss that comes from self-surrender. This living hillock bounds away, squeaking to itself, intoxicated by the fresh air . . .[1]

[1] B. Lesmian.

"Doesn't that little tale remind you of something, Naomi? Of our life on the surface . . . ?"

She dug her nails into my wrist.

"Mustn't fall," she was mumbling, "mustn't fall . . ."

The rhythm of this brief phrase was dictating the pace of our advance.

"Do let's go a bit quicker, Naomi. It can't be much farther."

CHAPTER 13

The Hospital

They were old, all three of them, these trusty, age-old land-
marks for drunks out late on winter nights and courting couples whiling away the fragrant spring evenings. The mill
and the bridge and the hospital in my town do not exist today. They were destroyed by flame-throwers belonging to the
army which, two years after the events that I am relating,
was to sweep from east to west and reoccupy our wooded
plains.

But before disappearing, the hospital and the bridge and
the mill were—in the days following our negotiation of the
disused tunnel—to pass through the richest hours in their
long, long existence.

As I said earlier:

The bridge led to the railway sidings.

Instead of silent grain, live meat was being stored in the
old mill—diseased with impatience.

The hospital—formerly a convent belonging to the Russian Orthodox nuns of the Order of St. Basil—was, and had
been from almost the very beginning of our great ordeal, an
important political and commercial meeting point. The sick
who came pouring in by the dozen were all at death's door,
true enough, but no more so than thousands of others who lay

in cellars or in the open street, covered with sacks and old newspapers, consorting with the dead. Sickness and suffering were certainly no denser within the walls of the hospital than without. In both places, the same afflictions, the same cadaverous faces, the same glazed eyes, and the same greenish hue of wizened flesh. Between the suffering outside and the suffering inside, there was assuredly no difference of degree. And yet, the hospital was an enchanted island, an island dispensing golden illusions: the fact is that sickness, spurned and despised elsewhere, came into its own within the hospital precincts. The doctors, the nurses, and even the merest orderlies were under the priceless illusion of carrying on a normal activity, of still leading their former lives and saving those of others. What did it matter if a patient on whom a hazardous operation had been successfully performed was going to be picked up within an hour of leaving hospital? What did it matter that, snatched from the jaws of death only by the use of vaccines stolen—regardless of risk—from an army sick bay, a typhoid case was destined to succumb next day, while still weak from his illness, to forced labor or to bullets on a barracks square?

Within the sacred confines of the hospital, invalids conscientiously plied their trade as invalids. Doctors remained doctors. Who else, apart from professional beggars and undertakers, could say as much?

Thimbleful by thimbleful, the doctors were doing their best to drain the undrainable ocean of suffering, and several of them were living more authentically, more fully, than ever before. Nursing was becoming a profession to be envied. The daughters of the rich and the aristocratic—pampered girls who had been kept from even the smallest glimpse of squalor— came flooding into this (to them) new and strange world. They would hand over money, a great deal of money, to secure a job as dishwasher. They would go to bed with the head surgeon, a fat, bald, red-faced man.

The sick, for their part, were drawn to the hospital by a kind of instinct, a preconception, a legend: a longing to die in bed. Actually, this was often only a dream, a mental picture seldom realized in this hospital where everyone was crowded together down on the floor, not only in every ward but along every corridor.

But what attracted them most of all was a myth—more than a myth: a concept based on reality. Immunity from the killers. Only in exceptional circumstances did the invader's troops, guards, and police set foot inside the hospital, and even then they comported themselves with remarkable restraint. This milieu whose continuing existence was purely a whim of theirs, this milieu which they tolerated for unavowable motives but which was becoming utterly absurd in the light of the general death that they were organizing phase by phase—this milieu still inspired awe in them, by reason of its intrinsic, vocational, and time-honored nature.

"The Hospital" was a tangible and respectable institution. In the eyes of the troops, it had nothing in common with the Department of Labor or the Council which they themselves had created, molded, and chiseled in the shape of their dream. A member of the State Police who, without a moment's hesitation, would have ground his heels on a festering sore and on the man surrounding that sore, had he found the pair of them in the neighboring street, would inquire with interest how a complicated course of treatment was progressing and would take care, as he threaded his way between rows of mattresses, not to jolt the bedding of anyone on the danger list, for "that might hurt him!"

The doctors' activities, which made not the slightest difference to anyone's chances of surviving, either the commu-

nity's or their own, were greeted with signs of marked respect on the part of the enemy, in sharp contrast to his behavior toward all that was not "The Hospital."

There were, to be sure, other, more tangible reasons for
this respect. From time to time, lady-friends of members of
the police and guard would incur accidents of the kind that
call for discreet and reliable surgical intervention. At the
hospital, one could stock up with ether and morphine without the risk of being reported to one's own authorities. The
doctors and the dispensary staff knew what the slightest in-
discretion would cost them.

All this made our hospital a positive hive of news true and
false, as well as of commercial and amorous contraband. The
only dealings I had there which could be described as more
than purely casual were confined to three individuals. Never
in my experience had distress, genius, and power been more
perfectly embodied than in Tamara, David G., and Dr.
Cohen, superintendent of the hospital and absolute ruler of
the herds cooped up inside it.

Tamara had been playing the nurse for only a few months.
Legendary accounts of her past affairs and her very real
wealth and beauty preceded her arrival at the hospital. How
can I describe her eyes, which set one dreaming of the silvery springs of antiquity, or her black tresses, weightier than
time, or the blest and reckless lines of her body? I was not at
all in love with Tamara. The few occasions on which she
lay on her back for me, in an empty operating theater reek-
ing of Formol, were more harrowing than grief. Death was in
attendance, just beyond the wall, within touching distance.
Was Tamara trying to escape from her unbearable loneliness? What, I would wonder, was this pinnacle on which I
found myself poised, yet whose slopes were not mine to as-
cend? I would feel dreadfully cool-headed. I would undo her

white nurse's apron, her maroon skirt. The skin between her thighs was smoother than Nothingness. I would think to myself: She'll never love me. This paltry "possession" of her body was perfectly designed to prove to me that I would never possess her. Well then, neither would I surrender myself. A kind of earnest indifference established itself between us, mingled with an ironic tenderness. As though she had said to me: "Well, here is my body, here is my whole self, the self I have become. So what?"

As though I, for my part, had said to her:

> "Whether we draw them
> Or do not draw them
> Of what importance (can it be)
> To these black lines—our daughters
> Whom our flaring brains
> Are preparing to engulf
> Without
> > till the moment of creation
> > > creating them."

It would have taken a mere trifle, a microscopic adjustment in time and in our destinies—as both of us knew—for this moment to become the very marrow of our lives. For us to be united. But this adjustment did not, could not, occur. Between what is and what isn't, there is only one small detail: Being, pure and simple. Tamara knew who it was I was seeking in the dark gleam of her eyes, in the silvery, fluorescent light of her bared skin. As for me, I knew that whatever happened, since I was not the one who had inflicted her incurable wound on her, that wound which had become Tamara herself, I could never become more to her than the shadowy companion of a few idle moments, of a few last moments.

When Tamara had presented herself at the hospital for the first time, the head nurse—old Mirele, a majestic, gray-haired woman—had taken her by the hand: "Listen, my child, I want to have a talk with you. Or rather, I want to ask you a question, a single question: Do you wish to be treated as a lady of leisure here, or as a nurse? Let me explain: we all know how much your father—may his spirit intercede for us with the Lord!—did for the hospital. We haven't forgotten WHO he was and how he died. In your case, if you just want to be sheltered, to have an *Ausweis,* a certificate of employment, there will be no need for you to ruin your hands. You can stay in the office and dispense smiles to the gentlemen visitors of our chief. Either way, our security is your security. And there is no such thing as security, whatever Dr. Cohen may say. As for carrying pails of shit about, we have dozens of girls who were born for no other purpose, who are happy to do just that . . . Don't feel awkward. You are ENTITLED to a place here, even if you never lift a finger. It's no special 'favor' on my part. How indeed could I, Mirele Yudin, just an ordinary woman, confer a 'favor' on the daughter of the great Reb Eli, who was the equal of the prophets . . . ? But if you are here for another purpose, well then . . . it's blood and pus right away. You won't have to grope about like a blind kitten . . ."

Old Mirele, awe-inspiring and dictatorial, feared and respected even by the doctors, had not minced her words, and Tamara replied briefly: "You know, Mother, that I am here for the OTHER purpose. And I am not so desperately eager to keep my hands white."

The very next day, Mirele had guided Tamara's first footsteps in the metropolis of human suffering. Tamara assisted at amputations and trepanations performed without anaesthetic. She bathed festering wounds and watched over the final moments of children butchered by the "Fight-Against-Contraband" Brigade. She became the perfect nurse, a superhuman nurse. All in all, the few brief months before the liquidation were the least distressing in her life.

David G. was at the very bottom of the hierarchic scale within the hospital. Smothered with soot, he stoked the boilers. Like giant prehistoric monsters, the big-bellied boilers —and they were very much alive—took up practically the whole of the little cellar in which he had installed his mattress. Too devoid of feeling to put down food for a cat or dog, he derived obvious satisfaction from cramming the insatiable jaws of the hospital boilers.

Squat, ginger-haired, and wily, David G. had a hunchback's expression in his bloodshot eyes. It was always with the same quickly concealed surprise that people seeing him rise from a seat for the first time registered the fact that there was no hump on his extremely straight back . . . Only eighteen, he assiduously cultivated his innate ugliness, and the few girls whom he attempted to woo in his brutish and offensive manner invariably dropped him after the first date. With studied and overemphatic brazenness, he would describe how his only honest and genuine moments of bliss came from his spells of masturbating which, alas, he was obliged to space out—"so as to keep in form." Obsessed with death, which he regarded not as a deliverance—there being no "deliverance"—but as the culmination, as the final, the only possible crowning of decay, of the successive disintegrations in which he wallowed more on his own account than out of malice toward others, it was with a connoisseur's delight that he savored the fruits of the enemy's occupation of our town.

He had hated his parents with a passionate intensity. Even before the war, David had made life hell for them. In spite of their normal bourgeois instincts, they could not bring themselves to have him committed . . . One day, he burned a cat alive by putting it in the oven, on top of a cake prepared for his fifteenth birthday . . . "It wasn't that I had it in for the cat," he later explained to me. "I didn't give a damn for the thing, one way or the other. It was purely a matter between my dear Mom and me. I wanted to straighten things out between us. A little family quarrel, you might say."

Twice—at the age of sixteen—he had attempted to poison his mother, and the only time I saw him deliriously happy was the day our fancy-dress cops marched his father off to the train that was bound for the gas chambers. With the black-and-yellow ritual shawl draped over his broad shoulders, David had begun to chant the prayers for the dead, a special performance for the benefit of his mother, who was trying to convince him (and convince herself) that "the train is on its way to a labor camp. Your father will be back. Stop your blaspheming."

Calmly and skillfully, he steered his mother's enfeebled mind toward open madness, and it was with a happy smile that he informed me, one day, of the results of his therapy: "Well, that takes care of that! Darling Mom finally took a cyanide capsule last night. None too soon. And I don't begrudge her the use of it, you understand—not in the slightest. She's very welcome, though at her age she might have made do with something less lavish. I used to own a capsule, too, for my own personal needs. What needs? I buried it in shit, and yet I could have got quite a price for it . . . I managed to pinch it from my father, an hour before the cops came for him. He must have got one hell of a surprise on the train, when he couldn't find it. Just think: he'd thought himself safe, up to that point! 'They won't get ME with their gas,' he kept saying, 'I've seen to that all right.' I taught him a little lesson. I bet he thought at once of his beloved only son. I'd have given a lot to have seen his face at that moment. As for his poison, I've already told you: I'm an idealist—I threw it into the privy. I'll never take the stuff. No suicide for me. I've even put it in writing, in my little 'chronicle.' The sentimental fuss made about suicide makes me want to throw up . . ."

I went to attend to his mother's shriveled-up little corpse and made the necessary arrangements for her burial with the Council officials and old Yaakov.

"If you want to meddle, you are welcome," said David. "I sympathize with all tastes. Even the most morbid. But count me out."

When the four black-coated males who made up the ritual group of pallbearers carried his mother out—a wax doll in its cardboard box—David hung back in the doorway and did not join the beggarly little procession. That very evening, he moved his few bits and pieces into the hospital boiler room.

Why, you will ask, this friendship with David, David the misfit, David the insufferable, David the (virtual) murderer? I'll answer you with another question, in accordance with our admirable racial tradition: How do friendships generally start? What is a friendship . . . ? At least this one was real, more real than the very reality we were living through. In the course of the nights we spent in the hospital, nights filled with gossip and shady deals and hasty love-making, we talked about things that I hadn't the nerve to discuss with anyone else, either before or since. David had a way of opening one's eyes. Also, being a born spy, and one who was left with plenty of time on his hands by his duties as stoker, he had undertaken what I regarded as a fine and noble task. He had set himself up as chronicler of the last remaining hospital in our town. Day by day he recorded events and his own thoughts in a fat yellow notebook, and—if you will forgive my saying so—this log of a vessel in her final hours afloat had a brass-like, a truly masculine ring to it. Later, owing to certain circumstances to which I shall be returning, I had the opportunity of glancing at David's notebook. Here are a few samples:

I adore the view. I abominate the view. I elaborate on it. I always think of myself as being, always feel myself to be, on the inside of the landscape—never on the outside. Even here. I gaze out of the windows. The view appears to be, strikes me as, a gigantic gob of phlegm. I am living on the inside of this gob, which, by solidifying, has formed a sort of diaphanous carapace about me.

Monday: When I had stoked up my boilers, they turned red and began to moan. I couldn't make out the tune. Several big flies, blue and green in color, have got into my room through the skylight. They are from the mortuary and are positively bloated with juice from the bodies. I can tell such flies by their solemn, their ponderous buzzing. I have caught one of them and, after plucking off one of its wings and four of its legs, have carefully deposited it on a heap of excrement. There it will live for a long time, unless the excrement dries up and becomes too tough for its jaws.

Since I am allowing the flies to go on living, this is a humane method of curing them of their exasperating nomadism.

Little Yenta, aged thirteen, who was admitted here with otitis, was deflowered by a madman (he must have been mad, for Yenta stank) who slipped under her bedclothes while she was asleep. She dared not scream, since Mirele had given her strict orders not to disturb anyone. Next morning, I took a long look at the kid's face. Pity I haven't a camera!

Gave Dr. V., one of the surgeons, my last two cigarettes in exchange for the stump of a leg amputated from the body of my old teacher. This made a wonderful toy. I kept putting a shoe on the foot and taking it off again, bending the stump and unbending it. I held forth to the stump, calling it "sir." I had someone to talk to. I enjoyed myself like a schoolboy. Why do we say that the leg has been cut off the master, rather than the master off the leg? I only parted with the leg when it began to stink too much. I'm dying for a smoke, but I don't regret my cigarettes. It was worth it. This is what is known as the triumph of mind over matter.

I spend quite a lot of time staring into garbage cans. The things that are thrown away as "useless," even in these hard times—all the garbage and the bits and pieces—lead an intense life, a life which is very much their own. This strikes me as symbolic, HIGHLY symbolic. May it not be that the Universe itself (along with that bitch, Eternity) is the refuse from something which manifestly doesn't exist? And God perches on it like a giant cockroach lulled to sleep by the sun. What can God's dreams be like?

To be on the safe side, I've started composing an anthem, the national anthem of garbage cans.

Last week, Sergeant Bach (Bach means stream) called on the chief and demanded the loan of four members of the staff "for an emergency job"—two doctors and two nurses. From among the best nurses, Cohen chose Chaja Krol and Annele Guzman. He had slept with both and wished to be rid of them. As for the doctors, they were of no interest: a starved-looking pair who were done for anyway. Well, the four of them were driven away. Next day, the chief asked the Council for five thousand rubles, allegedly to buy their release. The Council would not cough up more than two, and in circumstances of the utmost secrecy the chief received from Bach the body of one of the doctors. I knew that it was a put-up job between Bach and the chief and that they split the two thousand rubles between them. I'm referring to the financial side of the business, to the ransom money, for our chief probably had no part in the decision to remove the four. They were needed to perform a discreet abortion, which they were destined not to survive. As soon as the operation was over, the fetus's father addressed them as follows: "Thank you for your assistance. I really don't know what I'd have done without you. You're a splendid bunch of people. All this I say in my private capacity. In my public capacity I say: 'You have killed a child of pure and noble blood. You must die.' "

Apparently they mistook this for a joke at first.

I learned all the details by cornering old Hans, the medical orderly, and getting him tipsy.

As for the two thousand rubles, I witnessed a farcical scene between our chief and old Leo L., the Community Head. L.L.

got very worked up and started talking about "misuse of public funds." "It's a crime," he shouted, "to part with good money for this mangy corpse, when the children in the orphanages are dying of hunger. Aren't you ashamed? That isn't speculating. It's theft."

To which our chief replied: "I am not a speculator, but a doctor. And I am doing my utmost to save everyone and everything, even corpses. Thanks to my mediation, my unfortunate colleague will at least enjoy a proper burial. And at our expense, at the expense of the hospital, since you gentlemen of the Council are such skinflints."

Last evening, by the light of an oil lamp, I spent a long time gazing at my freckles in a mirror. I tried to incorporate them, mentally, in the heavenly constellations. Hard as I tried, I didn't succeed.

The night before last—Friday, it was—Boris slept with Tamara again in the operating theater. Why do they do it? Why shouldn't they do it? A few hours later, after Boris had left the hospital, I heard Tamara sobbing. She kept repeating the name of her younger sister and imploring her forgiveness. It was this sister who was arrested in the first sweep and with whom Boris, apparently, was in love. Boris remains forever courteous and obliging, in the most irritating manner. I shall have to see to it that one of these days the two of them are caught at it by the chief.

There is no doubt about it: everyone has gone mad, except me. If only I can preserve my clearheadedness, preserve it beyond doubt!

The thought often occurs to me that the entire Universe (not just the earth, but the Cosmos: space, time, etc.) is nothing more than the backside of a hysterical cat chasing its tail. Oh for a glimpse of the cat's face, of even a single whisker . . . just one glimpse! Who is its master? I don't know, but I'm sure the cat scratches his hands till the blood runs . . . It is even capable of drawing pretty patterns with its claws. Oh for a glimpse of those patterns!

If every being (human and nonhuman) were merely a symbol, a generalization (Plato in reverse) . . . then what ghastly plurality, what pullulation underfoot!

Yesterday morning, our own cops brought in the poet Horvitz—straight from the police station. He lived only for forty minutes. I didn't recognize him. His face, long and horsy in the old days, looked like a patch of cow dung. A smear of blood. Pus dried up by the sun, hard as a rock. His eyes were torn out . . . After he died, two of our surgeons entertained themselves by counting his wounds and fractures. There were fifty-eight. Good enough. I couldn't stomach his so-called poems.

The only form of constructive action that I acknowledge and am capable of: I spit on everything. Therefore I ALSO spit on spittle, my own and everyone else's. And I spit on the spitters.

Without such pertinacity, such iron pertinacity, it would be hard to get through these times. I INTEND to get through them.

I have given you only a few scraps from this journal—*said my customer*—which, after only a few months, already ran to hundreds of pages. The strange thing is that my friend David ended his days not as a killer, but as the killed. In the free part of town, outside the wall, there was a boy he was slightly friendly with: part pianist, part author of feeble sketches, the son of a caretaker. During the big sweep, when his beloved hospital was destroyed, David made a dash to the house of this friend, who, for a consideration, promised to shelter him till better times came. David had his diary with him.

After the war, the caretaker's son published a long novel that made him comparatively rich and comparatively famous. As I skimmed through this novel—the story of a murdered hospital—I came across hundreds of pages from David's diary, faithfully copied out.

In the capital of the liberated state, a party was given to celebrate the award of a literary prize to the caretaker's son, who had so generously taken David into his home. The hall was crowded, the dishes daintily served.

"What ever became of our mutual friend, David G.?"

The prize-winner gazed at me, with a faint smile of amusement deep in his eyes: "Why, didn't you know? He killed himself, took his life, poor fellow. Did it back home, at my place. Failure of nerves. Took cyanide. Such a pity . . . To get rid of the body—for there were far too many snoops among our neighbors in those days—I was obliged to hack our poor David to bits and carry the pieces out one by one, in a little bag . . . Luckily, nobody took much notice of my comings and goings. They'd have denounced me . . . I often think of David. I think of him fondly. He was a strange boy, it's true. But so gifted, so gifted. In fact, I'd go so far as to say something of a genius. Wouldn't you?"

I noticed that in the published volume these two short

sentences had been carefully omitted: "The cyanide that I had thieved from my father I immediately flung into the privy. I shall never take my own life."

The book ended with a few words that have indelibly entered my memory. Were they by David? Were they by his literary successor? I shall never know. Here they are:

"The memory of my rebellious moments is dear to me at times when my soul is at peace. I am happy, sometimes, during the night. I wander up from my boiler room and see, above the deck of my ship (for the hospital is a ship), the Great Bear to starboard, the Pole Star to port. Whither is the ship bound?"

CHAPTER 14

A nasty rain was falling on the town. Ensconced in a comfortable chair in the office of the hospital chief, Dr. Cohen, I was mentally conjugating: "I am a toad, thou art a toad, he, she, or it is a toad. We are toads, you (plural) are toads, they (masculine, feminine, and neuter) are toads." This had nothing to do with any moral indignation. It was inspired by the physique of my affable host, who put one in mind of something soft, something slimy . . . of a toad, in short. A toad invading and contaminating the world.

"Well now, my dear Doctor, you were talking about your philosophy and your responsibilities. It's fascinating. Do go on."

"My dear Boris, I know perfectly well what people are saying and thinking about me in town. They take me for a louse, a Quisling. They spin yarns about my lining my pockets by picking the bodies clean. About my having made a pile and being ready to pull out the moment things start to go wrong. All this is partly true. But it is true only partly. Introspection is an incurable disease with people of our race, so I'll let you in on a secret: prior to these last two years I had never lived fully, not at any stage in my life. I was always the filthy little doc, the skunk, the upstart, Old Baldhead.

The children of our faith derided the prophet Elisha for being bald. To their cost . . . The fashionable world, YOUR world, has never taken to me. It doesn't care for me today. But it respects me. It goes down on its knees to me. And that's only a start . . ."

I made to protest, but I couldn't get a word in edgeways.

"You will tell me that it is impossible to live without some form of morality. I have one. It's simple. I concern myself with the inventory of our people's blood, not of their honor.[1] A matter of pure arithmetic. If I can choose between nine deaths and ten, I choose nine. And the families of the nine detest me, for they know. And the families of the tenth detest me too, for they do not know . . . If I have a choice between the death of an old man and the death of a child, I choose the old man. I choose life for the person who has enough money to keep him going, rather than for the person who will starve to death. I could make no choice whatever, and die myself. Obviously. But—between you and me—I'm afraid of death. Especially at the moment, when life is spoiling me. And I am far more afraid of the life that may come afterwards. I have entrenched myself in the present. As for the future . . . whatever happens, I shan't be able to call it my own. I know that. In the meantime I have gathered a miniature court about me. I drink. I whore around. While we're on the subject of my court—I took your little friend David in without breathing a word about money. And, as you know, I could sell his job for quite a lot of cash, which would all go to swell our puny reserves. Naturally they would. But it pleases me to know we have a chronicler attached to our court —especially one who is not only alert but mad. He is not without talent . . . Incidentally, I've noticed that since Tamara joined us you have been honoring us more often with

---

[1] Dvorjetzki.

your presence. That delights me. To think that I, little
Dr. Cohen, have reached a position in which I am able to
offer hospitality to young Baron D. and his lady-loves . . .
Though, to be honest, I am tormented by a kind of dark fore-
boding. But it is none of my business. I agree, I agree . . . To
return to the question of MY morality, would you be so good
as to glance at this worthless little volume?"

The bulky tome was bound in green. The accounts were
balanced every evening, with unerring care: Dr. C. has this
day saved 679 persons and yielded 561. Profit: 118 persons
saved. He has received from the Council and his patients
67,000 gold rubles and paid out 44,000. Interim gain: 23,000
gold rubles, including valuables. Every neck saved corres-
ponds to such and such a sum.

Can the worthy doctor have detected a query, a hint of
a smile, at the back of my eyes? He adjusted his sights:

"Quite obviously, I do not regard this money as being in
any way my own. I am merely a trustee. It is working capital
for my venture, which is a rescue operation. I don't even
keep account of overheads: vodka, morphine, occasional
blow-outs for our friends. Let's not be stingy . . . One last
request, my dear Boris. Don't breathe a word about my accounts to our mutual friend L.L. He must average slightly
less than I do—per head, I mean. But don't let that fool you:
his turnover is so much greater than mine."

Throughout the first two days of the sweep, the hospital
—rising like a sudden, sheer rock in the midst of the waves—
seemed to be victoriously withstanding the enemy's onslaughts. It was the very absurdity of the situation that inspired people with something much like hope. The

enemy (they thought), who claims that he is only eliminating useless mouths, is engaged in killing thousands of young and able-bodied men. True. But precisely because he needs a conspicuous prop for his hatred, will he not allow this jumble of sores and sufferings—which we know as the hospital— to remain in existence? How could he possibly bring about the disappearance of this unparalleled collection of our stenches and deformities . . . ? Dr. Cohen's stock soared among those who were speculating in survival, however brief that survival might be. The manhunt had not prevented the more reckless from besieging the building. Like darting swallows, they cut across open streets, blind alleys, and tree-lined walks to come and hammer on the hospital doors. Those doors remained bolted.

"Everybody back to work, everybody back to their places!" little Dr. Cohen kept roaring, thick blue veins standing out on his red face. "Let anyone so much as mention the sweep and I'll chuck him out on the streets to die," he would snarl at his colleagues. "Why hasn't this piece of live carrion had its temperature taken?" he would bellow at Mirele Yudin, pointing at a thin, sweaty, sickly colored typhoid case.

"He was asleep, Doctor, I didn't want to wake him. Besides, what's the point? He won't last long."

"Are you too an idiot, Mirele? You too? I don't give a damn for the patient. It's the chart I'm concerned with. The chart! I intend this hospital to be EFFICIENT. Anyone who doesn't like the idea can clear out! I'm not holding them back . . ."

He was everywhere at once, little Dr. Cohen, shouting orders, puffing and blowing, self-important and imperious.

"Dr. Cohen, may I have a word with you? Just a brief word . . ." It was the Nestor among the doctors in our town, old Ginsburg, who was making so bold as to disturb his superior's administrative frenzy by tugging him by the sleeve into a quiet corner. "My dear Dr. Cohen, I've never asked you for anything. You know that. But now it's different. I'm not asking you on behalf of my son or daughter-in-law. They're grownups. Let them fend for themselves. But do allow me to bring my granddaughter. She is only fifteen, but what of that? She'll make an ideal nurse—that I guarantee. I'll help train her myself. Now LISTEN to me, colleague. Let's not fool each other. It isn't a matter of work. It's a matter of life and death. If that child is taken from me, I shall not survive her."

"Now see here, Ginsburg, aren't you ashamed of yourself? *Et tu*, Ginsburg? You're my old tutor. I haven't forgotten. That's the only reason I took you on—for, between ourselves, at your age . . . You know as well as I do: I need YOUNG doctors. Your long university experience is no use to me here . . . You don't impress me by saying you will not survive your granddaughter. Anyone can always survive anyone. We've certainly learned THAT here, if nothing else . . . If we are all going to start bringing our grandmothers and our aging aunts, the place will become a regular brothel— and I'll no longer answer for anything. Now get off my back and go see how things are with your consumptives . . ."

"And what about Dr. Hirsch? What about Hirsch! Now you listen to me, Cohen! He has brought his wife and three children. You know all about that—don't you, Cohen? If anything happens to my granddaughter, to my Miriam, I'll kill you with my own hands. You think we are all blind to your racket. You sold them employment certificates at two thousand rubles apiece. Come on, out with it—how much do you want? Let's put our cards on the table!"

There came the sound of a hard slap. Dr. Ginsburg's glasses flew off, shattering into a thousand small pieces as they struck the concrete floor. And Dr. Ginsburg, reeling about between two rows of beds, ran toward the exit.

David sidled up to the chief, his face quite impassive.

"Dr. Cohen, sir—old Wahl of the Community Council is here. He wishes to speak to you at once."

"Tell him I am in the midst of an emergency operation. Tell him anything you like, but keep that gang out of here . . ."

Councilor Wahl—long black beard, tall stooping body, shock of white hair—was already in the ward: "Dr. Cohen, could you spare me a few moments?"

In Dr. Cohen's office, Wahl lowered himself heavily into a brown leather chair. He was fighting for breath. In his blinking, watering eyes, Cohen saw something that he had not wished to see, something whose very existence he had been denying in the face of everything and of everyone: the reflection of the streets through which the old Councilor had just walked.

It was Cohen who was first to break the long silence.

"Now then, Wahl. I shall make no attempt to disguise the fact that your visit affords me no pleasure whatever. There is nothing I am more insistent upon, these days, than the complete autonomy of my hospital. You must cope with your troops and your special brigade as you think fit. I cannot help you. I have saddled myself with heavy responsibilities toward my patients and my staff. That is onus enough for one man . . . Bear this in mind, Wahl: should a single one of THEM have seen you come in, there is a danger of their mistaking the hospital for the annex or subsidiary, as it were, of your Council. Now, as you know, I have done everything in my power to avoid such a confusion. It has cost me a good deal of money and effort. I don't wish to boast, but my labors have proved singularly more effective and intelligent than those of your beloved Leo L. That man has been a disaster for the town. But we'll say no more on that score . . . You can see the result for yourself: it isn't I who go running to the Council, it's you who force your way in here."

"Let it be thy neighbor's mouth and not thine own which praiseth thee." The Councilor was quoting the Biblical saying in its original text. "Intelligence has nothing to do with anything that is going on here. As for the results of your labors, one should not speak well of the day before nightfall. But you have guessed right. I haven't come here just for the joy of it. I am fulfilling a mission entrusted to me by the other members of the Council. It isn't ourselves we're concerned with. Our angels of death have guaranteed—get that into your head, Cohen—have GUARANTEED the safety of all members of the Council. Lieutenant Ulbricht (may his name be struck from the register of the living)—our dear Lieutenant, as I was about to say, undertook to put in a word for us with Captain H. (may he die like a mangy dog!). You know what 'put in a word' means. What did it cost us? A trifling sum . . . And we have received 'categorical assurances.' Just look at this certificate, go on . . . But we're married. We've got children. What about their safety? Not one of us wishes to survive them. Woe unto the goat whose kids have been slaughtered . . . I'll be brief and to the point, Cohen: the President of our Sacred Community orders you—ORDERS you, do you hear?—to allow our families in. After all, the hospital is here to serve the community, not the community to serve the hospital. It is a matter of only thirty-seven persons altogether. Don't make our task even harder than it is . . ."

"Well, you can tell your President I refuse . . ."

"What do you mean, YOUR President? Isn't he yours as well? Are you setting yourself apart from the community?"

"That's beside the point. There simply isn't room. You

wouldn't want me to turn my patients out into the street, would you? Or my doctors? Or my nurses? You yourselves have given me a reputation as an extortionist, as a character with whom one can make any arrangement so long as one is prepared to pay . . . This time I'm not nibbling. Look at it from my point of view: my doctors could quite easily have enlisted in your constabulary. My nurses and orderlies could have put their names down for jobs in the barracks. Months ago. I got them to believe in the security of the hospital. They put their trust in me. I was right. Down at the terminus, the trucks are crammed with ex-Council workers and with women who used to wash dishes and scrub in the army camp. Inside this building, people don't know what the sweep is. My hospital is running efficiently. And now you would have me turn out those who believed in me . . . Besides, how do you propose to get thirty-seven people here?—March them along in a troop? They'd be picked up at the first street corner . . ."

Dr. Cohen paused for breath. From outside came the sputter of submachine guns.

"Come to think of it, I might just as well agree. Your plan is impracticable anyway."

"Very well, Cohen. So that is your final word. I shall deliver your answer to Leo L.—provided, that is, the soldiers respect my safe-conduct. Which is by no means certain. And now a question of a private nature: would you agree to shelter my wife and two daughters? I offer you ten thousand rubles. God knows, it's probably money down the drain. You may believe in your precious security, but I don't. Only, one has obviously got to do something. I can't just keep the three of them at home, and I can't take them to the Council Office either. We've been warned that anyone caught on the premises, apart from the Councilors, will be shot summarily. Well?"

A small flame came to life in Dr. Cohen's eyes. He wasn't passionately addicted to money, but he believed in its power. The proposition was on a par with his everyday transactions. To some extent, it conveyed the impression that life was going on. Besides, what was the point of making an implacable enemy of this man Wahl, who, all things considered, might one day be useful?

"I've no room for them, Wahl, really I haven't. But I'll try to MAKE room, as a favor to you. At seven o'clock there should be a letup in the sweep: the gentlemen go to dinner. Have your family come then, to the back entrance. I'll make sure they're let in, YOU make sure they bring the money . . . Councilor, my respects!"

Obviously he was cooking something up, the dear Dr. Cohen. He smoked, he strolled about, he stopped beside the beds on which his patients were piled in twos and threes. He walked on. Suddenly he knew what to do: Staff assembly. Dr. Cohen speaks:

"In the light of certain considerations that I am not free to disclose to you, I find myself compelled to send two nurses away . . . for a few days. You will not hold it against me, ladies, if I make my selection from those who concern themselves least with their work and most with their . . . private affairs, shall we say."

He looked searchingly along the row of women in white coveralls who stood rigidly at attention, army style, painfully holding their breath. For all the world like a graduation class posing for a photograph.

"Olga Bieriezovskaya and Sarah Levitt! I think my choice is not an unfair one. These two ladies devote their time here to something quite other than their patients. Besides . . . should the situation change within the next few days, I would be prepared to consider reinstating them."

Tiny, slender, thoroughly bewildered, Olga Bieriezovskaya did not dare raise her eyes—not for fear but shame. The daughter of a penniless carpenter, her stay in the hospital had anyway appeared to her as a constantly renewed miracle. Dr. Cohen had slept with her twice after she had joined his team. She had not dared to say no. Now she did not dare to meet the eyes of the man who was casting her out to face almost certain death, who was casting her out of this coveted, peaceful island. He was right. Her place was not here. Sarah Levitt, built like a scoutmistress—swarthy and muscular, dark-haired and bony, her big breasts almost bursting from her white coveralls, responded with a single scream: "Louse!"

The doctor preferred not to hear. ("Well . . . good luck then, girls.") His eyes seemed to be scanning the terrified group for a third candidate. Suddenly Tamara spoke up in her toneless, unconcerned voice: "I trust you will allow me to join my comrades, Doctor."

Dusk was falling. Together, the three girls stepped out of the impregnable fortress into the utterly deserted street. From the window, David followed them for a long time with his weighty stare.

Back in the privacy of his office, Dr. Cohen poured himself a glass of brandy. And a second one. For a split second, the amber-colored stream solidified between bottle and glass . . . Was it really necessary to go through with this final piece of sharp practice? Poor little Olga . . . Why the devil had he taken her on? She would have been dead long ago, and he wouldn't have had to face the blame. It was Olga's father, the carpenter, who had come to the hospital for some repair work and had succeeded in touching the doctor's soft spot.

"Listen, Doctor, now that I'm without my wife—they took her to the old mill and she didn't come back—I shan't live much longer . . ."

He looked like a huge plucked bird. There was more life in his Adam's apple than in his face.

"Everyone wants to go on living. I don't. But there is my daughter Olga. This war won't last forever. I've got relatives in America. They'll send for her and give her a home. She might still enjoy a small taste of happiness. I've no money, and the days when I could work hard are gone. I'm not asking for any favors, Doctor, just a word of advice . . . What am I to do with my child?"

To which Cohen had replied: "Send your daughter to me, Nahum, I'll make a nurse of her. I can't promise anything, you understand, but she'll be better off here than anywhere else."

And in the depths of his soul little Dr. Cohen promised himself: "Let this be one thing, the only thing, I do for nothing."

Next day the child arrived, shy and withdrawn. She was afraid of everybody, even of the sick beggars, even of the children. Humbly, she emptied the stinking chamber pots and laundered the bloodstained sheets.

And then, one day, Dr. Cohen was attracted by something that emanated from this girl. What had it been, this something? He no longer knew. The faintly golden gleam in her wide-set eyes? The firm line of the breasts that were only just beginning to show under her blouse? Her timid, childlike bearing?

Anyway, it happened. "Better I than a soldier in an army brothel, whose inmates are doomed from the very outset": had he bothered to justify anything so trivial as the deflowering of little Olga, such, doubtless, would have been his line of argument. But what was the point of justifying anything whatever? Death was all around them, tangible in its presence. The death of others was something he thought he had finally domesticated, if not mastered. The game was not unappealing. The future—if it existed—was to be sought in other places than the body of a fair-haired little girl called Olga.

But the fleeting affair had left Dr. Cohen with a slightly bitter taste in his mouth: once again, in all the vast ocean of his acts of redemption, there was not a drop of total disinterestedness. Was it on this account that he had today cast little Olga into outer darkness?

No doubt about it: the brandy wasn't doing him any good. With things as they were, it would be dangerous to resort to morphine. He must remain clearheaded, utterly clearheaded.

Dr. Cohen had no literary tendency. Yet all at once the comparison occurred to him, commonplace but satisfying: I am an engineer who must drive his locomotive at breakneck speed along a length of line where pointsmen are being killed at predetermined intervals. Keeping ahead of the killers calls for a steady hand. The Wahl women will be here at seven. It is now six. Nothing like a good piece of surgery for pepping one up. The doctor wandered through the wards. He stopped when he came to Aaron—a twelve-year-old, the baker's son. The baker had been delivering twenty white loaves a day ever since his son had arrived in hospital. Aaron was clean and well tended.

"Does it hurt, my boy?"

"No, Doctor. It's better since this morning. What's happening in town?"

"Nothing is happening. Nothing whatever. And now we are going to remove your appendix. Don't be afraid. You'll be all right again and live to be a hundred . . . I take it, Mirele, that my instructions have been followed and the child hasn't been given anything to eat since morning? Excellent. Take him to the operating theater and call Dr. Ginsburg . . ."

Aaron was afraid of being afraid. He tensed, he gritted his teeth, he smiled. If the doctor was to operate, the hospital couldn't be threatened. If life was still going on in here, it must still be going on outside. Aaron's hands were trembling, imperceptibly.

The operating theater. The surgeon's mask. The shadowless light. All this was thoroughly familiar and had its usual calming effect on Dr. Cohen's nerves. Aaron was asleep. Dr. Cohen, Dr. Ginsburg, and Mirele busied themselves in silence, intent on doing a good job . . . Toward the end, David came in. Dr. Cohen was scrubbing his hands. David whispered in his ear: "Mrs. Wahl and her two daughters are here."

"Very well. See that they are given white uniforms. Inform the secretary and tell her to fit them up with papers backdated a month."

The doctor whistled to himself. He was pleased. The operation had been successful. The Wahl women had brought the ten thousand rubles. The tide may be beating higher on the hospital walls, he thought, but they are standing up to it. I was right not to admit the "thirty-seven." My staff are safe. It's just too bad about Olga and the other girl. It's just too bad about that madcap Tamara. They aren't the first, and they won't be the last. At least they'll have eaten their fill for a few months and done some useful work . . .

David reappeared: "Doctor, a truck has just pulled up at the main entrance."

Then came the sound of rifle butts hammering on the door, and shouts of "Open up, and be quick about it!"

Dr. Cohen's cheeks, normally brick red, turned quite pale. And yet, he thought, I knew it, I knew it all along. If only it weren't for this damned buzzing in my ears . . .

Somebody was running in the long corridors. The lights had gone out. Light from a huge fire was mounting skyward.

A solid, shadowy tree stepped into the room: it was Dr. Striglitz, the army medical officer.

"Good evening, my dear colleague," he began. "How is the healing profession?"

Striglitz, in his bedizened green uniform, with a death's-head on his peaked cap, looked embarrassed. He offered Cohen a cigarette and ran what seemed a regretful eye over the operating theater, the white tables, the lamps, a slumbering patient.

"The time has come for us to say good-by, my dear Cohen, this barracks is to be evacuated within thirty minutes. I deplore the fact, believe me I do. Our collaboration has come to mean a great deal to me, but everything on God's earth has to come to an end. The trucks are waiting . . ."

And, very softly, right in Cohen's ear: "I'm sorry, old man, but this time there is nothing one can do about it. Orders from the capital. Be as quick as you can."

Dr. Cohen managed to get a grip on himself, making a final, a mighty effort. It was just like this, exactly like this, that I always pictured these last moments. The machine must function efficiently to the very end.

He called a staff meeting. The second that day.

"Get the patients out of the building. They are to be evacuated to another hospital. Those who are unable to walk have
to be helped. The Captain has given permission for each patient to take one blanket . . ."

Slowly the mudpit began to stir. Somebody whimpered.
His neighbors quieted him: "Ssh! Keep your mouth shut.
Soldiers."

The soldiers looked at the walls, uncertain, disciplined,
correct. Dr. Cohen was within an ace of openly betraying his
satisfaction: if they show restraint, he thought, it is because
I have trained them to do so. It has cost me enough. In addition to which, my approach . . . yes, that's it: approach
. . . my approach was right.

The fortress was disintegrating. The patients were making
their way down the grand staircase, which had always been
out of bounds for them till now. Wrapped in their rough
homespun blankets, they were painfully hobbling about in
the flagstoned yard. A scattered, reeling band. Some were
giving themselves a military air. They were trying to march
in step. Others were singing funeral hymns. Their woeful
chanting, which was already losing all human quality, carried
to the little office where Dr. Cohen and his colleague Striglitz
sat conversing. One ward was empty. All things considered,
there was a remarkable calmness about the proceedings.

Dr. Striglitz was talking about the stomach disorder that
had been troubling him for some time past. He tried to master his embarrassment: How can I talk about my health to
this colleague who will be dead two hours from now? It isn't
decent. Imperceptibly he changed the subject. The conversation became professional. In the capital they seem to have
developed a completely reliable treatment of erysipelas.

"And to think, Dr. Cohen, that when I took my course in

contagious diseases, there was nothing I was afraid of, not even typhus or scarlet fever . . . nothing except erysipelas. From now on, things will be better. The young won't know how lucky they are, will they?"

Dr. Cohen was thinking about his gold, hidden in the cellars of the hospital. Who would find it? And when? Perhaps this same Striglitz. He wasn't as dim as all that, even if he did go on and on about erysipelas. They had learned the tricks of the trade. In other towns . . .

The soldiers, a little embarrassed to begin with, had split up and were watching closely the work of the nurses, who were propping up the weakest patients. The doctors were doing the same. The whole operation was marked by the utmost calm. The first truck was driving away. Already. There was a good deal of straw lying about in the wards and on the staircase. Drs. Cohen and Striglitz strolled along the wide, empty corridor, where the lights had suddenly come on again.

All this straw will have to be cleared away and the walls given a new coat of whitewash, thought Dr. Cohen, and was instantly aware of the incongruousness of the thought . . . Mustn't tremble. It was he who took out his cigarette case and offered Striglitz a smoke.

All that now remained was the surgical ward, where critical postoperative cases were confined. The patients in here were beyond being "propped up" or even carried, without the aid of special stretchers. They were all in plaster and quite unable to move. In some cases, their pupils were stirring, slowly revolving around an invisible but undeniable axis. There were not many cases in this ward. Thirty-seven altogether. Exactly the number I wouldn't admit, thought Dr. Cohen: perhaps the Councilors' families will survive now, thanks to my refusal, thanks to me. He shot a questioning glance at Striglitz, who opened the door of the ward and beckoned to a flaxen-haired, jovial-looking Sergeant.

"Muller, help me tidy up this ward . . ."

Striglitz paused beside the first bed, discreetly drew his automatic, and leveled it at the patient's forehead. "There, that's taken care of. No more suffering for you, little brother," he declared with unfeigned tenderness. He proceeded on his way, followed by the Sergeant. A hefty gardener and his frail, slender assistant, full of trust in his master. Both seemed to be engaged in a soundless rite. The clicks were barely audible. The patients lay there waiting, long, white plaster dolls. Their eyes—fat June bugs, dark and shiny—flew up toward the ceiling, then fell back, sinking lower and lower, their wings broken off.

A curtness came into Dr. Striglitz's voice. He was no longer the silent exterminating angel. No use pretending. It was time the job was finished: "Have the nurses clear out all this meat." Dr. Cohen relayed the order in a tone of authority. He thought: It's all over. For this last half hour I shall be no more than Striglitz's stooge. His shadow. And that is all that remains of my life BEFORE death, a life that seemed so intricate and unique and many-sided. No mind, no will of my own—only Striglitz's. I did not know, and he will never know, how fond I was of him. Is this a punishment? Is it a reward? Here I am, approaching a land where all contradictions are wedded and resolved—or so they say. I don't believe it.

This very night, Striglitz will start searching for my gold. It might as well be he. He knows how to behave. It cost me enough to teach him. Mine wasn't such a bad approach. The results were bound to be what they are, in any case.

Among the nurses who streamed into the ward were the Councilor's three womenfolk. They were working conscientiously, in an attempt to fit into their new community. The ten thousand rubles would not have been shelled out for NOTHING. Blood was trickling gently from the small holes through which the Captain's bullets had entered. Demure, garnet-red streaks were forming on the concrete floor. The Councilor's wife—a fat, gray-haired, bumptious woman—began to sway on her feet. She sank onto an empty bed and gave a piercing scream.

"Well, calm her, somebody, for heaven's sake calm her," said Cohen.

The final task was accomplished. The hospital was empty.

The staff assembled in the courtyard. Once again. That's the third time today, calculated Dr. Cohen. Nobody took a group photograph.

Striglitz: "We have provided transport for the medical staff as well. Why don't these people get in?"

Two trucks were waiting, with green canvas tops. Dr. Cohen was first to clamber up. He patted the small capsule in his waistcoat pocket. Through a slit in the top he watched the silent embarkation of the crew whom he was to lead on the voyage to survival . . . I lead them to eternal life, he thought again, and grimaced, for he felt it was a cheap crack and one that he wouldn't dare repeat to any of his fellow passengers.

A Sergeant stood counting the doctors and their small staff. Laboriously, he read out the names recorded in a notebook taken from Cohen's desk: four nurses and three doctors were missing. The Sergeant was getting impatient.

"Well, we're not going to hang about here all night," shouted Striglitz. "Get going, boys. We'll go without them."

Dr. Cohen noticed that David was missing too. And the last trucks drove away through the silent town, along an avenue lined with tall chestnuts whose blossoms were uniting above the procession.

CHAPTER 15

Your narrator gets up, impelled by an indefinable feeling; a change of scene is about to happen. Do we have something to do with it? The pebbles are growing uneasy and turning aggressive. The river is changing its substance. There is no longer water at our feet, but black polish, tar reflecting little yellow lights that come from nowhere. The dark is dense enough, too dense, yet gives the impression of being worm-eaten. Solemn processions of small-hour rats gaze at the spot where the moon ought to be appearing. It is engaged in a battle with the clouds which it knows it cannot win . . .

A roughness has come into Boris's voice, so that it sounds very different from before.

We walk past the ex-minister's windows. A uniformed cop and four plain-clothes men keep lookout for the hesitant dawn. It fails to appear. It hangs back, in the grip of a stage fright so human that one could begin to love this baby sun, this embryo sun, so long as it doesn't grow up to be itself. There are plenty of misanthropes who love babies, who love ONLY babies.

O sun—O you hard, lewd abscess,
One of us will certainly have to go.

Fools have made you their cop-god,
And it is for this I hate you.

Watch out, though: one day I'll grow rich
And print thousands of millions of posters
And paste them up all over the sky,
My lovely antisolar posters.

And then a current of trillions of volts
Will finally impregnate the antisolar revolt.
It's us, this current, and no doubt about it: us trillions of cops
Up before dawn, singing our lewd song.

In one of the numerous languages of his tangled past, Boris recites this poem—of which I here try to give a faltering translation.

A window opens onto the night. From it emerge two voices: one grave, the other shrill and cracked.

GRAVE VOICE: Barking all night, howling away all night . . .

SHRILL VOICE: Who was, Professor?

GRAVE VOICE: Why, the moon! Are you honestly telling me you didn't hear it, Christiane?

SHRILL VOICE: Not me, Professor, I was asleep.

GRAVE VOICE: Barked and barked . . . The dogs cried quits. Upset, they were. The moon was robbing them of their livelihood. They came running to me with their tails between their legs. As if to complain.

SHRILL VOICE: So . . . ?

GRAVE VOICE: So nothing. I tried to pacify them. I took them to bed with me.

SHRILL VOICE: And were you alone in your bed, Professor?

GRAVE VOICE: Not entirely. That's to say . . . Before the dogs came, Lucie called in to see me. She wanted pacifying, too.

SHRILL VOICE: Then you weren't alone? You were with the little peasant?

GRAVE VOICE: Yes and no. You know Lucie, don't you? She was there, yet not there: an absent presence. She has always struck me as being a bit Gothic, Lucie has, as being a bit too geometrical. All the same, I was very fond of the girl. But in bed I found out that . . .

SHRILL VOICE: Found out what?

GRAVE VOICE: What did I NOT find out! One does not speak of such things.

SHRILL VOICE: But since we ARE speaking of them . . .

GRAVE VOICE: Will you keep it to yourself, Christiane? Promise? Well, then, since we ARE speaking of such things . . . At first I supposed that Lucie was geometrical, triangular. It was only later that I learned the truth. She isn't triangular. She is a triangle. She isn't geometrical. She is geometry . . . But there is another matter I wish to discuss with you, Christiane.

(The GRAVE VOICE becomes graver still.)

Like a seed, like a seed, may your exertions fall on good ground. May they not be squandered like a bank note in a night club. For "exertions" one might substitute "sufferings" or "prayer." But not happiness, since . . .

SHRILL VOICE: Oh, come, come, Professor! . . . To think that you, who barge into my dreams with your cock-and-bull stories about caterwauling moons and rebellions in the ant world, should come floating through the ether especially to address me in such vulgarly common-sense terms. I'm surprised at you, Professor (simperingly), I'm disappointed . . .

With Boris, we draw away from the wavering window.

Lurching about in the middle of an empty street, a man whose features we are unable to distinguish is screaming: "Men, women, shadows, God, quick, quick, quicker than that, fly to my aid, arm me with your manifold pity! Untold woe has fallen on my head, a mishap beyond compare, the most shameful a man can suffer: I am born! I exist!"

I simply cannot place the tune that Boris is whistling.

What fear we experience at the approach of this dawn for which I have no wish! Is the new day—a fetus whose arrival is viewed with abhorrence by its parents—going to cast its lewd glare upon the nakedness of this story, upon the nakedness of Paris?

Oh, to drown, to annihilate this moment with the aid of words teeming like black insects. I dread Boris's fluency—certainly I do—but I dread even more what would happen if one now gave the sun free rein. One must justify oneself, defend oneself, tear oneself away from this inept moment, project oneself elsewhere. I resort to a subterfuge:

"And since pity still resides in you, Boris, I am going to intercede with you and plead the cause of someone I love. In Archangel, kindness reigns. But here, in this foolish latitude, night—EVERY night—is condemned to irrevocable loneliness. Never do two nights meet, intersected as they are by dusty days, like landscapes scarred by trenches. Never does a night succeed in enfolding her neighbor in her arms, in touching her smooth skin . . . They are strung out like beads, then they scatter, going each to her own loneliness. Help them, Boris."

Whereupon, with his long bony fingers, Boris touched the paling sky. In one swift movement, he seemed to give a fleeting caress to the rising sun, patting it away as though it were the lightest of balloons . . .

New blood had started to flow in the veins of the moribund night. With a shy, happy smile, she was welcoming her younger sister, whom till now she had been condemned to pursue without ever managing to embrace her. She touched her with a black, smooth, and sparkling wand.

The night is beginning again. The night is multiplying.

CHAPTER 16

The notebook that I received through the post a few months after our meeting opened with these sentences:

"Clay pigeons, virginal ping-pong balls dancing on your sprightly, vibrant jets, good-humored meerschaums . . . how my heart envies you!

"Pitched into this giant fun-fair, when will it finally attain, my heart, to the dignity of being a TARGET? I am all awed expectancy for this future moment, so longed-for and elusive, when . . . when it will be my heart's turn to be a target. For, ladies and gentlemen, as I'll wager you don't yet know:

"Suicides constitute a crack, a bigshot, an ultra-exclusive club in the other world."

I trail it after me on a lead, my past, like . . . like (but naturally!) a dog. And it howls like an injured dog. I lick its blood.

The days leave their spittle on
This winding road, so cracked and hummocky,
Stretching and losing its way
As it climbs toward horizons barred and blue:
Can it be you?

Blue, too, are its loops, weary
Of looping the loop, of being loops.
The froth of time melts into Nowhere.
It is this Nowhere it seeks before vanishing
Through the tough scales of the resounding seconds.
Loneliness has furrowed your face, so like land and water.
The one-armed bandits jangle away.
The other racket you can hear
Is the jerky march of objects
Back to their plasma,
Back to the germ and the brain wave behind it,
Back to the dough whence they first wound their way.
When its spreaders are gone, Fear will remain, alone and in-
    effable,
A triumphant tailor's dummy, flapping its wings
In rooms that have long stood empty. Today
What pandemonium, this enforced transmigration of objects
    to their source.
Even the insects won't call you brother.

Gaudy clubs crashed down on what was left of his poor
understanding.
    The escritoire, that lively and rickety table, was screaming
at the top of its voice:

The brown, parched road
Breathing heavily,
Inhaling the sad springtime
Like a stricken beast.

The greenish, dreamy spittoon
(What can they dream of, verdant spittoons?)
The poster ripped from the old wall,
Inflated by rain-bearing winds,

Washed out by innumerable, unseeing stares.

The irregular verb of a language
That never was,
Victim of faddish, mutilating paradigms,
A lump of rotted flesh in a booming trash can.

Town which has never known
Inhabitants other than invaders,
Home of invasions, invaded by the weed of absurdity,
The groping weed, the stumbling weed,
The weed that is target of crimsoning invasions . . . !

I search for your name.
O, how I search for your name . . .

Those actions in life which are reputedly the tiniest, the most insignificant (catching the bus at such and such a stop rather than another; buying this newspaper and not that one), strike me as being so much more important, more "existent" than I, the supposed author of these notes. Paralysis results. Pray for my soul.

One by one, words—all the words of the human language —wilt and grow too weak to bear a meaning. And then they fall away, like dead scales. All meanings evaporate. But that is their normal condition. Man grows dumb. If such a thing happens to a writer, the writer ceases to be a writer. But that is his "normal condition." Creakings, yet more creakings.

With rusty scissors, I used to cut up bits of the sky. I used to compare clouds to dirty cotton, easy as preparing boiled eggs . . . Yet more comparisons, yet more metaphors. It's enough to make one throw up.

Can values continue to be, without a "scale of values," without a system? Is man to live without love? Without the love which alone could incorporate him in your wonderful systematized universe? (A turd that wishes to be bigger, even an inch bigger, than another turd—that's communal life for you, "social" life. A turd that wishes to stink more than another. To succeed, he is prepared to do anything: even to become sublime . . .) I can't stomach the high-soaring nowadays; it's the thing I can stomach least of all. So the spring has dried up. The only remaining ally is weakness, but it is a treacherous ally . . . However, my body believes in one magic word, one liberating word. Is it on the way already?

Métier

The festive crowd, in its Sunday best, strolling under the trees in a great boulevard. With a rustle, a scarecrow takes wing and flaps about in the air. Panic. The crowd flees.

The moment I bend my head over a sheet of paper, the images crowding my brain beat a retreat; all set to embark on a respectable public existence, they vanish.

It is an especially revered deity, the deity of Nonentity, that jealously stays my hand. More and more seldom do I try to escape from it. For nonfulfillment is like a soft fur. So, my brothers in Nothingness, fight Reality, crush it! There is no more degrading form of mass hypnosis.

Between the terror inspired in me by a blank sheet of paper and the sense of shame that the aforesaid sheet gives off as soon as there are a few hasty marks on it, will there never be a "neutral zone" . . . ?

Before the town was destroyed, Leo L. spoke of the vocation to be witness, the only one that matters.

At the moment, memory is letting me down. The colors

are fading. The town has died. For a second time. The memory of it has become a burdensome fetus no longer breathing.

The "I" who had lived through the walled-up town and all the rest, is flowing away, draining away. Now that my spiritual home has evaporated, I am left with only one conclusion, crisp and rational: when a whirlwind comes along, one must make the most of it, exploit it, start writing at once, lying at once. The only really vivid lies are those conceived in the heat of the moment. My terrain: Birchtree Walk, Silver Street, Fountain Street—syllables falsely vibrant.

But everything that comes along, or MAY come along, seems so microscopic, so footling, especially where allegedly "propitious" events are involved. A one-time multimillionaire, starving now that he has squandered his millions, cannot bring himself to gather up the few "honest" pennies that destiny sends his way.

The "literary manner" is an obscenity by definition. It is even more so by the nature of its constituent parts: process, process—the very notion is like the trek between office and home performed day in, day out by a civil servant suffering from piles.

Literature: anti-dignity exalted to a system, to a single code of behavior. The art, occasionally remunerative, of rummaging in vomit. And yet, it would appear, *navigare necesse est:* one HAS to write. So as to trick loneliness, so as to trick other people. But above all: loyal to my destiny, however DISloyal my destiny may be to me, I feel bound to emphasize my similarity to an insect; now, haven't you noticed that man never so much resembles an insect as when he engages in the activity of writing . . . ? Dissecting the world into tiny bits, covering paper with tiny scribbles that aspire to be unique: that is the posture in which the brotherhood of man

and insect—hideous, if the truth be told—manifests itself in
the purest form, with the utmost obscenity. And man's posture, and the movements of his brain at the time of writing—
are they not those of an insect to end all insects, fleshy and
podgy, soft and space-planning, rationalistic and swayed by
the ideals which emerge from that great foundry: PHYSIOL-
OGY?

The mirror

The past four nights are a smooth-sided well. Which way
to turn?

It is all defeat, Boris's face, defeat ecstatic. This face is fall
and jump: violent onrush of the ultimate cement, of the liberating cement destined to mix with the blood of the brain,
with the fibers and vertebrae jutting from the body.

Violent onrush of the hard cement lining the reversed
top, the topsy-turvy top of this well that is our heart, our ultimate heart. Our bodies invoke the end.

Boris's face is a competition: a thousand faces, a thousand
faces vying with each other, for the "personal expression" of
each, against the expression of the rest, of all the rest.

No possibility of staying in the town, which snaps shut
before their lives like a clamshell, so smooth and cold.

Will they succeed in finding it, in finding at last that time-
sunk hidden door? In escaping from the town?

Condemned as I am to the crushing task of perpetual recount-
    ing
(Musings themselves lack free momentum.
They embed themselves in the old worn grooves
Cut in that filth which habitués know as "Time Goes By.")
When you think "money," you must think "creation";

Whoever says "power" says "key to maiden-mounting."

O this fourth-rate symmetry! If I threw it
On the trash heap as it deserves,
I'd be all alone: above the merely tolerable.

But to efface this rhythm is more than to free oneself. The
enslaving mechanism would be destroyed.

If musings themselves are only bonds,
If the saw of smug recounting cuts ceaselessly into the living
body

To the rhythm of a song,
Why defend the hardships, the hardships that were many,
from the nets, the seines of recounting?
(Imagine a world where there was no recounting. Inconceivable!)
But today the hardships will no longer slip through the nets
of enumeration.
I shall not help them. An eye for an eye. And so:

Hovering over remembered regions
(And may it not be that these regions, seemingly vast, are the
inside of a geometric point, the inside of a flea's head?),
Looking back on my many pasts,
Among all these motley places
I can find only one that I could (at a pinch) regard as home:
And that's the walled-up town,
Of which I'd dreamed already, long ago,
A skinny child, stumbling on the loneliness of others,
Lingering in drowsy streets with funny names:
Silver Street and Fountain Street and Carter Street.

The town was condemned like a well. I am alone again, with
the same imaginings.

Given the similarity of my dreams before and after,
Could it be "FIDELITY"
This framework whereon God has spread the unspeakable rag
    which—in my day-to-day experiences during the past
    thirty years—I have fallen into the humiliating habit of
    calling "ME"?

A cry rings out in the town:
"Hey, you! All of you who aren't me! Die, can't you, kick
the bucket, give up the ghost!"

God has answered my prayer: you are all here, up and
about; you aren't dead. Which means you ARE dead, means
you are . . . ME.

To my enemies . . .
    (and you are all my enemies):
Go on living for ever and ever. And leave me, me, me
alone with the sweet prerogative of dying. God conferred it
on man in His great pity. He Himself, it seems, is afflicted
with immortality, cruel immortality. Poor wretch . . .

CHAPTER 17

in which the author speaks again

[handwritten marginalia: narrative is editing the manuscript.]

It was not without faint repugnance that I handled Boris's papers. That kind of intimate journal is like dirty linen, a stranger's linen . . . complete with its "mana." You hold it between your fingertips, longing to be rid of it. But a certain curiosity lingers . . . Not that the manuscript was grease-stained. On the contrary: the pages were clean and uniform. The handwriting was not devoid of a certain concern for elegance. A reasonably disciplined hand, on the whole, with occasional little eccentricities—doubtless deliberate, or at least conscious. Characters of moderate size, of which only a few—and not always the same ones—assumed grotesque shapes and proportions to match the whim of their creator. Could it be that my customer was striving for an additional means of expression, the words or the way he handled them being inadequate to convey, to pin down, what he regarded as his "message"?

[handwritten marginalia: language not adequate enough.]

Do I have to admit it? It was "the tool and the art of comparison," the details concerning "the walled-up town and all the rest," that I was trying to fish out of this mass of gibberish—though they were, in fact, far from preponderant. Too many different threads, too many snippety themes (misconceived, for the most part) got tangled up in a narrative in which I would have preferred, goodness knows, to see greater unity. I don't have it on my conscience, therefore, that I decided to discard everything that hadn't a direct bearing on the story that Boris had spun to me in the course of that one and only night . . . To hell with the endless procession of a failure's "states of mind." But cutting is easier than judging: in this great sea of words, what had and what hadn't a bearing on the precious story? Boris seemed sometimes to be sheltering from his human condition, too vast and too uncomfortable, by confining himself to his more personal condition: that of the man with the wound, that of protagonist in his own story. Had he not discerned the utter flimsiness of this fictitious and purely cerebral step: "from the general to the particular"?

However that may be, the task confronting me was clearly no sinecure: the notes—even those I had been able to isolate after removing the pseudo-lyrical bits—were extremely muddled. When speaking of himself, Boris used sometimes the first and sometimes the third person. Did this wavering betoken a hidden need to objectivize his own existence, a need generally experienced by those whose existence is giving them the slip? As though, in the treadmill of "what is" and "what is emerging" and "what is fading," the word "objective" corresponded to something other than a mental outlook.

The very language in which the notes were written was a hybrid compounded of snatches of French, Slavonic, and other tongues, snatches that were not always the best of neighbors.

I frankly admit my lack of preparation for such exegesis. That character Boris had played a dirty trick on me. And yet, little by little I fell victim to the temptation to salvage the remains of a story which wasn't one, or wasn't quite . . .

It was in a spirit of unfeigned humility that I stuck at my labors and now offer the fruits of them. I have quoted from the manuscript wherever I was unable to do otherwise. I have summarized as often as seemed possible, but first and foremost: I have CUT. And if I fancy I have earned the right to any gratitude whatsoever from any reader whatsoever— and I am in doubt as to that—it will all be due to this wholesale amputating. And now:

CHAPTER 18

At a given moment, therefore, in what he calls the big sweep, Boris found himself on the premises of the Garin Corporation. He could have acquired a cushy job in the Workshops months before, on the strength of his contacts or of the money he still had—perhaps also on the strength of his name, which impressed those who ran the place. At that stage, he hadn't wanted to give up his free time or what he regarded as his independence. He had packed Naomi off to this haven and, in the first part of his story, he himself has reported the bad temper which this place of work, exalted to a redemptive religion, had induced in his mistress, who for the first time in her life—let us not forget—was having to submit to the distressing discipline of a rigid daily routine.

But the isle of the blest had not lived up to its promises. At the very time when the bulk of the staff were basking in their spurious sense of security, when the foremen were ordering the little girls under their supervision to wear lipstick and sing cheerful songs, when they were bidding the elderly dye their hair and give color to their cheeks so that the Workshops should not invite the reproach of employing SHODDY human material, a detachment of troops arrived in the buildings. That gray hair and pale cheeks could constitute the infallible sign of moral decay, an unforgivable sin against the principle of life: this "obvious" truth was something the older workers, indoctrinated by their superiors, were prepared to allow. But the troops did nothing to confirm its obviousness: in the space of twenty minutes they removed two thousand of the loveliest, the richest, the most pampered young girls.

Those remaining amounted to no more than a general staff without troops. Garin's messianic myth—work: safe-conduct to survival—had come crashing down about their ears, but they still clung to their belief in the magic power of rubber-stamped scraps of paper. The Sergeant in charge of the detachment was enjoying a final joke at the expense of those whose lives he was sparing for another few days.

"I'd never have seized all those beautiful young ladies," he was saying, "had their employment certificates borne the obligatory green stamp. But, to my great disappointment, they were all stamped with RED ink. You didn't look properly after your employees' interests . . ."

One of the directors dared to answer back. It was more than an act of bravery.

"But, Captain! The stamp in question certifies that the holder of the certificate enjoys the protection of the army and is contributing to the war effort. That no one is to lay a finger on him . . ." And lowering his voice: "You yourself insisted on our paying a 'surcharge' before you would agree to that wording. You yourself stamped the documents, only a week ago, and you stamped them red . . ."

The Sergeant was clearly in a conciliatory mood: "Don't be so pedantic. Come, come. It isn't a question of words. After all, words are never of more than extremely relative value. It's a question of colors. Your documents were value-less because they were stamped with red ink. And now I'm going to stamp all yours green, and you'll be as peaceful as babes in a cradle. It's a great mark of trust, my stamping your new cards with green ink . . . I'm not a pen pusher, you know, and if I am concerning myself with this affair it's purely to give you a hand, a brotherly hand. Besides, read for yourself: 'The holder of this document enjoys the protection of the army and is contributing to the war effort . . .' What more do you want?"

The Sergeant's lucky questioner felt that to raise any further queries would be to exceed the limits of good taste. The small group clustering around him asked nothing better than to believe the Sergeant. They were even beginning to protest vociferously when Baral, the old chief engineer, ventured to ask: "But in that case, why couldn't you have used green to stamp the cards of all those girls your men have just seized?"

No doubt about it: the Sergeant was patience itself.

"Oh, come now, Baral, how were we to know yesterday that green was the right color? It's a brand-new regulation. Right up until yesterday, red was regarded as being just as valid—more than that: as being EXCLUSIVELY valid. I'm no prophet. Let me point out, though, that the authorities are absolutely right. Something certainly had to be done about this hodgepodge of colors. Strictly between ourselves: a rainbow like that was getting beyond a joke. As for the girls, I'm brokenhearted. Believe me, I had nothing to do with it. But you have to admit the green-ink idea is a good one . . .

"As I was saying"—he addressed himself to the group as a whole, which was eagerly lapping up his words—"as I was saying, with green ink on your cards you will have nothing to fear and will live to the age of Methuselah. On one condition: that you allow no one to set foot in the Workshops who doesn't belong here, no one on whom I have not conferred the privilege—yes, the privilege—of the green stamp. The police have a hard enough job in this town, without your making a flophouse of premises that ought only to harbor serious work and those engaged in it. Don't thank me . . . I shall rely on you, gentlemen, and look forward to the pleasure of seeing you again."

"The Maker—may His name be praised—never HAS played fair with our people," mumbled Baral, ex-personnel manager of the Garin Corporation, wondering whether his high office was reconcilable with the final and conclusive absence of the aforesaid personnel.

It was in the midst of all this that Boris, at nightfall, knocked on the door of the Workshops. He was not unaware of the catastrophe that had befallen the Garin Corporation. It was a catastrophe that he had always foreseen. Accused, in the past, of being a blasphemer and a Jeremiah, he made no secret of his lack of confidence in the work of redemption undertaken by Garin. The very fact that most of the people about him pinned such high hopes on the existence of the Workshops, the huge sums that the girls' parents had shelled out so that their offspring might enjoy the privilege of slaving away at a sewing machine: all these things constituted, in Boris's eyes, so many additional pointers to the fate in store for this unassailable haven. When certain categories of human beings are doomed to extinction, their very hopes embrace only those objects which are themselves fated to go the same way. The man whom God has condemned to drown will never clutch at any but a rotting plank. Thus did Boris reason.

As he stood knocking on the door of the Workshops, Boris knew that his past predictions would in no wise endear him to the survivors. He was obeying two imperative needs: the first, to see Naomi—who, as he had learned in the course of the day, had escaped the slaughter; the second, to find somewhere to sleep.

Naomi was not amazed to have Boris restored to her. At this stage in their relationship, she would have been utterly incapable of thinking of Boris as other than eternal. Since the walls around her were there, and the sun and the moon, Boris had been bound to come. Nothing was more obvious. The death of Boris was as inconceivable to Naomi as a four-pointed triangle.

Boris describes how, in an attempt to keep him out, those in charge of the Workshops invoked the Sergeant's prohibition and argued that the admission of somebody who wasn't on the staff, and who didn't have a card bearing the priceless green-ink stamp, could only bring further disasters down upon their heads. The massive roundup within the very Workshops had not entirely robbed the survivors of their sense of security. Buoyed up by the virgin green ink on their documents, the directors were trying to prove to themselves that they were in clover: were they not surrounded by solid walls, and could they not still exercise their authority by refusing to let Boris in?

Boris eventually bought right of entry by reporting the news from the town, from which the directors had been more or less isolated since morning. No sooner had Boris told them of how he had witnessed the almost casual shooting of their superior than the directors gave up all thought of dismissing the bearer of such important tidings. Boris had thus acquired the freedom of the deserted Workshops by carrying out this courier's mission.

He repictured the bluebottles buzzing about over the

crimson trickle that emerged from Garin's temple as he lay on the cobbles outside the Council Office. For the first time he thought of Garin with affection—of Garin who had never in his life been able to walk past a rock without imagining the torrents of running water which a Moses would have conjured from it.

Was it so inexcusable that for a split second he should have mistaken himself for Moses? He had visualized the torrents, the unending rivers that a Moses would have been able to summon from these arid rocks. "Would have been able to" and not "could." For, my dear Garin, is it not likely that "might-have-beens" are, in fact, the only possible consolation, the ultimate justification for existence? Knowing that one has missed the bus, that one has messed up one's life and even one's death—is this not sufficient reason for unbitterly falling into every rut . . . ?

By this time there was nothing but wailing to be heard in the Workshops, and all at once there rose the prayer for the dead, deep-toned and plaintive.

Boris tells two other little stories about the same night. Here's the first:

As the reader already knows, the staff of the Garin Corporation was made up mostly of the rich and the influential and the resourceful. A prosperous craftsman called Nathan Litovski—a broad-shouldered, rosy-cheeked, potbellied figure who owned a flourishing workshop and salesroom—had registered for employment there, together with his wife and small children and four of his apprentices. It was no small matter, getting hold of all that number of cards, but for once the worthy craftsman had been unstingy. Reasoning that here was a matter of life and death, he had paid up. On the day of the catastrophe, Litovski and his family and dependents were spared in a manner that was all but miraculous. His wife and children he shut in a small cellar, reached by way of a trap door which failed to attract the attention of the troops searching the building. His apprentices he ordered up a ladder, to repair an electrical fixture which showed no sign of fault . . . The enemy claimed to respect labor. This was true only in part. He was destroying the fruits of generations of labor. He was killing those who labored. But the very act of laboring, however illusory, frequently prompted the soldiers to hesitate, and even to shy off. Whether for this reason or for some other, Litovski and those in his care were spared.

Were his portly wife and his children and his apprentices now going to see Litovski, not merely as the exemplary husband and father, not merely as the firm but fair boss, but as the Man of Providence, the Savior?

Lying on the floor, with only a few bits and pieces for comfort and with Naomi's head nestling on his shoulder, Boris watched the Litovskis, mustered at full strength, preparing a quiet resting place. The master did not deign to speak. The apprentices were furtively discussing the day's happenings. Litovski's wife dared not break in upon the silence of her lord and master. She was savoring the greatness conferred on him by the miracle that he had wrought that morning. At the same time, like everyone else, she was caught up in the grief that had descended on the Garin Corporation. Like a bedbug in the folds of a sumptuous red plush counterpane, dear Mrs. Litovski, so respectable and bloated, had in the old days lived solidly entrenched in her familiar world. She and the order, the unshakable order, of things were as one. All the respectability of a medieval guild was reflected in her soul. But now, suddenly, the red plush and the trade guild had vanished. Mrs. Litovski was digesting this cruel transformation, but she would not surrender to it. She said to herself: One has only to set one's face against ruin, to spurn it and disown it, holding fast to a sense of Orderliness, then one cannot perish.

The Garin Workshops, which only that morning had echoed with thousands of voices, and the clatter of machinery, and the shouting of foremen, were now empty and silent. This emptiness was like a misty halo, like a lung-bursting vapor. Mrs. Litovski could stand the silence no longer. Through her hot tears, she addressed words of sublimity to the young apprentices:

"And to think that all this . . . this whole appalling human tragedy . . . is due to you whelps! All because you never do as the boss tells you! If only you did as you were told, none of this would ever have happened . . ."

Litovski did not say a word. But his silence was approbatory. However far beneath him she might be, his wife was not mistaken. Things would never have come to this if the whole world wasn't topsy-turvy, if it were to bow to his wisdom as a stern but fair-minded employer, as a sound and conscientious craftsman.

Boris couldn't contain himself any longer: he roared with laughter.

Later, at about four in the morning, the Litovski family was marched off in its turn, together with several members of the managerial staff.

Boris and Naomi survived. How? Boris remains silent on the subject. But he was witness to a scene that he describes in summary terms, and which it would be wrong of me not to relate in turn:

After the morning raid, a party of some forty children arrived on the premises. They had no connection with the Garin Corporation. None of them was more than twelve years old. A mixed group of boys and girls, they were chaperoned by three women, who shepherded them into a vast cellar.

How had this brood of youngsters managed to secure a footing within the sacred precincts of the Workshops? Certain good souls had found a way of cashing in on the latest disaster. Since the Garin Corporation, contrary to all expectation, had already been searched, there was little probability of the troops' returning. After the blood bath, the Workshops had become once again what they should never have ceased to be: the best hide-out in town. Had the Sergeant intended to return, why should he have given strict orders against admitting the common herd—in other words, those who didn't own cards stamped with green ink, the only valid ink . . . ? It was along these lines that the surviving directors must have reasoned. And since this was how things stood, would it not be possible to SELL this immunity to a few men of substance looking for somewhere to hide their threatened offspring?

Confronted by this storm, which had been whipped up by some and foreseen by others, heads of families were on occasion adopting the attitude of the gambler refusing to stake all on a single number. They were splitting up their dependents, lodging them in several more or less reliable hiding places. They said to themselves: "If I myself perish, maybe my son will survive me. Or else one of my daughters, or my old father." They wouldn't admit the possibility of the whole family's being wiped out, for that would take away even the hope of revenge. How could they possibly believe that there would be nobody, after they had gone, to recite the funeral prayers . . . ? As for the aforesaid revenge, it was so taken for granted that it was becoming more or less a contractual obligation: those who lived would HAVE to remember. They would HAVE to stop others from forgetting. And in that case, they thought, what difference does it make whether it is I or my brother who carries this burden?

If the truth be told, there was only a tiny minority who

thought in these terms, and an even scantier group who had the resources to adjust their tactics to such an outlook. Hiding places with a reputation for being safe were few and far between, and could provide shelter for only a very restricted number. One such hiding place was this cellar within the very precincts of the Garin Workshops.

Thick though the walls were, the children were under strict orders to stay silent. Their three chaperones had been given wide and explicit powers: should any scream or other noise be deemed likely to endanger the group as a whole, they had only to strangle the guilty child.

How did Boris discover the existence of this makeshift kindergarten? He is content to refer to a late-night jaunt through the Workshop cellars, a jaunt embarked on after a quarrel.

Anyway, at about three in the morning, he stumbled upon a vast room where the foul, almost unbreathable air was like an autonomous, hostile entity. Those few children who were not asleep were making a din that was far from reassuring. A little eight-year-old hunchback, daughter of the most prosperous miller in the province and till recently the focus of all the shame and love of a rich and powerful family ("they say there's a professor in Switzerland who has found a way of remedying children's humps . . ."), asked Boris straight out: "When our bodies rise from the dead, little uncle, as the Holy Scriptures say they will, shall I still have a crooked back . . . ?" Abandoned dolls, tiny shoes, a soft, silky teddy bear . . . nothing was missing that might serve to heighten the lyrical nature of the moment, asserts Boris, who—on his own admission—hesitated for a long time as to how he should answer the child's pertinent question.

"Can Yaakov be ten already?" he wondered, gazing at a pair of burning eyes set in a thin face that was surmounted by a shock of blond hair . . . Two years earlier, this same Yaakov had accosted Boris in a park, by Lomonosov's monument.

"Who is this guy?" Yaakov had asked.

"A scholar. A poet. A philosopher."

"And what's a philosopher?"

"He's a man who thinks about thought," Boris had replied, after a momentary hesitation.

"And he has a monument just for that?"

"Why certainly: not everybody does as much . . ."

"Oh, but you're wrong! Everybody must. How could anyone who didn't do it BE?"

This exchange had engraved itself upon Boris's memory. Oh, this insane love which the "adults" of our race bestow on the sayings that issue from the mouths of children!

But at this point one of the three women, having handed Boris a whole collection of safe-conducts, identity cards, and employment certificates, called on him to confirm, and proclaim aloud, that by remaining with the children she was performing a deed of great note—for her impeccable papers quite clearly exempted her from all the persecutions that had been unleashed up on the surface. "At this very moment, I could—couldn't I?—be sleeping peacefully, perfectly peacefully, in my own bed. But what wouldn't one do to save these poor children . . . ?"

The second woman displayed a similar assortment of papers in order to prove, likewise, the disinterested nature of her sacrifice, which her neighbor simply wouldn't admit. "But dear Helen," she said, "hasn't had HER papers stamped by the Fight-Against-Insects Branch. My husband paid ten thousand rubles to get mine stamped. No price is too high for him. I was completely in the clear. Whereas it must be a great relief to poor Helen to be allowed to look after these children. See for yourself: she hasn't got the most important stamp of all."

The third woman, Boris relates, had magnificent and beautifully dressed red hair and retained, though well into her forties, a surprising peacefulness and a calm, self-confident beauty.

He was reluctant to render his judgment of Paris: which documents were the better? Were both, or was either of, the first two women exhibiting a sublime sense of duty, or were they merely out to save their own skins? Had he the right to disclose to them that this scale of values, the last to which they apparently clung, was no longer applicable to anything on the face of the earth?

It was at this moment that the third woman, a bit ponderous and hefty of gait, began to comfort a child who had suddenly waked up. Taking the little girl in her big strong arms, she broke into a quiet song. It was all about an old miller who had just been turned out of his mill. Within this watermill he had raised his children, who, now that they were grown up, had turned their backs on their father and gone off to the town. It was in the mill that his wife died. Turns the wooden wheel, murmurs the stream. And within this mill he had left behind his youth and his strength and his dreams. Turns the wooden wheel . . . And now he is old and feeble and hasn't the strength to work. The harsh new lord has thrown the old man out, and he limps sadly off down the highroad . . . Murmurs the brook.

The little girl was fair and pale. The outlines of her frail body were barely distinguishable in the dim light. She was still crying softly, more and more softly, and Boris found himself wondering whether her hot tears were going out to the old miller or to something else . . . Something else, something else: the two words reverberated in Boris's brain, gradually shedding all meaning. Tiredness was like a warm bath, like a liquid seeping into his entire being.

As she wept like this, as she weakly stirred her frail limbs, the little girl seemed to be performing a rite that went back to the beginnings of time.

An Egyptian statuette, an Egyptian statuette—the banal comparison formed in Boris's weary head. Mechanically, to keep himself from falling asleep, he took the little girl from her guardian's hands.

Was it from tiredness, was it from tender feeling? A shiver ran through him at the touch of the child's infinite softness.

Just as the inevitable thought occurred to him—and this blond squirrel, must this blond squirrel go the same way as the rest?—the sound of rhythmic footsteps rang out in the distance.

The soldiers—there were only four of them—did not enter by way of the Workshops, but through one of the adjoining sewers. They did not realize that there could be any connection between the Garin Corporation and the hiding place that they had just discovered. The fact is, their working day was over. This "probe" in the sewers was an act of sheer conscientiousness on their part, undertaken completely on the off chance. They too were tired, and none too sure of themselves. Three solid patresfamilias and a thin, sweaty, rheumy-eyed Corporal. A few seconds' silence, strained as a violin string. Then a demand fired, curtly but correctly, at Boris: "Your papers?"

Not a single "valid" document on Boris's person. Not a single slip of paper stamped by the army or the police . . . Just an old passport, a prehistoric item which some years before had conferred, in the name of a state that no longer existed, the right to travel to a foreign country since invaded.

A fossil, a museum piece, grotesque and anachronistic, dog-eared and faded. Completely out of touch with the rules of the game that History was playing. A drop of oil in a milk churn.

You were born on May 4, 19 . . . ?

In Krasnoy . . . ?

Your father's name?

The Corporal's eyes remained impassive. After a moment or two:

"Thank you. That's fine. Your papers are in order." With a hint of melancholy he added: "If only everyone in this damned town had papers as good as yours, we'd have an easier time of it . . . You are free to go . . .

"As for these ladies and children . . ."

Still holding the little girl in his arms, Boris shot a sidelong glance at Yaakov. The boy was standing with his back against the wall, his dark eyes riveted on the Corporal's face. There was a kind of silent expectancy in his stare.

Boris thought in a flash: It is through him, it is through those eyes that this moment is going to shatter like a piggy bank. It is there that this suspense is going to crumble and pour away . . .

As the two women were waving their unimpeachable documents under the Corporal's nose, the Corporal finally caught Yaakov's eye, which was full of contemptuous hatred. The full knowledge of hatred is accessible only to children, thought Boris. Again there was that strained silence. Then the boy opened his mouth wide in the Corporal's direction and poked out a red tongue, so long and so wide, an endless purple-pile-carpeted corridor, a tongue that was only too real, appallingly real, in this setting which wasn't real at all. So this is the form in which this moment has elected to material-ize—a child's tongue, thought Boris, as he heard the Corporal articulate, slowly and distinctly, a phrase that was almost noncommittal: "What a badly brought up boy!"

Boris refrains from describing the slaughter in detail. The three soldiers held the resisting boy while the Corporal cut out his tongue with a bayonet that was too big for the purpose. There was blood, plenty of blood, more—according to Boris's estimates—than the whole of Yaakov's body had seemed likely to contain. Not a word was uttered by the group of children, who froze into complete immobility . . .

The little girl whom Boris had been holding in his arms was next. "She's got really lovely eyes," said one of the soldiers. "Like gems, they are. They'd look good mounted on an engagement ring." Even before Boris had time to reach the end of a silent prayer, intense as an electric shock, the rheumy Corporal had started gouging out the child's eyes with a hornbacked penknife, the very one he used for opening tins of corned beef. He entrusted these eyes to Boris, who took them in his palm and thought: A pair of eyes, useful enough items, when all is said and done, so intricate and hard to reproduce. There is none but the Maker, in His wealth and prodigality, who would permit Himself such waste!

They were slippery. They were trickly. Piercing screams filled the cellar like so many panic-stricken little animals. Yawnings, indefinable noises, monstrous crossbred sounds. Rendings of senses and skins. Geometric figures, geometry entire subsiding into madness the way one subsides into a hot bath. Somebody saying: "Geometry, that irrefutable proof that God is mad, stark raving mad . . ." The belly of the Universe, the belly of Existence was gaping open, and its filthy intestines were invading the room. The dimensions and categories of consciousness, time, space, grief, vacancy, and all astronomies were indulging in a masquerade or tussle, in a wedding or ride, and the stuff of dreams was sprawled on

the Throne of God, who lay in a swoon on the concrete, surrounded by His own vomit.

The quiet woman, the only one who at the outset hadn't
seemed to believe in the magic efficacy of official documents,
was stretched out and impaled. The magnitude of the rape
blossomed out in the room, a multicolored exotic flower.
What is mentionable persisted—gray, unassuming, basely
amenable to reason—side by side with the unmentionable.
The magnitude of the rape flowed between the woman's
spread-eagled legs without her making a sound. A dumb
show. Like gashed statues, thought Boris, whom the amiable
Corporal was inviting to share in the general merrymaking.
Boris doesn't say whether he declined the invitation. At a
given moment, he sensed something like a veiled threat in
the kindly Corporal. As though to say: "The gentleman
doesn't deign to participate in these vulgar manly festivities.
That could cost the gentleman dear."

Grenades thrown from outside. Childish voices moaning
and howling in the dark. A cat with its paw ripped off.

It wasn't till two hours later that Boris returned to the
same spot, together with a nurse armed with a syringe. Several mutilated children were still suffering. The nurse went
around distributing death, like portions of gingerbread
stuffed with darkness. For they do exist, Boris assures us,
cakes stuffed with darkness. He also compares the nurse to
the gardener who fulfills the destiny of the flowers and the
sunshine by picking them.

PART II

The Journey

CHAPTER 19

The train flowed on like time. Darkness reared on every side. Could it be that this flight we had taken upon ourselves was too burdensome? Yet it was all we had on our shoulders and at our feet: flight, capricious homeland of the homeless. My fair hair discouraged the vultures' stares. All around us, the whole great cop-world was asleep. And Naomi's head had found the inevitable hollow in my shoulder.

It was a soundless migration, but where on earth was the rest of the flock . . . ? Dimensions and categories were engaged in battle, within us and without. We were sinking deeper into our flight, which was bounding ever onward, clad in the heaving old train.

Early next morning, the fat woman snoring away opposite us, her supply of bacon tucked away under her wide skirts, might want to barter commercial success for ease of concience. And conscience, without fail, would bid her contribute to the task of liberation: of liberating our blood from the prison of our veins.

By leaving the town, we too had precipitated, had crystallized, the death of its life and the life of its death. This train, extending temporary hospitality to our flight, was one more trickle of blood issuing from our late home town. It was of little consequence that the others had spilled their blood directly into the soil and that ours continued to beat against the walls of our contracted veins.

And suppose it wasn't the fat woman, but the little boy who, prior to falling asleep, had whispered in his father's ear words that might constitute our death warrant?

At five in the morning, at Nigoriloy, we had to change trains. October is a cold month. It opens the winter—a drawer crammed with hostile gray objects. The sleepy little station was barely beginning to yawn. A draft coming from nowhere was caressing bits of straw on the dark wooden flooring. In the distance, somebody was whistling a Partisan song. The Partisans murdered us, just as those whom they were fighting did.

For a few seconds, curled up against a suitcase in a shadowy corner, I had a dream: I saw a red flame, extremely tall and slender. The wind—or was it something else? (though WHAT else? An organic force?)—was making it sway, slowly, in different directions. As the wind willed (let us allow that it WAS the wind), the flame bowed this way and that, as though searching for the four cardinal points. It was kissing the black and fleeing earth. A voice spoke out: "Hey, Boris, come on, Boris—cling to the tip of the flame! Hang on tight and swing with it, for all you're worth . . ."

I woke chilled to the bone and scared: for I was no longer Boris. This name which, in its Biblical version (only a few letters need changing), means "blest," I had just discarded. Together with my family name, which in some countries would have opened plenty of doors to me, and much else—everything, one might as well say, except the sign of the Covenant which, inscribed in my body, was prearranging an early death for me, or a dull perpetual fear. I was Yuri Goletz. I had at long last acquired a respectable occupation: farm hand.

I kept reciting my fictitious biography to myself, like one of the simple prayers of the religion that had stemmed from my own twenty centuries before.

Farm hand, certainly, but not quite like other farm hands. The deception would have been obvious to the first comer. After all, I could hardly chop off my unduly long fingers or use pigment to darken my hands, which remained hopelessly, appallingly white. Nor could I rid my voice of certain modulations which, heaven knows, were not those of a young fellow in the habit of herding cattle in the wide open spaces.

Yuri Goletz, whom I had created *ex nihilo,* must therefore have undergone experiences that would justify his present appearance. The son of poor peasants, having learned to read and write, he had discovered at sixteen the world of books. Intensive studying had drained the natural rosiness from his cheeks and left them sallow, as they were today. And it was studying, too, that had shown him the Way, the glorious, the one true Way of militant nationalism.

I had thus swapped races, bartering one that had for thirty centuries been regarding itself as Chosen for another that had been harboring a similar belief for only some thirty years. Both had been molded, sculpted, chiseled out of sufferings vaster and richer than those endured by the races around them. In different degrees, I was indifferent to the destiny of neither. But the second, with its Cossack past, its traditions of life in the steppes, its sad songs and incomparable landscapes, was joining in the task undertaken by the invader of exterminating my own people. The masquerade that we were enacting had a particular flavor to it: from a slave doomed to immediate cremation I was turning into a slave who assisted and vindicated the fire attendant in his task.

Naomi was quietly shivering beside me.

"I'm hungry," she said, "give me a bit of chocolate."

I handed her a bottle of vodka.

A small military procession—just five uniforms—appeared in our cramped waiting room. They were holding lighted hurricane lamps. Their leader had a little black mustache and a sickly smile that slowly traveled over the faces of the half-awake press of people. Men and women were camping on the benches and on the floor. They stirred sluggishly like pallid worms, and the waiting room was like the inside of a black pudding, that legendary choice delicacy of this dull-witted and mistrustful peasant tribe. In the distance trains could be heard fighting for breath. They seemed to be crawling over my tensed skin; like fleas. And my heart was thudding as I drank Naomi's hair. She, meanwhile, was opening the bottle.

This was not our first journey, though, since we had surreptitiously turned our backs on our town and our destinies. But they were all so alike, these endless journeys that toyed with our peace of mind and our racing heartbeats. Refuge itself was on the run, perpetually on the run.

On leaving our dying town, we had made for another oversized village, fifty leagues away. Our first steps had seemed sadly, appallingly easy. Our days were as grimy as empty eggshells in a garbage pail. The slowness of time laughed at our bodies and our futile longings. The first man we met who knew our real identity belonged to that section of the population which the invader had earmarked for degradation, for tasks that would never be more than those of underlings . . . but not for death. Andrei, with whom I had shared a year at the university, hated us—Naomi and me and everyone else of our race. But this hatred, which was mingled with contempt, was naturally bound to be less immediate than his high-minded and pathetic hatred of the invader. He regarded us as vermin, but since it was the invader who was attending to our liquidation, he would have considered it despicable to share in the task.

"You want a flat, do you?" he asked us, with marked offhandedness. "Nothing could be easier. Quite a lot of flats have recently been vacated by your crowd . . . All you have to do is call at the municipal housing office." And with a smile on his face: "Watch out, though. Where on earth have you picked up that insecure manner and diffident way of moving? If I were you, I'd try to make them a bit more self-assured. And I'd also be on my guard against that blur one sees at the back of your eyes . . . It's incredible what good psychologists and physiognomists the cops have become—and not only the cops, but every petty official. And all because of you people . . . Incidentally, Mr. Goletz (what a scream of a name you've picked for yourself!), you haven't by any chance got twenty gold rubles you could lend me? You'd be helping me out of a hole . . ."

I had to rummage for the coin in the hollow heel of my shoe. Leyzer, the old shoemaker who had made this artful hiding place for me, was no longer of this world. Grabbing the shiny coin and weighing it in his palm, Andrei condescended to address me again: "Thank you, Boris . . . or rather—I'm sorry—thank you, Mr. Goletz. This is a personal loan. And now we come to another matter: I see no reason why I should conceal the fact that I am treasurer of the local Resistance movement. I am sure you will feel impelled to make a small contribution. I put it to you as question, whereas I am entitled to demand. Your ancestors made fortunes out of the sweat of our peasants' brows. It is only fair that you should pull your weight, in this way if in no other . . ."

It was common knowledge that some members of the Resistance movement in whose behalf Andrei was speaking murdered members of our race with a zeal that their undercover leaders did little to damp down. But faced with Andrei and the extortion of this second gold piece I was compelled to adopt the attitude which, for endless centuries, had been that of Boris's ancestors, and not that of Yuri Goletz's.

Andrei was satisfied, disdainful, and polite: "Naomi may stay here in my room and rest. Now off you go to the town hall. I hope it all goes off without a hitch."

In the walled-up town that we had left behind, every square inch of living space had taken on a mystical value. The area allotted to the community had shrunk like Balzac's magic piece of shagreen, and its shrinking was always several steps ahead of the rate of extermination. The enforced promiscuity was that of a henhouse. The room that I had been sharing with Naomi, and with her alone, toward the end represented the pinnacle of imaginable luxury. But those who, in the walled-up town, had belonged to the so-called "middle" class had lived crowded together in mean little rooms, ten or fifteen to each. The great, the privileged, and the rich had taken small flats and brought their families together there. Into the lawful allocation of every square yard there had gone a fantastic welter of red tape, wirepulling, exhausting representations, and bribery.

And now I was standing in this dusty and frightfully normal town-hall office. No queue. And yet I could so badly have done with an hour of waiting in which to ponder, in which to prepare for, this unprecedented and crucial step: the struggle to secure a three-room flat for two! A deep-sea fish suddenly breaking through to the surface and deprived of the pressure without which life no longer seemed possible, I felt the blood throbbing madly at my temples as I addressed to the official in charge these deliberately casual words which to me, in my innermost heart, seemed sacrilegious: "I have just arrived in town, from the East . . . with my fiancée. I'm looking for something . . . something . . . oh, something —let's say—in the medium-price range . . ." And at the same time I was formulating a soundless prayer, so intense that it hurt: "God, don't let him find out who I am, don't let him suspect me. Grant Naomi a roof over her head tonight, and walls to hide our isolation . . . Or else, at least see to it that I get safely back to her." I mustn't leave her all alone at Andrei's. In the politest possible way, I was sure, he would not fail to turn her out if my absence grew protracted. He wouldn't go further than that. I knew him to be punctilious, arrogant, and loyal to his principles as an officer: blinkered, patriotic—honest even, according to his code . . . which wasn't mine. He wouldn't take advantage of the situation by attempting to sleep with Naomi, or to console her. Nor would he denounce her. But he would say courteously: "Boris hasn't come back. I fear he won't now. With my responsibilities to the Resistance movement, you will understand that I cannot incur any additional risks. It's getting late. I'm sorry, but I've got to go out and I must lock my door behind me. So, till I have the pleasure of running into you again . . ."

The official glanced up and directed his tired, myopic gaze at me. My raincoat was of elegant cut. My tie was discreet and expensive . . .

"But of course, sir, we have exactly what you are looking for: a cottage at the bottom of a walled-in garden, down by the river. It's suitably furnished, and you'll even find linen and china there. The fellow who had the place before has just been deported. He was . . . He was a . . . Well, you know what he was. These are hard times, but at least we're lucky in that we're getting rid of those people. Of course there are also a few decent ones, even among THEM. The same as every-

where, as we all know—don't you agree? But what is one
to do . . . ?"

With a conspiratorial smile, he handed me the form that
had to be filled out, and a set of keys. Was that all there was
to it? Could that really be all?

Thus we had a cottage all to ourselves, a wealth of fresh
air, trees, an autumnal riverscape, and long twilight walks.
I thought of Leo L.'s final wish. He had wanted, one last time
before he died, to stroll around the pond on his estate, and
breathe the all too taintless air, and gaze at the sunset. Destiny
had dealt him superhuman power and a death whose precise circumstances were unknown to me at the time. And it
was we two, Naomi and I, who were being treated to this
peaceful autumn, to this golden emptiness, to this rustic quiet.
I loved watching Naomi as she came up the garden path,
bearing water from the well in a pair of clay pitchers. These
were our origins, the origins of us all, the beginnings of a
small desert tribe, deep in a trance and sick with longing for
God . . .

But I was thinking of other girls and other women. Tedi-
ous quarrels spun around our heads like wasps.

I grew drunk with solitude, as though with vodka. Once
the heavy blinds were lowered, I would plunge into the huge
silence, which would gradually start to quiver, to hum.

"In its quintessence, the concept 'window' constitutes the
negation of the concept 'house.' There is no way out of our
isolation. Luckily, it is hardly voluntary. Besides: immobility
and death are a choice raw material. Haven't you noticed . . . ? One can hew trees and planets out of it, men
and women. One can produce suns and centuries from it. Our
empty hands, our inert hands would be mere orphans without

this raw material, without this cosmic dough . . ." When I would treat Naomi to these reflections, in my most earnest manner, they simply made her furious. The woman in her hankered after a more outdoor, public existence. She would have liked to show off our status as a couple, to exhibit the bond between us, which was at once existent and nonexistent, like the cotton candy that children are always pecking at on fairgrounds.

The ebb and flow of the ocean, synchronized and clashing at full tilt;

or again:

Two falls, equally precipitous, matched at full volume so that their waters bite and devour one another.

My need for solitude—a need experienced intermittently by the male, like a shooting pain—would collide head-on with the insatiable "determination-to-be-a-pair" that resided in Naomi and so obsessed her.

And at these times, our days would be like so many bellowings—anything alien to our fusion turning, as Naomi saw it, into the very substance of my perpetual betrayal.

To her totalitarian way of thinking, the universe was merely the embodiment of this union which I was sacrilegiously mutilating—I, who was organically part of it. In Naomi's eyes, and to her senses, I would become in such periods a fetus stabbing its mother's womb.

Our walks along the river or through the woods were taken in the twilight. For obvious reasons, we avoided treating the local people to a close look at our faces and at the movements of our bodies, which had recently experienced a life so different from theirs.

On one occasion, after strolling through an outlying district, we ran slap into a small detachment of police. It would have been rash to turn back. The men had spotted us and were beginning to laugh aloud, pointing at Naomi, who was exquisitely beautiful and so different from the girls they were used to encountering in these parts . . .

Automatically, our bearing grew haughtier, our movements more assured. We in turn began to laugh boisterously. A Lieutenant stationed himself in our path.

"You are on army property. This road is closed to pedestrians . . ."

He was the same age as I. He was weighing the effect of his words.

"I'm so sorry, Lieutenant. We didn't know. We didn't notice any sign."

"But the sign is just over there: see for yourself! The troops have orders to shoot on sight. There's a camp a bit farther along, one of those camps for . . . for you-know-who."

"We didn't realize; we've only just arrived in town."

"That's what I thought! I have never had the pleasure of meeting you, either in the mess or in the café . . . Anyway, you can count yourself lucky. This little stroll of yours could have cost you dear. You're lucky it was I you bumped into, and not one of my colleagues, the majority of whom—strictly between ourselves—are a bunch of louts . . . Permit me to introduce myself. Second-Lieutenant von G. . . ."

"Yuri Goletz. And this is my fiancée, Natalia H."

"How admirably you speak our language, my dear sir. I am lost in admiration. It bolsters our national pride to hear a foreigner express himself in our tongue as you do. And heaven knows it needs bolstering, for all our lightning victories . . . But since we have made one another's acquaintance, and in such an unusual way, won't you please do me the honor of joining me for a drink in our mess. It's no distance. And afterwards I'll provide you with two men who will escort you out of the prohibited area . . . and even through the town itself. That goes without saying. It's absurd, this curfew our police have been forced to impose on the natives . . . I beg your pardon: on your compatriots. These constant outbreaks of crime. *Mais à la guerre comme à la guerre*," he added.

He was a young man of friendly manner and good stock. He comported himself like a man of the world, conscious of his charm, which derived to some extent from shyness. No hint of the gulf between victor and vanquished. Our meeting seemed to have put him in excellent spirits. He complained of the deprivations of life in a remote garrison town. He lauded its beauties. He confided his lack of enthusiasm at the thought of fighting the enemy in the front line. Nevertheless, he was by no means insensitive to the more dubious aspects of life as an invader in a hostile region.

After a time, we came to a small clearing in the midst of the trees. Here, all was barbed wire, observation posts, and small towers. I was not given the opportunity of glancing inside the compound. Not yet.

It was quickly apparent that in speaking of the "officers' mess" our new-found friend had been guilty of a certain readily forgivable exaggeration. It turned out to be no more than a small pinewood hut where our host had to combine, for our benefit, the duties of bartender and waiter. It was warm. It was cozy. The logs crackling on the hearth yielded a pleasant aroma and emitted long-tailed glowing sparks. The poor quality of the brandy gave rise to a number of jokes and recherché allusions.

Unthinkingly, I wandered over to the window and in the twilight made out a little yard full of refuse, rusty tins, discarded pots and pans . . . and what looked like four or five cabbageheads, white and yellow, jutting from the ground. A number of bloated pigs were prowling majestically in an

idle search for food—with which, I thought, they must be
stuffed as it is. An elderly cook came out and emptied the
slops from her large metal bin. A cheery-looking soldier appeared, calmly extracted his white penis, and watered one of
the cabbageheads. All at once, my body was invaded by a faint
uneasiness, by a sense of insecurity. It seemed to me that
nothing existed in the whole wide world except for these
mucky cabbageheads, for these stumps so queerly planted
among the filth and rubbish. Through the sheer power of
their daydreams, these cabbageheads were conjuring us up,
fixing us all in our places . . . and the world with us. Then
were Naomi and the friendly Lieutenant and this hut in the
middle of the woods and the two of us—Boris and Yuri—no
more than the projection, the crystallization of a "thought,"
or rather of a moment of musing and putrefaction, to
which these urine-sprayed cabbages were briefly subject?

I averted my head. The conversation with the Lieutenant
flowed on. He had now reached the stage of confessing to his
passion for theosophy:

"Oh, to be the arrow and the bowman, the hunter and the
hunted! To be the great assenter and the great assent . . ."

My mind was elsewhere: I was barely attending to his
words. I was eager to get back to the window; a kind of
sixth sense told me that, behind all his eloquence, he was trying to stop me, to turn my attention to other things. A peculiar, almost inexplicable phrase crossed my mind: "A house-
warming in a condemned cell . . ." Then another, even
more absurd:

> Petrified tear
> Putrefied soul
> heavy within me
> as a dead fetus . .

Where on earth had I heard this foolish stanza? Better watch out. I was beginning to have hallucinations, and this was hardly the time or place for them. I must take myself in hand.

"You were saying, Lieutenant . . . ?"

He was all shyness. The slightest possible hint of a stammer created, as it were, an additional bond between us.

"You know, my dear sir, there must be something very strange about this country. About YOUR country. To tell you the truth, my duties aren't too taxing. They leave me with time on my hands. And then, what with autumn, and the countryside all around, and the long empty evenings, to say nothing of the loneliness . . . well, I've taken to writing little stories. Oh, without the slightest thought—believe me! —of setting myself up as an author. I'm the first to laugh at my pieces. We've never produced anything but army officers and landowners in my family, not in three hundred years. Never a single poet, or even poetaster. Now that I'm out here, I sometimes get the feeling that it is up to me to express everything that my ancestors kept bottled up. Not on my own behalf, for I'm just a cipher, but on theirs. I'm the last of the line. That sounds terribly melodramatic. If I'm sent to the front, it is more than likely there will be no more von G.s here below. Not for all eternity . . . Oh, don't think me more obtuse than I really am. I don't give a hoot for my family tree. It's this country—yes, it's this country of yours: it has awakened strange images within me, images that I was wrong to jot down."

I had to say it, to avoid appearing impolite: "I'd be grateful to you, Lieutenant, extremely grateful, if you would do me the honor of reading me a few passages. I should greatly appreciate such a token of trust or, if you would prefer me to put it another way, such a treat. To be frank, I am not

guiltless of a few such sins myself. You will find me an atten-
tive if not a qualified listener."

And this is the story that Second-Lieutenant von G. read
to me:

"Once upon a time there was a cockroach. But his eyes
were not at all those of a cockroach; or, if they WERE those of a
cockroach, they were less ignoble than you might have imagined. In the past, his life had not been unduly splendid.
As down-to-earth as down-to-earth could be: the life of a
cockroach.

"But recently, since his arrival in S., 'the-life-of-a-cockroach'
had given place to 'the-process-of-crushing-a-cockroach.'
Day by day, hour by hour, the process continues. The cockroach's armor cracks and tears. The whitish innards flow
out and start leading a life of their own, a life that would
strike terror even into a cockroach who was in the best of
health.

"If only it weren't for this continual shouting of 'Kill him!
Kill him!' "

His stammer was turning into a real stutter, and only a
few passages have stayed in my mind:

> "The pith of the story
>   Gobbled up by cockroaches:
>   Fancy having it in for cockroaches
>   For being only cockroaches . . .
>   Why, it's a high caste!"

Or again:

> "Phenomena suck at the squalid hour
>   That falls without a crash
>   As red flies
>   Suck at the carcass of a blind cat."

"Or would you prefer another version, my dear sir?" he asked.

> "Acts, deeds, events
> Swarm on each of these squalid hours
> That go on and on falling from the tree of time.
> They swarm like flies
> In the carcass of a blind cat . . ."

"Why 'blind,' why 'blind'?" I asked myself—or rather, asked the Lieutenant, who, all hot and panting from his reading, was looking to me for some comment or response. The bottle of cheap brandy was empty.

Naomi, who had been almost silent throughout, said with a quizzical smile: "You might be brothers."

The sense of intimacy that was building up within the room was almost tangible. It was only as a result of hard, conscious effort that I managed to rise from my chair, brushing aside the officer's hand: he was still trying to hold me back. I pressed my burning brow to the cold glass of the window overlooking the little yard. And suddenly, like the crack of a ringmaster's whip, a searchlight illumined the scene. The tiny, lunar landscape struck my temples like a club. I checked an instant desire to vomit. It wasn't cabbageheads that the pigs were licking and chewing. Five men were buried upright in the tiny garden adjoining the canteen. Their besmirched heads, covered with wet dust and other, unmentionable objects—their half-devoured heads were projecting from the soil like giant mushrooms. One of these heads with gaping sockets had just performed a clearly perceptible circular motion.

With a violent and unpremeditated swing of the arm, I smashed the pane and leaned out. And before feeling the chill revolver barrel on my streaming forehead, I succeeded

in catching a damp utterance—half death rattle, half song—
coming from a long way off, from farther off than the stars:
"Harken, my people, God is thy Lord, there is none like to
Him . . ."

Blood was pouring from the gash in my hand. With a
strength and determination that seemed superhuman to me,
the Lieutenant was dragging me back into the center of the
room. Naomi had flung herself, with all the weight in her
body, upon the hand holding the revolver. There was but one
thought in my mind: I mustn't faint! This was the supreme,
the ultimate problem, like the one confronting a sterile man
who wishes to create a world.

The revolver clattered to the floor. A sentry appeared in
the doorway. "Get out!" roared the Lieutenant, and the man
backed away. A mighty slap crashed down on my cheek, robbing me of my breath again . . . Should I hurl myself on this
boy, and die, and take Naomi with me?

"I apologize for that blow, sir," said the Lieutenant. "I am
to blame for all that has happened. The regulations are
plain, and it is I who infringed them. Local inhabitants are
not to be entertained in our officers' messes. The regulations
are quite right. I can understand your reacting the way you
did to what you saw. It would normally be my duty to have
you shot at once. But it was I who invited you, so I shall be
satisfied with your word of honor that you will not repeat to
anyone what has been revealed to you. We are compelled to
be implacable and we do not have to account for our actions
to any man living. Or so, at least, our superiors keep telling
us all day long. Enough said! However, to set your mind
at rest, I can disclose to you that those are not the heads of any
of your fellow countrymen. That item out there, those items
. . . belong to members of a tribe which we curse and hate as
much as you do. That, at least, is the official story. For hate

and I are birds of a different feather . . . But we'll say no more of that.

"As for the blow I dealt you, in normal times you would have been entitled to demand satisfaction of me, and I assure you I would have given it without hesitating. But since that is not possible, please believe that the blow was in no way aimed at your honor, but was administered simply in order to save you from a hysterical outburst which, in view of the time and the place, might have been fatal. I could hardly summon our medical officer to attend to you! And now, if my apologies seem adequate, do please give me your address. I shall be delighted to pay you a return visit—as a guest and as a friend—and to erase the painful impression that you would otherwise retain of our meeting . . . Sentry! You will conduct this lady and this gentleman out of the military zone and into town . . . Wait, while I give them a safe-conduct . . . I'll say *au revoir*, then, and hope to see you soon."

Had Naomi seen, had she glimpsed?

I went away harboring my secret as one harbors an undivided love.

CHAPTER 20

Next morning, while out to do some shopping, I was brought up sharp by a sickly, derisive expression on someone's face. The man whose eyes were scanning my features was not unknown to me. His heavy hand clapped me on the back.

"Why, my lord Baron, what a pleasant surprise!" he said. "Does His Lordship deign to recognize me?—Gerard Fuchs, who used to come courting the girl who was lady's maid to Your Lordship's mother. My wife still harbors fond memories of your family, and of you in particular. I've seen you out-of-doors several times with Miss N., and I even know your address. There's no need for me to ask after your family. I know all about them, you see. They're away on a long journey. Should you wish to join them here and now, just say the word . . ."

He jerked his eyes significantly toward a policeman crossing the road.

"But if you don't want my help, then it's up to you to help me." His hand closed on my shoulder again. "In an hour's time I'll be waiting for you right here in this street. In that little café over there. Fifty thousand, and not a penny less. For ten days now I've been wrangling with my wife about you. She wants me to lay off you, the little fool. Whatever next!

Maybe you'd like her to start waiting on you again? Maybe SHE would, too—who knows?—but times have changed . . . Thanks to you, I'm having scene after scene at home. You WOULD have to pick this town to try and save your dirty skin . . . And whatever you do, don't try anything silly! Don't think you can give me the slip. I've got men following your every movement . . ."

"Well now, Gerard, I might be able to tide you over. With a reasonable sum. But fifty thousand is out of the question. And I can't produce such money at the drop of a hat. It's true my father stashed away a certain amount of gold in our town, but you will understand that I don't walk around with a bank in my pocket. You are free to denounce us, certainly; but how would that further the interests of either of us . . . ? As old acquaintances, it would surely be better for us to settle things on a friendly footing. And over a drink . . . So drop in at the cottage for a moment and say hello to Naomi. Poor girl, her black hair keeps her from going out much. She never sees anyone except me, and—as you know—I'm not always the brightest of company. She'll be thrilled at the chance of chatting for a while with an old friend. Besides, I've got a bottle of plum brandy. Dating from prewar days . . . But look here, you haven't even told me what you and your wife have been up to, all this time . . ."

"You're trying to soft-soap me, but watch out: I'm hard-headed where business is concerned. It was your crowd who taught me to be so. Back in the prewar days, as you call them."

"But my invitation has nothing whatever to do with business. Or rather—it has, to be quite honest. As I told you, Gerard, I haven't got fifty thousand rubles on me, or even ten thousand. But it's just occurred to me: there IS that little ring of my mother's. Who knows? It may even be worth more than the fifty thousand rubles you need. As you'll surely remember, some of my mother's jewelry wasn't at all bad. Myself, I don't know about these things. But you, with things as they are at present, must have learned quite a lot about jewelry."

I wasn't looking at Gerard. My eyes would have given me away. Furtively I gazed down at the multicolored mud at our feet, where the flimsy blue sky was reflected in patches of oil.

The man stood hesitating—torn, as he was, between the desire to display his power directly, and at once, and that other desire, the desire for finesse, for diplomacy, so much more refined, so much more in the style of the white-collar class which he had been striving so desperately to copy all his life. Neither of us was new to the game. Merely from his semi-military appearance (gleaming boots, stout green jacket), merely from his sartorial attempt to pass himself off, so boldly and so lovingly, as one of the wielders of power, one could tell that I was not the first man he had betrayed, just as he was not the first blackmailer we had encountered in the course of our exodus.

After all, the man might believe me: fifty thousand rubles wasn't a sum one could lay one's hands on just like that. My mother's jewelry had enjoyed a fame which Gerard's wife, having been her maid, was bound to have inflated rather than diminished. And then there was the offer of a free drink.

What about these "men" of his, who were supposed to be following our every footstep? Did they really exist? I wasn't sure. The prospect of not losing sight of me for a moment till the deal was clinched could only reassure friend Gerard. Perhaps he envisaged tears and entreaties from Naomi. And suppose, he was probably thinking, I get the chance to take her pants down, the little tramp?

It was his servile lusts, so twisted and bottled up, that decided him in my favor.

"Very well, I'll come. But my time limit is unchanged. One hour. As for having a drink . . . you need one more than I do. You're as white as a sheet. You could do with a good bracer. I can understand that, and I'm a man of feeling. But a hardheaded one, don't forget. And time is running out . . ."

He stared at his solid gold watch. There was nobody following us.

I carefully closed the garden gate after us. Naomi was standing in the doorway in her dark blue dressing gown. She turned a bit pale when she saw I had someone with me. She recognized Gerard and sized up the situation in a flash.

She's got what it takes, she's got what it takes, I thought with fleeting satisfaction. She became cajoling, bubbly, all smiles.

"But, Boris, what a lovely surprise! You've brought such a dear and unexpected guest. Somebody from the good old days . . . But what about your wife, Mr. Gerard, what about dear Martha? Why isn't she with you?"

"Well you see, Miss, I'm here on business . . ."

"Business, business, these men are insufferable with their business . . ." A small icy gleam appeared in Naomi's eyes. A gleam that was new to me. She was affability itself. "But come in, come in. I'll be back right away, and I'll bring a tray of drinks." Her voice grew lilting. "And for once I'm going to have a drink too. Do you know, Mr. Gerard, Boris never allows me to drink. So I'm jolly well going to take advantage of your being here . . ."

She went out, leaving the door ajar. It was imperative that I should join her, but I was afraid to leave Gerard unattended and thus destroy the flimsy shell of camaraderie that at the moment enveloped our relationship.

The urgency of his greed came to my rescue.

"Well, Boris, what about this ring? I'm itching to see it. Haven't you got it on you?"

"Wait just a moment, and I'll get it for you. It's under one of the tiles, out in the kitchen. Here, have a cigarette. I'll be back in no time."

Three glasses and a bottle, set on a silver tray. With the aid of a carving knife, I slit open the small inside pocket of my jacket. Inside a round metal container, as thin as a child's little finger, the white capsule reposed in its cotton wool, as truly in place as an embryo in the maternal womb. My hands were trembling, and it wasn't on account of Gerard but of my own parsimony. This white powder was painfully valuable. More valuable than life.

Naomi poured the red liqueur into the three glasses. There was no way of introducing a distinguishing mark. It's in the lap of the gods, I thought.

And to Naomi I said: "If only this tray were square, the odds would be more in our favor. One thing more: don't choose a glass before he does. And wait a second . . . give me your ring."

It was an old ring, handed down from one of Naomi's grandmothers. An emerald mounted in gold. It wasn't worth much.

With Naomi following close behind me, I returned to the living room, tray in hand. The eager stare that Gerard directed at the ring quickly turned to anger.

"But you said it was diamond and platinum!"

"I'm going straight back for it, Gerard. I've brought this one merely to ask your advice. We're nearly broke and we're going to have to sell it. I thought perhaps you could tell us roughly how much it's worth. But for heaven's sake let's have a drink first . . ."

My poor little stratagem! The glass with the white powder in it was full to the brim. On the other two, one
could make out a glistening, transparent halo. Were these
two or three millimeters about to turn, for our benefit, into a
world of freedom? My hands grew as heavy as two rivers enfolding a vast country.

"Help yourself, Gerard, help yourself . . ." But it was
Naomi who was first to take one. The fool, the slut, the bag
. . . I'd TOLD her to wait. I'll have to knock some sense into
her, I'll have to thrash her, I said to myself in my great joy,
which had blossomed forth in a second, like a plant at a fakir's
touch. For the glass that she had chosen was not THE glass. She
was eliminated, eliminated for good and all, and now it was
between the two of us, just Gerard and me. For a moment I
felt a kind of fondness for him, a kind of solidarity from
which Naomi was now excluded.

Now it was Gerard's turn to take a glass, not mine. With
people like him, especially with people like him, such trivial
points of etiquette had to be scrupulously observed. Furthermore, something told me that if I tried to hurry things to
their conclusion by reaching out before he did, an avenging
inner voice might put him on his guard. The situation
called for slowness: I must let matters take their course.

"Come on, Gerard, help yourself!"

"What about that diamond ring?"

"In a minute, in a minute. I'm thirsty, and I can hardly
take a glass before my guest does . . ." (Wasn't I going
too far by NAMING the moment in this manner?)

Our fingers, our hands—a motionless race to attain survival, an unwitting race, just as there are soundless cries and
clear-sighted blindnesses.

A set look came into his eyes. A decision. He reached out.

"Your health, Miss, your health, Boris, and here's to our transaction!"

He drained the overfull glass at a gulp. Calculating, petty, greedy, he was bound to choose the glass with most in it, I said to myself—but my soul rejected such glib psychological arguments. It was singing the praises of Him who was about to destroy one of His creatures, one on whom I wished a slow death. A fat fly was buzzing about over our heads. I studied the second hand on my watch . . .

Dr. Cohen had explained to me long ago how the powder acted on the system. By the end of a minute, Gerard would no longer be capable of taking the few strides that would enable him to reach the door. But he would remain conscious—even if things grew a little blurred toward the end—for another twenty or thirty minutes. That was all the time I needed. He would suffer no intense pain, his limbs would grow heavy, they would become alien objects, and within four or five minutes they would no longer obey him. It wouldn't matter if Gerard screamed for help—even if he were able to. The windows were shut, and we didn't have neighbors.

Naomi was pouring a second round of drinks. From a barely perceptible expression on my face, or from the set of my hands perhaps, she must have suspected that the battle was won.

"Aren't you due home before noon then, Mr. Gerard?" she asked, firing the question in a harsh, crisp voice that made me shudder. It was a voice I didn't recognize as hers.

"Why, no! You don't think I account to my wife for my comings and goings, do you? If I feel like drinking, I drink . . ."

The child running through the tall grass leaves a momentary wake. The grass closes after him, and the wake is gone.

This is what passed through my head: the tussle with Gerard, and the victory I had reaped, and the righteousness of my cause, and the scurviness of his, and even the smell of the cheap eau de Cologne with which he smothered the crinkles of his smugness, and for which I could forgive him least of all: all these things were of such small account in comparison with the extent to which—involuntarily and thanks to me —he was about to outdistance us two. Another few minutes, and Gerard would be striding through planetary landscapes and oceans, or else through gaudily colored empty spaces or nonspaces . . . the only worlds that still mattered to me. It was I who was opening up these vertiginous plains for him, these abysses deeper than depth.

And if this slick and able-bodied man was about to turn into a sewer, if talk of an Elsewhere, of spaces opening up after death, was all eyewash . . . what wouldn't I give to know the color of those stagnant waters, to glimpse—if only for a moment—that pure corpsehood to which old Gerard was going to be reduced in a few minutes' time.

> "Rusty centuries
> Danced a jig
> Around your cradle . . ."

As they will likewise dance one around the coffin you will never have. Yes, my dear old Gerard, this is precisely what is meant by "the eternal cycle."

Might I compare each of the millennia that have elapsed (or, worse still: that have still to elapse) to a squashed bedbug? But I have resolved to kill comparisons, to expunge them all, to exterminate the whole tribe, the whole pernicious breed. And if that figure, that poor, worn-out "figure of speech," dies out forever, I shall be left with no choice but to engage in mere recounting, mere enumeration, so pullulating, and so ugly. I shall be left with that mere enumeration worthy only of a storekeeper: "Item, the squashed centuries . . . Item, the bedbugs . . ." Mere recounting just goes on and on, and addles, and palls . . .

And then again: in compliance with a mistaken social convention, when "we" are inclined to sympathize with suffering, we are concerned with what caused it, with its origins, and not simply—as we should be—with its specific intensity and color. Instead of losing her children, Niobe, all thrilling tranquil beauty, Niobe the desired, loses a front tooth. Between her lips looms a monstrous gap—a scandal. Niobe's suffering, and her shame, are more acute, for sure, than those prompted by the death of her sons. They are more deserving of compassion. But this compassion is not forthcoming.

None of these words was spoken aloud. However can one heap so many thoughts upon the poor back of a second, of a single second . . . ? Hate your enemy, humiliate him if you can, but do not kill him. Procure life for him, unending life if need be . . . The broken pitcher of my brief triumph was discharging poison into my soul, and I must wrestle with my soul, I must "knock some sense into it" . . .

"Gerard, I shan't be bringing you the diamond ring! Gerard, I've got fifty thousand rubles on me all right, and a HUNDRED and fifty thousand, but you aren't going to get them. Want to see the notes? Here they are. Look! And here are the gems. See how they sparkle! You are a lackey, and to lackeys one gives tips when they are loyal and know their place. When they are correct. As you were, in your time. That is the way of the world. There are those to whom one hands millions on a plate, and those to whom one gives no more than coppers. You belong to the second breed. Or rather, you did. Large-scale transactions—fifty thousand rubles!—are not for you. Take my word for it. But when lackeys get out of hand, one boxes their ears."

I rose unhurriedly from my chair. His muscles were straining. He supposed he must be dreaming. He thought he must have gone out of his mind. He couldn't believe his eyes, or his ears, or his skin. The blow caught him full in the face.

"Naomi, bring me the kitchen knife. And a pair of rubber gloves. Yes, that's it: the gloves you wear for peeling the vegetables. And then get out of here: I've some unfinished business to attend to with Mr. Gerard."

He made a mighty effort. His veins and muscles stood out. He was dribbling saliva and blood.

"Gerard, you are going to live, but you are going to live mutilated. You won't be able to denounce anyone ever again, for you will be blind."

I produced a slight gash on his left cheek. Gerard was clean and well-shaven. The touch of his male skin filled me with revulsion. I hurled the knife into a corner of the room and sank back into my chair. I didn't feel proud of myself after this macabre bit of play-acting, which I had been childish enough to embark on but not plucky enough to carry through. A piece of third-rate cinema.

"You rats, you swindlers—oh, you dirty rats!" Gerard's moanings were muffled, but still articulate. "You'll pay for this. The Chief of Police is a friend of mine. I hate your guts. I've always hated you—you and all your kind. All that's being done to you is nothing to what you deserve.

". . . My lord Baron, I was only joking. Let me go. Stop fooling. I'll be your slave. We'll hide you at our place. We'll-wait-on-you-again—wait-on-you—wait-on—wait-on—wai . . ."

He was growing tongue-tied, but there was lucidity in his eyes. The immense lucidity of a body rebelling against annihilation. A few drops of blood dripped from his nose.

"Naomi, pack our things! There's a train to the capital at noon, and we must be on it."

Like a forsaken child, Gerard began to burble plaintively, faintly, more and more faintly.

CHAPTER 21

Landscapes were dancing like mileposts. Their blood was dark and sluggish and coagulated. Our endless peregrinations had started again. Sometimes night brought us our only respite; on those occasions when it descended far down:

"When the army of dreams descends on your destiny,
  To acquire substance itself and devour the substance of your
      incredulity,
The substance of your life . . ."

A jumble of distinctive gestures, handed down from our forefathers and resuscitated by our life in the walled-up town, seemed the greatest threat to our survival: relics of sign language; fugitive expressions in the eye which did not resemble, which did not sufficiently resemble, the expressions of the people around us; quiverings of the taut skin of our cheeks; a gait which strove to be calm and which, in a slightly too obvious manner, curbed the swiftness, the spontaneous swiftness, which alone would have matched our constant fear.

We had to scan other people's faces without their noticing —not wishing to scan them, yet scanning them all the same. We had to hide our terrible aching for the countryside, and fresh air, and rivers, and open skies. We had to restrain the

sense of humility, the obsequiousness, that we were bound
to feel in the presence of human beings not liable to immediate extinction. We had to conceal our immeasurable pride
vis-à-vis these same human beings.

And all this in the endless succession of towns, villages,
railway carriages, and hotel rooms that paraded before our
blinded eyes. Uprootedness became our only homeland,
and there was nothing cozy about living in that sprawling
country. Daily I smashed the inkwell of Eternity, the way one
smashes the wings of static glassware angels. All this talk, all
this activity—in an attempt to draw nearer to the God, to
the fleeing God. For our God was flight. Not refuge.

The occupied capital was ramshackle and ribald, debased
and running wild. On the trams, conductors were refusing to
take money for tickets, since it would only help to line the
invader's pockets. Graffiti foretold the downfall of the masters of the moment. Handwritten prophecies, popularly attributed to great figures of the past—Paracelsus or the
Queen of Sheba or various Martyrs of the Church—circu-
lated undercover, proclaiming the imminent destruction of
the Beast. Onslaughts directed against the enemy were devised somewhere in the hidden depths of the city; they
seemed to stem from the bottom of the river which enfolded
the southern half of the capital with its sturdy arm. Armed
resistance and the black market captivated the hearts of these
barely urbanized, country-rooted folk, who maybe found in
these lacerating disturbances the sole key to their grim happiness, to their true happiness. They ate and drank their fill
of humble pie and the spirit of heroism. Their requirements in matters of love and hate were regally met.

True, but this hate was in no way exclusive: it was vented
on the enemy, certainly, but it was also vented on those few
members of our race who had so far survived. Like ivy en-

twining a pillar, it surrounded our movements, our faces, and our thoughts. The selfsame men and women who braved death in the fight against the invader applauded his relentless campaign against our survival.

In this state capital, conquered and unsubmissive, I realized that Gerard, who had died as a result of my stratagem, had been merely a bungling small-town amateur. Whole armies of blackmailers and unpaid Quislings set traps for us and treated us to their unsleeping watchfulness.

In this city of several hundred thousand inhabitants, how many of us WERE there, trying to evade prying eyes and murderous hands? A hundred, or five times a hundred? I didn't know. Occasionally, glances would be exchanged of a kind that strove to be anonymous, that strove to be noncommittal, and that were identifiable precisely on account of this striving after anonymity. Of a kind that instantly aroused demented, unbelievable love.

How many of us? I still cannot say. But in that very city, which aroused the admiration of the world by the way it fought, I learned that great boulevards could hurt like an aching heart, that a park in autumn, with its dwindling number of visitors and its golden leaves rustling underfoot, and with the miracle of its lingering sunlight, could be a cold, cruel enemy. That a tram was a monster spying on its victims with a hundred hostile eyes.

Through the help of a few contacts, of a few distant "friends" who had no inkling of my true situation, I got a job as manager of a variety theater. The staging of brainless revues—which, on his own admission, the enemy tolerated merely in order to bestialize the soul of the conquered state —brought me into contact with girls eager to become singers and dancers. Physical fidelity to Naomi was becoming burdensome to me. Would not our partnership, this union sus-

tained by the blood of the spirit, have been purer if rid of a
sexual exclusiveness so artificial and nonsensical, deriving
from cautiousness and fear? This was a problem with which
Naomi was quite unacquainted; she was blind to the dangers
of conventionalizing a relationship and tempted, in her entirely pardonable inexperience, to mistake the inevitable advance of one's body's indifference for a moral defect. It was
this moral defect she supposed she was fighting, assured of
the righteousness of her cause, resorting now to fits of drearier
and drearier melancholy, now to violent scenes in which
she sometimes came close to real grandeur. The maledictions
that she heaped upon my body and my soul; the punish-
ments that she called down on every thought of mine that
might originate outside what was common to us both; this
world of hyperlucidity and cause-and-effect, spikier and more
inhuman than the whole of mathematics, and closed forever
to all chance gestures or even hints of gestures; this world
in which, even before conception, every seed became its frui-
tion and its own corpse—these were the great tracts that Naomi opened out to me, there to receive my love and my betrayal.

All about us, a thousand darknesses were cutting each
other's throats. Locked in Naomi's monologue, that splutter-
ing yellow lamp that was likely to burst at any moment like a
weak heart, I contracted till I was without area. A geometric
point wavering and dreaming. Grieving in the knowledge
that once it penetrates the noble substance, the living substance which it deifies, it can't be anything but a sore in the
eye, can't be anything but the Hurter. Is it possible for a
geometric point to dematerialize, to melt away, to efface the
ruts, the painful traces of its journey through the world? The
suicide's prerogative, the sweet favor of extinction, is denied
him who has been hewn from the hard clay of immortality.

Oh, how I cursed it—this pitiless immortality in which the Maker had tricked us out, as though in a clown's costume. Inside my body, that hateful quivering which was God. In the meantime, I knew it, I knew as much: like birds of prey on the attack, you were going to swoop down on me one day— you, my new thoughts that I hadn't as yet conceived; you, all the sights that I hadn't as yet glimpsed . . . But I don't want anything to do with you. You are the future, and the future is foe.

I fingered the outer walls of the flame. I stroked its infinitely soft skin. Will I one day softly penetrate the injured flesh of the flame?

To Naomi—so mulish, so peevish, and looking to me only for the supreme hurt—I used to relate a story that opened with these words:

"Hundreds of years ago, inside a candle flame, there lived an old man."

She would kiss my hands. To her it seemed that the fear which held us in its clutch was her only ally. Would not the sign of the Covenant inscribed in my body betray me to the very first tart I picked up?

Eyes, windows, street lamps: so many poisoned springs throbbing with the water of our extinction.

"What are the thoughts of a cockroach when it sees, when it senses, a heavy boot about to crash down and squash its casing and bring its numberless white innards spurting out? Does it imagine the Crunch and the Stench, the last two products that its departing life is going to leave on earth? And what would be the fruit of crossbreeding—is such a thing so impossible?—between a male spider and a human hermaphrodite?"

The stagehand at the theater, poor fool—part madman, part *agent provocateur,* clad in dark threadbare overalls—

would embellish my idle moments with such questions, worthy of Second-Lieutenant von G., as I dozed in my tattered armchair.

I would do my best to answer them . . . In a fireless crucible I would try to stir the magic of his obsessions, but the crucible had grown cold and the magic was stillborn.

Autumn was advancing, and yellow leaves were strewn thick on the surface of the river. The days were so spare and indistinguishable that they barely merited their names and dates. Often they were abortions of days, featherless chicks the color of ashes, as heavy as lumps of clay.

One day the mad stagehand was arrested as a hostage and shot with plaster of Paris in his mouth to stifle the seditious final shout that he would not have uttered. The long line of men doomed to execution gave like slipknots in a children's game.

Shortly afterwards we had to move on, for a newly engaged actor suspected my true identity. Naomi was relieved, greatly relieved, to see me turn my back on the aspiring actresses.

CHAPTER 22

And then came a mountain resort, and a small town, and a
big town, and steep paths, and inns, and peasant huts, and
railway carriages, still more railway carriages, and city slums;
incoherent stages in the development of a pure and coherent
whole. Naomi was getting thin and pale, and as transparent as
certain childlike thoughts. And I had nothing to offer her,
apart from this wretched handful of gray nights. It was visi-
bly dwindling, this handful of nights which my blood was no
longer rich enough to turn black. These short, anemic nights
were a flimsy shelter, a tattered garment.

Occasionally, solemn birds would wheel above our heads.
Occasionally, we would be enveloped by clouds of reddish
dust. In a mighty condensation, this red-brown dust would
turn into lumps of sandstone, from which tombstones are
carved—those stones of my childhood. The sacred characters
expelled from the old cemetery had hidden themselves away
on pieces of waste ground, along the edge of bumpy roads,
under withered trees. They were weaving our destiny, they
were weaving the clown's costume that one day I should have
to don.

We moved on and on, and the journey would continue to
confront us, set and grinning, like an ancient mask. It was

leading us through the boundless realm of "Choice." The act
of choosing or the semblance of "Choice" multiplied by
the seconds of our lives would buzz in our hyperattentive
ears like a swarm of wasps: the street opens out into a square;
turn right, and we may meet with torture and shame, and the
shame of being ashamed; turn left, and we may be safe; or the
other way round . . . This constant gamble would feed our
quarrels and feed on our brains and thoughts. Suppose that
one day all four points of the compass were to lead to death,
and death alone; we should never know, confronting the ultimate wall, that the three lines of escape that we had rejected
had been likewise sealed off.

There follows a long chapter in which Boris pores over the
significance (or lack of significance?) of the act of "choosing":
lawyer or doctor, pediatrician or phthisiologist, phthisiologist or specialist in pulmonary tuberculosis, scholar or
tradesman, etc., man or beast, man or his thought, man or his
shadow; mammal or bird; existence or nonexistence; mentionable or unmentionable; perceptible or hidden from all
"conceivable perception" . . . or even from all "inconceivable perception"; "reality" or concave reality; unreality or
concave unreality. Bifurcations, endless bifurcations . . .
This realm of "Choice"—concludes Boris—was a well full of
lizards, some half alive, the rest very dead. The feel of them
—it seems—he found more than a little loathsome.

Returning to his story, he continues:
And then the little railway station, the waiting room: the
inside of a red sausage full of white grubs moving about with
deadly slowness. In that period, which my brain transforms
into a damp, ashen twilight, gaily colored with the glow of
cigarettes and twinkling with small occurrences each of

which took on planetary proportions (though how small the planet was!), in that breathless period I would often gaze intently at Naomi, who was the link, who was the continuation. Quarrels, outbursts of jealousy, differences of outlook would fall away like filthy rags when my eyes scanned her sleeping face and the lines of her body, as though they were a manuscript penned by myself, long since forgotten, and suddenly rediscovered. Immortality for him who thirsts for life, easy death for him who craves for nothing but his own extinction. Both cries, equally true and equally mendacious, were ringing out somewhere within the inner walls. And by the sheer power of her presence, Naomi had the capacity to trail them on a leash, these two cries, like a pair of goats—one white, the other black.

Once, arriving in a small mountain resort at the end of a crawling train ride, and finding it impossible to remain in the tumble-down station, which was teeming with spies, we took shelter in a railwayman's hut. Outside, nothing but endless snow and the spotless, crystalline frost; a few distant lights. We got into the big bed, under the vigil lamp which stood flickering in front of the icon, a bed gaping open near the pillow like some great red fruit bursting with overripeness. So all the roads that I had tramped in the past, stretching the length and breadth of a continent, ended in this grappling wherein man at last approached the sluice gates that had always remained hidden, wherein the object of his long craving lay finally within his grasp.

"I was thirteen," Naomi related, "and they had just made us move into the walled-up town. My parents had brought all their gold with them, and plates and dishes, and mattresses,

and carpets. They had been preparing for this move, but at the last moment they were not prepared for it. My mother worked herself into a state. She could have been worse, though. My father—you remember him, don't you?—did his best to stay calm; he had wrapped a huge sheepskin around me. He told my mother—I heard him when they thought I was asleep—that he could face the thought of the three of us dying, but couldn't bear to think I might be cold. My lungs were none too strong, it seemed to him. I had a big cat, and I put him in a bag and carried him to our new home inside the walls. My parents gave me ham, and fritters cooked with real butter, and everything that was as scarce as could be. And on the sly I used to put it all out for the cat, who turned his nose up at it. I'd been told that cats attached themselves to nobody, only to walls and neighborhoods. And because I loved him so, I was torn between two attitudes: the fear of his running away, and the determination to be like him, to love nobody, not even the cat, but only walls and neighborhoods. And after only four days of it, the cat vanished. On the very day that yellow notices were put up to say that any of us caught on the other side of the walls would be shot summarily. But I crept out, just the same. Father had gone to the Council meeting at Leo L.'s. Mother was trying to get some butter. At three o'clock in the afternoon I stole out of the gate in the wall. I had been afraid of being caught BEFORE, in our own town. Later, in THEIRS, I ran like a mad girl. None of them, I thought, has raven hair like mine: 'I was dark as another is naked.'[1] You remember those words. For ages and ages I stood in the gateway of our old house. The major lived there now. I'm sure you recall: there was a garden surrounding the house, and a little gatekeeper's lodge. When the gatekeeper saw me, he nearly jumped out of his

[1] Adolf Rudnicki.

skin. But he was one of the best. He pulled himself together and said: 'I know what's brought you, Naomi. Your CAT is here.' And the cat clawed me till he drew blood. He didn't want to come. But I caught him again and slung him over my shoulders, and on the way back I felt quite safe. My parents didn't say a word; they just kissed me when I walked in. But when my father held me in his arms, there was a certain mistiness in his eyes, such as one seldom sees. I shouldn't tell you that, you don't deserve it, but just occasionally a similar mist appears in yours. Perhaps it's for that reason I came away with you. And perhaps for another. Listen, I've never told you this. It wasn't till long, long after the incident with the cat. My parents were still alive, but everything was quite plain to me by this time, and I knew they might take their lives any day. And I hoped they would, for I loved them. I loved them in my own way. You know what I mean. No need to explain it to you. You called at our flat and you took me to the Council Office to get me fitted up with a card saying I was a scrap-iron collector, or something of the kind. It was supposed to protect me when there were roundups. You didn't believe it offered any such protection, and neither did I. But I went so that my parents should think I believed in it. And then we took a stroll at the back of the old synagogue, where there was a bit of a view: a bleak one, but with a spot of green here and there. It was twilight. You talked about the 'organic landscapes'[1] that your friend David had described. David with the ginger hair. You said that we were all just part of the landscape, perhaps the most impatient part. And that the landscape was inside us. And you said a lot of other things that I couldn't repeat now, but which I understood at the time as though your brain were inside my head. You didn't try to make love to me. I was disappointed. And I knew I wasn't

[1] Adolf Rudnicki.

going to die or be arrested before I had slept with you. Young as I was, I had seen you going about with girls: with dark-haired Rachel and with Tamara, who was so much more beautiful than I. I was jealous. I was furious. And none of the things around me existed any more. I hardly noticed my parents, or the soldiers, or the sweeps, or the disappearances. It was as though I was cut off from everything that was going on. And you gave the impression of seeing everything but me. Things went on like this for far too long. Half the people we knew had gone, half the town had vanished before you came to our flat again . . . Even while the town was being ravaged, even while sick men and women were being slaughtered in the hospitals, I had no thought for anything except getting even with you. Every night I used to beg God to send you a dream, a bad dream about ME. Had I been given the power either to save us all or to arouse in your mind the dreams, the longings that I wished you to have, the dreams about ME, I'd have chosen the latter . . . If only I could paper the walls of your brain with pictures of me every night. And if only those pictures could shimmer with the hue of the Impossible, of the Unobtainable.

"But when I met you in the street, I would find no trace in your eyes of the dreams I had implored God to send you, so that they might take hold of you. You weren't even cool toward me: just politely affable and not quite there.

"And even now, when we are both confronted by this dark wall, we aren't together. Perhaps one day you'll regret it. But it will be too late, and the world around you will be bare . . ."

"You are a verdant aquarium, Naomi. The plants quiver. The goldfish cleave the heavy space like arrows. Like swallows. I love you, Naomi."

CHAPTER 23

Again there occur in Boris's papers notes which it is hard to attach to any particular part of his circuitous tale. He was reading the Upanishads, but apart from a few fleeting references to some of the titles, the only visible evidence of these dippings takes the form of a tiny quatrain, almost classical in mold and quite different from his usual mode of expression:

> For the sap of a poem
> And the rhythm of a plant
> Are not, Brahmachari,
> Two different things.

And for that matter, observes Boris, what is the "difference" between things? If it is a juice, its flavor seems too hostile to my palate. And I reject it. That is my last remaining luxury.

Also to be found among the papers is a brief profession of faith—or rather, a few lines relating to Boris's conception of prayer. I quote them exactly as they appear:

Life and its experiences—the proverbial dash of cold water; or rather of boiling water over a head that is endeavoring to stay cool—have not succeeded in curing me of my inherent faith in magic. With every fiber of my spirit and of my
body, I believe in the possibility, in the necessity, of acting
upon distant objects by a concentrating of the body's mind
and soul. That is the one faith I adhere to. I believe in the
efficacy of prayer, which transforms all known or assumed
facts, which clasps and loosens the folds of time and space. An
acquaintance—all too cursory, alas—with certain tantras and
a mania for the practice of gematria have something to do
with it. The host, the motley host, of prayers rises (or descends?) from prisons, camps, hospitals, sewers, and palaces.
The fruits of these prayers could not be displayed in a shop
window. Is it a question of modesty . . . ? An earnest voice
(one that has not won my heart) assures us that it is only lame
prayers that remain unanswered. Rump prayers, cripple
prayers, abortion prayers: it is to them my pity goes out, and
perhaps even my love.

Let us recall the vast spaces around the Nigoriloy cemetery.
When they shot my "brothers" there, that cemetery became
a cemetery twice over. The cemetery of a cemetery. To be
sure, the quotation marks are offensive here, as they are everywhere; but honesty forbids me to dispense with them.
Quotation marks: that anti-prayer . . . And are not quotation marks an international sign, a universal phenomenon?
Just imagine a universe without quotation marks, without
the possibility of resorting to quotation marks—what cruelty!

Another fragment:
Praised be the Lord! As regards filth, I am self-sufficient.
I have no need to import filth from that desert which goes by
the name of the outside world.

Self, antiself, aself.

God, antigod, agod.

I see myself as I am: a gentleman with graying hair (which isn't true; I am not turning gray) walking down the street between tall buildings. I see his thoughts. They stir, slowly, like reddish entrails. The candle flame is covered with a skin, with the skin of the flame. The skin covers the flesh and entrails of the flame. Oh, to cleave the surface, to penetrate the flesh of the flame . . . To what purpose? I reject the igneous world.

Must I enter a temple? If God exists, He ought only to love atheists. And for my own part, I am afraid of any form of love: God's first and foremost. Still, as an eminent director told me with such massive discernment, "The idea of God has been superseded by science."

A column of ocher dust goes by, staggering from the heat of this summer afternoon. I see its scattered thoughts. They are like dark roots. Like a head of hair, disheveled and scalped.

The sunbeams are torturing me. They are cutting and welting me like ropes fraying the prisoner's skin and his spirit.

My hatred, my real hatred, is not aimed exclusively at the sunbeams. It goes out to the grains of dust as well. And the two hates bite and devour one another like a pair of proud waterfalls set face to face and unleashed at full tilt. That's it: at full tilt.

And now it starts up again. All over again:

The walls of the flame. The interior of the flame. The skin of the flame. The flesh of the flame. The flesh of the injured flame. "Inside a candle flame there lived an old man . . ."

Pray extinguish it (with Thy gaze), pray extinguish,

O Lord, this stupefying flower—the flaming flower, the impatient flower of my heart!

> The blood
> Boiling
> In the snow
> And giving
> The mud
> A ruddy glow
> In turning to mud
> This blood

Is no trite
Symbol of love
It is
The blood of the Jews
Shot
At the sixteenth kilometer
Of the road
> running
To Zbarazh from Michnia
AAAA—
"Of the Jews," one says
But see here
What were they, what were they like?!!!
> They were:
> A lath
> Of a man whose
> Adam's apple
> Turned in the moment of truth
Turnsole sunward
As the globe turns
Round his fear
Or perhaps round

His reflection
Or perhaps round
Nothing
    And the next was
    Like a vulture
    He loved women
    And the Cabala
    The glistening of his silvery skin . . .
    His eyes: two pink mice
And the third
Whose body had the
Gift of song
Of frail songs of the snuffed-out flame
She was like
The blood-smeared standard
Of love . . .
    But enough of these old embroiderings
    Trampled in the mud
    And hurrah for the Savior,
    For the Eternal Savior:
            Mud

Another brief note, which I append to this chaotic chapter with a reticence even more pronounced than the reproaches I would have leveled against myself had I left it out. Such childish excursions into "ontology," it seems to me, must have contributed greatly to the final clouding of Boris's brain. Perhaps it will help the reader to a fuller understanding of Boris than I have attained to?

a) In every gaping moment (they are like swarming insects, our moments: they buzz), in every moment we reinvent (unless—though by whom?—it is reinvented for us) the eternal functioning of Being and Non-Being. You're lying: the functioning of Non-Being is closed to us, or else it doesn't exist. But the functioning of Being . . . it is iridescent with painful and absurd nuances: the subfunctioning of Evolution and of "De-Evolution," the superfunctioning of "Re-Evolution" or of Being-Through-Collapsing. At night, these labels are pasted up in an illumined factory. A sickly darkness pulls its weight.

b) A foul-smelling dough in a kneading machine—that is Being, the whole of Being. How does it think of itself, how does it strike itself? As being "Me," as being "Us," or as being "You People" and a whole series of "concepts" which do not fit into the grammatical categories of any language? It is kneaded by "Nameless Hands," this dough. Small lumps detach themselves: numerous—and for me alone, innumerable—"me"s. They feel pain, hunger, ambition, love; one turd strives to be bigger than another turd, if only by a fraction of an inch . . . until they drop back into the "kneading machine" and are reintegrated with the maternal dough, with the brownish "Primeval Dough."

or again:

c) An interminable roadway (?) thick with mud. It is the mud alone that "exists," the roadway being (it's my impression) merely an "impression," a decorative detail indispensable to the clarity of my image.

A black limousine (?) comes bowling along. At the touch of its wheels, small lumps are splashed up from the "Matrical Mud." And there, before they drop back and are reintegrated, is the whole of "Existence," is our life with its duration, its emotions, its hates, its loves, its eternities . . . and its entire repertoire.

But is it possible (even if it is certain) that in the space of that moment, between departing from the Matrical Mud and returning to it, I have been able to experience the Walled-up Town, and the longing for that town, and the loves which—coming before and after—belong to it?

The catalogue of voids

. . . For there is the diseased, sickly-looking, rickety, feverish, and gasping void, and the void that is repose. The creaking void. The void that yields despair and the void that is the last quietus. The red postsuicidal void and the circumscribed void. The vibrant void and the still, soundless void. The region of pain and the ultimate cure . . . Out of all these brotherly voids there emerges a hollow monument.

This top-hatted gent was a collector of voids. But, running short of money, he began to sell them. Reluctantly, if the truth be told.

A triangle groaning: "Oh, let me find it, let me find it; I can sense its existence, its presence in some far-off world or even somewhere close at hand . . . this third . . . dimension. The restful haven from which my soul was expelled before the beginning of time. Lord, O Lord, where shall I find it? It is only within its pale that . . ."

(Man in pursuit of the fourth dimension, feeling it in his bones but unable to capture it.)

But how do these virginal extra dimensions, how do these unoccupied dimensions, so slippery and elusive, spend their free time? Where are the green pastures of these white sheep?

Shall I ever find my way to the dormitory occupied by these boarding-school girls, whose maidenhood is an endless temptation to me? Shall I ever succeed in putting them in the family way, these blonde, brunette, and redheaded dimensions, these dimensions so anemic and innumerable?

I should not forgive myself were I to end this chapter, even though it in no way advances the main story, without adding the description, the record of a dream. This note is dated. It belongs, without any doubt whatever, to Boris's last writings. It is not because of any intrinsic value that I am adding it to this collection. In my labors as an editor trying to impose a certain shape—and what a shape!—on this jumble, I have quickly had to abandon any ideas of fishing for authentic "values." Rather, I am acting from a sort of pity, from a sort of weakness, in not casting this fragment into outer darkness. Has not Boris himself conferred on this scene —unexceptional enough, in all conscience—the title of "my crucial dream"?

I was in a large synagogue which, in the second half of the dream, became imperceptibly the True Temple. Ancient bronze candelabra. A good deal of gold. Even more brass. Plenty of light and shade. They were engaged in stately and skillful games with one another. Their blood commingled. True magnificence and true holiness. To begin with, I was overjoyed to see devout, bearded figures wearing their ritual shawls.

Which synagogue WAS this? How could I fail to know such a place? Was it the one in Fountain Street? Why no, it was more spacious and more awe-inspiring . . . Hard as I tried, I could not place this palace, which to my wondering eyes seemed like a cross between the Temple of Solomon and the hospital in our town, that Byzantine hospital flanked by the old cemetery, as embellished by the imaginings of a six-year-old.

After making my way through the twists and turns of the corridors and passageways, I came out onto a kind of terrace. In the middle there rose a cupola, an opulent cupola built of pink sandstone. (Perhaps it was this cupola that had put me in mind of the hospital?) A splendid view from the terrace. The light was resonant. It sighed. A dated, a medieval landscape: battlements, turrets, bridges. One felt like dissolving, melting away, existing only insofar as was strictly necessary for the purpose of experiencing this scene. Another moment, and a Saracen merchant would appear, his camels and mules laden with precious burdens. Or a group of lepers would come into view, clad in flowing yellow robes and sounding their rattles.

The time was obvious to me: a summer afternoon, still gilded by the declining sun.

I came down from the terrace and found myself in a kind of hallway, where a score or so members of the Temple Guard were striding about in small groups, dressed in "Biblical" robes (as seen through the eyes of the seventeenth century). Their attire was reminiscent of that of the heroes of *Athalie* . . . I made for one of the doors, which (seen from inside) was on my right, but it seemed to be locked. Then for another: a pair of guards barred my way, clashing their swords together. "You shall not leave!" This recurred several times, and I felt a gnawing disquiet. Could all this blissfulness be a trap? Back in the hall, at least a dozen guards (this time, despite their ancient garb, they made me think of Sergeants at a barrack-room inspection) stood around me in a ring. They were gossiping with one another, taking no notice of me. I learned (though from whom?) that I was under sentence of death, a penalty that I associated with asphyxiation. I was afraid and had difficulty in pulling myself together. In the hands of each of the guards I noticed a small red brick. A thought flashed through my mind: So that's it! Stoning. I'm to be stoned . . .

All at once a woman, reading my thoughts, said to me: "If you had rather it were done another way, here—take this knife and open your artery . . ."

I applied the little knife to the left side of my neck and was afraid. I would never be able to bring myself to drive the blade into my flesh.

Signs of hostility and repugnance from the guards. Nevertheless, one of them whispered in my ear: "You're racking your brains as to WHY you are to be killed, aren't you?" Then something like: "It isn't on ideological grounds"—though the word he used wasn't "ideological"—"it's because the old boys are having a row." I knew he was referring to the High Priests. "They both need cash. And when that happens, they'll concoct any high-sounding excuse . . ."

The atmosphere of no exit, the feeling of being stifled and walled up, was intensifying. I knew it was pointless, but fear impelled me to act. (Which is unlike me.) I began to edge my way toward the left-hand side of the hall and then, thrusting my way through the guards (who seemed contemptuous of me, as butchers are contemptuous of animals' carcasses), I made a dash for one of the doors. I was in the temple garden, racing toward a gate set in the wall. Somebody was running in front of me; he seemed to be escaping too. I felt a certain warmth for him, as for a companion to whom one is bound by fate. But as soon as he reached the gate (breach in the wall, blockhouse, convent judas), he pulled up sharp, stationed himself calmly in front of the gate, and swung around to face me: he too was a guard. I could see that now. But when I in turn came to the stout gate set in the wall, he opened it wide and stood aside to let me pass. He bowed to me. No perceptible irony in his gesture. I went out. And I found myself confronted by a second wall, much higher than the first and gray from top to bottom. No exit, in either direction. Just a long dusty road confined between a pair of towering walls. And that was the end.

I have derived much satisfaction from this dream, which to my mind, even in its trite symbolism, retains a certain robustness. I have called it "my crucial dream."

CHAPTER 24

That same night—or was it perhaps on another, identical night?—I lay beside Naomi and stared through the curtainless window at the broad expanse of wintry sky. It was years since I had given any thought to my uncle Zachariah—Zachariah the washout, who had long been in his grave. And all at once a peculiar thought came into my mind: it was he, Zachariah, whom God had strewn with the stars upon this splendorous glittering sky.

Uncle Zachariah had died before the war, before even the beginning of my tale, but the stuff he was made of tallied far better with the things we had seen and lived through than did that of any of us direct participants. The relatively colorless segment of time in which his death occurred struck me as nonsensical and unjust. Not that I would have wished my uncle Zachariah to come to any harm. I was glad he had been spared the physical privations, the spectacular terror. But at the same time a voice was whispering to me: Perhaps this epoch amounted to no more than a projection, to no more than a realization of the innermost nature of this dead-and-buried uncle of mine. It was like casting one's mind back, in the aftermath of a victorious revolution, to the revolutionary who had not lived long enough to witness the crowning of his dreams. Not (absurd hypothesis!) that Uncle Zachariah would have been on the side of the killers. But why had this silent craftsman in suffering been denied the privilege of seeing, of relishing, the martyrs' passivity? Hadn't he deserved to be of their number, so much more than those who today were leaving the world without the capacity to appreciate the flavor of their own deaths? It seemed to me that I was in process of piercing what had always intriguingly struck me as the enigma surrounding my uncle, the ultimate projection of a destiny that he had been unable to work out to the end.

In a family that, for generations past, had devoted itself to the accumulation of fortunes and of what are regarded as "honors," Uncle Zachariah had always appeared in the light of a straying lamb, if not of a black sheep. He was gray-haired, drooping, old before his time, and extremely silent. He never raised his voice. Indeed, he very seldom spoke—not from any thought of bolstering his prestige by the use of silence, but from an inherent aversion to communicating with the outside world. This boundless pool of silence within a single human being, this infinity of silence, would catch at one's throat.

According to family accounts, even his parents lavished less affection on him than on their other children. Once— Zachariah, who was the eldest, must have been eleven at the time—he was playing in an unused room with his two brothers (one of whom was my father). The winter evening dragged on and on. Suddenly the boys upset an oil lamp, and their clothes caught fire. The uproar brought my grandfather running to their aid; he wrapped furs around his two younger sons, to put out the flames. It was only some seconds later that he realized that Zachariah had received burns far more serious than his brothers', without uttering a sound.

The flames were extinguished. Uncle Zachariah recovered

from his burns within a week, and his brothers even more quickly—thanks to the furs.

But this attitude on the part of his own father was simply a foretaste of the attitude that life itself was to adopt toward him.

My father was a famous lawyer. His younger brother, who had chosen an academic career, was the author of published works that earned him a wide reputation on both sides of the Atlantic. Uncle Zachariah had failed to graduate from high school and at the age of thirty was still living in a tiny straggling town ringed by a few villages: the nucleus of the family's landholdings.

It was at about this time that he married a girl with almost too much money, thoroughly unattractive looks, and an extremely trying nature. The marriage took place chiefly because Uncle Zachariah couldn't summon the energy to stand up to the old professional matchmaker. Having not only his own belly to feed, but those of his large brood of children, the matchmaker could not be expected to brook celibacy in a man of thirty who was well off and came from a brilliant family. Uncle Zachariah must have said to himself: "What difference does it make in the long run whether it's she or someone else?"—assuming that he said anything whatever to himself.

All the same, the first spring and summer in the small town (where the bride had come to join Zachariah) had sorely tested even his angelic patience. His young wife demanded to be entertained, to be taken out, to be paraded so that the neighbors might feast their eyes on her dresses, which were made for her in the capital. She wished to be surrounded by an atmosphere of billing and cooing, she wished to be SPOKEN to. In the absence of every one of these attentions, she began to show her claws, to make noisy scenes, to indulge in tearful hysterics. She filled my grandparents' old house with new furniture and derived endless hours of entertainment from keeping it spick and span and moving it from one place to another. By the end of eight months, Uncle Zachariah had come to the conclusion that the estate of marriage could not be suited to him. He took a decision, probably the one and only decision he took at any time in his life, which was indecision itself.

Without a word to his wife, he had three horses harnessed to the large sleigh and set off for the town where his in-laws lived. Ahead of him lay a journey of several hundred versts. Zachariah wished to apprise his in-laws of his firm intention to seek a divorce. The only person to whom he confided the purpose of his mission was my father, who happened to be staying at the family seat just then. Winter held the countryside firmly in its grip. The elderly coachman was obliged to make frequent use of pick and shovel in order to clear away the snow. At sunset, the snow would fill the air with a spectrum of the most amazing colors. Innumerable silver mirrors dancing before innumerable suns. The silence would groan and sing like brass subjected to mighty hammer blows. The wolves would kneel before the hillocks of snow, and the dawn play symphonies of faraway worlds.

Sitting huddled in a heavy pelisse, Uncle Zachariah felt sorry for the wolves, for the snow, for the veiled sun, and for the glittering stars ("they must be cold up there"). He dozed, he dreamed of things that he never confided in anyone, either before or after this journey.

He gazed regretfully at the peasants' sleds, which were left far behind as his troika sped like lightning through the unsullied landscape. He closed his mind to all thought of the discussion in store for him with his wife's parents. Luckless pair! By marrying off their daughter to him, they had banked upon drawing closer to his forefathers, and—owing to their Learning (long since defunct) and to their legendary piety—had imagined they were securing better seats in the theater of future life. If only they had known what a painful burden these renowned ancestors, so well versed in the Scriptures, were to Zachariah!

A swallow—though was it really a swallow?—clove the sky at vertiginous speed and fell stone-dead . . .

"I'll have to explain to them," Zachariah would mutter, "I'll have to make it clear to them that . . ." His big gray eyes, shortsighted and weary, would gaze out at the world as though through a mist. "They're decent people. They'll realize that their daughter cannot possibly be happy with someone like me. Besides, there's the dowry. They are going to get all those millions back. Even as a divorcée, their daughter will be in a position to make a good match, to marry someone who is alive, really alive. Our natures are not suited to one another. The whole thing's my fault, but it simply cannot go on. They are bound to understand, they WILL understand . . ."

He felt a sharp pain in the pit of his stomach. He would have liked to stop and exchange with some peasants a few of those ritual words that mean nothing but which would have brought a touch of human warmth even to a silent recluse such as himself. This warmth was something he failed to find in even the most penetrating commentaries on the Holy Scriptures which his forefathers had left behind. It was as though there was a layer of cotton wool between him and the outside world: there was no way of telling what stage the journey had reached. Was he still in his troika?

"I must explain it to them, explain it ALL to them . . . What say we go back home?" The temptation was like a tiny worm. It had been present from the very beginning, but it was not until this moment that it had betrayed its presence by making a first, barely perceptible movement.

"I should be spared the talk with my in-laws, true enough, but not the endless and infuriating talks in store for me with my wife. Besides, how can I possibly tell Ivan the coachman to turn back after all the trouble he has gone to, clearing away the snow? It would be a poor reward for the way he has battled against Brother Winter . . . Anyway, we must stop at this inn. Ivan must rest for a while. I must buy him a drink. Another twenty leagues to go yet. There is still time to come to a decision. We'll see in the morning . . ."

At the end of a week, after visiting his in-laws, Zachariah went home to his wife. He kissed her awkwardly on the cheek; he even brought her a little ring with a big stone, and in a trice this present had sparked off a quarrel: the size of the stone, it seemed, was not in keeping with the requirements of fashion. Only a hardhearted fool like my uncle could possibly be oblivious to such an obvious fact . . . The woman's hands were like two great lumps of meat on a butcher's stall, red and podgy, with streaks of blue.

My father was a silent witness to the scene. He was itching to get Zachariah by himself for a moment.

"Well? What about the divorce?"

Zachariah's shortsighted eyes were searching for an excuse. My father wasn't going to give in.

"What about the divorce?" he repeated.

"Well, the truth is, dear brother, there's not going to be a divorce. I couldn't do it." Zachariah muttered these words in his old familiar way, as though he was making excuses for refusing to lift a weight that would be trifling to anyone else but was too heavy for him. "I couldn't do it. We got there at about midnight—Ivan the coachman and I. We were cold.

The old man welcomed me with a broad smile. He threw his arms around me and inquired after the young bride. Out came the drink. Before I had time to breathe a word, he was telling me that marriage was a difficult undertaking, that he was well aware of his daughter's abominable nature ('just like her mother'), but that she had a heart of gold ('just like her mother'). Could I contradict him? I couldn't get a word in edgeways. Well, anyway . . . I was there for two whole days, and I didn't say anything. It was all shows of affection, and drinking, and stories about the holy men of the past and the miracles they used to work. Poor devil, he was so proud to be talking about OUR family! And such brightness all the time: he'd lit every candle in the house in my honor. My eyes still hurt, even today. He kept saying that my visit was a great occasion for him. 'As though the Messiah had set foot in my home.' I don't care for light, as you know. 'Window' is a contradiction of 'house.' But one has to be fair, he was doing his best, poor man. How could I let him down? I had only one thought in mind: to get out of the house. I left without unsealing my lips. After all, life doesn't last forever."

Zachariah was destined to drag out that life which "didn't last forever" for another thirty long years. Within the walls of his silence there teemed shy half-deeds that hadn't the courage to grow into "happenings." His movements and his daily tasks were like the smoke from his everlasting cigarette —sketches that never rose to the status of definitive drawings. Perhaps it was this unlived life that gave a leaden weight to every gesture Zachariah made. And indeed he made so few! But did another life—the true one, the real one—genuinely exist somewhere, or was this yet another mischievous invention on the part of his wife, who was constantly abuzz with preposterous activity?

He had four children by this woman, two girls and two

boys, and the very least one can say of them is that they in no way inherited either their father's serenity or his attitude of resignation. The big house seemed small, it was so full of constant shouting. From time to time, Zachariah would escape and come to us for a week. Growing ever grayer and paler, he would sprawl on a wide divan and devote his time to silent smoking, and to reading, and to digesting thoughts which he never communicated to anybody.

One day, at the age of eight, I asked: "Tell me, Mama, how did Uncle Zachariah come to have so much death inside him?"

Uncle Zachariah loathed and feared dogs. He loved cats, with a shy love that seldom manifested itself. He had never allowed himself to be tempted to the point of getting into a car or going to the cinema. The conservatism and anachronistic nature of his habits in no way stemmed from any preconceived theory. They derived from something deeply rooted, something innate. Sometimes—very, very occasionally—he would allow himself to be lured to the theater; but it had to be clearly understood that the work in question was a play by one of our own classical authors, written either in the ordinary, everyday language of our people or else—failing that—in language that at least represented a bridge between our present and our past.

His health was being slowly undermined by a duodenal ulcer. The wan smile that very infrequently appeared on his lips had the beauty of a landscape run wild and doomed to destruction. Whenever I looked at Zachariah's head I would think of a shattered, lifeless gas lamp, its glass panels broken by stone-throwing children. Zachariah was like a black silk scarf throwing out somber, unwieldy sparks at lengthy intervals.

"How are you feeling, Zachariah?" my mother would ask,

when she happened to go near the wide divan which was reserved for his use in our home.

Which would bring forth the reply (almost invariably the
same one, accompanied by that sagacious smile, by that
smile which now, in the middle of this night in a snow-bound
railwayman's hut, was lighting up my long spell of sleepless-
ness): "Praise be to God, we don't live forever, my dear
Ruth. We must give thanks to the Everlasting for that. We
don't live forever."

CHAPTER 25

Through the carriage window, I gazed at the wasteland on the outskirts of a town we had just left. Once again, too many people were getting to know us by sight, too many men were showing an interest in Naomi's Oriental, consumptive's face. Already the caretaker was asking indiscreet and outwardly friendly questions about my family and my business activities.

At the inn where we sometimes went for our meals, in an all but empty dining room, a lingering customer was subjecting us to a weighty stare in which there was no longer even a trace of doubt. We were in the middle of our nonstop daily performance as a pair of lovers quite oblivious to the outside world. A huge cat sprang into Naomi's lap, and she stroked it lightly. We were just getting over a quarrel—not a particularly violent one, actually. Ferreting among my papers, Naomi had come across a note that had apparently hurt her deeply before sparking off her anger: "The first angels to turn their backs on heaven did so from a desire to be alone— a pleasure and an ecstasy from which angels are still rigidly excluded."[1] It was notes such as this, trivial remarks often made unthinkingly in the course of conversation, that opened

[1] Chekhov.

the floodgates of her anger—more surely than any act of open betrayal. The erosion of love . . . Had I begun to live it? To die it?

If only—oh, if only!—I had known what to say; but in all the wide ocean of language, it was beyond my powers to find the very word, the only word, that might have soothed Naomi. Was the love I bore her deceitful, then, or contemptible? It went out to the history, the great history, of our race —a history that we were living through and that was possibly about to be extinguished before our eyes, and together with us. It went out to a past whose contours were present in Naomi's features and in the blackness of her mop of hair.

I loved Naomi's forefathers, who were also mine and who, by dint of strange and inhumanly systematized meditations, had succeeded in approaching what was godlike in the human condition as no one else had ever done—or so, at least, I thought. I loved the landscape of our past, a commingling of the Biblical desert and of the steppes through which the Scythians had roamed. Where else would I have found this cocktail of the Oriental and the Slav, this union of two races, each of which had fashioned its own unique yearnings, vaster than death and just as deep?

Yes, but Naomi seemed to shut her eyes deliberately to these regions of my love. She would have preferred me to be constructive, at least insofar as our everyday relationship was concerned. Yet I suspected that she would not have loved me had this been so. At first, our reconciliations were easy and gentle, like fresh betrothals, like backward journeyings to the earliest days of our relationship, before we had set up house together. This conjugal life, which had been imposed on us by the times in which we were living, hung limply about us like adult clothes on a child . . . But as time went by, not even our reconciliations succeeded in compensating for the violence of the scenes that my partner inflicted on me. ("I'm going to denounce us both . . . May your body be smashed to bits like my soul. May it be as eaten up with pain . . .")

I would endeavor to justify her, I would invoke, for my own guidance, the extenuating circumstances: I was the first man in her life; there was every danger of her being the last woman in mine. Both were good reasons for excusing her outbursts and curbing my own . . . Would it be so hard to summon afresh a strong desire, to re-create a passionate feeling? Somewhere in the depths of my being I thought I could detect a layer of barrenness, of aridity, the existence of which would have explained, if not justified, Naomi's explosive anger.

Did she not deserve patience, infinite patience? I was cruelly devoid, however, of any vocation as a father. The only real lacerations, the only real wars between two human beings are those inflicted and waged, not by their personal interests or even by their skins, but by their dreams. The blood and pus of dreams are a perfidious poison.

A transparent dewdrop that would begin to boil and shriek . . . During the spasms that she herself provoked, Naomi would threaten to denounce us both. She had only to imagine that my eyes had strayed momentarily in the direction of some woman in the street, and she would start railing at me —in the thick of the crowd!—in one of our mother tongues, in precisely that tongue which could so easily prove our undoing . . .

But this time, sitting in the restaurant, we had been quarreling only mildly. We were all smiles, both of us; the artificial gaiety of our gestures, the artificial brightness of our faces were for the benefit of our silent neighbor, who was gobbling his eggs without any apparent thought for us; acting out this comedy scene together was reuniting us more joyfully than hour after hour of "thrashing things out."

All of a sudden he scraped back his chair. He was powerfully built. His face was gleaming. Glancing to one side, and not addressing us, he slowly and distinctly articulated just one sentence: "The fools always give themselves away!"

My failure to react to this extraordinary soliloquy betrayed me more surely than any hysterical outburst. Would not a man who had no fatal secret to harbor, a NORMAL man, have responded with at least a questioning glance?

Naomi's rather swarthy complexion turned deadly pale. Thirty seconds later, in a voice that was meant to sound firm, I called for the bill and we left the restaurant with a falsely assured step. But the street afforded even less shelter than usual. The daylight was harsh and naked. It infected us with its nakedness. We set off on our travels again that very day, and suddenly, as the train progressed through the province, my eye fell on a group of workers who, under the supervision of a few sentries, were shifting heavy sections of rail. These workers wore on their backs the hexagonal sign of our king, who was shepherd and poet in the sight of God. Their faces were haggard, and they belonged to the past. Imperceptibly, I drew Naomi's attention to these barely real figures.

She smiled and then, as though confiding some lover's secret, she whispered in my ear: "You see, we aren't yet the last . . ."

Already the train was gathering speed again, and before our hungering eyes the workers merged with the trees, which in turn disappeared into the dusk.

CHAPTER 26

The mountain resort, till recently so elegant and generally regarded as the state's winter capital, greeted us that October with emptiness and calm. Both quickly proved spurious. I knew the place well, having gone there frequently before the war, when my visits had been enlivened by a few easy climbs, spells of bathing in the icy waters of the lakes, and a series of short, sharp amorous adventures. In the past, poets and artists and prominent politicians had flocked to O. and had created, with considerable assistance from the scenery, a highly individual atmosphere, the like of which I have encountered nowhere else on earth.

Nestling among the mountains, intersected by foaming silver torrents, and consisting in the main of a host of wooden chalets dotted about among the pines and built in a style that derived its name from the district, O. was populated by a race of mountain folk who, for predominantly commercial reasons, clung rigidly to their sartorial and other traditions.

A fad that had survived for several generations required all visitors, even the most illustrious, to display open-mouthed admiration for the allegedly eagle-like posturings of the local inhabitants.

Accustomed to this admiration, which was frequently supplemented by clumsy imitation, the mountain folk lorded it over those on whom their livelihood depended. The cheeky coachdrivers would keep their passengers waiting for hours whenever they fancied a drink in one of the taverns where tourists were strictly prohibited from setting foot. In their uncouth dialect, the locals would revile as whores the cabinet ministers' wives who hired their carriages for the purpose of paying the traditional visit to the valley or to the famous mountain lake.

It was the poets from the plain who saved the legendary tales of highwaymen from complete oblivion, and now conjured them out of thin air—thus embellishing the somewhat drab history of these parts. It wasn't long before the mythmakers began to believe in the authenticity of their own fictions, and after that there was no end to the arrogance of those whose humble ancestors were thus aggrandized. The increasing number of tourists soon brought a high level of comfort to these peasants who, for generation after generation, had known nothing but extreme poverty. Pampered, admired, invited to wild drinking bouts by nobles with whom they condescended to associate, exhibiting an air of quite unfeigned superiority, the mountain folk of O. became infected with a feeling that had nothing whatever to do with gratitude: the feeling that they were a race apart, totally unconnected with the rest of the country.

The invader had turned this excessive sense of autonomy to account, employing it to weaken the spontaneous solidarity of the conquered nation. He needed a sheltered spot, a handsome resort endowed with villas and luxury hotels to which he could send wounded and convalescent and meritorious troops. The men of the mountains escaped the deportations and were exempted from forced labor. Once again, but this time on an entirely official basis, they were elevated to the rank of a breed apart, a breed altogether nobler than their compatriots down in the plains. Their one duty lay in creating an environment, in contributing to an atmosphere conducive to getting the sick on their feet again and to softening the deaths of the dying. In O. and the surrounding countryside, the price of drinks was lowered, with the aim of reviving the gaiety of old and of creating a thoroughly artificial oasis of freedom amid the surrounding desert of slavery. Princely titles were conferred on the handful of genuinely ancient local families. Age-old peasant cautiousness whispered in the ears of their offspring that such titles and splendors couldn't be anything but ephemeral. To silence these whisperings, some organized active resistance to the enemy, others toadied to his representatives: both groups took to drinking more and more while waiting to see how things turned out.

It was in this period that a few surviving members of our race came seeking refuge in O. What drew them to the place? Was it the real, if chancy, freedom of existence there, or the absence of large-scale roundups by the police, or was it a longing for nature, for the fresh mountain air of which they had been deprived throughout their sojourn in the walled-up towns which had now vanished? Did they reason that, in their neighbors' ears, the murmur of the mountain streams would muffle their dangerously, their fatally foreign pronunciation of the language that they were compelled to use from now on?

The autumn evening on which we arrived in O. was a cold one. The bracing air in our lungs and the scenery, whose grandeur we could sense even though it was now hidden from view, added to the weariness of our bodies. The lounge of the hotel where we had put up was decorated with ancient coats of arms. The log fire teased the imagination and the

skin. The soft, springy carpets rendered movements soundless. Dinner was served on Dresden china. Eight persons,
in all, were seated around an old, massive carved-wood table. The owner of the villa, who impressed one as being more
like "the lady of the manor" than a mere landlady, endeav-
ored to steer the conversation around to noncommittal subjects: the beauty of the mountains in the off season, the local
traditions, and even the WEATHER—what it had been like
at the same time last year, and what it would be like tomorrow. Enveloping us strangers: a layer of mistrust, thin but
undeniable. The guardedness of the conversation sustained
the awkward feeling that had taken hold of me the moment
we had set foot inside this lovely house. But if there WAS an
awkwardness, I was certainly not the only one to be infected
by it. The invisible threads of a complicity, whose nature remained concealed from us, seemed to connect our hostess
and these customers of hers, with their relaxed attitudes and
their display of well-being. But were not this very relaxation
and this very well-being exhibited rather ostentatiously?

A gentleman in a well-cut country suit was in the middle
of describing the jaunt that he had made to a famous waterfall that very morning. He sought to give the impression of
being oblivious of Naomi and me, but his story, without question, was entirely for our benefit: You see, you two strangers,
you two intruders, I go for walks, I am sufficiently relaxed
to enthuse over the charm of these mountains and these torrential springs. I am not even addressing you, who may have
the keys to my destiny tucked away in your suitcases. Which
ought to make it clear to you that you have no key and that
my destiny eludes you; it is equal to yours, in no way inferior.
I have nothing to worry about. I'm not the man you might
take me for. Though, as to that, why should you take me for
the man I'm not . . . even if I am he? And if I did have

something to hide, I'd hide it well enough. All the same . . . what a rotten idea of yours, putting up at this hotel and not at another!

The gentleman was still plugging away at his casual yarn (describing the tracks of a wild boar, which he had allegedly discerned on one of the steep paths) when I saw a kind of cloud, ever so small and fleeting, darken the gaze of our amiable hostess. And always this morbid need to interpret the gestures of the people about one . . . It was as though she was saying to her guest: "Watch out, my friend, your performance is becoming a little glib. You are attracting attention. Those whose anxieties are less deadly than yours have no need to hide them, and they don't make fatuous speeches about the beauty of nature. For all my experience as a landlady, I've no idea who these two characters might be. But it would be wiser to talk about the black market and the latest stock-exchange prices, rather than the tracks of wild boars. The attributes of your race may well have become those of mine, but the attributes of my race have certainly not become yours. Leave the wild boars alone. I have taken several hundred thousand rubles from you for hiding you here—or rather, for allowing you to take a holiday which, God willing, will last as long as the war does. I shall abide honestly by the terms of our contract. But if you allow yourself to be carried away by your role, if you will insist on overdoing things, if you stray beyond the reach of my protection . . . then I can no longer answer for anything."

Addressing me aloud, she said: "Do have another piece of chicken. Would you prefer a wing or a leg?"

For a fraction of a second, our eyes met and the hostess understood: we were not the hunters but the hunted.

When the samovar was brought in, the old lady gave a smile in which relief was mingled with compassion: "I forgot

to tell you, Mr. Goletz—the room I am letting to you tonight
is booked from tomorrow on. I'm terribly sorry . . . You
will have to look for something else. It shouldn't be difficult, out of season like this . . ."

A look of relief flickered over the face of our neighbor at
table, and this time it was genuine.

God bless him and may he live, I thought, closing my
weary eyes.

The little villa at which we called next day was reserved
for convalescing officers.

"The only person who could authorize you to take a
room here is the commander of the local garrison . . . Actually, he himself is one of our guests. Would you like me to
tell him you are here? He seems harmless enough."

The landlady thus addressing me was in her forties. She
had a kindly smile and was surveying us with the cordiality
appropriate to persons of good soil, well rooted in their exist-
ences. A wave of almost carnal fellow feeling passed between
the plump old dear and my eternal thinness. Something
from which Naomi, thin as she herself was, was to remain
excluded.

"Please go in and see the Major, Mr. Goletz . . . Your
wi--, or rather—I'm so sorry—the young lady can wait here in
the hall. Here is a magazine for her to read."

He didn't look so very terrible, this officer to whom I was
compelled to apply for lodgings. His eyes, of a worn and
somewhat washed-out blue, were gazing at me with rather
weary benevolence. There was something familiar about his
sad smile. It was with just such a smile that the manager of
our country estates had been in the habit of informing my

father that there was a drop in the annual revenue because the tenant farmers wouldn't pay their rents, "and we aren't going to take them to court just for that, are we, my lord Baron . . . ?"

The Major was grizzled, extremely grizzled. There was nothing aggressive about his elderliness. To be sure, this man was bound to spend a good deal of his time silently justifying, to his brother officers, the prolongation of his tour of duty in these parts. The true origins of his life were submerged by the heaving, turbid waters of history. But he retained the memory of these origins, and it was to this memory he must have clung in his moments of solitude.

But wasn't everything that I was secretly telling myself about this enemy officer just so much unwarrantable nonsense? Our destruction—both my own and Naomi's—might very well be lurking somewhere among the wrinkles on his broad, tanned forehead, as a bug lurks between two brushstrokes on a mural.

Between this officer and me, the petitioner, arose a whole cascade of avowed and unavowed relations. In the role that I was adopting I certainly wasn't his enemy, but I was very much his inferior, a scion of the vanquished race, a fragment of the conquered landscape, less than an object. But if, beneath my garb, his eyes succeeded in detecting my true skin, or what had taken its place for the past twenty-two years, then I would become a negative entity, a prize corpse, a gap, a chasm, the very existence of which, at the foot of the rock constituted by the Major, would be viewed as an unthinkable affront to the Established Order. Once the cards were on the table, relations between us could only be those of life and death . . . But suppose he too, for other reasons, bore a chasm within him, suppose his aging and yellowing

skin surrounded nothing but empty space, an emptiness
skillfully camouflaged in the presence of his subordinates and
his superiors . . . ?

"Pray take a seat, Mr. Goletz," the Major said courteously, scanning my features. "I was intending to ask you how
I could be of service to you, but that will now be my second
question. Let me assure you straight away that if what you
seek is within my modest competence, I shall do all I can to
help you. But before we come to that, permit me to ask
you another question: What were you thinking about as you
walked into my office just now? You needn't be afraid. I have
a warm regard for youth. My curiosity is entirely disinterested, which makes it all the sharper. Not that I wish to be indiscreet. If your thoughts consisted of anything to which you
cannot own—or not, at least, in present circumstances—I
shall not press you. If that should be the case, don't say anything. And, above all, don't INVENT anything—either to suit
me, or to suit the time and place. That is all I ask of you . . ."

"Well now, Major, I was thinking about the fraternity of
chasms, about what would be the result of a contradictory
gathering, of a party, of a syndicate of chasms. I was reciting
a short stanza to myself:

> "O chasm my friend
> You may contend for me
> With a stone clock
> In which I am imprisoned . . ."

At once I cursed my rebellious tongue and cursed myself.
It wasn't bravado, it was suicide to allow myself to be carried away, to go rummaging in the vocabulary of surrealism,
in the presence of this little officer who in civilian life might

easily be a village schoolmaster. Yuri Goletz would never have indulged in such wild talk. To abandon my loyalty to Yuri Goletz was to abandon the very hope of survival. Naomi was waiting for me. Once again, I had only one desire: to get out of that room. By what crazy reckoning could I expect any spark to fly from the collision between this officer and the image—though was it really an image?—that I had just cast in his face?

"The fraternity of chasms! What a conception, my dear sir! Or rather, what a sound . . . ! As for what it all means, I am inclined not to ponder the problem too deeply at the moment; I am even inclined to admit (forgive my offhandedness) that it is devoid of meaning, at least at present, in this year 194. . . . However, should this war come to an end one day, I should be more than glad to reopen this little chapter. Hostility of chasms. Fraternity of chasms. Fraternal hostility and hostile fraternity . . ."

Suddenly he snatched a small notebook from his pocket . . . A most unpleasant feeling took hold of me. The Major jotted down the little phrase: "Fraternity of chasms." His action was distinctly reminiscent of police procedure. Interrogation was bound to begin in a similar manner: the noting down of the words uttered by the accused at the time when he is least on his guard . . .

The officer handed me his notebook, wishing to make quite sure that the three words which he had recorded did indeed tally with my ineptitude. His handwriting was calm, controlled, and serene, but this serenity seemed to have been achieved at great cost, at the cost of renunciations the nature of which it was impossible for me to determine.

A wave of serenity flooded the room. I glanced out of the window. The mountain ranges rose immutable as TIME in certain invalids. The peacefulness that was descending on us extinguished all fears. I might have been back in the cradle. I didn't disclose any of my deadlier secrets to the Major—had I opened the door no more than an inch or two?—but our two-hour conversation was "fraternal" enough.

We were allotted an extremely comfortable room between two suites, the first occupied by a General in the enemy army, the second by the local Chief of Political Police.

Almost every evening, after several drinks in the hotel lounge, I would accompany my neighbors on the piano while they sang love songs, lullabies, and military marching ditties. Some of these songs expressed a sorrowful tenderness and pity for creation, a resignation capable of arousing limitless love. Others voiced happiness at the final victory over my race. This was likened, now to a plague, now to vermin. As though by chance, the Major never joined in these fireside concerts. Whenever she heard me accompanying the General and the Chief of Police on the piano, Naomi would turn imperceptibly pale, and I had the indefinable feeling that our relationship was undergoing a change, the nature of which was hidden from me and perhaps always would be.

The General and the Chief of Police both had fine deep voices, and they displayed a friendliness toward me that was even attended by touching little tokens of consideration. When the weather turned cold, the General brought me a fur-lined jacket and refused to take anything for it: "Good heavens, Yuri my boy, our shops are crammed to capacity. This jacket was issued to me free, and you are dressed as though winter never came to these mountains . . ."

The Chief of Police made me a present of a slim volume of esoteric poems, which he had inscribed in immensely flattering, if not the most tactful, terms: "To the most amiable and charming of Slavs . . ."

Long mountain walks, autumn leaves, occasional random dippings into literature, hours of loving one another (loving one another sadly, to tell the truth); a snatched flirtation with a consumptive Resistance fighter who was seeking health in the mountains, well knowing that, once cured and back in her plains, she would return to the battle that could only lead to death . . . all this composed the setting of my last days of freedom. It was as though the hatred in my heart had burned out, and the wish to survive had to some extent stopped fulfilling its role as guide and pilot. The notes I made at the time were subsequently lost, and it is hard for me to re-create the color of those days. Sometimes it would seem to me that I was surrendering too fully to the part I was playing, and that as a result of my rubbing shoulders with the enemy a genuine solidarity was springing up between me and the companions of my musical evenings. Fog and apathy. Was Boris any closer to me than Yuri? Was he any more real? My two halves seemed to be melting away into the giant landscape that surrounded my days.

Can it be that what we regard as "authenticity," as "tangible truth," is even more false than falsehood and fiction itself? This hypothesis may be absolutely right, for "truth" and "reality" are invested with an arrogant and outrageous pretentiousness that is even less justifiable than the most reckless of lies and the least consistent of fictions. It was all very well Boris's presuming on his "legitimacy" vis-à-vis Yuri: the latter was not without weighty arguments of his own. Their quarrel, if quarrel there was, went on so long ago that it no longer even succeeded in "harrowing" my inner self. Though (and this was the main question) was there anything whatever to harrow?

Sometimes I would derive a strange pleasure from reviling

my race and my family; from applauding the destruction of all the people I had loved.

The Law promulgated by God forbids members of my religion to touch dead bodies. Should I have conformed with that other Law which enjoins us from living in the company of murderers and making friends of them?

The ethnologists know that any contact with the Unclean, or even a single glance in its direction, is sufficient to cause defilement. It is simply a matter of determining what is clean and what isn't. That is the whole game, but what is he or she to do who no longer gets any fun out of it?

Had he existed, Yuri Goletz could only have been flattered by the friendship shown him by these holidaying murderers. To have rubbed shoulders with superior beings like this would have crowned his highest ambitions. But ought I to deride poor Goletz, who was doing his best to ensure that I should continue to drag out my empty days? My boundless tenderness, my profound fellow feeling, was always going out to things that didn't exist. Slowly but surely Yuri Goletz, the Nonexistent, was conquering the cells of my brain, the receptacles of my soul. He longed for his masters' victory, he would have given his life's blood to procure it; their affability was filling him with happy pride. Was I capable, at the time, of distinguishing between that pride and the one that stemmed from the feeling that I was pulling a fast one on the enemy?

It was about that time that the Major offered me a job as superintendent of a convalescent home for enemy police. Under such a camouflage, it was unlikely that anyone would ever entertain suspicions as to our true identity. The problem of survival was receding into the background.

Thus, clad in the conqueror's uniform, receiving army rations, and secure from all roundups, I was going to slip arsenic into the food of likable lads whose recovery would be left in my hands. I was going to live with Naomi among these mountains and pay back the locals in their own coin for the part they were playing, side by side with the invader, in tracking down our people. I was going to swell the black market with food intended for enemy consumption. And—who could say?—by expending a good deal of skill and money and securing contacts in the right places, we might manage to slip into a neutral country, where I'd relate a few of the things that had been done to our people. Perhaps hate, that vivifying ingredient, after being lulled by contact with the enemy would reawaken in the presence of those notorious neutrals, the indifferent? But, first and foremost, Naomi and I wouldn't have to worry any more about finding a roof for our heads. At last there was to be a break in our interminable and superhuman travels. Naturally I accepted the offer.

"Thank you very much, Major, I shall be back in a fortnight. I have to go east again, to fetch somebody—an invalid—whom I'd like to have with me. For the climate here in the mountains is, as I'm sure you will agree, incomparable."

CHAPTER 27

All his conversations with the Major were like that. Boris
didn't lie: he told half-truths. There really was someone in
the eastern sector of the country whom he would have liked
to have with him. Someone whose life meant as much to
him as Naomi's. What Boris had NOT told the Major was
that this "someone," if indeed he was still alive, was a prisoner in one of the last walled-up towns whose existence the
invader still countenanced (though for how long?) in this
nation which he had turned into the graveyard of our race.

There was nobody who could fill the role of witness, to
which Leo L. had once alluded, as could the man whom Boris
was preparing to smuggle to his mountain retreat.

Europe was pouring away like silence. Quick action was
called for, the quickest.

> On the tightropes of thought
> (Straining upwards, leading nowhere)
> You clamber like a spider.
> Mate then, toads and chasms.
> > The impossible you'll breed will
> > Be as smooth as smooth can be.

"Be on your way, then, and come back soon," the Major said to Boris. "Though I don't believe in returnings. May the landscape that my countrymen have wrought in your nation not be too cruel to you, and should an arrow hit you may its poison be strong enough to kill you outright."

His laughter grew forced. Was it ambivalent, that cracked laugh?

"Come along, young man, show some reaction! No one has any right to be as dead as that! I'm very fond of you—and between you and me, you ought at least to leave your fiancée with us. Traveling isn't easy. The trains are so crowded, and then there are roundups. The young lady could wait for you here, with us . . . You mustn't forget your fraternity of chasms . . . How are you to know that interpreting symbols isn't my greatest passion? Don't make fun of me, when you are my age you may find yourself in the same boat. Not that I would wish that upon you . . ."

Imperceptibly, Naomi pressed closer to Boris. The key words had been uttered: roundup and poison. Did the Major sense the truth? Was there a suspicion at work in his mind?

And already Boris was wondering whether it would be safe to return. One thing was certain: they must leave, and leave at once.

And so they returned to their travels, as though donning a last piece of clothing. Large holes were appearing in it, great gaping holes.

PART THREE

The Tool and
The Thwarting of Comparisons

CHAPTER 28

"The universe viewed as a nurse tending our passions. So as to fan them? Or so as to douse them all forever? The nurse turning into a whore . . .

"The 'other moment' has lived up to one's past dreams, to one's cruelest dreams."

Were one to make an inventory of the impulses that pass through one's body, one would find merely the fear of blows and of nakedness. (But the time of blows and nakedness has come already and is stretching endlessly on and on.) Then there is curiosity—ready, in its turn, to catalogue everything. But what if only a single category were to figure in that catalogue: that of physical pain or that of anticipation?

Boris's arrest corresponded almost too closely to the way he had often pictured it in the course of his long peregrinations. A November night, dense and cold, the few dim lights of a forlorn railway station barely scratching its surface. A routine prowl by the police. Your papers . . . ? A "kindly-come-with-us." Final glimpse of Naomi asleep with her head on a suitcase in a corner of the waiting room, full of smoke and spittle and rubbish and scruffy, sleepy men and women. Crunch of boots on the thin layer of ice coating the mud.

Mixture of drizzle and frost, the drizzle more or less theatrical. Raindrops pattering on the grimy windows of an overheated room. Harmless questions concerning the domicile, place of work, origins, and attachments of Yuri Goletz, whose overelegant valise has caught the greedy eye of the officer on duty. Two plain-clothes men with blurry eyes, wherein there lurks the stock derisive glint. The first contemptuous familiarity and the first blow: "What do you mean by keeping your hat on in the presence of the Leader's portrait!"

And then, the all too tame reaction, which was really non-reaction, to this breach-opening blow. The factitious piece of décor bearing the inscription "Yuri Goletz," that high paper wall, which was meant to hide the turncoat from the crumbled world, crumbles in its turn. The duty officer's eyes suddenly lit by a mocking flame, thrust at this wall like a pneumatic drill:

"And what if your name WASN'T Yuri Goletz . . . ? That would be a laugh, wouldn't it? But first things first: just take your trousers down for a moment, my much-traveled friend. Come on, let's have a look . . ."

Boris puts his hand into the small inside pocket where the capsule is hidden. If only—oh, if only he had time to swallow it, he would be transported out of the reach of all these cops and of this unbearably oppressive moment. But Boris's hands are slowness itself. They barely exist, these hands. And suddenly two men are leaping forward and clutching him by the shoulder. The slightly asymmetrical face of the duty officer lights up again. From a long way off, Boris makes out half a dozen lumpish, purply hands, like slaughtered turkeys after plucking. These hands are busying themselves about his body.

"Poison! He was trying to swallow it. Typical! His kind always go around with whole dispensaries on them. But this one didn't get away with it. We were too quick for him, weren't we? And now we'll find out where he got his forged papers from. Just look at him . . . He's as white as a sheet."

Boris stares down at his hands: they are not shaking, for they are lifeless. If only it could be over and done with . . . His mind revolves about these words without managing to get to the pith of them.

Now he is handcuffed. The phial of poison lounges on the desk, flaunting itself like a desired body lost forever. The ripped trouser-fly reveals the bluish penis. On it, the sign of the Covenant is inscribed in indelible lettering, all too easy for these bustling men to read. The tool and the art of comparison. Though to what is it possible to compare this matchless moment, in which the entire universe converges and recedes and rears till it becomes a ring, a steel ring: cold and painful, this steel ring encircling Boris's tool.

The blows fall, monotonously, and Boris's swollen face embarks on a new life, turning into a mountain, turning into a precipice. There is no longer any such thing as an Outside. Boris's head is sensed by him as a hollowness. A wind is blowing from that land which was there before, before the past began.

Boris's body sags about his faded consciousness.

CHAPTER 29

First thought, coming from far, far away and slowly crystal-
lizing round a dull ache: They haven't shot me.

It is a hostile thought. It steals closer and closer, like a tire-
some and thoroughly mischievous insect. Naked time flows
past; like a relentless clock, physical pain—growing ever
more precise—invades the cramped confines where Boris's
wavering consciousness lolls.

He is lying on concrete, and his first sensation is an ambiguous one: it's good, this coldness emanating from the
concrete. It eases the pain. It's bad: those parts of the body
that are not battered are begging for a little warmth. Boris
is shivering, but the tiny movements resulting from this
trembling add to the pain. He tries to check the shivering—
but the effort of doing so likewise reawakens the pain. A
buzzing (no: a buzz, an animated buzz, shrill and obscene)
traverses the entity that used to be known as "Boris." What
if I was turning to sound? What if nothing was left of me but
a sound?

The shabby gray walls of the cell are fainting away. A
smell of vomit, so strong that it becomes almost a solid, hits
Boris full in the face.

*　*　*

Feeling as though he were sitting in a washbasin, Boris is wheeled to his first interrogation on a barrow. After the cell walls, it is the trees that are fainting away now. The sky is swooning, as well. ("How melodramatic can you get!") The plain-clothes men stroll along beside the barrow, wearing fraternal expressions. The snow is croaking like a frog. So my own past and the past of all the planets were merely a preparation, merely the logs fated to kindle the flame of this second.

"As from this moment, my dreams could not possibly come under any heading but entomology. Cockroaches' dreams. Dreams which ARE cockroaches."

"On your feet, Jew-boy! So you claim your name is Yuri Goletz, do you . . . ?"

The odd thing is, Boris DOES get to his feet. His legs support his frame as though it were a foreign body. Every movement is a discovery. Everything in Boris seems destroyed, apart from the sense of smell: there is a strong reek of polish and stale piss.

The first interrogator is a gnome. He has to stand on his toes to hit Boris. And Boris doesn't fall.

The second resembles an icon. His face gleams. He is stately and solemn, like a national anthem sheathed in a black overcoat.

Boris's valise is there, on the desk, ripped open. Lying beside it are a good many notes, a good many letters, a few books written in the language of the local race—not Boris's race, but the race of Yuri Goletz the Fictitious. How childish these precautions seem when set beside the deadly obviousness of the tool, now laid bare again.

The kicks in the balls are like a prolonged howl. The point at issue—the penis—has indeed chosen a fatal environment: that of the testicles. Boris feels like smiling, but the smile fails to negotiate the aching zone of the jaws.

"First of all we're going to find out through whom and from whom you got your forged papers. And also, who these addresses in your notebook belong to. And the names and whereabouts of the people who sent you these letters. You are going to be quite sensible and tell us all that, aren't you?"

He who consorts with and abets the Unclean becomes unclean himself and must be exterminated. Boris ponders what is known as the magic thought. This thought lies at the very root of the conqueror's legal code. The five letters from friends that had strayed into his valise may easily earn their writers an interrogation just like his. It is all so predictable. All courage ebbs from Boris, even the courage to betray, to succumb. For what is courage, if not the capacity to bring about a change, or at least to glimpse it? Boris can no longer summon this capacity. Twilight is descending on the room. The walls are papered with eyelids. Interrogator No. 2 is sprawling on his desk. He produces his lighter, raises it to his cigarette, and flicks. But the lighter doesn't respond. The machinery creaks, for the very first time. And yet its functioning ought to be entirely dependent on the interrogator's will.

From a side drawer, the interrogator produces a bottle of lighter fuel. The bottle slips from his grasp. Can it be that there was an unextinguished cigarette end in the ash tray? The letters lying on the desk are ablaze. The names and addresses inscribed in them are now inscribed only in Boris's head. He addresses a silent and intense prayer of thanksgiving to his God.

The interrogator shrugs unconcernedly. His casualness is

directed as much at Boris as at the burned papers. For the true facts are blatant in Boris's tool and his fear.

Organs roar out in a deserted temple. The oaths that are being shouted no longer have anything to do with Boris. He is taken back to another cell.

CHAPTER 30

The coldness is like a tangible and hostile object. There are six persons in the cell, besides Boris. A father with his two little daughters. A seven-year-old boy—all alone. A young couple smelling of trees and snow.

The fair-haired girl, wearing leather boots that are too big for her, has nothing to say for herself. Her smile is leading a life of its own. It takes wing; it flutters about between the narrow walls. She loves us, this girl, but scarcely notices us. She is not with us, who would like to be with her. She would prefer to exist only for her companion, only with her companion. Our presence isn't even embarrassing; it is superfluous, like that of close relatives around a newly married couple. With a barely perceptible movement, she touches the boy's tousled hair. It would be good to die in the warm. It is only nine hours since they were brought here, this little couple, so silent and so earnest. The frozen earth fleeing and shooting up around the trees, the ambush in the secluded forest, the hasty fighting, a loyalty which—though shy—was vast as the ocean: all this still lingers in their eyes. True, the boy has received a minor wound, a mere scratch on the shoulder which doesn't hurt. But how handsome it is, this wound. How it elevates this boy above all the rest of us, who have never wielded a gun. He is like a shining candlestick during the Feast of Hanukkah. The girl radiates happy, maternal pride . . .

The father is talking to his two little girls. The little boy, looking rather ridiculous in his outsize lambskin, is listening attentively, not yet daring to join in the conversation. Boris, who has not confessed to his origins, isn't supposed to understand his neighbors' language, the language of his own people. It is possible for anyone to be a spy, for anyone to be indiscreet. Without a word, the reasons for Boris's silence are acknowledged by those about him. Unresentfully. And a lump comes into Boris's throat, resulting from an indescribably tender feeling for these people, as though for a hidden memory.

The policeman set the bodies of the two Partisans down in a corner like a bundle of washing in a workhouse. The click from the gun had been discreet. The boy had qualified for the first bullet. The blood was trickling onto the concrete, drawing indecipherable arabesques. A few minutes later, an elderly warder came in, accompanied by a prisoner on fatigue duty. The two bodies were stripped of their clothes. Boris glimpsed a nakedness that took his breath away. He felt alone, alone and mutilated.

"We'll have to send them to be disinfected," growled the warder. "They're alive with fleas. But sheepskins are mighty comfortable. Those two must have been nice and warm, even in the forest."

The girl's eyes, full of arrested sparks, were far from dead. They looked as though they were covered with a layer of ice so thin that it was almost nonexistent.

And the living continued to surround the couple like five torrents poised hesitantly above a great river.

"My father will get me out of here," the little boy pipes

up. "He certainly will. He's a dentist in Orava. That's a big town. Haven't you heard of it . . . ? He fixes the teeth of all the local police, and of the garrison commander himself. They come specially to see my father, through the gate in the high wall surrounding our quarter. They say that none of the dentists in the open town can hold a candle to my father . . . But there was to be a sweep in our town. Everyone was scared. And my parents sent me to stay with our maid's family. Mama unsewed the stars from my clothing, back and front. Papa gave the maid some money. It was two years since she had worked for us: she wasn't allowed to live inside the wall. But from time to time she would sneak in just the same, and we would buy butter from her, and cheese, and even fruit. I just love apples. My father promised her that if her family would look after me till the end of the war, she'd get a house when it was over . . . On the train, she got talking to a policeman. The two of them sat there laughing. Later, they drank some vodka. They gave me a drop, too. And the policeman put his hand on her breast . . . They were laughing again, and all of a sudden she told me to let my trousers down. 'Go on,' she said, 'show us your little dickey-bird.' And the policeman saw I was circumcised. He called in some more policemen, who were in the next compartment. They all laughed, and they took me off at the next station. As for the maid, Eugenie, she stayed on the train. They were very nice, the policemen, very gentle—all except one, who tugged at my ears. But the others told him to lay off. They gave me some chocolate. We got into a car, and they said they were going to take me home to my parents. I sat next to the driver. But they brought me here, to jail."

The steel door opened, and the head warder came in with a plain-clothes man. The plain-clothes man wore thick spectacles and a Tyrolean hat with a feather tucked in at the side.

"Listen, my boy," said the warder, "you complained of being cold last night. We've brought you a blanket—look! You'll be better off, this way, just like you were back at your mother's."

As the plain-clothes man put the barrel of his small pocket revolver to the back of the little boy's neck, the warder looked embarrassed. The child began to flutter—resembling, all of a sudden, the smile of the young girl who had been shot earlier.

And the cell was turning into a henhouse, a henhouse in which a fox had slaughtered the hens.

Why did Boris, the latest to arrive in the cell, feel as though he were the host, as though he were the master of the house? What gave him this sense of responsibility for the well-being and comfort of his guests? His lie, not yet totally demolished, gave him one chance in a thousand of surviving, whereas his companions—the father and his two small daughters—had no further rivers to cross before going to join, in the same cell corner, the two young Partisans and the son of the skilled dentist. "What a peaceful night I shall have!" Boris was thinking, even while that fictional character Yuri Goletz still clung by his nails to the glassy wall of earthly existence.

Suddenly, Boris seemed to be gazing at the old cemetery back in the town of his birth. The elder of the little girls, the one who was nine, was so like the bas-relief goats on tombstones.

As the plain-clothes man had used his revolver, her father's face had gone to pieces, had disintegrated into primary elements. And suddenly Boris was filled with the urge to recover these elements, and rearrange them, and mold a new face. Which meant embarking on a strenuous chase between the cell walls and the grimy partitions; between the dusty baseboards, the sinuous, juicy past and the pungent present.

In the eyes of the condemned, the survival of others, or even the faintest chance of surviving, was frequently—as it were—a sign of elevated rank, a badge of nobility. In many cases, as if by infection, the enemy had succeeded in imposing his own hierarchical system. Was the terror that bade the little girls' father avert his head from the bodies heaped in the corner fraught with a certain disgust, with moral condemnation, even?

For Boris, on the other hand, accession to death constituted an initiatory step which was being taken, all around him, by those he loved, by everyone but him. Should he press this antithesis into service?

Having once elected not to understand the language which was as much his own as that of the little family with him, he couldn't start a conversation except by some clever stratagem. There was a danger of the man's mistrusting Boris, of his linking him with the murderers or with those who were not marked for extinction. Wasn't that the same thing? But then again: terrified by the death that had come to reside in the bodies of his companions heaped beside the wall, repelled by that death, he was bound to cling to this chance, to this spark, of survival that still resided in the body, in the instance, of Boris.

The minutes were falling from the invisible ceiling.

To get the man talking, he must display a carefree independence, he must make it clear that they were not entirely in the same boat; but he must do so without undue brutality, otherwise the man might retreat into his shell, overcome by the awareness of his different and inescapable destiny.

Boris heaved himself up to the small barred window just below the ceiling.

Used as he was to defining, to describing, he started turning phrases over in his mind:

A physiological landscape? A man's entrails, not as seen by a medical expert, but as pictured by a child. The alarming, worn greenness of the undisturbed puddles. Trees whose upward-straining branches are so many isolated, unattuned screams. Trees on the lookout for people to hang. They have grown for no other purpose than to receive a cargo of flesh. Stones firmly rooted on the banks of a pool, slippery stones, green and moist, which will never suffer being detached from the ground. A sky neither blue, nor green, nor red; white rather, white as lime, an absent sky.

No, it wasn't a prison yard; not unless the whole world was just that—a prison yard, a universal prison yard.

When Boris got down he was already, for his companion, "he-who-had-dared-to-look," he who had dared to infringe regulations in such a carefree manner. And might it not be that the hint of a miracle, a spark of survival, was going to emerge from the breach of this deadly regulation, for the benefit of the two little girls?

"My story is simple," said the man. "There was to be a sweep in our town, a sweep directed against members of our race. What wouldn't a father do to save his own flesh and blood? So I sent my two little girls to live with a neighbor, one of my oldest friends, a blacksmith by trade. He and his wife had a small daughter who had played with ours for years. I gave the blacksmith a lot of money, two thousand gold rubles."

The man seemed to choke, as though he had put a burning-hot potato into his mouth. His long neck grew longer still. His smile was begging forgiveness for a blemish, a short-coming that Boris could not pin down. Was the man seeking pardon for possessing a sum which, though certainly considerable, was far from huge? True enough, Yuri Go-letz who couldn't speak his cell-mate's language, Yuri Go-letz endowed with the survival that was inherent in his race and in his status as a farm hand, Yuri Goletz was bound to be dazzled by the vastness of the sum. On the other hand, in view of present circumstances and particularly in view of his own nature, he was unlikely to be moved, to any great extent, by the fate imminently in store for the children . . .

Did the man suppose that, by conjuring up this picture of his wealth (now vanished, in any case), he had slammed the final door or—quite simply—snuffed out the final spark of a friendly compassion?

Quite suddenly, Boris felt weary of the game. With a ges-ture that could only belong to the great-grandson of the Doc-tors of the Law who, by God's will and by direct as well as devious means, had led this man and his daughters to this blood-smeared concrete, he stroked the older girl's hair and planted a kiss on the younger one's cheek. Nothing was said, and everything became clear . . . After all, let him think what he likes. If, now that our fundamental link has been brought to light, he retracts his confession—then so much the worse or so much the better. The outcome will be in no way different, either for him and his little girls, or for me. But the man was going on with his story:

"The blacksmith's wife assured me that she would take as much care of my daughters as she did of her own. 'I love them just as dearly,' she kept saying. She also asked whether there wasn't something more I could hand over, in addition to the two thousand rubles. 'You know what I mean,' she said, 'it would be a shame if the fruits of a lifetime's work should fall into the hands of the soldiers. Now that it's all up with you (what difference does it make whether the end comes tomorrow or a week from now), at least make sure your savings go to your daughters and to the decent folk who have taken them in. Food is terribly expensive today. And haven't we always lived like one big happy family?'

"I turned all this over in my mind and decided that I didn't like the look of it. 'Fine family!' I said to myself. 'They've no thought for anything but the inheritance.' And my girls didn't want to stay with them. The older one—Esther here—kept looking at me and looking at me, and all she could say was: 'Papa, don't let's split up. It won't help, anyway . . .' And all next day, from early morning till late at night, I went on racking and racking my brains. The knowing smile that the blacksmith had exchanged with his wife was gnawing at me like a worm. So long as it was daylight, I couldn't set foot in the street. It was a long day, as long as our exile . . . As night came on, I hurried to the blacksmith's and I said: 'Thank you for your kindness, but I've changed my mind. Give me back my daughters and the money. We may be going away. I've had a letter from my brother-in-law in Minsk, saying that things are fairly quiet there.'

"At which the blacksmith stared at me and said: 'Hey now, why don't you just cool off . . . How can you leave here, you fool, when they won't even let you on a train?'

" 'Don't worry,' I said, 'I've arranged for a peasant to hide us in his hay-cart.'

" 'Listen,' said the blacksmith, 'you've got your brother-in-law, I've got mine. He's in the police. If you want the kids back, take them. But as for the money, I haven't got it any more. You'll just have to wait a couple of months . . .'

"He grew quite red in the face; I saw several empty bottles on the table. He started shouting. 'That's the thanks one gets for trying to help YOUR kind!'

"And suddenly his brother-in-law breezed in, with three other hooligans. He's a skunk, that brother-in-law. He used to be a carpenter before the war. He even made a cradle for Esther. He has grown quite fat, since then. Anyway, he breezes in with his friends and says to the blacksmith: 'Jospeh, old boy, don't worry your head over him. If he won't see the light, he just won't. Stop worrying. Now we'll MAKE him see the light.'

"And they took us straight to the police station. If I'd been alone, I'd have made a run for it. I'd have shoved past them. They were drunk. And I'm brawny enough. But with the kids there, it was out of the question. 'Don't let's split up, Papa,' said Esther, 'don't let's split up.'

"And so now we're here. And we're not split up, that's one thing to be grateful for. And my money is at the blacksmith's."

"Why, just look at your hair," said the older girl to her sister, "it's all over the place. Show me . . ."

Whereupon Boris took a comb from his pocket and looked on as the children tidied themselves for the last time. For a long while afterwards, his comb retained a faint smell of camomile.

Boris is alone. Twilight descends on the room. Like a weary insect, dying and deadly slow, Boris's gaze creeps along the colorless walls. This gaze is pulled up with a jolt by a crevice, a barely perceptible chink. His eye weds this tiny window: an old woman is there, lying on a heap of ocher bricks; a painful smile, a mechanical smile, imprinted on the features of the lifeless face like a flower on a piece of material.

This room is no ordinary cell. Its spirit has not been shaped by countless human presences. It is what used to be the prison linen room. In the old days, this part of the building had been set aside for the service rooms of the prison. Since the war, the number of prisoners had been on the increase. The number of their needs, recognized as such by the administration, had been on the decrease. The linen rooms and laundries and shops, so recently regarded as indispensable to the lives of the inmates, were now put to another use: that of storing bodies. Bodies that were still alive and those that were no longer so. The presence of inert objects in this room is normal. It does not disturb the sensibility of the walls.

Boris's gaze remains faithful to the crevice:

A dying fowl, wreathed by its chopped-off neck as though with a broad sash—and how it trickles, how it drips!—this moaning Sabbath wakes with a start; it whimpers, it shrieks. Like a little brood of chicks, its tremulous cackles disperse in all directions, instantly swallowed up by the reddish dust. Multicolored streaks carve its featherless body. Body: islet. Body: source of sacred vibrations, impossible to create anew. How resonant this dust!

The woman's body says to Boris:

"I have to keep my nine children and my husband fed. They are like the Ten Commandments to me. My old bones are tired, my life is tired, my skin is tired. Even my tiredness is tired. Yes, my weariness is weary.

"Everyday hunger is a sin that God commits against us, His creatures. Hunger on the Sabbath is a sin that we, His creatures, commit against God. If any of you heathen (to whom I address this utterance, the way one hurls a bottle to the very bottom of the sea) is capable of understanding, let him do so.

"Now, God may well commit sins against us who are hungry: in vain does He commit them, day in, day out. He is still holy. His back is broad. His back is robust. But is it right for us to commit even one more little sin against God, however trifling?

"My back, our backs are nothing like God's. See for yourself . . . Even though it is written that we were created in His Holy Likeness, that likeness must reside somewhere else —not in the back. My back is bent, it is weak. It will not stand the burden of a further sin against God: that of starving my husband and my nine children on the Sabbath; that of being hungry myself on the Sabbath.

"My husband earns neither bread nor living, for himself or for us. He devotes his days and nights to study. In the Holy Scriptures, he is learning how to win a future life. He hasn't time to win the present one.

"My back is bent. It is stooping. My husband and my nine children are like the Ten Commandments to me. My husband is the crown, the blazing crown of my life.

"I run an onion stall down at the market, and am myself an onion. I run a fish stall, and am a fish.

"On the Sabbath, on this Sabbath . . . they come, they came, helmeted like angels. Oh, for the panting—for the panting of this Sabbath—to end . . ."

The smartly uniformed police perched on the clouds stand motionless above the town and its Sabbath. The little boy hidden in the folds of the sky is captivated by their proximity. He marvels at the gleaming bayonets.

His eyes grow dazzled by their shine and, looking down, he

glimpses the blackish, brownish earth. The earth recoils. Its calm surface grows disturbed: tremors, whirlpools, islets. But how far away it is!

Heave then, earth coated with brown, burned meat, boiling earth!

CHAPTER 31

Bare cold days, like scales, formed an armor plating around
Boris.

Since he persisted in denying his origins, he was trans-
ferred to another cell—this one inhabited by people who
were not doomed to immediate extermination. Among
them was a village shoemaker, a weak and sentimental man,
who had killed his wife in a drunken fit. He would cry bit-
terly and relate the lives of a number of saints who seldom
figured in the history of the Church. His huge head, bald and
sickly-colored, shed a sad autumnal light in the cell. He was
a just and upright man who wouldn't normally have hurt a
hair on anybody's head, but he hated lies; it was he who,
after Boris's arrival, was first to call a spade a spade: "You
aren't one of us. What's the use of trying to hide it? Tell your
judges the truth, and you will be granted an easy death.
Which is more than my own death will be."

The second shoemaker, a wiry, venomous man, nodded
his head in approval: "There was one just like him back
home in the village," he said. "He was blond and blue-eyed;
you could have taken him for one of the local boys. He was
hiding with the Count's family, up at the manor house.
They gave him food and drink. He pretended he had been

an officer. He gave English lessons to the Count's children. And then suddenly he started to get fresh. He came out of hiding, he went riding through the fields with His Lordship's daughter, he was high and mighty to good Christian people—thinking they would never know who they were dealing with. But these things show, they have a stink of their own, you sniff them. Some of the village organized a hunt. We went after him with pitchforks. How he struggled when we caught up with him, poor devil! How he struck out with his fists and feet . . ."

A peasant charged with illegal slaughter of pigs (which, under the law of the times, might cost him his life) treated Boris with unbounded contempt: "If God permits your kind to be killed, it's because you are all bloodsuckers and filthy sinners. The measure of your sins is filled to overflowing. It's because of you this war broke out, because of you that the blood of Christians is flowing in torrents. You provoked it, you brought it about. In the prophecies of the Queen of Sheba, it's written that the Beast will devour not only the Just, but its own children as well. You are the children of the Beast. To celebrate your Sabbaths, you used to drink our babies' blood. Today, the Beast clamors for YOUR blood, in preparation for its own Great Sabbath. You're an educated man, I can see that. You'll have heard and read about what I'm saying . . ."

A fair-haired boy of sixteen—shy and nice to everyone, even to Boris—was awaiting trial for escaping from a forced-labor camp. He knew an old peasant fairy tale and would start telling it, monotonously, every night. "In a faraway country there lived a bird with golden feathers. By means of spells that he had learned from a witch, the poorest peasant in the neighborhood summoned the bird, who offered him one of his feathers. This golden feather, inlaid with precious stones, was worth a king's ransom. But, in exchange, the bird demanded an object of his own choice from his debtor's mean hovel. The peasant quickly agreed to this condition, thinking it innocent enough, and immediately the bird flew off, clutching in its beak an old iron cross that the peasant's little daughter used to wear around her neck. From then on, one disaster followed another, striking not only the peasant, but the village and the entire province as well. Children died, fires and Tatars ravaged the countryside. A strange illness broke out, carrying off the cattle and wiping out the happiness in men's hearts . . . The peasant set off in search of the bird, hoping to get his cross back. After many adventures, he came to a land where cannibalism was considered the highest of virtues and the greatest of privileges. Where children were taught false swearing at school, as elsewhere they are taught multiplication tables. The king of this land was an infidel bird with golden feathers . . ."

At this point in the story, the audience's eyes would invariably turn toward Boris, fastening the whole burden of the crimes attributed to the bird and its subjects on him. The treatment inflicted on Boris by his cellmates was caused by the imperative need they all felt to re-establish the moral equilibrium upset by the bird's treacherous carryings on.

A highway robber, arrested on a charge of murder, relieved Boris of his shirt and socks, insisting on his rights as one who was going to survive, as opposed to the absence of rights of one who was soon to depart this life anyway.

A notary, who, as the one representative of the "intelligentsia," enjoyed considerable prestige in the cell, would enliven the hours of forced leisure with regular lectures analyzing the baneful role that Boris's race had played in the nation's economy and politics and culture:

"They are now, gentlemen, reaping the rewards that they have richly deserved for their age-long abuse of our all too generous hospitality. They led us into unclean ways. Their money-grabbing nearly poisoned the spirit of our splendid race. They contaminated our young people by the example of debauchery which they had exalted to an ideal and to a system. They repaid our endless kindnesses with the blackest ingratitude. But luckily God is with us, gentlemen, and now they are brought low. Which is consoling and irrefutable proof that heavenly justice is no idle phrase. Isn't that so, Mr. . . . , Mr. . . . (oh dear, I keep forgetting what name you go under!), Mr. Yuri Goletz—is that it? What's your opinion? You say nothing, and yet this is a subject on which you must be bursting with knowledge . . .

"Just look at him, gentlemen, he's shaking, he's as white as a sheet. Between ourselves—and heaven knows there should be complete trust between companions in misfortune —allow me to confess that I don't believe a single word of our Mr. Goletz's story. In my humble opinion, his name is certainly neither Goletz nor Yuri, and he has never been a farm hand . . .

"You ought to be ashamed of your lies, young man. At a pinch, I could understand your continuing to pull the wool over the eyes of the police—although I, for one, don't believe in lying . . . But here, in this cell, you are among decent folk who are not informers. Unless you think the opposite? If you do, say so and we shall behave accordingly."

The peasants were staggered by the notary's elegant turns of phrase. They would endeavor to imitate him. A collective protest was even organized against Boris's presence in the cell—"occupied, Mr. Prison Governor, by persons who are certainly on the wrong side of the law, which can happen to anyone, but whose blood is pure and whose origins are beyond dispute."

There were collective lessons, too: fifteen overseers set about teaching Boris how to sweep the floor of the cell, how to hold the broom, how to clean—without implement of any kind, with his bare hands—the pail full of excrement and urine. All that was left of the broom was the handle, but the floor had to shine. The cleaning of the pail had been entrusted exclusively to Boris. He began to love shit: a patient substance, humble and completely unaggressive.

The inmates were summoned to the interrogation room. They returned with swollen faces and with lilac weals on their skin. Some were shot, others released. Night and morning they chanted solemn, weighty prayers in chorus, prayers that rippled like a wheatfield.

New tenants would arrive in the cell where Boris had become the oldest piece of furniture, a kind of pail or spittoon. Occasionally his companions would receive food parcels from their families and ceremoniously share them out, without tossing so much as a crumb in Boris's direction. Hunger became an obsession; it was like a tangible substance. The hungry went on and on about food, so much so that their conversation resembled a weird and wonderful cookery book. Their dreams were devoid of fresh air and open skies, but were crammed with bacon. In their dreams, they wandered in unknown climes strewn with chapels and churches whose walls were built of this fat, silvery and universal fat.

They stuffed themselves with succulent dishes, whose only defect was nonexistence. But to some—to the tough and to the harsh—these effortless excursions into the Enchanted Land of Bacon would come as all too painful a wrench. Whereupon, although rendered impotent by the gnawings of hunger, they would start rummaging in the trash cans of sex. Here is a tale dug up by the skinny postman:

"In our town there was a widower: very friendly he was, quite a gentleman. He must have been getting on toward fifty and was developing middle-aged spread. Everyone looked up to him. He was Chief Cashier at the Municipal Slaughterhouse, a good position, and no doubt about it. More than that: a high position, an exalted position. Always smartly dressed. Always in a dark suit. A silver-topped cane. Every Sunday he used to go to church and sit right behind the Mayor.

"He had two daughters. The elder had married a pub-lic-works contractor. A man of substance; more than that—a man of the world. As for the younger . . . my, she was pretty! Just the way I like them to be. Well-cushioned, and with her hair in curls—hair as blonde as blonde can be. A real angel. And big innocent eyes, which maybe weren't so innocent after all. And plump rosy cheeks. She must have been about twenty-two at the time. Had quite a dowry into the bargain. The boys used to hang around her like flies around a honeypot. But Papa was proud, it seemed. Not a sin-gle suitor was good enough for him. Just think! And him nothing grander than Chief Cashier at the Municipal Slaughterhouse. People started whispering; but no one took much notice of the stories. There are envious folk in all walks of life. It's one of the laws of nature.

"They had a pretty little house, with a garden to it, and geraniums in the window boxes. Decent, respectable, good-class folk.

"I was their neighbor. I rented a room from the old woman who owned the place next door. And every day, as I came home from work, I would raise my cap to the girl sitting idly at the window. She acknowledged my greeting with just the faintest nod of her pretty little head, as befits a girl of good family dealing with a man whom she hardly knows and who in addition—what's the point of hiding the fact?—is just a poor post-office inspector. I would dream of her as one dreams of a princess.

"One winter night I was waked up by the sound of shrieks. It was like pigs being slaughtered. I quickly put on my trousers and rushed outside, just in time to see the girl leaping over the wall, covered with blood and with nothing on but a bra and a pair of pants. The wall was only a low one. She was screaming for help like crazy. 'If I haven't killed the old swine already,' she shouted, 'I'll go back and do him in with my bare hands . . .'

" 'Can I be of any help to you, Miss?' I asked her, all politeness. 'You must put something on, it's cold.' And I handed her my jacket.

"It was as though she hadn't heard. She just kept on yelling: 'I'll kill the old swine!'

"People came running from all directions, bringing lamps with them. We went into the house. The cashier was inside, moaning and screaming. He was writhing on the floor, in a pool of blood. The bedclothes were in a mess. 'The little whore!' he was shouting. 'Oh, the little whore! I'll settle her hash for her. She didn't respect her own father. She didn't respect his gray hairs. I've been too good to her . . .'

"I was one of the first to get there. I slipped on something soft . . . without realizing. And then I bent down, and then I DID realize: it was a pair of balls, the cashier's balls. By the time the doctor came, I knew what it was all about. And later, when the old boy had kicked off—which didn't take long, two days at the outside—the girl explained the whole story to the judge. Papa had been making advances to her. He'd wanted to sleep with her. The girl had taken it as a joke. That night, he had doped her tea to send her to sleep. In her sleep, she felt something between her legs. And when she came to, Papa was on the bed with her, probing her with his prick. At this, the girl pretended she was still asleep, still dozing. And then, in a single movement, she picked up the razor that was lying on the bedside table and sliced off his bollocks . . .

"After the old boy's death, she inherited the works: house, garden, money. The court acquitted her. But she seemed out of her mind. Wherever she went, the kids ran after her, shouting: "Hoy, where's that prick? Hand over that prick! What have you done with that prick . . . ?"

Accompanied by a duty prisoner, the warder would bring in a canful of steaming soup. The inmates would wait their turn in a long line, mess tins in hand. To whom would this one last potato go, or this shy piece of marrow clinging to the very bottom of the can?

Everyone was alive with fleas, but a firmly established tradition ruled that one man alone was to blame for the invasion of these fraternal insects: Boris. It was he, the Unclean One—newcomers were informed—who had brought the vermin into the cell. This myth influenced Boris's attitude. During the delousing rites, which were celebrated on Saturday evenings, when, barring the unforeseen, it was virtually certain that none of the occupants of the cell would be summoned to the interrogation room, Boris would pretend to imitate his companions and squash the parasites. But he would spare their lives. He would take off his shirt like everyone else. To avoid physical violence and recriminations, he would go through the motions of searching the seams of his underclothes, but his fingernails were snapping at thin air. The giant fleas—lazy and bloated and yellowish, with crosses on their backs—would emerge from these sham searches quite unscathed. They were loyal and hung together; they were fraternal. Having to give a present to somebody, Boris made them a gift of their lives.

On Sunday evenings, tired of interminably hunting these small mobile rubies, as numberless as the stars in the clear July sky, the inmates—enveloped in the warm mist of their own breaths—would start relating their dreams, dreams that "descended in swarms on their lives, to become flesh themselves and devour the meager flesh of their incredulity."

Boris was not insensitive to the strange beauty of these tales and of the trancelike commentaries that attended them. But naturally he was likewise excluded from this communion woven from the thread of dreams.

The first shoemaker had seen a clock, which the second interpreted as follows: "You will be released before long."

Vassili, the robber, had dreamed of plums. Interpretation: "You will be flogged next time you're interrogated." A pair of boots meant transfer to another prison. "A field of clover—last night I saw myself walking through a field of clover," this from the boy who'd deserted from the labor camp. And the shoemaker who had murdered his wife commented: "Poor boy, that's grim. No one in your family is going to come through this storm alive. Neither your father nor your mother. You are an orphan already. It's hard on you, hard . . ." And the boy would shed bitter tears.

Boris, too, was visited by images made all the richer by the colorlessness of the four walls. But he kept them to himself.

It was at about this time that he was sent his "crucial

dream," which he set down on paper some ten years later and which is related in Chapter 23 of this book.

Every four or five days, Boris was taken to the interrogation room. A small, dapper Lieutenant asked him the same questions every time: "What is your name, where are you from, who gave you these forged papers?" He would slap Boris's face and lash his back and hands with a whip. Boris would stay silent. Was it by "instinct"? Had not everything in his life been the expression of an "instinct"? He would try to shrink his vital processes, to stop breathing, to contract, to disappear between the walls; would try not to think, as though thoughts themselves might betray him.

After a week in the common cell, during which he had thoroughly gauged his companions' predispositions, he decided on an attitude which, when its advantages and drawbacks were weighed, seemed to him the most auspicious—indeed, the only possible attitude. He acted dumb. For two whole months he didn't say a word to anyone. In this absolute silence, which he drew from the depths of his being, he found a kind of grim happiness, a solid and ever-strengthening support. This silence was like an ardent faith. Often he would choose an object at which he would stare for hour after hour as the grayness of the autumn twilight turned to darkness. Sometimes it was the smooth, shiny surface of the cast-iron stove, which was stoked from outside, in the corridor, behind the heavy cell door. At such moments Boris would grow lighter and ever lighter and hover in empty heights from which he could gaze down at will upon the dark, rent earth. And upon the multitudes of his fellows rotting in mass graves.

As for his external fate, it was subject to only one incident

throughout this whole period—and even that was insignificant. The successive generations of prisoners who moved into
the cell, only to move out again soon afterwards, always passed
on to one another, like a baton, a small piece of glass which
they used for cutting their nails. In the course of one particularly cold and black night, Boris got hold of the little object.
Lying on the bare concrete, under a coat which served him as
a blanket, he broke the glass into small splinters and carefully swallowed them, one by one. The operation lasted an
hour. He didn't want the others to catch him at it. His theft
of this item of public property would have earned him
further blows. Furthermore, a suicide attempt could only
confirm the general opinion concerning his origins. Finally,
the act in which he was engaged was strictly private, at the
very least, if not shameful, and the presence of even one witness would have robbed Boris of all pleasure, as though he
was indulging in a particularly ecstatic spell of masturbation.

When the disappearance of the piece of glass was noticed
next morning, Boris's companions were distressed without
exception.

"It was so useful to us, that harmless piece of glass." As
usual, it was the notary who summed up the situation. "Now,
who could have gained by depriving us of it? It is deplorable,
gentlemen, but there are those among us to whom not even
our common misfortune has taught the elementary rules of
community living. Oh, if only I could get my hands on the
stupid and mischievous thief . . ."

Oddly enough, nobody ever suspected Boris of this piece of
petty thieving. For it constituted, in the eyes of every man
there, a virile action, however trivial, and Boris struck them
in this context as too shadowy, too lifeless—too nonexistent,
one might almost say.

To Boris's deep disappointment, the glass that he had

swallowed didn't even give him a stomach-ache. Deprived of its expected consequences, entirely isolated, this action— the only one that Boris allowed himself in all those weeks— vanished like a fish in the meanderings of a torrential stream.

Once a fortnight the prisoners were taken to the showers. In the overheated room, beneath the low ceiling, their cut and bruised bodies emitted, under the impact of hot water, fumes that were unlike anything Boris had ever before experienced. They seemed to emanate from animals of a zoological species quite unknown to him. The men would indulge in ponderous jokes about the genitalia and their uses, jokes which eventually settled upon Boris's bluish tool. The sign of the Covenant was inscribed in it and constituted, for these men, the most scathing rebuttal of Boris's allegations to his judges. This tool likewise afforded irrefutable proof of the stupidity of the invader, who was "allowing himself to be made a fool of by this dumb oaf."

"Just look at the damned thing! And with a tool like that, he thinks he can pass himself off as one of us, as a 'Yuri Goletz.' Some hope! Why, you rascal, do you even know how to make the sign of the Cross? Hey, don't hide your little tool so quickly. We're going to have a good look at it . . . That's better. Now then . . . What's happened to your foreskin? Here, look at my prick. Can't you see the difference?"

Boris would stare at the subject of contention: so this was the instrument, the poor instrument, of all his past metaphysics? Of all his metaphysics which in the past had seemed so personal, so exceptional, and which today were no more peculiar to him, no more "individual," than are the entrails of one squashed cockroach as compared to the entrails of another?

A halo of hilarity would surround the group of men in the washroom. The warm steam enwrapped them like pity. At the sound of the guard's shrill whistle, the game would come to an end, and the prisoners would return to their cells.

In the dim light, Boris would stare once more at the smooth surface of the red-hot cast-iron stove. By sheer force of imagination, he would draw geometrical figures on this virgin surface, and as soon as he relaxed his exertions these imaginary figures would topple into madness, dragging Boris—Boris the everlastingly silent—with them. "Geometry, that irrefutable proof of God's madness"—where had he heard those words . . . ? Yes, but would a NORMAL God, a God devoid of madness, be bearable?

"I shall plunge into insanity the way one plunges into a hot bath." He would formulate this idiotic phrase over and over again, yet not a sound ever passed his lifeless lips.

His companions having fallen into a particularly heavy sleep, Boris lay awake on the bare concrete, keeping watch on the immense darkness. His senses were skillfully savoring this precious wakefulness, which he supposed was solitary. From out of the darkness a hand emerged and settled on his shoulder. Its touch was soft and wary. The shoemaker who had murdered his wife whispered in Boris's ear: "They haven't understood a thing, poor fools; even our august friend the notary hasn't. They spend their time strangling and trampling on their own kindness and pity, which are vast, really . . .

"Now me, I knew from the very first, I could tell at a glance: you think you are innocent, for you love them. They think they are innocent, for they hate you or make out they hate you. In fact, your love for them and their hatred for you are twins . . . The mistake was fundamental, radical. I paid dearly for the truth, paid for it with my life and with my soul's salvation, but now it is in my grasp and it will not escape me again. Listen, Goletz:

" 'Love one another'—none but their skinny and anemic God could have voiced such an injunction, worthy of a village mayor. Pity is mawkish, when limited . . . It is worse than the worst cruelty. Had the fortunes of your world still concerned me, I would have imposed another commandment on you all, my own: Fall in love, desperately in love, with everyone around you. Become sodomites and lesbians, when necessary. Let each of you fall madly in love with every man and every woman. Let each of you raise himself to the only height worthy of MY God: to that of the crime due to love, the suicide due to love! Let the Universe wear itself out in perpetual orgasm, in the ultimate *crime passionnel,* perpetrated by every man and every woman, on every man and every woman. May the one true God serve as an example to you . . . !

"As for all that humanitarian twaddle—'Man is the only one who matters. Man is the measure of all things'—why, it just makes me laugh. Every word of it. Francis of Assisi and certain Hindus, yes . . . They glimpsed the truth, they sensed it without grasping it clearly. The ultimate *crime passionnel,* the ultimate *suicide passionnel,* not omitting beasts, mountains, rocks, precipices, thoughts, and images . . ."

The shoemaker's whispering grew impassioned: "Now you know why I killed my wife, Goletz. You know why I am urging you toward death. Same as they do, but for different reasons. Am I right? Meanwhile, take this piece of bread.

Go on—take it, you fool! And, whatever you do, don't comfort me. We're too much alike. As you must have guessed. Answer me! Answer me!"

But Boris, Boris the everlastingly silent, kept his lips sealed. He averted his head, while his heart reverberated with an extremely calm and extremely rational speech, the speech of a stranger:

" 'He who abhors life has only to choose death.' 'Suicides constitute an ultra-exclusive club in the other world.' But what of him who is equally repelled by life and death, those two poles of an eternal magnet, coated with filth every bit as eternal? What action is he to take? What explosive would be capable of blowing up that mangy old bitch, eternity?

> Death—that pale satellite of life.
> Life—that insipid satellite of death.
> *Taedium vitae et taedium mortis.*

"Oh, my God, beloved Master, my Lord, boss, chief, governor, my poor beloved shoemaker, my God . . . have you really nothing else to sell, no other goods to offer me in this grubby shop?"

. . . When their eyes met in the cell next morning, there was no trace of this nocturnal dialogue in either Boris's or the Shoemaker's. In his innermost heart, Boris was grateful to the Shoemaker for this absence of complicity, and he made no further attempt to stave off the feeling of warm friendship that was invading his entire being. He said to himself: "To rip open this membrane—the most delicate that exists, produced by the wound that cannot possibly close in a scar—there are obviously countless means, great and small, all equally efficacious. Indeed, every act, every gesture, every show of rebellion and every submission are merely one

of these means . . . My poor Shoemaker, my beloved Shoemaker, if only I had a Kingdom I would say to you: 'You
will enter it.' Far more than that, I'd have given you the keys
and the scepter. I'd have set off myself and found you in your
village. But I have no Kingdom. My poor beloved Shoemaker . . ."

Such, then, was Boris's life in the prison of S. From time to
time, he was still summoned into the presence of the ex-
amining magistrate, who would promise him the death penalty, to be carried out at dawn next day, but who was
clearly too lazy to sign the order. There were always more
urgent things to be done, more important examinations to be
dealt with. Boris and his "case" were shrinking as though in
a dream, were getting lost as though in a fog. Like an extinguished lamp covered with dust, his destiny was dying before he himself died. In the course of time, half forgotten,
Boris was turning into an object to which it was barely possible to give a name, into a thin carapace, into a withered in-
sect-frame.

The nights were growing long. Winter had taken possession of the land. Snow covered the prison yard, the roofs of
the adjacent houses, the tall lonely trees that could be
glimpsed through the barred window of the cell. It covered
the men and their daily activities and seemed mightier than
even time itself. Until the day of December 22nd. And then
everything changed for Boris.

CHAPTER 32

He woke in the early morning and desperately tried to assemble the small fragments of night that were receding upward and downward, to the left and to the right. He would have liked to wrap himself in night as though in a garment, but night was fleeing from his hands and from his eyes. Almost every day, he would engage in this exercise of holding back the receding night. In time, he had acquired a certain skill at it. He succeeded in making the night last or, at least, in dallying longer in vast intermediary zones which he sheltered in his coat. He contrived, almost at will, to halt the invasion of the hostile day. Sometimes he would resort to certain incantations, which he himself had composed. Here is one of them:

The night lows above the black cows
Barks above the black
                    dogs
                        because the night.
The empty compartment flies away (to an unknown destination)
        flies away
                because the train and the rails.

The gasping night dies
With a crack of bones. Dark day approaches.
Your companions sleep with a heavy sleep
With the sleep of statues. With the sleep of stones.
They sleep[1] cows, dogs, nights
They sleep the whistling train
And the greenish entrails.

Among them, among "us" . . .
You alone, O notary, king of this subterranean world,
Lie awake. Keeping watch on the night and on humility.
She keeps watch—your Grandeur,
Your mother, mother of a little back-street thief,
Of a great king of Hades. Did she win
This dark throne for you through silent entreaties?
She was a streetwalker in a not too scruffy
Quarter of Hamburg, not even a . . .

But that morning, Boris felt too exhausted for the effort of will that the game demanded. The feeble daylight was beginning to draw intricate signs on the grimy windowpanes. It was a Sunday—no doubt the warders were sleeping late, and the roll-call was delayed. The morning ritual was not even begun: no reveille whistle, no issue of coffee. A no man's land in time and space, this prisonful of men sunk in a heavy sleep. What wouldn't Boris have given to be able to scribble a few words, even if later he had to destroy the notes himself. But there was neither paper nor pencil in the cell. Even if there had been, no one would have given them to Boris. Be-

[1] "Sleep" *cum accusativo*, "sleep," transitive, appealed to Boris more than "dream of." And there does indeed seem to be a slightly different shade of meaning.

sides, he wouldn't have made notes simply to have them stolen and chewed over and talked about as soon as they were written. Perhaps this complete impossibility of externalizing anything was a blessing. Perhaps it was toward this impossibility that Creators strove in that most shameful of activities: creation. Boris started dozing again: "I loathe death almost as much as life. I do not at all loathe my companions. Hate: a particular form of vibration which in the old days used to awaken the feeling of *déjà vu* and *déjà vécu* . . . I don't experience hate any more. Just weariness."

He reopened his eyes and stared at the window. No sooner had he fixed on the arabesques engraved on the glass by the first rays of the invisible dawn than he was seized by an almost unbearable tremor of excitement: in the now shrill confusion of the arabesques, he perceived the Sign of Terrestrial Life.

In the course of his thirteenth year, at the approach of ritual maturity, Boris had learned to distinguish this pattern, unique among all others: a transverse line giving rise to three stems, each surmounted by a small flame. A wandering Jew with sallow skin, prominent cheekbones, and a black beard had been given hospitality by Boris's parents. The servants had made fun of him, though without spite. He seemed lost in the world. He was making his way across the plain on foot, in search of a goal that he would discuss with nobody. For a few months, he paid for the hospitality that he was receiving by initiating Boris in the mysteries of the Book of Creation. Between the pages of the old tome hairs were inserted —some gray, others black—and their presence was explained to Boris as follows: Whenever a God-fearing man devotes himself, on the Sabbath, to the study of the Holy Scriptures, and whenever—searching for a hidden meaning in the text—he tugs at his beard and pulls out a hair, a huge pipe falls with a clang from the mighty organ set behind the Creator's throne. In order to avoid this disastrous clatter, all the pious student need do is to put his hair between the lines of the Book. And this was how the hairs of Boris's forefathers came to be lodged between the pages of the Book, which was faithfully handed on from one generation to the next. One day, the man with the black beard had gone off in search of new horizons, but his teaching remained graven on Boris's memory. The Sign of Life, known to the simple as the sign of the miracle, and standing out from the general host of objects, lines, shapes, and colors, had visited Boris on four previous occasions; he knew the forcefulness with which it ruled and commanded. The Sign drove things, phenomena, developments, thoughts back to their point of departure, back to their seed and even to the seed of their seed, whence they might re-emerge along different paths, following different curves, in accordance with the wishes of whoever was capable of recognizing the Sign and grasping it. The Sign returned the elements of the visible and the invisible world to that matrix where they were not yet themselves, but pure, free concepts; crossings and intercrossings of limitless possibilities, strings of a musical instrument as yet unplucked by any hand.

With one last tiny movement, a pilot who is fatally wounded, but in whom training proves stronger than life itself, gets a supersonic plane off the runway and is then lulled into unconsciousness by the drone of the engines. Boris was still questioning himself: Was it worth all the effort? But there was no way of escaping the Sign. Just as there was no way of escaping his own movement or his own immobility. Already the Sign was invading his being, taking control of his reflexes, infiltrating the channels of his senses and of his will.

But now at last there were sounds of movement from the corridor. A massive key grated in the lock. The door opened.

"Try and wash some of the dirt off, Goletz," the warder said, without arrogance. "You're due upstairs in twenty minutes."

In a mental state akin to a luminous dream, Boris wandered through the decrepit prison corridors. His nostrils no longer detected the mingling smells of urine and polish. His feet didn't touch the floor. Ready-made expressions, sentences devoid of meaning, drummed lightly on his consciousness: "Truly, the only enemy of beings is Being . . . But against the Sign, even lowered eyelids offer no protection . . . Emptiness bites on bald space . . . but it is powerless. Emptiness . . . that smiling, friendly substance. The body of History, attacked by cockroaches . . . but they will not devour it . . ."

Incoherent fragments, poems, and strange forms of words were lighting up and going out like neon signs. Boris's case was completely routine. By now, it could only be a question of disposing of a piece of unsettled business, of attending to an everyday formality.

Boris walked into his interrogator's room as he might have walked into a post office. He was faraway and inattentive—and yet, and yet . . . his pulse quickened.

Lieutenant Lesch—fair, fat, and good-humored, like a round red flower in a flowerpot—was sitting at his usual place. The whip and revolver were there on the desk. The plump white hands stirred at regular intervals, like a pair of performing mice. A few seconds went by in silence. Lesch began to speak: "Well now, my dear Goletz—since that is what I must call you, even though the name is a false one . . . Well now, my dear Goletz, it's time you and I had a serious talk. All honest men and women in this world of ours have a job to do. I have mine. I am the tracker-down of your race. With my own hands, I have shot nine hundred and ninety-four Jews in this little town. I am the king of the Jews here in S. Your case is no ordinary one. You yourself have realized that. You were in the condemned cell. When Jews come to this building, and into my hands, I accord them a brief respite—one day, or two, or three at a pinch. Not longer. Yet you have been eating our bread for . . . let me see, now"—he stared at the file open on the desk—"for sixty-six days. Three ounces of bread a day. Not much, you will say. And yet, in this war forced upon us by your race, we have to keep account of even such trifles as that. If we are compelled to act meanly at times, that again is your fault. But we won't go into that. Even you must admit, though, that there is something scandalous about this sixty-six-day record you have established . . . Another two days, and it will be Christmas. I'm going away on leave, to the town of P., and by hook or by crook your case has got to be closed before then. I propose an honest deal. You are a Jew: we both know that. So I suggest we come to a gentleman's agreement: if you will confess, if you will give me your real name, and the names of the people who fitted you up with your forged papers, then I give you my word of honor as an officer that you will be shot at once, without any further beating or interrogation. A bullet in the back of the neck doesn't hurt. Why make such a fuss about it? It isn't as bad as a visit to the dentist. You will go to heaven and see the world from above. For my part, I shan't be staying indefinitely in this town behind the lines. Once my job is finished, I shall be sent to the front and required to shoot at those damn-fool Russians. And I shall be alive with fleas, even more alive with them than you are now. I may lose an arm or a leg, and perhaps even my nuts. Not everyone has the opportunity that I am offering you now, the opportunity of being killed neatly and cleanly, with a single bullet. As for you, my little angel, you'll be free to look down on me and gloat over my misfortunes. For the sincere liking I feel for you isn't mutual, is it?"

As he spoke, the Lieutenant sat playing with his hands; and Boris, who was staring at them, perceived the Sign in their movements—the Sign which, from that morning on, was never to leave him.

Can this be a "dialogue" going on between Lesch and me? wondered Boris. Are we really sitting at the same desk? No, each of us is standing—and what a din!—on a separate balcony, overhanging a large square. He is shouting, but I cannot make out a word he is saying. In a moment, it will be I who am shouting to him, from a balcony set higher than his, a little higher, but my own voice is likewise too weak. The whole of humanity (though what an ugly, pedantic word "humanity" is!) is nothing but a mass of lunatics, of disturbed minds, each of whom is standing on his own balcony—set a bit higher or a bit lower above the big square—and hailing someone else, who is in turn apostrophizing someone else. But what a motley square it is, and how full of chariots and trees and dust! Resonant dust. This eternal resonant dust! My own balcony is set higher than Lesch's, but I am no better than he. Just as wretched, just as disturbed. Weary of this quest for the Essential that has been imposed on us—though by whom? For the Essential which may not exist. What a din! As though from the crow's-nest, I am now going to try to answer this little Lieutenant. But the wind is tearing our words to shreds . . .

After a pause for breath, Lesch went on: "Obviously there is another possibility, and one which frankly, for my own part, I would rather not contemplate. You may be stubborn and still refuse to confess, as you have done till now. In that case,

I can make you only one promise, and that also I am backing with my word of honor. According to the books that you people claim are holy (not being a theologian, I shall express no opinion on the subject), a human being—yourself, for example—has three hundred and sixty-five bones and ossicles in its body. Not one will be left intact. Just take a look at yourself in a mirror!"

He broke off for a moment: "Why, there IS no mirror in this room. Sentry! Hey there, sentry! Bring this gentleman a mirror, as quick as you can . . ."

Lesch put a cigarette between his lips. Four matches went out, one after another, before he managed to light it. The four matches, tossed heedlessly onto the desk, formed the Sign. And Boris, sure now of the safe outcome though less sure of his right to it, fell to wondering, like a distant, unconcerned onlooker: The breach exists, but when and where is it going to appear? He was no longer impatient for the answer. It was present, at hand. It was bound to come.

A mirror, doubtless stolen from a house whose inhabitants had embarked on the long journey, a large mahogany-framed mirror, was brought in by the sentry and set before the Lieutenant. From his jacket pocket, Lesch produced a comb and a small brush and started tidying his slightly tousled hair. It wasn't till several minutes later that he seemed suddenly to recall his visitor's presence.

"Well, come along then, Goletz! Take a look at yourself! You're not a pretty sight, you know. And if you don't confess, you'll be even less pretty—but you'll have no eyes to see yourself with."

For the first time in sixty-six days, Boris was looking at his own face. He felt sick. This face was more alien to him than Lesch's. Shall I really, he wondered, be obliged to wear this blue and yellow, this swollen and shapeless thing for the rest of my days? The wounds may heal, and the bruises and bumps fade, and the little red veinlets vanish from the whites of my eyes . . . A certain truth concerning my face has been revealed to me. I shall mistrust it, I shall hate it my whole life long, like a jealous lover who never forgets the single night that his mistress has spent in another man's arms. So this is one of the uses to which a face, MY face, can be put! Why, the knowledge is a release . . .

The breach that Boris was no longer troubled about finally appeared in the shape of a single word which Lesch, growing impatient of the silence, let fly as a closing argument:

"We've seen more than our share of 'Poles' like you . . ."

So that was it: the word "Poles" was the springboard which could not fail to propel him onto the grass of survival. And the game started to unfold, swiftly and in accordance with pre-established rules and moves:

"Yes, Lieutenant, you are quite right. I am not a Pole. I am a Ukrainian. I know you are going to kill me. You cannot possibly release me now. You have worked me over too thoroughly. None too proud of the idea of my parading myself with a face like this, are you? I've no illusions on that score . . . All the same, I'm not a Pole. Nor a Jew. And if I am to die now, I want to die as I was born: as a Ukrainian. I don't give a damn about your threats and your promises. I know what you are capable of. But just send for a single intellectual—yes, that's it: a single Ukrainian intellectual— and any doubts you have on that score will be removed at once. He'll perceive at once that I know things that no one else—whether he's Polish or Jewish or German—could possibly know. Traditions that are handed on from father to son in old Cossack families. Zaporozhean rites and customs unfamiliar to even your most erudite ethnologists, to even your most learned Herr Doktors . . . Go ahead, don't be afraid, send for somebody. And before you pack me off downstairs, allow me to tell you, Lieutenant, that you don't know your job. That's all!"

The vehemence of this speech was as great a surprise to Lesch as it was to Boris. Up to this point, the Lieutenant had regarded Goletz as a slow, defenseless insect, incapable of quick reactions, incapable even of intense fear, imprisoned in his colorless silence and immobility. And now suddenly this animal was bestirring itself. And what if he was telling the truth? After all, in the majority of cases the Ukrainians are our allies in these parts. We rely on them to administer the defeated nation. Obviously, it isn't of the slightest importance whether we gain one or lose one. But if I am a professional Jew-detector, if I have made extensive studies in typology and character reading, if I have learned to recognize the Untouchables, and to know their smell, and to spot their gestures, have I the right to be mistaken to such an extent?

All at once, Lesch felt like a mathematician who had stumbled over a multiplication table. Doubt stole into his heart, even though he still pretended to be wonderfully sure of himself: "Don't get so worked up, little Goletz. Your brazen impudence would give away your origins, even if nothing else did."

He made a show of playing with his revolver, but his absolute conviction had deserted him, and neither of them was taken in. With a magnanimous sweep of the arm, Lesch lifted the receiver: "Very well, you shall have your intellectual. And I'll bet the details he will concoct to add spice to your execution will handsomely repay our little venture. You will have brought it upon yourself. If I were in your shoes, I'd change my mind. The Ukrainians are thin-skinned, and my friend Humeniuk will be far from pleased to learn that a Jew is trying to pass himself off as a compatriot of his . . ."

There was a faint click.

"Hello, is that you, Humeniuk? Could you come to my office? That's right: at once. I've a case here that can't fail to interest you. That's right. A Jew who claims he's one of your countrymen. That's right. He claims he's a Ukrainian. Quite a novelty. Generally such customers try to pass themselves off as Poles. It's easier for them, because they know the language. This one is trying a completely new dodge. I'm relying on you to show him the folly of his pretense. See you shortly, then."

Still standing by the window, Boris gazed out at the branches and rooftops, covered with gray snow. He was sculpting his own weariness, carving little statuettes and toys and small objects of weird and wonderful design. And again and again, quite independently of his will, the shapes and outlines were disintegrating and re-forming in the pattern of the Sign.

They were waiting for the Ukrainian intellectual, Mr. Vassili Humeniuk, doctor of philosophy and member of the enemy police. Boris did not know him. Somewhere outside, Mr. Humeniuk was cleaving the cold air and splashing through the snow and mud on his way to join Lesch, whom he was to help reach a decision concerning the case of Yuri Goletz.

CHAPTER 33

Rinsed in waters clear and waters turbid, tall, rather stooping, with a face that retained a constant, animal attentiveness, even though its sensitivity and curiosity in things seemed to have been quite washed away, Humeniuk sported the invader's uniform the way some people sport celestial grace, grace sent from heaven a little too late. Doubtless he had greater density, a higher specific weight than Lesch, who had summoned him, but it was in Lesch that the power of life and death resided, and Humeniuk could only bow to the other man's congenital superiority.

All the same, the natural and supernatural gulf between the conqueror and his native-born assistants was not a thing that could properly be displayed in front of such a shady character—especially one suspected of impure origins, and consequently doomed to extermination. The two gentlemen therefore exchanged courteous salutes (though they didn't, it's true, shake hands) and even a knowing smile. But something whispered to Boris that there was a crack at the bottom of this smile.

Was a fellow feeling between men of the great plain, between heirs of the Scythians, developing between Boris and Humeniuk the Horsy? If so, Boris said to himself, it will be against my will, without my seeking. And yet, may not Humeniuk's forefathers have worked on the estates of the princes to whom my own forefathers lent money? Or again, when the opportunity presented itself, did they not slaughter my ancestors, whose children they fondled, in the good old days when pogroms, cruel though they were, were at least not final and conclusive? Be that as it may, I know you, my good Humeniuk. I know the landscape that molded and nourished you. I know the songs that surrounded your cradle and the colors of the ceremonial costumes worn by your mother and your peasant grandmothers. Likewise, I know the road that led you from the stable to the palace antechamber, and from there to the lecture room and to the cheap lodgings you had as a hungry and painfully earnest student. I can picture your winter afternoons in a strange town, which to you seemed immense and inhuman, and your evenings in shabby, unheated rooms, and your humiliations and your longings. And the latest stage in your journey, the one that brought you here to this room, in their pay. You can scent yourself as much as you like with that ghastly eau de Cologne for which junior officers trade their coupons, but you will never be able to dispel that smell of hayricks and stables which is yours and which it is impossible for me not to love, just as I love your past daydreams and love this love—such a delicate vibration, as though it already belonged to the past, to A past . . .

Lesch broke in upon the silence: "My dear Humeniuk, I explained the situation to you over the phone. You are exactly the kind of Ukrainian intellectual by whom this Jewboy asked to be confronted. Question him, wear him down, hit him, do as you like to him, but let's get it over. I'm hungry and I've really had enough of this case!"

Humeniuk did not even glance up at Boris. Clenching his

teeth, he flung out a question like a sour village schoolteacher, displeased with his pupil's answer even before he hears it:

"Who is the greatest Ukrainian poet?"

It was then that the game began to amuse Boris. His brain was working as it hadn't worked for a long time. He thought: If a man wishes to prove he is an Englishman, and a well-educated Englishman, he will prove nothing by answering "Shakespeare" or "Byron" to such a question. Of course not, for everyone has heard of Shakespeare and Byron, whether English or not. On the contrary, what he must do is imply, and get his interrogator to acknowledge the implication, that it is unthinkable he should be asked such a question. He must immediately mention some such figure as Eliot or Edith Sitwell. In the same situation, a Frenchman, a REAL, well-educated Frenchman, could not possibly answer "Ronsard" or "Victor Hugo." In that way, he would be proving nothing. It is only by alluding to a Lautréamont or a Milosz that he would give proof, if not of his French origins, at least of his degree of initiation in matters pertaining to France. Well now, in asking me who is the greatest Ukrainian poet, our friend is expecting me to voice one name and one name only: that of their bard, Tara Shevchenko . . . But everybody here—not just the Ukrainians, but the Russians, Poles, and Jews living in the Ukraine—knows that this singer of the serfs' hardships and of Cossack pride IS the glory of your nation. That's stale. If I were to cite Shevchenko, I'd please you, my good Humeniuk, but I wouldn't appeal to your imagination and, most important of all, I wouldn't prove anything to you. I need, or rather YOU need, something quite different.

And Boris named an avant-garde poet who had died not long before, at the age of twenty-nine, an old friend of his, known and loved by perhaps two hundred readers. Like a Horace aiming to transplant Hellenic rhythms onto the soil of Italy, this man—Ihor Hranich—had tried to graft surreal-ist shoots onto the tree of young Ukrainian poetry. Much good did it do him. Shortly before the war, he succumbed to the inevitable and proverbial tragic tuberculosis, in his parents' cottage. Massive and inconsolable was their grief at the death of this son, whom they had raised and educated at such cost to themselves and who, had he only followed their heartfelt wishes, might have made a good country priest, and perhaps even a bishop.

My poor Ihor, Boris said to himself, to think that I should be using your name—the name of somebody dead and buried, of somebody I loved—as a life line. It deserved a better fate, as we both know.

Humeniuk leapt up in protest: "What else could I have expected from a gallows-bird like you! You have the nerve to say that Hranich, poor twisted devil, is our greatest poet! That he is a poet at all! Why, you're joking! I knew friend Hranich, he used to make me feel sorry for him. To be frank, I've never understood a word he wrote, and I don't think there IS anything to understand . . . His work is a crazy quilt of gibberish just about on the level of a child of four . . ."

"That may be your opinion," said Boris "but it isn't mine. You asked me a question, and I answered it as honestly as I could."

"Honestly, honestly . . ." Humeniuk was entering more and more fully into his role as a schoolmaster called upon to examine a pupil, who might be brilliant but who was also alarming and eccentric.

"Well, we don't see eye to eye on that score. Not by a long shot. We'd better forget about poets and turn to more down-to-earth matters."

The Ukrainian in which Humeniuk was expressing him-

self was somewhat artificial. A sensitive ear would have detected traces of the years he had spent in non-Slav countries.
But his usage was correct, elegant even. As for Boris, he was
familiar with every refinement of this tongue, which for him
was filled with the scent of summer evenings on the banks of
the Dniester: marsh tongue, steppe tongue, twilight tongue,
water tongue.

Humeniuk was proceeding with his task: Name the leading prewar Ukrainian newspapers.

Name the chief political parties.

This examination was a witches' Sabbath, a Walpurgis
Night. But Boris was in supreme control of its successive
starts and finishes. Like a turn performed by white mice, intoxicated by drink yet obeying the finger and eye of him who
holds the threads, who prompts and checks their every leap,
their every trick, their every skilled *entrechat*—this discussion, down to every detail, was going exactly as Boris's will
intended. He gave the wires another jerk, and the conversation degenerated, just as he had wished, into a quarrel. They
wrangled. They raised their voices. Poor Lesch, quite forgotten, looked on—dumb as an oyster—at this tussle between
two men of the East, conducted in a language that he couldn't
understand. And even if he had understood it, he would have
been quite lost in this welter of claims and counterclaims, of
recriminations mortal and venial. Humeniuk wasn't cheating. He was defending, with all his heart, his opinion that it
had been only right for the sons of an oppressed nation, which
had been prevented for hundreds of years from becoming a
state, to don the uniform of the conquering power. Boris, on
his side, was arguing: "But can't you see they are leading us
by the nose? They aren't letting us enjoy the fruits of a victory which may be short-lived. Which WILL be short-lived.
But if they meet with defeat, we shall be associated with

it. Our young men are fighting under foreign banners, yet though he promised us our independence, the invader wouldn't even proclaim Kiev the state capital. A gesture that would have cost him nothing, since the real power remains in his hands anyway, for as long as the war continues. He didn't even deign to recognize the government which we had prepared, even though it would have been his staunchest ally. As for our ministers, you know as well as I do what he did with them. It hurts me to speak of such an outrage. Your bosses want everything for themselves. In the end, they will be left empty-handed."

Boris's nationalism was pure and wholly messianic. He loathed compromising.

Humeniuk: "You are unrealistic, young man. With your insane intransigence, you and your likes are going to rob us of the only opportunity that has come our way in decades. Partnership with them, whatever our private feelings, is our one hope of achieving anything real, anything tangible. We mustn't besot ourselves with big words like independence and sovereignty. We must begin with small concrete tasks. This is the first time our generation has had a say, a small say, in the running of this country—which is, after all, our own. They are ridding our land of the Jewish pestilence. To do so, they need our help, for without it they would be incapable of tracking down and unmasking and identifying those Jews who are in hiding. True, we would rather they began with the Poles, but for political reasons which are theirs and not ours they will not or cannot. Not yet, at least. What is our role in all this? Are we to sulk and hang back because their timing of events doesn't entirely coincide with our wishes? No, and no again! We must make ourselves useful and indispensable. We must learn whatever we can from them. Away with false ambitions. We must accept any parti-

cle of power that is offered to us, irrespective of its size and
origin. How are you to know that, once the Jewish chapter is closed, we won't be called upon to rid this country of
Poles and Russians and gypsies . . . ? And if that happens, then whatever the outcome of the present military campaign we shall have a homogeneous territory, truly our own.
Call it what you like: independence, autonomy, or protec-
torate. There are plenty of dependences that end in freedom,
and plenty of independences that get further and further
away from it. What difference does it make to us? Our goal is
still the same. And if they help us to draw even an inch
closer to that goal, it is only right for us to co-operate. And
that is our SOLE duty at the moment."

He looked Boris straight in the eye. It was Boris's turn to
ask a question:

"Do you know Kiev, Mr. Humeniuk? Have you ever been
to our former capital . . . ? I've lived there."

He was scanning Humeniuk's face. That face in flight, that
flight of a face. Once, while he was still only a child, Boris had
seen the body of a hare that had been killed by an eagle. This
hare had lain on the roadside for three whole days, devoured by the ants and washed by the rain. Humeniuk's face
was at this moment the very image of the dead little animal's.

Humeniuk was stupefied. Could he have misheard Boris's
question, a question so incongruous and astonishing?

"Kiev?" he said. "Kiev?"

"Well, Mr. Humeniuk, I've been to Kiev and I've stayed
there. It is the most beautiful town in the world. A miracle,
THE miracle of humility. When spring comes to its
outlying districts, the smell of the earth isn't something vague
and fleeting; it is yearning and the object of that yearning,
passion and its appeasement. It is lovesickness and its remedy.
At first, you feel a yearning. Then you are no longer capable

of that, and all you feel is a yearning for your own yearning,
and so on. That is the path that leads away from life. But
what if we turned our scale of values upside down . . . What
if yearning became more precious than its object, and yearning for a yearning became purer and more precious than the
original afterimage? There, perhaps, lies the enigma, the
immortality of Kiev. I have watched the current of the Dnieper in March, full of ice and uprooted willows. The whole
scene is gray, but I wouldn't swap its universe-containing grayness for even the loveliest girl or the most radiant landscape. Kiev is the stained-glass window of a cathedral which
no one has ever yet dared to build. I know the caves and the
underground passages which, as used to be thought in the
old days, and as I still think, lead directly to Mount Athos, to
Jerusalem, to Paradise.

"There are little wooden cottages in pink and green, quite
clearly reflected in the river. In a procession around you
are cherry trees—yes, miraculous cherry trees, the equal of
those in Japan. It was in this town—all river, all honey, all
fresh breezes—that our destiny took root, twelve centuries
ago. The town where our spirit was born . . . They stole it
from us. They arrested the members of the government
which we had constituted there and which was, as it were, the
heart of a free man. They didn't even shoot them. That, presumably, would have been too noble, too chivalrous. They
transported them, ignominiously, with common criminals,
with Jews, with the very worst kind of riffraff; they made
them peel potatoes and polish boots. Their boots. That was
the ultimate outrage. All we asked was to be their allies, to
die for the common cause. They spat on the fraternity that we
had offered them.

"And after all that, Humeniuk, you strut about in their

uniform and feel happy when they entrust their dirty little jobs to you . . ."

At this point, Boris ran out of breath. His spirit was appeased. He had just thought of his uncle Zachariah, who had been dead for years. Zachariah would neither have lied nor have made a speech like Boris's. He would have remained silent. Can it be, he wondered, that our only real betrayal is the one we commit against silence?

Meanwhile, Humeniuk seemed to be searching desperately for a reply; but it was not forthcoming. The time for arguing had passed. Now was the time for bidding, for rivalry between two loves, and Boris's was the stronger.

Humeniuk stammered: "I know Kiev, too . . ."

Then, in a voice turned suddenly furious: "But what has that to do with it? You stand accused of . . . you know what. You've got yourself in a fine mess. You're all the same, when it comes to the point. You're irresponsible. You're criminals. Look at my uniform and look at your rags . . ."

So this is his only argument, thought Boris. He has no other. And he knows it. He will try to save me. Otherwise, he won't be able to return to his rut. My love for the town, his town and mine, is more convincing than his instinct, than reality . . . As for his rage, he loves me really, he loves me already. My words have sunk in like a seed. There will be no peace of mind for him after this. I've turned a policeman into a knight-errant in a cause that isn't my own. Not quite my own . . ."

Humeniuk looked up. He shouted hoarsely at the sentries: "Get this heap of dung out of here, and be quick about it!"

And, turning to Lesch: "That's no Jew. Take my word for it, he couldn't be. He's trash, of course. Politically, I wouldn't trust him an inch. But as for being a Ukrainian—alas, he is . . ."

"Good God!" said Lesch. "I'd never have believed it. You mean to say even a turd like that can entertain political ideas? Why, how absurd . . . You amaze me, my dear Humeniuk . . ."

The observation was ambiguous. It could be aimed equally well at Goletz and at his compatriot, who had just been having such a heated argument with him. The shaft went home, yet Humeniuk continued, imperturbably: "As I said: politically, I wouldn't trust him an inch. A pernicious character, on quite the wrong side of the fence. But he isn't a Jew. No question of that. He speaks our language too well, he knows too much about our history, our literature, our way of life . . ."

Lesch: "But he is circumcised."

Humeniuk: "True—I'd forgotten that! But it makes no difference. We must ask him how it happened. His circumcision amazes me every bit as much as it does you. But as for his being a Jew, I'll never accept that. Not in a thousand years. I'm not mistaken. I cannot be mistaken . . ."

Boris was summoned back from the corridor into the comforting presence of Humeniuk. Humeniuk was more horsy than ever. And Boris loved horses.

It was Lesch who spoke—and who spoke, in spite of everything, with renewed interest. The surgical nature of his question harmonized better with this police smell than did passionate speeches concerning a nation's legendary past:

"How do you come to be circumcised?"

Boris was silent. The town of Krasnoy is on the other side of the front, he reasoned. They'll have no means of checking my story. But they won't admit that. Not one of them under the rank of General is prepared to confess that they don't lay down the law in New York and in Moscow and on Venus.

They have no *raison d'être* other than ruling the world, the whole wide world. The absolute is not prunable; if it were, it would cease to be absolute. Their minds are incapable of accepting the slightest limitation to their omnipotence.

Then Boris spoke. The fire had gone out with which he had conjured up pictures of Kiev and the Dnieper and the skiffs of the early Varangians. A little village idiot, rather bewildered and too obtuse to tell lies, was relating his little tale:

"In 193..., I lived in Krasnoy. In the narrow street beside the mill. I went to see a tart: Olena, Fat Olena. Everyone went to her, and one day my friends took me along. Three days later, it started itching and discharging. I kept hoping it would clear up of its own accord. I was ashamed. I went about like that for weeks. In the end, I couldn't walk another step. My glands had swollen up like a pair of apples. I was completely laid up.

"So I helped myself to some of my mother's money and went off to see Dr. Stankivich. Getting on in years, he was. Wore a goatee. He lived in . . . he lived in Fountain Street. He put me on a course of treatment. It lasted two whole months. Not a day went by without his injecting me in the prick. And I pissed red and blue and green . . . All the colors of the rainbow. No, not all. I never pissed black.

"Anyway, as soon as he saw my bollocks this doctor said to me: 'Your little tool's in rather a bad way. You should have come and seen me sooner. You're all alike, there was nothing to be ashamed of . . .' Well, to cut a long story short, I had an inflammation and then . . . phimosis. So I had to be circumcised. I cried openly in front of the doctor—I was just a kid, you know. 'I don't want to look like a Jew-boy,' I told him. To which old Stankivich said: 'You needn't worry yourself on that score, sonny. Any doctor will always be able to tell that, by the time you were operated on, you were already a grown man. Besides, it will be healthier for you, it will be cleaner . . .' "

Long shadows were settling on the walls of Lesch's office. Boris was staring at the small square patch of sky beyond the frosty window. Between the hovering bird and the sky, there is flight, unaccomplished flight. We are all at the bottom of a spittoon, and I'm there for just the same reason as these characters. If only a shell could burst . . . Why are you so long in coming, where are you hiding your glory, O incandescent, O fraternal shell? Coherence, you say? All coherence is a spittoon . . .

This was what was passing through Boris's head, while his tongue and his parched lips were still retailing their merchandise.

Now they were convinced and satisfied. Humeniuk would no longer have his country's blood on his hands. Lesch's conception of the universe would not be upset.

A faint smile lit up Lesch's face: "If you are telling the truth"—*and he knows I am, he knows I am,* a voice was shouting in Boris's brain—"if you are telling the truth, we are going to get a doctor to look at you. He will settle the matter. But if you are leading us up the garden path . . . that would be a pity, a pity for you and for all the trouble I have gone to. Never before has a Yid made me sweat blood the way you have . . . Well, we must wait and see what happens. You will now be taken back to your cell. I shall give orders for you to be taken to the prison medical officer tomorrow. We must settle things one way or the other. The joke has lasted long enough . . ."

In polite reproach, Lesch's eyes came to rest on Humeniuk's impassive face.

CHAPTER 34

Had it not been for the smell of disinfectant, the tiny prison infirmary would have been cozy. Pine logs gave a white heat to the cast-iron stove. Boris stood eying the plump nurse. In her misty hazel eyes he saw a glimmer of interest, perhaps of fellow feeling. He was trembling inwardly at the sight of the twin globes rising and falling beneath her white coveralls, to the rhythm of her heavy breathing. How disappointing: this bluish tool, this factory for producing metaphysics, all my metaphysics, has come through my shipwrecks. Yet shall I ever be freed of this obsession? So the death that I am now cheating is not mighty enough to prevent the first pair of breasts I have seen in months (though what breasts!) from still seeming the magnet of existence, the fountainhead of the divine. "O man—impatient flame!"

Outside, the squall was forcing the army of snowflakes to carry out queer, impassioned maneuvers. It was warm in the infirmary. Boris wasn't out of harm's way yet—far from it!—but he was thinking of the burden of existing without restrictions, a way of life that was threatening to become his again. "And the Word will fulfill its destiny by becoming flesh, so that flesh may fulfill its destiny, turning to smoke . . ."—was it Leo L. who had once uttered these words . . . ? When one is hand in glove with death, life is a betrayal. And a betrayal that doesn't pay.

When all was said and done, what reason could the doctor have for ratifying this tall story about contracting phimosis? All might not be lost. With a hint of nostalgia, Boris envisaged, as though it were a lover's tryst that had not been kept, the bullet in the back of the neck which the worthy Lesch had once promised him. But at this point, the gears of salvation began to turn: the doctor walked into the room. He was a slightly stooping figure, with black hair and prominent cheekbones. He looked consumptive: good-natured and consumptive. A pair of hefty prison warders stood behind Boris as he fumblingly undid his fly buttons with his manacled hands. He was sure of himself and perhaps too sure of the doctor's reaction. He spoke as a man of the world, eager to clear up a slight misunderstanding which was rather embarrassing, but primarily absurd:

"Well now, Doctor, this is the situation: they've arrested me and locked me up in here, claiming that I am a Jew. Would you believe such a thing? Now, I'm no Jew, I'm a Ukrainian. That, I should have thought, was obvious to everyone except the police, whose minds are inevitably dulled by the practice of their trade. I am relying on you, Doctor, to show these gentlemen—if nothing else—how little they know about anatomy. It's getting beyond a joke. Some years ago, I contracted phimosis, and the doctor I had at the time carried out an operation. He was quite positive that any surgeon would be able to spot the difference between his handiwork and that of the Jewish mohels . . . And that is the whole story."

Was Boris's casualness exaggerated? Had his immediate impression of the doctor been too hasty? By averting her head from Boris's exposed penis, was the nurse trying to convey a message to him, trying to show him he was making a blunder?

The bulb hanging from the ceiling was casting its reflection outside: a second bulb hanging amid the multiude of snow-flakes. Boris gazed out of the window. He knew that he had no other home, apart from this prison to which destiny had brought him. Even vagrancy was timeworn. Even if things turned out in his favor, what would he do? Would he find Naomi and his family and friends anywhere but in the abyss of the past, where he would figure shabbily as a latecomer?

Attentively, as one ponders an abstract idea, the doctor pondered the depersonalized, humiliated penis whose owner, in turn, was pondering the nurse: This is one I shall never have, not even if I DO get out of here. Not unless she's a necro-phile . . . Passive necrophilia: an experience one has yet to reap . . .

As though unwilling to perceive it, the doctor declined the personal bond hinted at by Boris's free-and-easy remarks.

"Look, Mr. Goletz"—he laid stress on the "Mister"—"it may be that your story is truthful. That is for the police to decide, not for me. As for my pronouncing on the anatomical problem that you have laid before me, the responsibility seems to me a very grave one . . . Besides," he added, as though to himself, "I have a wife and children. And I am not a surgeon. Thank God. If these gentlemen think it worth while, they have only to send you to a surgeon. That is all I can say."

In the intricate mechanism of survival, something was creaking. Did a cogwheel, a piston, need changing? But now that it had been set in motion, the performance must proceed. There could be no dropping of the curtain.

CHAPTER 35

Early next morning, the warders came and got him from his cell. He was weak and shivering. He was afraid of leaving prison, just as some people are afraid of leaving life, like fetuses unwilling to emerge from the womb.

" 'Time goes by.' The phrase doesn't mean much," one of the shoemakers had explained the night before. "Every day, heaven sends every man and beast and object a tiny scale that links up with the armor of their past. Woe betide him who has been robbed of this armor . . . ! But sometimes there is an exchange of armors: between animal and man, between man and house, between man and man. And when that happens, there is confusion on earth and in heaven."

He will live, Yuri Goletz will live, this laborer from a farm that existed at no time and in no place. He will drag his bones toward that no-place, toward that emptiness which had bitten into Boris's substance. Boris should have gone to the grave long ago, to join his spirit and his fellows. But he himself and all that surrounded him had mostly been no more than a caricature of tragedy, no more than a caricature of eruption. Just as my notes, *writes Boris,* will be no more than the caricature of an eruption. Obsessive hunger has nothing in common with normal hunger.

* * *

The sky was invisible. Like an infinitely sharp knife, the fresh December air took Boris's breath away. Shackled hand and foot, and surrounded by four guards, whose rifles were aimed at his body, Boris was on his way to the military hospital where the surgeons were to deliver their verdict. He was dazzled by the pale morning light. As though in some grotesque ballet, trees and cottages would leap up and waltz, silently accompanying the procession formed by Boris and his guards.

The nurses, in their nunlike headdress, silently withdrew and lowered their eyes in mawkish compassion. The whiteness of the walls and the smell of carbolic were like a mallet blow to Boris. He nearly lost consciousness, but the dizziness did not last.

And there he was, unbuttoning his trousers with his manacled hands and baring, yet again, the organ on which the sign of the Covenant had been inscribed years before.

Did this door still open onto God? Did it at least open onto the Divine . . . ? Dull rites, dull symbols, and those which are less so: are the Covenant with God and physical passion, sharing the same site and founded in the same crucible, the same thing . . . ? Could the Biblical patriarch, that forefather clad in the red desert and resonant dust, have foreseen this thought of mine? Did he set me a playful riddle, one that I am succeeding in solving after thousands of years —at the LAST moment?

Boris trotted out his fabricated little yarn to the two medical officers, and felt no shame at doing so, merely a slightly amused weariness . . . It was the doctors who looked embarrassed, in their brand-new uniforms, with their firm, assured gestures. After a momentary hesitation, the younger one took hold of the piece of bruised, bluish flesh, as though handling an inert object. From the pocket of his white cover-

alls, which now inadequately concealed the uniform under-
neath, he drew a slim torch and conscientiously examined
the wrinkles and cracks on the surface of the depersonalized
skin. He seemed oblivious to Boris's presence. His eyes, devoid of all expression, stared clean through Boris, who just
stood there, motionless.

The doctor said, addressing his superior: "Quite honestly,
Major, I cannot give an opinion. It looks like a ritual circumcision, but it might equally well be something quite
harmless, the relic of an operation performed more or less
recently. Kindly look at this fold . . . and now at this scar.
How insane of them to expect us to determine whether the
job was done five years ago or TWENTY-five. The present condition would be the same in both cases."

With a helpless look on his face, he turned to the Major.

The latter was a tall, corpulent, rosy-cheeked man, with a
distinctly rustic air. Boris didn't know whether the Major
had heard a word of his story. The Major's thoughts—if indeed his fat shiny tomato of a head contained anything whatever at the moment—must have been far, far away, hovering
perhaps over the kitchen garden adjoining the Major's
little house in some medium-sized provincial town, a university town no doubt, where he lived in the bosom of his large,
his homely and respectable family.

Pitched into this barbarous region, as head of a military
hospital behind the lines, he was bound to regard the people
and things around him as beneath his notice. It would be
asking too much of this doctor in uniform to expect him to
pay much heed to the destinies of the people he encountered
in these parts, or to try to fathom their peculiar needs and
desires. So there was still a chance . . .

Now it was the Major's turn to take the disputed item in

his rubber-gloved hands. A ghost of a smile flitted across his face. But it was gone so quickly that long afterwards Boris was to wonder whether he hadn't simply imagined it. The Major didn't say a word to Boris. He turned to his assistant; he seemed to have barely glanced at the small expanse of whitish skin, which to Boris felt a distinctly foreign body. In a professorial and slightly domineering tone, the Major made a series of quick points to his junior: "You are mistaken, my dear colleague. It is perfectly possible for us to make a conclusive pronouncement. Why, just look at this! And this . . . !" He produced a small magnifying glass and handed it obligingly to his associate. "This fellow is quite right. As I'm sure you know, in the case of Jews one is dealing with a circumcision. In the case of this man, all one can see is a concision. Here you can see the scar left by the operation. It's still quite distinct even after six years, and who can wonder? But had it resulted from a ritual act performed twenty years ago, one could never have detected such a scar. And that isn't all. Just look at that! And that! Feel for yourself . . ."

With his manacled hands, Boris refastened his trousers. He was going to have to live. Between fear of dying and repugnance for living, would no "neutral zone" ever emerge?

He could hear the Major, in the next room, dictating an official certificate to a shorthand-typist:

" 'On the person of Yuri Goletz, a Ukrainian born in Krasnoy on November 4, 19. . . , an oval-shaped scar, length as follows, has been authenticated as the result of an operation made necessary by an attack of phimosis . . .' And rubber-stamp it, Lise. Yes, that's right: use the military hospital stamp, the one with the eagle and swastika on it."

Boris emerged from the hospital, surrounded by his guards. The sharpness of the air and the shrillness of the light, unfiltered by bars, made him reel. One of the guards handed Boris a cigarette. Another rushed forward to give him a light.

By now, they were right out in the open. The sparkling snow crunched under the weight of heavy army boots.

"Why, you're mad," said one of the guards, "to travel about with such a defect in times like these. Has it even occurred to you that you were within an inch of death? The amazing part of it, to me, is that they should have gone to all this trouble, with doctors and such, to get to the truth of the matter. It was touch and go with you—you don't realize. When we come across a suspicious-looking character with a tool like yours, our orders are to shoot him immediately. For the Yids are emerging from their ghettos by the hundreds now. Like rats from a sinking ship . . ."

Another of the guards bent his head toward Boris's: "Poor fellow, what a mess they made of your face. And I don't suppose you'll get anything out of them by way of damages. But hell, you've been lucky, incredibly lucky . . . Our Lesch has done a good job. Isn't your name Goletz? My wife has some relatives called that. I suppose you don't come from Tarnopol way, do you?"

"No, I don't," said Boris, "but I seem to remember we had cousins in that part of the country . . ."

"Poor devil, poor devil . . . As soon as they let you out, come and look me up. My wife will be delighted. She'll cook something special for you: a bacon *kasha*, say . . . Why, you poor devil . . ."

These words were all that he now had ears for. For the first time since it had all started, he was being shown obvious human warmth. He records that the experience gave him a certain pleasure. The killers were making a little room for him at their table. He was becoming an associate—not a full member, but an associate all the same—of the "Uncircumcised, the associates of death." [1]

The prison governor received Boris in his room. The prison smell, which was more or less that of urine itself, was not absent even from this office. The smell of bare bones, of chilled steam. The room seemed magnificent, after the cell . . .

The governor rose from his chair: "My dear Goletz, I deeply regret the treatment that we and your cellmates have inflicted on you. Naturally, I knew all about it. In our profession . . . But I let things take their course. I have just informed them of the results of the inquiry. I am taking steps for you to be freed as soon as possible. Perhaps this very evening. Anyway, we'll see about that . . ."

Back in his cell, Boris detected a sense of occasion around him. As in the past, he spoke to no one, but simply lowered himself onto the concrete floor in one of the corners and shut his eyes. He thought of Naomi, and a huge fear gripped his empty bowels; within the walls of his skull, a fluid, a slimy fluid. His brain was curdling, was it? "My thoughts are with you, O my little queen Karomama" [2]—was that it? Without uttering a sound, he murmured to himself:

Whole worlds were bristling inside his head, full of klaxons and hostility. Their stiff black hairs were rubbing against the walls of his brain. The pain, secreted by rubbing, and solidifying in a flash, without treating itself to the gentle luxury of remaining a liquid, if only for a second—this pain was floating like a battleship in the liquid. And what was this liquid? Was it I, was it she, was it "everything"?

[1] Czeslaw Milosz.
[2] O. Milosz.

A hand settled on Boris's shoulder. The notary was standing over him, looking rather embarrassed, in an attitude
which he supposed was that of a man of the world.

"My dear Mr. Goletz, it is not simply in my capacity as a
private human being that I am addressing you now. I have
been unanimously entrusted with the task by our comrades.
They have 'elected' me—that is the word. Furthermore
. . . my own conscience impels me to redress the wrongs
that we have all perpetrated against you. Throughout the
long weeks of enforced cohabitation and shared sufferings,
we have treated you harshly—yes, harshly and in a manner
which, to be quite blunt, was inhumane. Do not deny it.
We are deeply sorry, and we tender our apologies, our heartfelt apologies. But I have another purpose in speaking to
you . . . We wish to enter a plea of extenuating circumstances.

"You will admit that in this tragic—yes, tragic—misunderstanding, all the evidence pointed against you. We were
not pretending: we really believed that you belonged to that
accursed race, and we treated you accordingly. Be honest—
had you been in our shoes, would you have acted otherwise?"

This was apparently a purely rhetorical question, but Boris
could stand no more of this flow of eloquence. He was thinking of Redheaded Helen, Abracha's aunt, and of the loneliness that she had predicted for him.

"I quite understand, my dear sir," he said, "and—yes, had
I been in your shoes, I should have acted in precisely the
same manner. Indeed, I make myself a promise: I SHALL act
in that manner, I SHALL follow your example, should the
circumstances arise one day. But what do you want of me
now?"

The notary refused to be put off.

"What do we want of you? Why, we want your forgive-

ness, your forgiveness and your fraternal friendship. I am a
Pole. You are a Ukrainian. There may have been misunderstandings of a political nature between us. Hatred, even.
But all that is over and done with. The same blood—Slav
and Aryan—flows in our veins. In the face of this common
disaster, we must help one another and—let us not be afraid
of the word—love one another. There is no real gulf between us . . . Don't bear us a grudge, Mr. Goletz. We were
unfair, but our conduct was pure in origin. Here is my
hand . . ."

And, slowly, Boris extended his own as a trite thought
flashed through his mind: My hand is no more mine, now,
than is my penis. It belongs to Goletz. Let us give ourselves
over to the joys of fraternity. But how does a man like Goletz
give expression to joy? I'd almost forgotten him.

A broad smile appeared on his ravaged face.

"Very well then, sir, let us be friends. And may our Lord
forgive you, as I forgive you all . . ."

The scene was not yet over, however. There was a catch
in the notary's courtesy.

"Mr. Goletz, you will be leaving here shortly. My colleagues and I would like to ask you to perform a number of
more or less delicate services for us. If you COULD, for example,
call on my sister, Mrs. B., and tell her that I haven't faltered,
that my patriotic zeal is quite unsapped, and that I expect AT
LEAST one parcel a week from her. You don't need telling
what the food we get here is like . . . Then Z., poor devil,
would like to have his family informed of his needs, and he
also wishes a number of papers in his house to be destroyed
. . . Since we have no pencil in here, and since, in any case,
there is a danger of your being searched when you leave, you
had better learn the addresses by heart . . ."

The village shoemaker, the one who had killed his wife,

had no requests to make. Deep in his steady eyes, Boris thought he could detect a quiet hint of irony. Boris made no comment. It was at this moment that, after exchanging winks with the others, the notary came out with it:

"Naturally, while you were away today, there was the usual issue of broth. I know you always used to receive the least substantial portions, with no potatoes and no meat. We have, so to speak, pooled our wretched resources, we have clubbed together so that today your meal shall be somewhat less frugal . . ."

Eight potatoes, plump and white as little lambs, were produced from a hiding place at the back of the cupboard and solemnly handed to Boris. Was this an attempt at bribery, with an eye to the errands that they had entrusted to him, or was it really an act of moral reparation? Boris ate the potatoes with genuine emotion. It was the most important happening of the day, and of all the preceding months, perhaps.

At all events, he told himself sleepily, no more interrogations; a chapter has been closed.

The rays of the setting sun were struggling through the grimy panes of the barred window. The sordid interior of the cell displayed itself to Boris's gaze as though he were seeing it for the first time. The metal pail, the old straw scattered over the concrete, the faces of his false companions in fate, who were already receding into the past . . . Leo L. had maintained there was only one thing more horrible than Horror: the routine day, the commonplace, ourselves without the framework imposed by Horror. "God created death. He created life. I'll grant you that," L.L. would declaim. "But don't tell me it was He who created the 'ordinay day,' 'everyday life,' as well. My impiety is great, I'll admit. But it shrinks from that slander, from that blasphemy."

So I've got away with it, thought Boris. And what good has that done me? Outside, it's cold and naked. In here, I had a home. I love them, I always have loved them, for my false hatred and my false contempt were enjoyable. That isn't the only reason.

Perhaps one day I shall try to capture this scene. If I do, a niggardly demon will do its best to rob me of every destitute word that might serve to describe the objects and human beings surrounding me here and now, so close and so tangible— human beings with whom I don't know what to do, except love them. I shall have obstinately to snatch from this jealous demon every word that is even slightly appropriate, and it will be a harder battle than the one in which I have just gained victory. More shameful, too, like everything that serves to describe, to debase reality. Only one sin is graver: that against unreality.

"Is it not the act of writing, of wielding the pen in pursuit of dispersing images, that most closely relates man to insect? And the laborious dissection of phenomena and space? And the movements of the brain, so ugly and so crafty?"

Was Boris already perceiving what language and, in consequence, the simple-languaged (who exist as surely as the simple-minded) generally term "the future," though it is really no more than a linear sign engraved on the skin of our minds and of our bodies, than a sign sometimes multiplied by prayer?

In his light sleep, Boris saw the Man buried up to his neck among refuse and garbage whom he had formerly seen in the little camp lost in the heart of the forest. How am I to go on? Where will my future paths lead me? The only lively hatred of which I am capable, I dedicate here and now to

those future paths. What of Naomi, the child who was entrusted to me? Shall I find her again here on earth? Where am
I to look for her and where am I to take her?

Soon I shall be free. The future is an abscess to be lopped
off. And, softly and testily, he added: I shall be far from this
warm and pacifying frame which used to contain me, which
still contains me. Its absence has too bitter a taste . . .

But Boris was mistaken.

Coda

The story of the tool ends here, with this remark and with this image which might be denounced as a happy ending. But it does not end entirely. Do not let this amaze you. There are many things that have to end but that do not manage to "end entirely." Which is just too bad for logic.

The story of the tool had repercussions in the great Plain of the Birches, the plain that was to make the world rub its eyes in wonder. But I shall spare you those, for the moment . . . As for the Plain of the Birches, in addition to its inexpressible greatness it likewise harbored stories no less gripping than that of the tool. For example: the story of the flowerpot-man who, buried in the eternal mud, like Francis of Assisi exposed to the birds and the flies, and to men as well, his noble if somewhat soiled and awesome head. If God permits, and if such is your pleasure, I shall tell it to you, along with many others.

To assuage your curiosity, and to satisfy the rules of composition, so ill-treated and discontented, I shall confirm what you no doubt guessed right at the start: the man with the tool steeped in shoddy misfortunes and the head brimming over with comparisons, the fellow who figured as the hero in this tale—has come through it all alive.

From time to time I take a corner seat in this vile café in the Boulevard Montparnasse where, one August afternoon, I had first met Boris and opened this story, which is his, "the way one opens a shop." The damned of the earth are there; they haunt the place, and will go on haunting it for all eternity. They are poor and they sweat, "those at least whose bodies retain the paltry gift of sweating."

On each of their faces, the same printed notice: "What's new?" And the answer: "As though anything could be new in this dreary world . . ." And, one stage higher, another question, shyer this time, and more veiled: "Is it quite necessary to term the world 'dreary,' in view of the fact that we are part of it, we sitting here, we the sublime . . . ?"

Out of all this crowd, there is one man who is beginning to intrigue me. He has had a dazzling career: he has become his own nose, endowed with a network of ultrasensitive nerves, like the wing of a bat in a museum or a grotesquely complicated ordnance survey map. What a vigorous and independent life this network leads! A nose that dreams, smiles, apologizes . . . He is beginning to sense the interest that I take in him. Perhaps one of these days he will honor me with a long story. I try to be cautious.

Once I managed to pick up a little sentence that he had just uttered, and which made me ponder long and hard. It may have been only a stanza, but it seemed to carry the weight of a philosophical treatise:

> Well then, every one of us
> Is only a hearse,
> A fairly battered hearse
> Transparent and almost empty.

This "almost empty," I must confess, I found sublime, "almost sublime." Be that as it may, the host of dark cracked hearses crawls slowly between the bar and the outside tables. Relentlessly.

As for Boris, I've seen him in the distance on several occasions, but we haven't spoken. The life on which he afterwards embarked in your hospitable West may have included prisons, illegal frontier-crossings, morphine, and a mass of other peccadilloes, but it has been no more than a miniature, no more than a "rough" . . . And heaven knows I haven't much liking for miniatures.

I don't wear a hat. I don't even own a hat. Nonetheless, I remove it from my bony head and humbly prepare to pass it around. If you haven't a copper to spare, ladies and gentlemen, at least let me have a nice dry Gauloise. If you haven't a Gauloise, then pay me with a smile. After all, a Gauloise— had you ever thought of it?—signifies a woman or girl from Gaul . . . For it's ready to scream, my loneliness is. Oh, I'm sorry. Am I rambling on . . . ? You're going to toss a few bits of old rubbish into my hat, a few laxative pills, and I'll be overwhelmed. Many thanks, ladies and gentlemen. From the bottom of my heart, I thank you!

Postscript

This book is not a historical record.

If the notion of chance (like most other notions) did not strike the author as absurd, he would gladly say that any reference to a particular period, territory, or race is purely coincidental.

The events that he describes could crop up in any place, at any time, in the mind of any man, planet, mineral . . .